PAPER OVER IT

For Mum, Simon and Jacob.

Thank you for everything x

-1-
THE QUARTET: MILLENNIUM

25th December 1999

Christmas lunch - quickly, quietly and expertly expelled.

A well-practised routine. One flush (more than one would be suspicious). Quick wipe of the mouth and chin. A petit-pois of toothpaste. One sheet of loo paper purposely placed on the settled water (to disguise the slight residue, the skim of oil).

Job done. Paper over it.

Jen - the bouncing Tigger, the life and soul of the party. Jennifer, aged twenty. Born and bred in Manchester. Jennifer Jones, already expert at papering over it.

31st December 1999

"Jen!"....... "JEN!" shouts Em.

"What?"

"Which one are you in?"

"This one," as Jen shoves her hand under the toilet cubicle door and waves it.

"Let me the fuck in!"

"It's open."

"Right, we've got fifteen minutes – we need to get the shots in and the bar's rammed. Move over. I need a wee."

As Prince (will always be 'Prince' to Jen and Em – it didn't symbolically change from 'Purple Rain' to 'Golden Showers' did it?) marks the millennium conclusion with his partying like it's 1999, Jen and Em make their way back to their 'cop a spot'. Em carefully balancing a tray of tequila, salt and lime.

"You cut that bloody short, knob 'eds," Lou shouts as she helps herself to a tequila trio while spilling Hooch over Kate's prized white capri pants and onto her new, ambiguously acquired Dolcis mules.

Em rummages in her bag for her Nikon Coolpix. "Take a piccie will you?" she shouts at the person closest to them. He does what he's told. People tend to when Em asks.

The quartet 'cheese' at the flash, then (on Em's command) do 'frightened face' on the second flash and then 'pout face' on the third flash. They collectively stick out their tongues for the final flash.

As the countdown begins, the four girls sprinkle salt on their hands, pick a lime wedge each and wait for all computers to crash, for times and dates to be fucked by Y2K, planes to fall from the sky and for the world to generally end. They don't, it doesn't.

And where is 'Auld Lang Syne'? Bloody Robbie Williams. Could he not have written a more exciting song than his slow Millennium? More of a 'Let me entertain you' vibe? Or could some other bugger have not? Fatboy, Britney, Madonna, Steps even – you could have proper exploited this and made a Millennium banger without falling from grace. Epic fail.

The girls lick their salt, down their shots, suck their limes and create a circle of heads and limbs - and bounce. Tigger bounce. Bouncing is what they do best. More specifically bouncing is what Jen does best. Bouncing helps, and has always helped paper over it.

Jen - on the short side, blonde haired and green eyed with white skin that tans irritatingly easily. Jenny – bright with great teeth from four years of braces, one normal rounded ear and one which goes into a little point at the top, dimpled cheeks, a wide smile and a supposedly 'perfect' little size six body. Jennifer Jones – pretty much perfect on paper, yet riddled with insecurities.

As the quartet welcomes in the New Year - the new Millennium - none of them know there are five of them bouncing.

None of them know the year that is in store for them.

That stars would be directing their fate and some, at times, would be praying it wasn't too late.

1st January 2000

"Fuck a fucking duck, I feel fucked."

Em – or to expand, Emily Roberts - spouts.

A privately educated, pony club graduate, filthy minded and equally filthy mouthed twenty-one year old from Hertfordshire. Em's confidence is legendary, her slight Manc accent fairly newly acquired and peppered with posh (highlighted by the way she pronounces 'fuck' and 'fucking' – which she pronounces every other sentence). Her analogies always phallic, sense of second fiddle to her big brother and desperation for attention from her father an undercurrent to all her brash bravado.

"I need sausages, bacon, eggs, toast... and tea. I need tea! Is there any fucking milk?"

She chose Manchester uni, even though Durham was her father's 'path'. The quartet are staying in the flat her father had bought for her in her first year. Yes, a whole flat. A flat fit for his little star.

She likes to call it her 'Pretty Woman Condo' – the Gere effect is still just a nine-year-old fantasy. She had explained once (pissed) that her dad had called her his 'little star' when she was younger, and had treated her like one too. But over the past few years he had become a bit detached. "He buys me things to make up for his lack of attention," she said. She never mentioned it again, and the girls didn't ask.

Jen met Em at registration on their first day at uni. Jen had been in her cargo pants and crop top (à la All Saints) while Em wore nice formal pants and a navy blazer a bit like the Appleton sisters before All Saints cargoed and crop topped them. Neither Em, nor the A-sisters, would never ever wear that shit again. Until, of course, they grew up and had to. Em never actually bought any cargo pants, couldn't understand why you would want pockets down by your knees. But she did, however, reassess her wardrobe.

Jen was immediately fascinated by Em. She was aloof and didn't give a shit, or that's the vibe she gave off. She held her head high, which made her appear even taller than her 5' 8", and had a way of flicking her long brown hair and glaring with her auburn eyes which caught people off guard. She had pale skin and thick dark eyelashes. Girls and boys alike were fascinated by her. She had a way of looking at people with her chin slightly raised – like they were beneath her. And her 'fuck-off' face was epic. If she was a cheese she would be Stilton. Full flavoured and slightly nutty, with a stingingly blue mouth.

But Stilton and fuck off faces aside, she has the most wicked of laughs and her wit is unbelievably dry and quite cutting. She sometimes cutely says 'oopsy daisy' like Hugh Grant in Notting Hill, before quickly checking herself. It isn't really 'on brand' Manchester

Em. Her ability to describe any situation in a 'can you fucking believe it?' way makes everything funny. She embellishes and adds drama to all she says, does and sees. Jen loves Em's ability to fantasise. From that first meeting it was love at first sight. Jen loves living in Em's world. It is a world Jen feels doesn't need any papering over, because Em has no cracks.

How wrong could she be? Stilton has cracks, deep cracks. Deep blue cracks. Or are they actually green?

Jen grew up very middle-class (she was told) in a fairly large Victorian semi-detached house in South Manchester. Manchester is peppered with Victorian semis due to its prime during the Industrial Revolution. Manchester, and its success, were built by labourers and working people living in terraced housing. Worker Bees. The best they got was an end terrace.

Then came the semi-detached. The further from the city centre you got, the fewer terraces there were and the larger the semis became. As you got to the heady heights of Sale then further south to Hale, the semis became larger and were bombastically termed 'Victorian Villas'. Then we hit the even headier heights of unconnected houses in places like Alderley Edge and Wilmslow. Detached houses. Jen had never lived in one of these houses, yet she had always felt slightly detached. Which, in fact, made her semi-detached childhood home rather apt.

Jen always wondered what middle-class meant. Did a semi-detached denote middledom? Was an end terrace in fact a semi? What did class really mean? Attending the local grammar school, Jen met loads of girls. Terrace girls, semi girls, detached girls. But no-one ever quite like Em.

"Is anyone there? Just check the milk for fridge, will you?" Em shouts.

"I'm here – I'm right here Em. Will you stop with your shouting. My head is banging." Jen is lying right next to Em on her bed, ignoring her inability to string a sentence together. In fact, loving her for it. She goes all back to posh when she is very drunk or highly hungover. "I'll go and check."

There is milk – but it stinks. And in her daze, Jen allows her nose to meet the rim so the spoiled milk lingers in her nostrils. How transient milk is, Jen thinks. Good one day, off the next. Things can sour in a second. Like the curdle of life. She laughs to herself and her alcohol addled chewing of the cud, like a dairy cow's stomach regurgitating a portion of its contents back into its mouth for a second chew.

"I'm going to the shop. I'll be right back."

Lou stirs as Jen slams the flat door. She face-planted the sofa at 4am and has been comatose since. Her mascara has left two moons on the vintage cream throw the girls bought Em from Afflecks Palace for Christmas to say thank you for all the city centre sleepovers. Afflecks is the shopping mecca for all things vintage and second hand in Manchester's Northern Quarter. A bohemian maze of independent traders where you can also get a piercing and a tattoo, or go for a smoke and a brew. Lou opens her eyes slowly and starts to tongue the crusty saliva in the corner of her mouth. It is surprisingly tasty. Her hangover hits her like a tonne of breeze blocks. She face-plants the sofa again.

Lou is from Liverpool – LiverLou the girls sometimes call her. She'd never been called that before uni, but then why would she? The second eldest of the quartet after Em, already twenty one, she had never lived anywhere but Liverpool before heading thirty five miles east to Manchester two and a half years ago. She never realised she had an accent, and was continually bemused when people copied what she said, trying to sound like her. "G'wed LiverLou!" when telling her to go ahead.

Right now Lou's liver is not in the best of states. It is more LiverBlue. Being an Everton fan, this is probably quite apt.

As Lou makes her way to the loo, she trips over Kate and knocks over Em's huge prized Swiss cheese plant. Steve the Cheese. Kate, fast asleep lying on the floor spooning the footstool (or pouffe as Em calls it), doesn't stir. Who has a pouffe as a student? Or even a footstool? Or, in fact, a Swiss cheese plant called Steve? The only plant Kate and Lou have is the cannabis one they have been carefully cultivating in the cupboard under the stairs in their terraced house in Withington. 'Hairy Potter' they call it.

"What the fuck was that?" Em bellows from the bedroom.

"Nothing Emmie," Lou scouse sings whilst trying to scoop up the cheese beast and reacquaint it with its soil, soiling Kate in the process.

PAPER OVER IT

Kate blinks awake, brushing away something gritty from her face. Kate is from Glasgow, from a gritty part of Glasgow. The first in her family to go to uni. Kate has a very tight and strong relationship with her mum, dad, little ten-year-old sister, two big brothers and extended family. Her first few months at uni were sprinkled with a melancholy yet merry mix of pride and homesickness. Kate is in a fairly serious relationship, but also works hard and plays hard. She is the only one of the four girls who has a full grant, but she still works up to sixteen hours a week at Dolcis shoe shop on King Street to make ends meet.

Kate is quite opposite in so many ways to Em. She is openly kind, warm and giving. Whereas Em, although all of these things deep down, has a hard shell. Like a Trebor Softmint. But the girls have a bond which is hard to explain. In their own ways they want what the other has. The strong, loving family unit versus the monetary ease. In a way their slight jealousy seals their friendship, like a toastie needs cheese.

"I need water!" Lou hollers, heading back from a dehydrated, unproductive loo visit.

"I need a new head," Em groans, lurching into the lounge from her bedroom.

"I need a shower," the well-soiled Kate exclaims. "Why am I covered in soil? And where the hell is Jen?"

So this is Jen, Em, Lou and Kate.

Jennifer, Emily, Louisa and Catherine.

A quintessentially quirky quartet of differing backgrounds, unique experiences of love, idiosyncratic ideals, insecurities, hopes, dreams and fears.

A tight troupe all acting in their own way, but with a strong understanding of the roles each are playing in their lives.

They genuinely love each other and are hugely protective of each other, collectively enjoying the madness.

Because they know deep down, at some point, it may fade away.

Millennium.
Robbie Williams.

-2-
JEN: IT FEELS SO GOOD

26th January 2000

A day like any other day. Jen just eats what she is supposed to, without causing suspicion for not eating enough. She is not anorexic. That would be wrong and bad – but above all, everyone would notice her not eating. She just eats normally, like a 'regular' person, and then gets rid of it. She doesn't ever eat loads and make herself puke, she never 'binges', therefore she is not bulimic either. That would be wrong and bad too.

Is she bulexic? Or anoremic? She doesn't know – or care. If it doesn't have a real name, it isn't really a thing. She is just in control of something. It feels so good. She looks great. She looks fit. Her abs are on fire (formed from two hundred sit ups a day, Britney style). No one notices anything wrong – they haven't noticed anything for years. Perfect. Paper over it.

"I'm treating you and the girls to dinner tonight. We are going full on!" Em's dad has sent her some money to celebrate the end of her penultimate set of exams. Another attention deficit cashola injection, the girls thought. "Call or text Lou and Kate will you, Jen? Booking is for 8pm. Tell them to get their best shit on. And tell Kate to not be fucking late!"

The recent phenomenon of text messaging is still in its infancy. You can only type 162 characters and your phone can only hold fewer than ten messages. Word abbreviations are just coming in to counter the frankly frustrating max character rule, and your thumbs almost get calluses from having to press every number key numerous times to get to the letter you want.

These word abbreviations have recently been termed 'SMS language'- LOL OMG L8R BTW IDK FOMO and WTAF to mention a few. Older, more traditional people are horrified and see this as the beginning of the end for the English language.

Example conversation:

MU m8. HRU? - Miss you mate. How are you doing?
OK U? LTNS :(- I'm ok. How are you? Long time no see (sad face)
Mt up? - Fancy meeting up soon?

PAPER OVER IT

On a D8 2nite - I'm going on a date tonight
WTAF! New BF? - What the actual fuck! Have you got a new boyfriend?
Ye - Yes I do
2moz nite? - What about tomorrow night then?
GR8 wher? - Sounds great to me! Where do you want to meet?
No space for new messages ... Argghhhh.

Em has had a mobile for over a year (she had, of course, had a pager before this). Jen and Lou got their first mobile phones (properly proud of their matching nifty Nokia 3210s) for Christmas, but still don't really know how to work them – apart from playing Snake. Em got a new computer for Christmas with a dial-up modem. Lou and Jen don't have a computer. Kate doesn't have either a mobile phone or a computer. The only way of contacting Kate is the payphone on the little table by the front door in her and Lou's student house a few miles south of the city centre. In Withington. No. 52.

"Wassup!" Lou answers said payphone in the style of the recent Budweiser phenomenon.

"Wassuuup!" Jen replies.

"Is that you Jen?"

"Yup"

"Wassup B?"

"Watching the game. Having a Bud."

"True, true."

"We're out tonight for dinner celebrating the end of our exams – Em's daddy dinner donation," Jen explains. "She says she needs her quartet fix."

This is exciting! Kate, Jen and Lou don't often eat out in restaurants - doner meat and chips or cheesy garlic bread from the kebab house near the infamous nightspot Jabez Clegg on Oxford Road (or another equally sticky-floored venue - bar and takeaway alike) is as much eating out as they tend to do. They are more than happy to eat out to help out.

"Where we goin'?" Lou asks.

"Cocotoo."

This is the newer incarnation of the original Coco's restaurant launched in Manchester in the early 1980s. A smart Italian built in an arch under Oxford Street Station with an incredibly impressive replica of Michelangelo's Sistine Chapel ceiling. Coco's and Cocotoo were originally owned by a barber called Carlo Distefano. In 1992 Carlo also launched his first San Carlo restaurant in Birmingham.

"Why can't we go the Dutch Pancake House?" Lou scouse pouts. She doesn't really like Italian food and has a long term obsession with pancakes. She also quite likes getting her own way, is a tad competitive.

"I know, I know – but she's paying, so Italian it is. And you haven't seen the amazing ceiling! You'll love it, I promise," coaxes Jen. "Pre drinks at Em's at seven. Bring drinks. NO TRAINERS OR CARGOES! Let's glam it up tonight! Tell Kate."

"She was out last night for Burns Night. I had to help her in. She's rancid," Lou snitches.

"Well get her a brew and tell her to give her 'ead a wobble," Jen orders. "And make sure you tell her for once to not be bloody late!"

"Wassup!"

"Wassup!"

"True."

Jen has been staying at Em's a lot recently. She has never had student accommodation. She, in theory, lives at home in her semi. She is semi there, semi at Em's, and had been semi at her ex's until a few months ago. Her choice of Manchester uni had been mainly due to her ex, if she was brutally honest. She had adored him in the early days, had been with him since fifteen. Had met him at McDonald's and lost her virginity to him a few months later on Valentine's Day night in a car (a black pimped Ford Fiesta XR2 with a rampant roaring exhaust to be precise) in a muddy field.

But he had controlled her in a way no one should ever be controlled. And he cheated – over and over again. He was an extension of his rampant roaring exhaust. This bare-faced, bare-back cheating had given her a few 'gifts' along the way. The chlamydia contribution was an inconvenient classic.

It all started, she remembers, around when she met him, living in her semi middledom. Doing well at school, in fact doing brilliantly at school. A maths brain with a strong ability for English and storytelling. A pianist (hated every second – including the bitch teacher who often slapped her hands with a ruler) and a naturally talented athlete. Winner of many awards, never 'most improved' or 'best effort'. Always the 'best' ones. Whatever 'best' was

Home was not a place of sanctuary. It didn't feel so good. It had become a quiet war of fighting, tears and disappointment for many years. Jen's older sister had struggled physically and mentally through no fault of her own. Money had been eaten up through recession-forced family business decline. Her much-loved mother had become miserable, downtrodden and disappointed. Her father equally as disappointed, but also angry and blaming. She felt her home had been built on paper notes, not emotional oats. And as the paper notes dwindled, 'D' for disappointment reigned.

When her father had recently left to live with a wealthy widow, Jen was neither surprised nor particularly upset. In fact she had told Kate, Em and Lou almost in passing.

One day, many years back, just as her ex came on the scene, she felt full – really full. Downstairs her parents were fighting again about their situation and her sister. They never fought about Jen. Jen was never in trouble. Jen was Tigger. Jen was fine. Jennifer was always fine. Jennifer Jones was always absolutely fine.

She just wanted to clear her head. She couldn't clear her head, but she felt she could clear her body. So she did. It was easy. It was liberating. It had nothing to do with losing weight. It had everything to do with control. It made her feel good. It felt so good. It made her feel powerful. It made her feel in control. It made her feel high. This was the start of the addiction, the self-harm. The start of papering over it.

It's a Wednesday so 'sports afternoon' at uni. For the majority who do absolutely no sports apart from running for the bus, it is drinking, sleeping or do whatever you want afternoon. Em has found a hair salon with an open session – hair students cutting students' hair free of charge. What could go wrong?

Em doesn't need to find such a place. Her dad would just pay for her to go to a top salon. She has an M&S card to buy her food, a seemingly bottomless credit card to buy everything else, a new Renault Clio (Papa, Nicole) with a central Manchester parking space and a fully expensed Pretty Woman condo with air conditioning and a balcony. But Em loves playing the student game. And, it appears to the girls, she loves pissing her father off even more than playing the game.

Jen has really bad stomach pains and isn't really in the mood. Has lost her Tigger recently, somehow. She's just about bracing herself for the night at Cocotoo, knowing Em will be on one and want to large it up later on the hunt for a cock-or-two.

"Let's goooo, Jen!"

Jen titivates her Tigger within, acknowledging it means she won't have to wash and sort her hair later.

With Em in the lead, having checked the location of the hairdressers in her well-thumbed Manchester A-to-Z, the girls brave the sunny yet chilly Manchester streets. Jen sparks up a cigarette. They have no idea exactly where they are going. They contentedly amble along together with linked arms, listening to Em's CD Walkman through an earphone each.

"We're here!" Em shouts over the music, far too loudly.

Jen sparks out her cig, only half smoked, and pops the future fruitful fag-end into the front pocket of her canvas military shoulder bag. Yet another purchase from their much-loved emporium Afflecks Palace.

Sitting in the slightly sticky reception area, flicking through old glossy magazines and contemplating Kate Moss's pixie cut, the girls wait their turn. They have given their bags and coats to the bored receptionist, who all but threw them into the cupboard behind her.

She had greeted them robotically, in a staccato fashion, "Hi, I'm Rachel. Welcome to Hair Me Happy. Take a seat."

"Hair me fucking happy?" Em giggle-whispers. "More like glare, no glee and snappy."

Em is funny, she is proper funny. She always makes Jen smile when she's feeling down. But then Jen is proper funny too. Everyone loves Jen. Jen lights up a room. She is the life and soul, makes people howl with her stories. But she doesn't really understand her power, her aura, and it's all such an effort at the minute. She feels tired. All the time.

'You're braver than you believe, stronger than you seem, and smarter than you think,' said Pooh.

"Fire, fire," the receptionist screams.

PAPER OVER IT

"Where?"

"There, in the cupboard!"

The whole salon erupts and water is quickly sourced and showered onto the blazing baby bonfire.

"What the fuck is that?" the receptionist points at the offending smoking article.

"Oh shit," Jen whispers to Em. "It's my bloody bag."

Jen and Em decide not to get their hair done. Em is laughing so uncontrollably, her fringe would have never been cut straight.

Word to the wise, never spark out a fag and put it back in your bag – unless you are 100% sure it's been suitably de-sparked.

The girls leave Hair Me Happy with a slightly ruined canvas military shoulder bag, dirty hair, coats smelling of burnt burgers and a gaggle of giggles. They bounce out. They say sorry and goodbye to rude receptionist Rachel and the rest of the HMH crew. Jen pees herself just a little as they Tigger bounce down the road, exploding with laughter.

"Seriously Jen!" Em spits. "Could you be any more funny?"

As they link arms and giggle their way back up Deansgate, a man calls to them. "I think you've dropped something, ladies."

The girls stop, clock, drool up at his frankly gorgeous face then look down to where he is nodding his handsome head.

A slightly charred and half open tampon has escaped from the newly burnt hole in Jen's military bag and is now on the road. Jen hasn't needed tampons for a while, her bulexia/anoremia stopped her flow a while back, but she always keeps a few of the long tailed little fellers in her bag, just in case.

"For fuck's sake, Jen!" Em points at the tampered tampon. "That is so embarrassing."

If anything is to happen to someone, it will happen to Jen. Especially recently. "Oh shittedy shit shit," Jen embarrassed laughs.

"You literally make me howl," Em screams as Mr. Hottie smiles, winks at Jen and walks off. "You blew that one Jen!"

Jen knows she constantly blows it. But like most girls, she dislikes blowing it. Loves Axl Rose but not his anagram - oral sex. It doesn't feel so good. And it in no way keeps her satisfied.

"I literally make myself howl sometimes," Jen admits whilst

13

shaking her head and giggling, unsure whether to retrieve the slightly burnt, dirty tailed tampon from the floor. Just staring at it thinking how much it looks like a legless lifeless mouse. "Howl in pure personal embarrassment," she admits, head in hands.

"Well, let's face it, you're never inserting that fucker are you?" Em points at the roadkill rodent. "Or, more unfortunately, that fucker!" she adds, pointing to the retreating back of Mr. Hottie.

Jen falls about laughing at Em's instantly accurate yet crude assessment of the ridiculous situation, grabs her arm and they both run down the street towards Em's flat to wash their unstyled hair and get ready, giggling like two schoolgirls.

Jen feels blessed to have Em. It feels so good to be semi living in such a funny yet faithful friendship.

She isn't really used to 'faithful'. Or feeling good lately.

It feels so good.
Sonique.

-3-
THE QUARTET: NEVER BE THE SAME AGAIN

26th January 2000 – continued

The lasagne and garlic bread, second time tasted like a cow and her cud, leaves a temporary torrid tang while Jen goes through her 'post' routine.

In public toilets the pre, during and post routine are, as a collective, a little more complicated - though no less well practised.

Noise becomes more of a factor when in a public loo. Even though many years of perfecting 'muting the motion' has left little to hear, but like putting a silencer on a shotgun, there is always a tell-tale tone to give the game away.

Try and hang around until there is no-one in the toilets. If this is not possible, wait until someone puts the hand dryer on or flushes their own loo. You can flush your toilet before you start so the cistern filling noise prevents any silence if the dryer or other toilet noise stops. But this can, for slow filling cisterns, mean you have to wait a while after the deed to flush again.

Always, always make sure there is loo roll. This can be placed pre-purge as, like with a poo, it can dull the splud (splash thud) of the purge. The loo roll will also obviously be needed at post-purge stage to wipe the seat of any evidence, and of course, to paper over it. You can use the same piece to do both jobs as long as there is not any noticeable evidence on the paper after wiping the seat with it.

As said, a little more complicated. Bulexia/anoremia ensures everything is a little more complicated, assures toilet visits will never be the same again.

The temporary torrid tang of vile bile is removed through a quick rub of toothpaste on her teeth followed by a cursory check in the mirror and a swipe of lip gloss. Less than sixty seconds. Job done. Jen is a pro at papering over it.

Back at the table in Cocotoo, Em has ordered shots. Of course she has! Jen looks around at her friends with affection and bemusement.

Em has the most silky mane of brunette loveliness. Her pale skin and elegant nose look particularly perfect when she is sneering at people. You wouldn't call her classically beautiful, but she is ethereally classic. Like a Roman muse.

Em is studying Management Science with Jen. Em took maths, biology and chemistry at A-Level, Jen took maths, English literature and French. Both had done the useless yet obligatory, completely un-revisable, multi choice general studies exam too. If it wasn't a question on the impact on ordinary people in 1514 of Copernicus saying the Earth travelled round the sun, it was an equally random question like:

'50 parts per billion' means:
A) 50 oxygen molecules for every billion molecules in the air
B) 50 oxygen molecules for every billion ozone molecules
C) 50 ozone molecules for every billion molecules in the air
D) 50 air molecules for every billion ozone molecules

Who actually gives a fuck?

Neither Jen nor Em really knew what they had wanted to be or do, after Jen decided she didn't want to be a journalist, so chose something quite generic. They had both chosen to specialise in marketing in their final year – simply because the guest marketing speaker from ToysRUs was hot, and (in fairness) made a lot of sense. The guest guy from IKEA, who explained why they first launched in the UK in Warrington (geography and road network, for interest), also made a lot of sense. And was also appealing on the eye. And they had found HR, Finance and Supply Chain a bit dull.

As Em flicks her mane, Jen's attention turns to Lou. LiverLou is a dancer, a performer. It literally emanates from her like sweet smelling sassy sweat. Every extreme of her body performs. Even the way she kills her shot is delightfully dramatic, as is the buoyant bow she always takes afterwards.

Lou danced all over the North-West as a kid, even at the ballroom in Blackpool. It had made her tough. Competitively tough. Her family were as proud of her as her wardrobe was of the luminous Liver-lycra that proudly filled it. Lou can also sing beautifully, but dancing is her absolute passion. She had been offered a performing arts place at a prestigious college in London, but she didn't want to be too far from home, her boyfriend Eddie or her family.

Lou has crazy, curly, riotous red hair. The kind of hair that everyone wants (if they don't have it). And if they have it, don't want it. Anne of Green Gables with a beautiful bonus bounce. Her eyes are the type of bluey green that draws you in, you just want to swim in them, like perfect liquid aquamarines. Cute freckles frolic on her fair skin. Lou is small, like Jen. In fact, when they first became close, they did 'shoes off, back-to-back' numerous times to establish who was the tallest (or shortest). Lou's bouncy hair height advantage possibly skewed the result.

Lou also has a crazily long tongue which she can touch her nose with. Her party trick. She can be crazily competitive at times and is the bendiest girl Jen has ever met. She is jam packed full of mischief, like a Jammie Dodger. Jumping into a perfect box split is another party trick Jen is particularly envious of.

"Bored now, where's next?" Lou blasts. "I wanna go dancing!"

"What day is it?" asks Jen.

"It is Wed-nes-day!" sings Lou.

"Love Train?" offers Jen.

"No!" screams Em.

"Yes! Brutus Gold!" yells Kate. "Royales!"

The other collectively more 'posh' and mature Cocotoo guests start to murmur at the excitable quartet.

"Veto!" Em shouts.

"No chance! Democracy!" Kate challenges. "Hands up for Love Train."

Kate is a politics student on a four year course. She is socialist and Scottish Labour to the core.

Six hands go up for the Love Train vote.

"Motion motioned."

"What the fuck does that even mean?" Em spits.

"It means let's gooooo!" Lou points at the door theatrically.

"For fucks sake, I need different friends," Em sulks. Though they all know she will be up on stage tonight I Will Surviving, Staying Aliving and then, on the way home, making all four sing Bridge over Troubled Water with the high shit on the last verse assuring it's right behind and it will ease your mind.

So the quartet set off on the short walk to some solid seventies bangers at the questionably salubrious Discotheque Royales nightclub on Peter Street. Royales had previously been the location of Pete Waterman and Michaela Strachan's 'The Hitman and Her' TV music program, and has had a strong whiff of cheese ever since.

Brutus Gold's Love Train has been a student fave for a good few years and, according to Manchester's Finest, is 'a hazy combination of platforms, flares, ridiculous wigs and an over-abundance of camel toe... all with enough cheese to make the Laughing Cow take a long hard look at her life choices.'

Brutus Gold himself is a moustached, loud shirted, Cuban-heeled seventies legend and impresario who conducts all the mad hat disco-inferno capers and owns Wednesday nights.

Brutus Gold is actually a short balding bloke called Nigel from Middlesbrough.

One of the key highlights of a Love Train night is the legendary dancing competition. A few 'lucky' love trainers are invited to have a dance-off on-stage with resident dancers Disco Dick, Angel de Lyte, Chad Valley and Krystal Crest. Generally pissed, the contestants think they look like John Travolta, however they tend to look like absolute dicks. It is positively hilarious. Somehow Em has been asked up at least four times in the past – and had won three of those. Much to the annoyance of Lou.

Unsure whether it is flared fate, or a pre-prepped platform shoe-ed plan, Jen spots Kate's boyfriend night-fevering over to the foursome.

"Will!" Jen shouts. "Get the beers in!"

They all love Will. Kate and Will met a few years back one early evening in Dolcis shoe shop when Will asked her if they sold Oxford shoes. Kate had responded, "What are they?"

Kate had no clue what Oxford shoes were, neither did Jen or Lou. Em knew, of course. She also knew the difference between these and brogues. When Kate regaled the meeting, Em had questioned, "Surely you know the saying 'Oxfords not Brogues'?" She was met with three blank faces.

Dolcis girls are allowed to be sassy. They are also allowed to wear hot pants and crop tops ('footfall drivers' the manager said) and to bully men with their batting eyelids into buying insoles and shoe protection they don't need as it increases their shit weekly pay packets through small bonuses.

Dolcis girls are, however, not allowed to steal the odd small handbag by sneaking it in their larger, non-stolen bags or a pair of shoes by putting them outside the back delivery door under the big blue bins. But they do. Neither are they allowed to punch £29.99 into the till but £2.99 into the card machine for their mates. But they do. At £2.78 an hour, Dolcis girls do what they have to do.

"Sorry, I've never been in here before. I just need a pair of shoes urgently for something tonight. I left mine at the Rugby Club", Will explained, dragging his eyes up from her ample chest.

"The boy's shoes are over there," Kate pointed, emphasising 'boys'.

"Sorry, what was that?" he asked, struggling to understand her Glaswegian accent.

"There," she pointed. "Boys."

"Ok, thanks," he didn't rise to it, but he was definitely already hooked. Feeling the stirrings of a physical rise.

Kate checked out his cute arse and wide shoulders as he turned. As he ran his hair through his 'Four Weddings' fop in a confused Hugh Grant way, something stirred inside her too.

"Can I have these in a size ten, please?" Will asked, turning to face her from the 'boys' section.

"Sit there and I'll go and grab them," Kate pointed at the bank of stools.

"No time, they'll do. I'll just take them."

"I'll get your box."

"I don't need a box," said Will, "A bag will do."

As Will followed her to the till, he got a chance to really check her out. About 5'5", he thought, and the sexiest body he had ever seen in his life. Curves in all the right places, with her deep olive skin skimming over them perfectly. Like silk shimmying over a classic statue. Her thick, dark hair danced around her shoulders as she turned to face him. Her rich dark eyes reminded him of expensive chocolate, but had a kindness and warmth in them which he found intoxicating. And her blow job lips were a cock teasing continuation of her incredible curves.

He thought of his mum's favourite Delboy moment as he tried to nonchalantly rest on the till counter whilst taking out his wallet, "I think we're on a winner here Trig. Play it nice and cool son, nice and cool".

Kate took his Coutts card from him. She had never seen or heard of this kind of card, even after years of working in shops and bars. 'Cute's card', she called it to the girls later.

"Want some protection?" Kate asked from behind the till.

"Want some what, sorry?"

"Are you deaf?"

"Ermmm, no." Why is she asking him about condoms already?

"Protection for your shoes," Kate repeated. "Want some?"

"Ermmm, no." The realisation that she was not asking him for sex in a subtle way waved over him like a flustered tsunami. He was acutely aware that he was coming across as an ignorant, inarticulate oaf.

"Big mistake. Big. Huge."

"Alright Vivian," Will laughed, understanding her immediately "I'll get some bloody shoe protection."

"It's Kate, actually," she laughed too. Her kind eyes crinkled as her face was overtaken by a big, warm, beautiful smile. She loved the fact he got her Pretty Woman reference.

"Want to know my name?" Nothing ventured, nothing gained.

"If I must," Kate scoffed, hoping it was Edward. Eddie.

"I'm Will."

"Can I call you Willie?" Kate flirted, looking up at him teasingly through her ridiculously long black eyelashes.

"Not if you expect me to answer," Will responded quick-as-a-flash. He and his brother had watched Pretty Woman so many times he knew every word, though neither brother ever admitted this to anyone. "Are you here tomorrow?"

"No, got uni all day."

"Ok…" He had assumed she was a full time shop girl. He berated himself for doing so. He wouldn't have cared either way. He was smitten.

"I'm here Thursday night though. Late night shopping again," Kate offered.

"See you Thursday then," Will smiled as he reversed out of the shop, tripping over the bank of stools before pushing the pull door.

"You've forgotten your shoes," Kate shouted as he managed to correctly navigate the simple glass door.

Little did Kate know that in that instant, he'd opened up a door in her. And she had in him.

From that night, neither would ever be the same again.

Never be the same again.
Mel C.

-4-
JEN: PURE SHORES

14th February 2000

The first Valentine's Day of the Millennium. Relationship statuses as follows:

Kate

Since meeting Will in1998, Kate has been a one-shot Scot. From completely different backgrounds, social views and political persuasions, the two connected like Vivian and Edward. They are very similar creatures. Both deep-down want the fairytale, and love Prince. Kate and Will are just made for each other like a cork and a screw, crackers and cheese. Like Brad and Jen. Pure shores.

Em

Footloose, flirty, feisty and fancy free. Many men have tried over the years, but after one or two dates Em always finds an issue. These issues have historically and hilariously included: dodgy feet with toe number two being longer than the big toe, too like her brother, rampant ear-lobe sucking, small sweaty hands, too like her dad, skinny dick, pointy tongue and slightly inverted nipples. She just can't find a man that ticks her boxes, but does like her box room having a lick of paint regularly. Hasn't found her pure shore yet.

Jen

Her experience of men, on the whole, has not been massively positive. Having broken up with her ex nearly five months ago, she is still very much single – but still in his grasp. It has been five years to the day since he popped her proverbial cherry in the rampant roaring XR2. He pops up in places he shouldn't know she will be, even though one of the many reasons she had split up with him was because he had perpetually 'popped up' in places he shouldn't have been throughout their five year relationship. Their shore hasn't been pure in any way.

Lou

Madly in love with Eddie who she had known throughout school. An older brother of her friend. She had written 'I love Eddie' on her Garfield pencil case, her 7Up Fido Dido ring binder and the exercise books her mum had carefully helped her paper over and then cover with transparent sticky film. All written discretely obviously. Unlike the obvious bubbles in the sticky film that even the skimming of a long metal ruler couldn't completely remove. She had spent hours practising her future signature with her full first name, Louisa, and his surname. They first got together when she was in fifth year, just before her GCSEs, and he was in the second year of his mechanics apprenticeship. A genuinely lovely and caring guy, Lou always says. Quiet, calm, composed – the perfect foil to the vivacious, boisterous, loud Lou. Much taller than Lou and rather on the skinny side, like the Fido Dido character she had loved as a teen. She sometimes calls him 'Fido' as a pet name. Eddie still lives in Liverpool working as a mechanic. He comes to Manchester some weekends to see Lou, or she goes home to see him. He would rather she go home to him every weekend, and says this often. Rather she had just stayed and studied there, or got a job. Lou wants to marry Eddie, she already knows she wants his babies one day. Pure shores.

It is a Monday, a rubbish day for Valentine's. Kate and Lou had double dated it with Will and Eddie on Saturday night to celebrate. Lou had made sure it was her beloved Dutch Pancake House. Em and Jen aren't interested in the slightest in the Clinton Card con, as they term it.

The girls decide to spend the evening together. They call it 'Galentine's' thinking they are really clever and wondering if Clinton will ever think of it. They had planned to go to Blockbuster and rent Ghost, Em's fave film, but Will said he could get them hot property tickets to see 'The Beach' which has just been released at the cinema.

Jen is at Em's waiting for her to get dressed. They have a lecture at 10am and it's already 9:30. Jen's ex has already called her six times. Her new mobile phone has become a perpetually poisoned chalice. She still has no idea how he got her number. She ignored him. The last thing she wants is to talk to him on Valentine's Day. She puts it on the silent mode she recently located on her phone while playing Snake in a dull lecture.

"Shall we sack it off and go and get some brekkie?" Em asks. Jen knows it isn't really a question, and is not in the mood for a lecture either. She feels tired again. They can easily get the lecture notes off course friends later.

"Ok, where do you fancy?" Jen asks.

"Greasy spoon!" Em had never even heard of a 'greasy spoon' before heading up north. In the queue for registration, she had asked Em if Manchester had a McDonald's yet. It was 1997. Thirteen years after Manchester got its first Ronald restaurant. The only greasy spoon she had ever encountered was a silver one filmed with over-oily soup that her stepmother served last Christmas. Her stepmother, Eve, is only eight years older than her. This disgusts Em even more than the odious oily soup and the resulting greasy spoon.

"What's happening to your job applications?" Em mumbles, tucking into her full English.

"Going to London next week for that final M&S interview," Jen replies, slurping her tea and taking a chunk out of her buttery toasted teacake. She has been shortlisted for the M&S graduate scheme. "And I've just sent off that BA application too."

Jen doesn't really know what she wants to do, apart from get away from the semi and her ex. She loves her mum very much, but feels like she needs to get away. She loves the idea of a big graduate job in London town, but she also wants to travel and fancies being an air hostess for a year. She has A-Level French, just about meets their minimum height requirement of 5'2" and is 'slender' with a 'weight proportionate to her height'. All prerequisites at British Airways in the year 2000, alongside being aged twenty-seven or less. Although not an active feminist, she had laughed when she read all these 'requirements' a few months ago, but thought 'fuck it'.

"Where are you up to?" Jen asks, knowing full well Em still has no idea what she is going to do after uni. She also checks her phone. Five more missed calls.

"Barbados baby! Take me to my beach." Em's dad has a beach house there. "Then wherever the Caribbean wind blows me," Em wafts her sausaged fork, accidentally letting the half-eaten banger escape and land in a mug of tea minding its own brewing business on the table next to them.

"Oh, I do apologise," she says to the table's middle aged male occupant as he wipes his tea-stained t-shirt with his paper napkin.

"I appear to have porked you. Let me get you another cup of tea," as she flirtily removes the phallic floater with her fork with absolutely zero shame.

Jen loves Em's total confidence that everything will always work out fine, including a banger bobbing buoyantly in a stranger's brew.

"I love you, my sassy southern belle," she laughs after their neighbour decides to just leave. Soiled, porked, slightly stimulated and perfectly puce.

"Ditto," Em ghosts, Patrick Swayze style. "My knockout northern bird."

"Ha! So 'knockout' I'm still single?" Jen counters, smiling whimsically.

"Still single because he'd bloody kill any man who came anywhere near you!" Em explains what didn't really need explaining. Seeing Jen's slightly broken expression, she adds, "Let's take your mind off him and being semi-single, and go get that single you want."

The music single 'Pure Shores' had been released earlier that day. 'The Beach' movie theme tune by All Saints, a song from their upcoming Saints & Sinners album.

Heading back from the big Our Price store on Market Street, Jen gets a text from her ex. She stops to read it.

ND 2 C U. R U IGNORNG ME? ND TO SPK 2 U.

"Ignore him," Em says firmly, ripping Jen's phone from her hand and putting it in her bag. "You need a break from this shit. From his shit. Let's go back to mine, have a drink and listen to this bad boy," she coaxes Jen whilst patting the Our Price bag safely still in Jen's other hand.

"Sounds good to me," Jen smiles. "But it's Monday lunchtime. We can't get pissed. We've got lectures this afternoon, we've already bloody missed this morning."

"We'll only have one," Em winks. "And maybe a cheeky joint to balance it out."

"You are incorrigible!" Jen laughs, linking her friend's arm and lighting up a little at the thought of lighting up. It isn't really her thing at all, more Em's thing, she is more a standard legal light up kind of girl - but she goes with the Em and the flow. Thinking a little illegal smoke might cheer her up, or chill her down - either would do right now. "Let's do this," she links her arm into Em's and starts to bounce them down Deansgate.

Back at Em's flat, with a pair of nearly downed Buds, one large spliff on the go and a second splendidly rolled one sitting on the table, Jen opens the Pure Shores CD.

"What the actual fuck!" she shouts when she realises the lyrics aren't printed in the CD wallet. "So annoying! Why would the Appleton sisters not insist on it?".

"Do they not know we need the fucking lyrics?" Em adds, like Jen, rather brewed from the blend of the Bud and the bud, 'fucking' even more than usual. "We're just going to have to fucking do it ourselves."

"True," Jen replies. "True."

At the same moment Jen's intercom buzzer buzzes. They know who it is. He just keeps on buzzing.

"Ignore it," Em says. "He doesn't know we're here. Just have the rest of this," and hands her the end of the spliff.

After a while the buzzing stops so the girls crack open another pair of Buds, find a pen and paper, slip the disc into Em's CD player and lie on their fronts on the floor with their elbows holding them up. Em proceeds to stop and start the CD whilst Jen writes down the lyrics word by word. Both concentrate very hard on their specific jobs in their slight stupor. "Rewind," "Stop," "What was that?" and "Rewind again," Jen shouts while Em shouts back, "Can you not write faster?" "I'm coming, not drowning," and "I am fucking rewinding."

They swap jobs as Em is absolutely a faster writer than Jen, though Jen is undeniably a better writer than Em. She has always loved reading and writing. Had wanted to be a journalist at one point. Had done work experience at The Guardian newspaper in the northern office on Hardman Street.

After about twenty-five long minutes they have it nailed, unlike their lecture notes from earlier that day.

"Have we really just done that? Are we eleven listening to Kylie?" Jen giggles. She has the proper giggles. She is in a far better mood.

"No. Because the fabulous Kylie did insist on the lyrics in the tape cassette sleeve!" Em verifies vehemently. Em is always quite vehement when half stoned, or pissed. Or, in fact, sober. "Do you remember her first album? What was it called? And that cool half black hat she wore on the cover with all her curls spilling out of the top?"

"I remember my mum buying one proper Kylie cassette and one blank tape," Jen recounts, her giggles rapidly replaced by her own personal vehemence. "She then copied the proper copy in the double tape deck in the lounge to the blank tape. My sister got the proper one for Christmas and I got the fucking dodgy one with a white sleeve with 'Kylie' hand-written on it! At least she got the album name right, although I'm not sure she did it intentionally," Jen fumes. "So no. I don't fucking remember whether she had insisted on the printed lyrics, and I certainly don't remember the cool half black hat and the fucking curls."

Em's vehemence is quickly replaced with giggles as she rolls about with laughter at Jen's indignation, frenetic 'fuckings' and slight PTSD from her eleven-year-old Christmas Kylie crisis.

"What's more, the cassette was the wrong length so 'I should be lucky' was split between the A-side and the B-side, and I didn't have the end of 'The Loco-fucking-Motion'. It just stopped when she was telling me to swing my hips, now," Jen's indignation and sense of injustice still alive and kicking.

Em can't speak, she's on her knees bent over. "The Loco-fucking-Motion! Stop! You're killing me!" The poor, long suffering Steve the Swiss Cheese gets knocked over yet again, "Oopsy daisy. Sorry Steve."

With that Jen also can't hold it in. Her umbrage unravels like her dodgy Kylie tape had a few weeks after Christmas and she joins Em and Steve rolling around the floor in laughter.

They catch their breath, wipe their eyes, pick up Steve the Cheese and look at the clock on the CD player. "Fuck, we're gonna miss this afternoon's lecture too," Jen yells.

"Well, we don't want to be late," Em says rationally. Jen thinks she's going to say they'll have to run. "No point going if we're going to be late. May as well spark this bad boy up," she further rationalises, completely irrationally, and grabs the second spliff.

A few hours later, with two more lectures missed, but the proud owners of fully and accurately penned lyrics to 'Pure Shores' and aching mouths from laughing, Jen and Em head out, slightly wobbly, to meet the other half of their quartet. Hoping Jen's ex isn't outside, waiting for her.

"Thanks Em," Jen says, relieved to see he isn't. "I needed that. I'm so fed up, honestly. I'm so tired." Jen's normal bouncy self a little squashed, her Tigger trampled. She starts to cry.

Em hugs her. "I know," she says knowingly, "I know." She knows she has to help her friend, enough is enough. While guiding Jen down the road, she thinks that she might ask her if she fancies joining her in Barbados for a while this summer. That it may be just the break she needs, miles away from home and her ex. Just some time in the sun, chilling on the pure shores of her beach. They both sing the newly learned Pure Shores chorus with its moving and coming, its drowning and swimming. It makes Jen smile.

Heading down Oxford Road, after meeting at St. Peter's Square, the quartet realise they have an hour to spare before the 7:45 showing at The Odeon, so they pop into 'The Thirsty Scholar' for a quick one.

"How was double-date night at The Dutch?" Em asks Kate while Lou and Jen head to the bar.

"Flipping brilliant!" Em eye-rolls at Kate's crap crepe reference. "It was really nice to be fair. The boys do get along well, even though Will doesn't speak football and Eddie doesn't speak rugby."

Kate is wearing her favourite Affleck's Palace vintage bright yellow top that she cropped with kitchen scissors, with a Harvey Ball smiley face on it. Yellow is her favourite colour. Em thinks it makes her dark hair and olive skin look annoyingly stunning. She knows she would look shit in it with her pale skin.

Kate is studying politics at Manchester University. A socialist with a quaver note of communism. She is fascinated by Marxism and had visited Chethams, where Marx and Engels studied together and discussed the ideas that spawned The Communist Manifesto, and the John Rylands Library in her first week of uni.

She is also a little conflicted as she understands that total class equality or a classless society is not achievable, and that her coming to university is, in itself, quite a capitalist thing to do. Or so some of her extended family had told her. She was only seventeen when she came to Manchester and her ideals evolved as she became more informed. She is also very aware that Will is capitalism personified. A living counteraction of communism.

Lou and her family are also 'left', but less left than Kate. Both families had loved Tony Blair's victory three years earlier, with its D:Ream 'Things can only get better' soundtrack.

Jen had been brought up to think Maggie Thatcher was a brilliant powerhouse with her 'right to buy' and 'the problem with socialism is you eventually run out of other peoples' money'. She still loves her feminist sayings: 'It may be the cock that crows; but it is the hen that lays the eggs' and 'If you want something said, ask a man; if you want something done, ask a woman.' But she has been re-educated by Lou, and even more so by Kate. She now sees the Iron Lady in a definitely different light.

Em says she doesn't do politics. This infuriates Kate. "It's easy to 'not do politics' with an M&S card and a fully expensed flat, you bourgeois bitch. You don't want or need anything to change," she had almost shouted at her a while back. It was very unlike the normally calm, gentle Kate. Many things about Em infuriate Kate, but she has a crazy soft spot for her. And when she had invited Em to stay up with her family in Glasgow quite some time ago, she could see how much Em had loved her homely little home and close loving family.

"When can we get you to thruple up with Lou and me?" Kate quizzes Em. "One day it'll happen to you – it'll be like 'boom' and it'll hit you right in the chest like a carthorse back buck."

"If he's built like a cart horse, I'm in," Em deflects, like a horse whipping its tail to whisk away a pesky fly. Em doesn't really understand why she can't let any man get close to her. Why she seems so mentally incapable of opening up and letting a man in, when she is so physically capable of exactly the same thing.

"Beers me dears," Lou sings carrying two bottles of Moscow Mule, followed by Jen with the other pair.

"I carried a water-mule-an," Jen quips, grinning.

"Oh no – that was truly shocking," Kate hides her face in her hands at Jen's dodgy Dirty Dancing watermelon misquotation. "For fuck's sake, put yourself in the corner baby," she eye rolls as Jen takes the corner seat, laughing.

"No. Go to that corner. Way over there!" Lou cajoles, pointing at the other end of the pub. "Go on!"

"No-one puts baby in the corner," Em says, suddenly a little over-protective of Jen after today. Also still a little stoned and drunk.

"Alright, knob 'ed! What's your beef?" Lou asks Em.

"We've just had a day of it with my ex," Jen explains. Her turn to be defensive of Em. "I've honestly had enough of it. She's been looking after me, keeping me busy. Making me smile."

The quartet proceed to spend the next thirty minutes discussing Jen's situation with her ex. The police had been called a few times over the past few months, but nothing was ever done. Jen had just been told to keep a diary. As if words on paper were going to stop his harassment and stalking. She had loved writing her diary as a child. Remembers one which had a little lock and key. She filled the pink paper full of stories. Some true, some fabricated, but always animated. But in this circumstance she feels paper is far better used to paper over it. It does absolutely nothing for the prevention of stalking.

The girls, as always, make her feel better. Promise they will come up with a more positive plan than the 'stupid diary' that the police had repeatedly proposed. They are all being saints.

As they head to the cinema, arms wrapped around Jen, she feels a little more positive. She just wants a personal sanctuary, a place where she can feel at peace and truly herself.

As she flows with the tide of her friends, Jen sings silently to herself about a piece of something to call hers.

Pure Shores.
All Saints.

-5-
LOU: THE REAL SLIM SHADY

14th February 2000 – continued

"Well that was a barrel of laughs for Galentine's, wasn't it?" Em exclaims as they exit the cinema on to Oxford Street.

The Beach had been a hit to their senses. Euphoric utopia which travelled to totalitarian dystopia, with a soundtrack to die for. A brutal, shark-infested, drug-induced, murderously mystical paradise version of Animal Farm. George Orwell's Napoleon and Alex Garland's Sal proof that a totally equal society is impossible to achieve. That someone or something will always want power, and that currency will always exist in some form. Paper or not.

Knowing that Kate is just about to open her mouth to ruminate over the societal learnings and the impact of the narrative within the film, Em pleads "Can we please not talk about the deep and meaningfuls – and just celebrate Leo?"

"Yes please," Jen says, even though she is more Billy Zane than Leonardo di Caprio. "One for the road?". She actually really quite fancies discussing the ramifications of 'The Beach' and 'Animal Farm' as Orwell is one of her favourite authors, but she doesn't have the energy. Thank god she is staying over at Em's. There is a main door, lift, corridor and intercom buzzer to protect her from her ex.

"Really sorry, I know I said I wasn't seeing him but my Fido is heading over. He texted while we were in the cinema to say he wants to come see me," Lou guiltily explains.

Em fake pukes, "For fucks sake, you and Eddie make me vom. Especially with your corny shit 7Up pet name. Kate?"

Kate, also looking sheepishly guilty, admits that Will is probably already at her and Lou's house. Probably already in her bed. Probably has already visited Hairy Potter under the stairs and was probably already sparking up a nice Valentine's spliff. Probably already naked.

Jen rolls her eyes, "Well Em and I will probably just fuck the pair of you off as friends then!"

Em gives the love birds the bird, American style, while Lou and

Kate laugh, blow kisses and Tigger-bounce to the bus stop.

Kate presses the bell as the bus rolls along Wilmslow Road towards Withington library. It has started to rain heavily and the huge windscreen wipers splash the girls as they hop off the bus, both eagerly anticipating their V-Day shags.

It is that Manchester kind of rain which immediately wets you all over like a posh hotel rain shower with a massive head. Lou had quite quickly noticed on arrival in Manchester that the rain was different to Liverpool rain – and there was definitely more of it. She had asked her dad why.

Given any opportunity to diss Manchester versus his beloved Liverpool, and with a penchant for talking about the weather, like all Brits and The Daily Express, and for regaling the story about Michael Fish's fishy forecast of 1987, he was in his element. In his element talking about the elements. He could still not quite believe his fiery haired, fiercely natured, beloved dancing daughter had headed over the M62 to uni in Manchester. But he was happy that at least she was close by.

He had explained that the weather is better in Liverpool because Liverpool is in the beautifully protective rain shadow of the Welsh mountains and has the River Mersey and Liver Birds to protect it. Whereas Manchester is on the shitty, rainy side of the Pennines in a dirty, dark valley with the filthy Ship Canal protecting it from nothing. Apart from its grubby self.

Lou had laughed, not quite believing her dad and his fishy information, but knowing it would have some geographical, meteorological elements of truth.

The two girls race giggling down the terraced street towards number 52, splashing through huge puddles which had miraculously appeared in just a few minutes. Like stick-kids in a Lowry painting. Lou wins, of course. Their other two housemates are out so they have the place to themselves. Will has used the back door key always hidden under the armless gnome called Norm in the little back courtyard. He had to go down the ginnel to get to Norm and his hidden key.

"What on earth is a ginnel?" he had asked when Kate initially instructed him on Norm's location.

"Did you never watch Corrie, you posh twat?" she had teased him.

"No, funnily enough they didn't show it at boarding school. It may have sullied our superior minds," he had teased her back.

Kate races in to see if Will is there. No mobile means she couldn't check. She really does need to get one. But they are so expensive. As she jumps up the stairs, two at a time, she laughs remembering a year or so earlier when her and Lou had found a life-sized cardboard cut-out of a male model outside the back of Burton's Menswear shop on a night out (whilst wild weeing).

They had named him Charles Hetherington-Smythe after some drunken deliberation, due to his tweed jacket, and had brought him home with them on the late bus, before quietly placing him on the landing at the top of the stairs. Stifling their giggles to not wake their sleeping housemates.

One of said housemates got up in the early hours to have a non-wild wee. Terrified by the intruder, she cried out and punched him square on the nose, only to increase her screams as her hand hit the wall as his head fell off.

Charles (and his rather smirky catalogue pout) is now a permanent resident at No. 52. His head carefully Fab lolly sticked and sellotaped back into place. He is now blue-tacked to the wall in the lounge. A permanent reminder of girl power. Will is quite the permanent resident in Kate's bed, which is exactly where he is when Kate bounces up.

Lou goes to put the kettle on to make a brew while waiting for Eddie to arrive, after checking her wet face in the mirror above the telephone table in the hall.

She races to open the door when she hears the knock. She had only been with Eddie the day before, but she always looks forward so much to seeing him. She genuinely adores him and knows they will be together forever.

As she opens the door, she immediately knows something is wrong from his expression.

"Lou, we need to talk."

"What is it? What's happened?" Lou demands, concerned.

"Let's go inside, I'm getting wet."

Instead of heading upstairs to Lou's bedroom as normal, he makes his way into the kitchen.

As the kettle switches itself off, its simple job complete, he simply says, "I've been seeing someone else, Lou. I'm really sorry."

Lou doesn't register. "Sorry, say what?"

"I am really sorry. It just happened. You're always here. I just don't get enough attention from you. It just happened."

"It doesn't just happen," she spits.

"Well, it has. I didn't want to hurt you – I don't want to hurt you. I still love you, I always will," Eddie mutters rather pathetically.

As the situation starts to dawn on Lou, the awful reality infuses her like osmosis. Highly concentrated emotion seeps into her empty body.

"What the fuck? Who is she? Why have you done this? How long has it been going on? What did I do wrong? We've been together for years! We talked about getting married, having children! We were planning our future! We had sex two nights ago without a condom, you fuck!"

Kate races down the stairs to see what the commotion is. She finds Lou bent over in pain, physical pain. Eddie is sitting at the kitchen table with his head in his hands, not answering any of Lou's questions.

"I'm sorry Kate," Eddie says. "I had to tell her. It just couldn't go on like this. It just happened – it's been six months now."

"On Valentine's. You had to tell her on Valentine's Day?" Kate screams. "Get out! Get the fuck out, you shady snake."

Kate scoops up her friend and holds her tight, stroking her hair while she starts to heave. Kate gently manoeuvres her to the kitchen sink where she vomits. Violently vomits. Kate holds her hair and strokes her back. She has held Lou's hair often in the past, but never like this. Never for this purpose.

Eddie lifelessly sits on his chair, their chair. The skinny, shady fucker just sits. Not standing up.

Kate feels a stab of tears prick her eyes as she witnesses her friend's confusion, clarification and heartbreak – almost all in one go. It is hideous and harrowing. "Six months? Six months? But we spent Christmas together. Just two months ago." Lou quietly wails in-between her body's violent convulsions. Kate just holds her tight, she can't bear to see someone she loves in so much pain.

"GET. THE. FUCK. OUT," Kate screams, commanding his attention. Not saying please. Loud as she can.

Eddie remains seated, head in hands. Not standing up. Feeling sorry for himself. Showing his real, selfish self.

Will enters the kitchen after racing down the stairs in reaction to Kate's screams. "What the hell is going on, Kate?" he asks, reacting to Kate's rare ferocity.

"What's going on is that this shady snake has just decided to tell Lou he's leaving her, that he's been cheating on her for six months. On fucking Valentine's Day!" Kate is trembling with fury. She rarely swears like this. "I'm going to fucking kill him," as she releases Lou and launches herself at the still seated Eddie.

Will grabs her, surprised by how fierce his usually calm girlfriend was being. He sits her down on the other side of the table to Eddie. "Stay there," he warns her.

He crosses over to Eddie's chair and puts his hands on Eddie's skinny shoulders. "Come on Eddie, stand up. You'd better leave."

And with that, Eddie finally stands up - and leaves.

The real slim shady.
Eminem.

-6-
LOU: SHACKLES

19th February 2000
It's been five days since Eddie's brutal Valentine's bombshell.

The girls tried everything they could do to help her, but all Lou wanted was her home and her childhood bed with its Garfield duvet cover. The pull of her family and Garfield was stronger than the dreadful thought of seeing Eddie with another girl, so she went back to Liverpool. She saw her old Fido Dido ring binder on her bookcase. Why had she kept that all these years? She shoved it under her bed so she couldn't see it.

Her dad was furious. Her mum fussed, baked for her, made soup and ached for her. Her sisters tried to do anything and everything they could. Offered board games and favourite films, musicals and cheesy dance CDs, face packs and ice cream, vodka and cranberry, even proper Smirnoff vodka. Nothing worked. Even the offer of tickets to watch Everton play Aston Villa at home on Sunday didn't work. The dance and fight had been drained from her like Superman losing the sun's energy. Her pride became her kryptonite.

Lou simply could not get out of bed for the first few days. She was lie low Dido, trying to think of anything but her Fido. She didn't get out of bed at all, apart from to go to the loo. Let every cup of tea and bowl of homemade soup she was brought go cold. Everything was grey. She ripped the pictures of him off the photo montage on her wall.

She was on a mixed up, ruthless merry-go-round of sobbing, rage and despair. She didn't wash. She wouldn't take any phone calls and could only eat plain biscuits and toast, everything else made her feel nauseous. Lou and her pride were genuinely traumatised.

She had trusted him implicitly. Had put her full faith in him. She had made him a part of her family, they had made him a part of it too. He had even spent Christmas with them. She felt so stupid, so embarrassed. She just hadn't seen it coming. The pain was overwhelming, but the shock to her pride even more devastating, savage and crushing.

"Supposing a tree fell down, Pooh, when we were underneath it?" said Piglet.

He was her first love. That all-consuming kind of young love. She felt like she had been split in two, or two split into one, she wasn't sure. Like the Spice Girls' 2 become 1, like a split atom. She remembered one time when Kate and Jen were stoned discussing the history of Manchester in the lounge at No. 52 in Withington, Charles Hetherington-Smythe watching, smirking proudly in his tweed.

They had been talking about some firsts of Manchester. Like Marx, Engels and the Communist Manifesto. Jen started telling her about the first electronic digital computer with the ability to memory-store. 'The Baby'. It had been designed and built by Williams and Kilburn at Manchester University in 1948. It was certainly no baby at seventeen feet long, seven and a half feet high and weighing in at over a tonne, but its birth was monumentally game changing. Lou had listened fervently in her Hairy Potter haze, surprisingly fascinated at the Manchester manifestations.

Then, after rolling up again, they rolled onto the atom. Apparently in 1917 a chap called Ernest Rutherford, from Manchester Uni again, had split the atom. A brilliant breakthrough that resulted in the birth of nuclear physics, the beginnings of nuclear power and the creation of cancer fighting radiotherapy. Not to be confused with nuclear fission which ultimately created the nuclear bomb. That was invented years later in 1938, six hundred and fifty-five miles east in Berlin. Manchester was apparently not responsible for fission, or the bomb. Lou, in her fog, had felt very pleased about that. She had told Charles so.

She had absolutely no idea about nuclear physics, but at that moment she had felt like an atom which had been split. She felt ripped apart.

She would never trust a man again quite like she had trusted Eddie, her first love, her pure shore. She was absolutely sure she would never want anyone to have her so completely handcuffed by love and trust. In these first few days Lou experienced her first desperate stinging stab of rejection and heartbreak. Her rite of passage from girl to woman.

"Supposing it didn't," said Pooh after careful thought.

Piglet was comforted by this.

On Saturday, today, Lou gets up. She certainly doesn't bounce down the stairs, but she manages a slight smile when her mum asks, "Fancy a brew love?".

"Three sugars please, mam."

"It will get easier love, I promise," Lou's mum assures her whilst tucking a rogue, greasy red curl behind her ear.

"I know mam. It just hurts so much. And I feel so, so stupid. I honestly felt I was gonna lose my mind."

"Come 'ere love," Lou's mum pulls her daughter close to her chest trying to lift the load off her, and holds her through her silent sobs. Then she dries the tears from her eyes with her thumbs – as she had done when Lou was a child. Her thumbs gently, carefully pushing the hope back into her distressed Rapunzel daughter.

"You know we never thought he was good enough for you kid, not for our Louby Lou," her dad confesses, his large frame walking in from his garden, from his beloved greenhouse. Puffing slightly, he takes off his huge, well-worn garden coat. Lou inhales the sweet smell of his cigar. It calms her for a second. "He was holding you back, shackling you - and he would have continued to hold you back. You need to dance, Lou. You're not like most girls. You need to fly."

"Mam?"

"Your dad's right, love. You know he never wanted you to go away. He wanted to keep you here. To clip your wings. He wanted to have you all to himself," Lou's mum confirms.

"And he didn't even really like you dancing, Lou," her dad says. "Did he? Be honest. Never really liked it when everyone was watching you."

Lou just listens. Tears starting to well again. Tears of realisation.

"And we didn't want to tell you because we didn't really know, but we think he's been seeing that girl for a lot longer than he's letting on," her mum says, taking her daughter's hands.

"Really? The bastard! The fucking shady bastard!" she throws her mum's hands away.

"Language, Louisa," her dad scolds.

"No Len, leave her - let her get angry!" Lou's mum counters, grabbing her daughter's hands again, forming them into fists. "Come on Lou – where's that famous fiery red-headed fight? Our chestnut mare? Compete, Lou. Feel the beat. Get mad! Get fucking mad!"

"I am fucking mad," Lou yells, clenching the fists her mum had made for her. "Fuck you, Eddie Taylor."

"You bloody pair of filthy-mouthed, mad bitches," Len laughs.

"Len!" Lou says indignantly. She often calls her dad by his name. She likes the way Lou and Len fit together so nicely. The perfect pair. "This is not the time to laugh."

Len turns up the radio in the corner of the kitchen. His fave Frank's dulcet, melodic tones start singing about times you knew and biting off more than you could chew.

He takes his daughter's fists off his wife and uncoils them. Taking her unfolded hands in his, he starts to dance his eldest daughter around the small kitchen and they collectively sing about doing it their way.

"You're a tough one, kid. Not like most girls," he praises his daughter, offending 'most girls' in the process. "Shackles off, Lou?"

"Shackles off, Len," she laughs at her dad's anti-feminism, but slowly starts to feel the beat again. Starts to dance.

Shackles.

Mary Mary.

-7-
THE QUARTET: YOU SEE THE TROUBLE WITH ME

29th February 2000
Lou returned to Manchester yesterday. Bruised, troubled, sad and angry, but with a new fight in her she didn't know she had. Her inner confidence and innocence dance replaced by a slightly different samba. A slightly wiser, more wistful dance. A more cautious Lou and definitely a less trusting Lou. But a more resilient Lou.

When she got back she immediately went to a clinic and had a thankfully negative STI test. She picked up a bag of free Durex condoms too - just in case.

It's Kate's birthday, her 20th birthday to be precise. Being Scottish and starting uni at seventeen makes her a year younger than the other girls. Or is it her 5th birthday? Being born on leap day, 29th February, in 1980 means that three quarters of her birthdays have been celebrated on the wrong day. Her 18th was celebrated on the wrong day, and her 21st will be celebrated on the wrong day. How shit is that?

She had once wondered whether her 30th or 40th birthdays would be celebrated on the wrong day, but then quickly realised she probably wouldn't give a shit by then so didn't calculate it. She'd be far too old to care.

"Isn't it ironic that Katie-Pie's so crap at dates and times, and is so late for everything – and her birthday is the wrong day most years?" Em had once mused.

"That's not irony, Alanis. That's just, like, shitty," Kate had responded.

Lou and Jen started to murder the four-year old non-ironic classic about spoons and knives, men of dreams and beautiful wives.

On the subject of marriage, it also means that every four years Kate could, in theory, propose to a man on her birthday. She has absolutely no intention of proposing to any man, on any day of the week. Although she likes to talk the feminist talk, she is a traditionalist at heart and requires her ample bamboozles (as she likes to call them) to be firmly secured in an unburnt push up bra as much as she requires a man to do the proposing.

'Eddie-twat-gate', as termed by Jen, had only been two weeks prior and Kate had suggested to Lou they postpone her birthday celebrations for a few more weeks until she was in the mood to go out. Lou still didn't really feel like having fun, but she knew she could do with a night of fun having her. So she had laughed and said, "I'm not letting that shady snake deny you your fifth actual birthday, ya knob 'ed!"

So it was done. The girls are going out dancing.

"Fifth Avenue?" Jen asks. They still missed the Hacienda, which had shut down eighteen months earlier.

"My choice! My birthday! I want to go to The Village," Kate puts her foot down.

"Prague Five or Via Fossa?" Jen offers.

"Let's see where the wind blows us!" Kate says whimsically.

They are all getting ready at Em's. Em in her bedroom, Jen in the bathroom. Both doors wide open. Kate on the floor with a small mirror she had brought from their house propped on Steve the Swiss cheese's plant pot, and Lou using the mirror over the fireplace. These are their spots, have been their spots for years – for makeup anyway. Hair is more of a battle. Em had tried to make the 'plug socket meet mirror' mare as easy as possible, but like many beautiful, expensive hotel rooms, her flat had clearly been planned by a man. A possibly bald man.

The flat's air is packed with shimmery frosted eyeshadow, bronzer and a heady mix of Vera Wang Princess, Clinique Happy and Body Shop White Musk.

"Lend us your Juicy Lips, Em," Kate yells from her spot by Steve.

"Juicy Tubes, Kate, they're called Juicy Tubes," Em corrects her for the fifth time.

Lancôme has fairly recently launched this iconic high-shine pucker pout producer.

"Ah yeah, sorry – keep getting confused with what Will calls my minge."

"Kate!" Jen cringes at 'minge'.

"What? What do you call yours then?" Kate giggles.

"My fu-fu," Jen says proudly.

"Fu-fu!" Lou screams. "Fu-fu!? That's the name of my auntie's poodle!"

"You've just made me mess up my bloody eyeliner, ya bitches!" Em howls as Kate spits out her Bacardi Breezer over the long-suffering Steve the Swiss cheese.

"I've got a stitch," Lou exclaims, doubled over with laughter. "I've also got a snatch," she blurts out.

"Snatch! Louisa! That's fucking worse than minge!" Em says in disgust.

"Well what do you call yours then, ya posh prick?" Lou asks. "Your lady garden?"

"No," Em replies. "I have spent the last two and a half years proving I am not a lady, and is it a garden if there's no lawn or bushes?"

The other three girls are wide eyed at this revelatory question. They have no idea she had upgraded from a Brazilian to a Hollywood. Jen only really mowed her lawn for a purpose. Having only had sex with one boy meant that holidays, swimming and really little hot pants were the only reasons she got her mower out. The majority of the time her fu-fu was actually more 'growler'.

"I tend to swap between Minky, Fandango and Hot Box depending on what mood I'm in," Em grins. "Can never decide - that's the trouble with me."

Steve the cheese is yet again Breezered, Lou's frosted pink lip liner skis off-piste up her cheek and Jen has to quickly sit on the loo before she pees her pants.

"Thanks girls, this is just what I needed," Lou admits while correcting the rogue frosted pink. "And happy fifth birthday, Minge!"

"Happy fifth birthday, Minge," Jen and Em sing.

Clad in an eclectic array of low-rise jeans, boob tubes, crop tops, capri pants, handkerchief tops, hot pants and mules, the girls set off to The Village.

'The Village' is in fact Canal Street. 'The Gay Village' to give it its tourist name. A street where its road sign keeps having its 'C' painted out by dick head tourists.

In the 19th century, cotton was one of the most important trades in the world and was initially fuelled by slavery. In those first several decades, to feed King Cotton, millions of Africans were enslaved and shipped to North America, where they were forced to work in the vast cotton fields of the South, the Cotton Belt.

Both Manchester and Liverpool had their own specific parts to play in feeding this brutal slave trade and horrendous abuse of power.

Liverpool

Cotton boats came into the Liverpool docks from America. This helped make Liverpool one of the wealthiest cities in the world, at times eclipsing the wealth of London. Cotton and slavery helped build the city's beautiful buildings, including St. George's Hall, The Royal Liver Building and The Albert Docks.

Manchester

Cotton was transported by water from Liverpool to the numerous state-of-the-art mills in Manchester – nicknamed Cottonopolis, the world's first industrial city – to be spun into yarn or cloth. Successful cotton spinning relied on high humidity and low-paid women and child labour. The city's wet climate and damp position under the Pennines (as confirmed by Len) plus its generally poverty-stricken population made it perfect to exploit in more ways than one. Manchester mill owners would then export this yarn and fabric to all four corners of the earth. At its peak, Manchester produced a third of the world's cotton.

Greed, brutality and exploitation of power – that's the trouble with capitalism at its ferocious exploitative finest.

This is the real root cause of the eternal Liverpool v. Manchester rampant rivalry. Not football. Cotton.

In short, Manchester was massively pissed off having to pay Liverpool merchants excessive handling charges and import / export taxes. The Manchester merchants needed to find a way of getting cotton to its mills and back out to the world without going through the Liverpool docks. It built an inland port just outside the city centre and, to get from the sea to the port, constructed the Manchester Ship Canal. Bypassing Liverpool. This obviously massively pissed off Liverpool. Manchester and Liverpool continue to be pissed off with each other to this day and football is the most recent incarnation of this rivalry.

Manchester is packed with a network of canals initially built to keep the cotton moving throughout the city. Canal Street sat at the heart of this network, with the New Union pub built in 1865. When commercial bust followed the cotton boom, Canal Street and its neighbours became deserted and many LGBT+ people moved in and started to make it their home and community.

From 1967, when homosexuality was partially decriminalised, until (shockingly) the late 1980s, venues were raided for ridiculous reasons like 'Licentious Dancing', with the Chief Constable at the time famously and frightfully saying that the trouble with gay men was that they were 'swirling in a cesspit of their own making.'

But the community stayed firm and launched its first Pride celebration in 1985, as a charity event for those with HIV and Aids. Now, in the year 2000, Pride is one of the biggest and best events in Manchester. Canal Street is a brilliant destination for all genders and sexualities with an amazing atmosphere in each of its plethora of restaurants, bars, pubs, clubs and hotels. No longer on the fringe.

Back to Minge's fifth birthday on Canal Street.

Kate opted for Prague Five. Its huge dance floor always a favourite for luckily now legal licentious dancing and mistakenly displaying a thong or two.

As the girls bounce, strut, pout, reverse into each other, wriggle and writhe, Lou removes herself from the group and stands back for a minute, looking confused and concerned.

She grabs Jen and shouts to the others, "We're just going to the loo."

"What's up?" Jen asks as she is purposefully escorted to the toilet.

Safely inside a cubicle, Lou looks down at Jen's ever so slightly swollen glittered midriff.

"Jen, I think you may be in trouble," Lou says seriously.

"Oh fuck," Jen had been in complete denial but knew something had been going on. Had been papering over it.

Her hands shoot up to cover her face, trying to hide from the all-consuming emotion that she is never meant to be the one in trouble.

But that is exactly what the trouble is with her.

You see the trouble with me.
Black Legend.

-8-
JEN: SILENCE

1st March 2000

Lou and Jen had not discussed anything with Kate and Em last night. Silence for now.

They had agreed, in the toilet at Prague Five, to meet the following morning, today, in Piccadilly Gardens at 10am. Lou said she knew a place near there - in fact she had only visited it the day before. They had carried on with the night as if nothing had happened. They had papered over it. For now.

Jen's ex had turned up at Prague Five a little later, somehow yet again knowing where she would be. Lou and Kate thought it was the bouncers (a very tight knit, insular community in Manchester which Jen's ex is a part of). Em thought he had inserted a tracker into Jen's fu-fu one night without her knowing. Jen bailed early after that and got the late bus home. She didn't want to stay at Em's, just wanted to be alone.

His appearances were not a daily occurrence anymore, and he hadn't turned up at Em's flat or Jen's semi-detached for a good week or so. It had been over five months since she had split up with him and the police had, as previously stated, been useless. It had been five months of looking over her shoulder, never feeling one hundred percent at ease. He was not a bad person, she argued with the girls, he was just a bit obsessed with her – or to be more precise, obsessed with owning her. He just couldn't cope with the rejection.

Sitting on the top of the bus heading for Piccadilly Gardens, Jen tries to think about anything other than what she is heading into. She tries to fill the silence. She remembers one of the first times Em had met her ex. It was early in their first year and he had turned up at Em's flat, somehow (as always) knowing where Jen was. Jen and Em had chosen a new blind for her kitchen window and were trying to put it up. They were making a complete hash of it and were in fits of giggles when he buzzed her buzzer.

"What are you up to?" he had asked, stupidly.

"We're painting the wall," Em bit back. She had met him just twice before and they already had a love/hate relationship.

Slightly blind-sided, he countered her bite back with, "That blind, it's proper hangin'."

"Well it's not quite hanging yet, as you can well see," Em helpfully explained, having absolutely no idea that he was saying how much he disliked the blind. That her blind was being dissed.

"Are you taking the piss?" he questioned, unaware she had no idea of his dislike of the blind. His diss.

"You two," Jen had berated the pair and proceeded to educate Em, yet again, on the dictionary of Manchester. "Hangin' means horrible," Jen explained.

"Why are you saying that my new blind is horrible?" Em asked indignantly but with a hint of a wry smile.

"You must be blind yourself if you think it's in any way not horrible," Jen's ex retorted, slightly snorting. "But come on, let me help you get the fugly thing up."

The trio had merrily managed to effectively erect the 'hanging not hangin' blind. Her ex was really rather handy. He had replumbed the waste pipe in her family's kitchen many years back, right down through the cellar and out to the Victorian drain. But right now, he is just a very modern, current drain.

Jen remembers fondly this love/hate relationship between her ex and her friend in the early days. She annoyed him with her poshness, he irritated her with his cockiness. But they did make each other laugh – a lot. It was a unique relationship that neither had ever had. It was only when he started to get so overly protective and controlling of Jen, or when his need to control became more obvious, less hidden by Jen, that the relationship between the two had started to sour.

It's cold and wet when Jen climbs down the stairs from the top of the double decker bus. The huge wipers battle against the relentless Manchester rain, squeaking and squawking with the effort. Waiting for the bus to pull into the station, Jen thinks of a childhood song, 'The wheels on the bus go round and round' and her favourite bit of it - 'the wipers on the bus go swish swish swish.' It is a satisfying, rhythmical motion. Like a see-saw. It transfixes her for a short while as the bus snakes into its stand at the station. The balance of it reminds her of one of her favourite quotes. A quote that Einstein wrote to his son in a letter:

Life is like riding a bicycle. To keep your balance, you must keep moving.

That's what she needs to do now – keep moving, keep her balance. One step in front of the other. Moving forward towards what deep down she knows and has been subconsciously unwilling or mentally incapable (or both) of facing into.

The rain is almost horizontal like a white wave. It stings her cheeks like jellyfish tentacles. Like a smack of jellyfish. She thinks how apt it is that 'smack' is the collective term for jellyfish. She isn't sure anymore whether she is being stung or smacked. She doesn't care.

She passes a little shop selling gifts and trinkets that she has never really noticed before. There is a little figurine in the window that commands her attention, speaks to her, draws her in. She can't take her eyes off it. It transfixes her. It is a pregnant woman in a long white dress with her hands protecting her bump. Such a natural, positive and complete form. Her head looks down to her unborn baby contentedly, peacefully, protectively.

She finds herself inside the shop, out of the storm, asking the shop assistant if she can take a look at her. She is beautifully carved out of some sort of clay. About 20cm tall. The lady says she is called Cherish and the tag attached to her says 'Awaiting a miracle'. She is £10. Jen knows she can't afford her, but also knows she can't leave without her. She is carefully wrapped in tissue paper and placed in a box with 'Willow Tree' and 'Susan Lordi' printed on it above 'Cherish' and 'Awaiting a miracle'. The box is then placed in a bag and given to Jen which she puts in her bigger bag.

She finds herself outside again and the sky is not as dark as she thinks it should be for this type of storm. It's oddly bright. It's white. Everywhere looks white. She is absolutely drenched again, but at least the wind and fierce rain break the silence.

"Keep swimming," she says to herself as she tugs on the Chelsea knot of her beloved and battered cream, chunky Chelsea Girl scarf and hugs her bag with her Cherish inside. She just puts one foot in front of the other, with no real destination.

Lou shouts at her and waves her hands. Jen is almost in a trance-like, slightly delirious state. Head down, keeping moving, keeping swimming. Lou runs over to her and grabs her shoulders.

"Jen, where are you headed? You don't even know where we're

going!" she shouts over the din of the deluge.

"Oh yeah," Jen just about forces out.

"Come on you. Let's go and get a brew before we get going," Lou links arms protectively and guides her up Oldham Street. Both heads go down to protect their faces against the stinging white wave.

Jen is pleased when Lou doesn't try to talk. It means she can fill the white silence with her own thoughts, let her think about something innocuous like some of the other Manc or Northern words she had had to explain to Em over the years.

'Brew' being a classic example (cup of tea). Em had thought she was offering her drugs when she offered her a brew for the first time. Was disappointed when she realised she wasn't. Now she uses the word quite often. Other Bs included barm cake (bread roll or bun), brassic (skint or broke), butty (sandwich) and buzzin' (excited or very happy) – and that was only one letter out of twenty-six.

With 25 being a square number and 27 being a cube number, 26 is uniquely placed as the only whole number that is exactly one greater than a square and one fewer than a cube. A rare, isolated number nestled between two exceptional number beasts. A lonely number, silently solitary and separate.

This is how Jen feels right now. Jen feels like a 26.

"Let's go face this Jen," Lou says kindly, when the empty mugs signal it is time to go. "Everything will be fine. We just need to understand the facts and then we can work out what to do with them. I am 100 percent here for you, we all are. We can be brave for you, whatever you need to be brave for. You can do and be anything you want to be, whatever you choose to do. Nothing, no choice you ever make, will define you. You can bounce back from anything. You're Tigger, right? Ok?"

"Ok," Jen says rather feebly after her friend's big speech. But something is swelling inside of her listening to her friend's wise words. Something is clicking in her head. Something is starting to make sense. A pure shore is starting to form, to fight against the white wave.

"Honestly Jen, you are one of the strongest, most thoughtful, most caring, most special people I have ever met - even though you're a bloody Manc! We will get through this, whatever 'this' is.

You have to believe me. You do believe me, right?"

Jen slowly and silently nods, starting to believe. Looking out into the white storm, she finds some ethereal strength. "A bounce back is always bigger and better than just a bounce," she thinks to herself. She tells herself.

"I've got a test, Jen. We can do this now and then head to the clinic after. If necessary," Lou encourages, forcing Jen's eyes to look at hers.

As she looks up at Lou, Jen thinks of the outcomes of pregnancy tests. How the results can be positive and negative in so many positive and negative ways. It is so personal to your own situation.

It can be 'positive positive' when you want a baby and are pregnant. It can be 'positive negative' when you don't want a baby and you aren't pregnant. Another can be 'negative positive' when you don't want a baby but are pregnant. And finally it can be 'negative negative' when you desperately want a baby, but there is no pregnancy.

So many different emotions from the outcome of one little test. A quartet of emotions. There's no wonder pregnancy testing kit adverts never show emotion, neither joy nor grief, excitement nor fear. As the feelings and reactions from the results are so personal and disparate.

"Do you want me to come into the loo with you?" Lou offers, breaking the silence.

"Yes please," Jen says, almost silently.

—

—

Jen and Lou head back into the white storm wave with linked arms, no more words needed. Silence is fine for now.

Two frightened, not quite yet believing girls keeping each other from sinking in their silence.

Two very strong blue lines ensuring they both believe.

Silence.
Delerium.

-9-
JEN: CAN WE FIX IT?

1st March 2000 – continued

Jen was sick earlier this morning.

Not bulexia/anoremia sick. Just sick.

It felt really weird.

She is thinking about it whilst she and Lou are sitting in the clinic waiting room.

"JENNIFER JONES!"

"Fuck me," Lou says under her breath. "Does he want to tell the whole of bloody Liverpool you're knocked-up as well as bloody Manchester?" Jen can't help smile at her protective, supportive friend.

Jen and Lou follow the rather large, middle-aged man and sit opposite him. The room is oppressive. No windows and lots of dark wood. Paint peeling from the walls. Yellowing polystyrene ceiling tiles display a history of drips, a smell divulges years of damp. A hard looking bed which splits in the middle covered in crusty fake red leather. Tatty posters randomly stuck on the dirty walls. 'Living with HIV', 'Chlamydia and Infertility' and 'Abortion: The Risks' to name just three of the welcoming pieces of art.

"I'm Doctor Krishnan. What do we have here then? Students I assume? I also assume you need something fixing before free condoms are of any use to you?" the man asks in an accusatory tone with a strong focus and deliberation on the word 'fixing'.

"My friend is pregnant," Lou states.

"Has she taken a pregnancy test?" the man questions Lou, ignoring the fact that Jen is sitting right next to her.

"Yes."

"Not married? A mistake? Need it fixing?" he assumes. That word again. Like they are in a car garage with a broken alternator.

"You are assuming a lot," Lou could not bite her tongue. "And she is right here, sitting right here. Her name is Jen. It wouldn't hurt to be a little kind!"

"Do you know how far along you are?" his tone starts to thaw slightly as he turns his attention to Jen.

"No, no I don't know. But I do know that I have not had sex for quite a long time," Jen says, her eyes rooted to the stained square carpet floor tiles.

"How long do you think?" he encourages.

"About five months," Jen slowly raises her eyes to meet his softening gaze.

Saying this out loud makes it true, frighteningly true. Not gradually, but instantly. Like a light switching on with no flicker. Lou glances over at her friend as it dawns on her how far gone she may actually be – how far gone she absolutely has to be. Jen continues to hold the man's eyes, searching for something, waiting for him to say something, anything. He slowly nods and gradually pushes himself up from his chair.

"Ok, let's take a look at you then," he walks over to the rotten red bed and pats it. "Up you jump."

It is an odd turn of phrase, like something you would say to a child. But something Tigger-like stirs in Jen. She is definitely not bouncing, but is sure she can manage a little jump. So she does exactly what she is told, as a good child should.

"You're absolutely tiny, but I would say this foetus is anywhere from nineteen to twenty-three weeks. It is definitely doing a great job of hiding itself," The doctor says as he prods and manipulates Jen's stomach. Jen stares up at the offensive ceiling tiles and the flickering fluorescent light which hums in a strangely comforting way.

"We will have to get you scanned to get a more accurate view, however, depending on what you choose to do, your time is running out so I would suggest we now sit down, go through the facts and discuss your options."

Jen nods as she covers up her stomach and goes back to sitting on the chair next to Lou, exactly as she is told to do.

Back in his chair, the doctor folds his arms and takes a deep breath in. He goes on to explain the law and her choices.

The Abortion Act of 1967 was, at the time, a big step forward for women and their right to choose what happens to their bodies. The details of this Act have not changed in the thirty-three years since. Abortions are legal up to twenty-three weeks and six days.

After twenty-four weeks they will only be performed if the woman's life is in grave danger, there is a severe foetal abnormality or the woman is at risk of grave physical or mental injury. At any stage of pregnancy, two doctors have to be in agreement that having the baby would pose a greater risk to the physical or mental health of the woman than a termination will.

Jen and Lou listen intently to this information. They had absolutely no clue about what was and was not legal before, what was and was not possible. Neither have private access to the internet, and going to a library asking a small, bespectacled woman for a book on abortion is not at the top of their bucket list.

"Have you got any questions so far?" the doctor asks the girls.

Lou and Jen just look at him both slightly open mouthed. At each other and then back to him. They literally have shit loads of questions, but they somehow won't come out of their already open mouths. They both slowly shake their heads.

"Ok. So I assume you want to consider the abortion route?" the doctor is back in modus-assumous. "I shall give you the facts. I am happy to sign for you to have the termination, and I will ask my colleague down the hall to do the same - so you have the mandatory two signatures. The only place you can have an abortion, at the late stage I believe you are, is in Leamington Spa."

The girls are sponges sucking in all these frightening facts like dirty dish water, and neither have any clue where Leamington Spa is.

"Your issue is, however, that it could take about two weeks to get you an appointment and they will not perform the procedure if they deem you to be over twenty-three weeks and six days on the day of the appointment. Therefore, if you are currently over twenty-one weeks, it is possible they will not perform the termination."

The information overload is quite intense for Lou. Jen has stopped really listening, or at least stopped processing. She doesn't want to hear any more – has no interest in hearing any further detail.

Lou was just about to start asking the questions which had been brewing in her brain when the doctor cut in with the most brutal piece of information.

"Earlier stage abortions use suction, however with later stage abortions you have to deliver the baby. You will be in labour – but will have a forced miscarriage. The foetus will be given an injection to ensure it is not alive when you deliver."

As Jen wretches, Lou's hands cover her mouth in horror.

"Could be worse. Not sure how, but it could be," said Eeyore.

The doctor, to his credit, soldiers on, "I am going to give you some literature. You don't have to make your decision yet. I want you to go off and have a think about it. Talk to whoever you feel most comfortable talking to. Maybe speak to the father? Or your own mother and father? Do some more research if you like."

He pauses for a moment or two waiting to see if Jen or Lou has anything to say.

Assuming their silence means they want the 'fix', or simply trying to ensure Jen's options are still potentially open, he ends with, "I will get the termination forms dual-signed now and posted to the clinic so that we don't waste any time and we ensure you have the best chance of fixing this. You will hear from them with an appointment date very soon."

Jen just wants to leave. The room has become even more oppressive and it feels like the air has been slowly sucked out of it. She can't breathe. She feels dizzy. The fluorescent hum is no longer comforting, it has become so loud it hurts her head and the stale smell is pervading her lungs. She needs to get outside, to get some fresh air. To never, ever hear the words 'fix' or 'fixing' again.

The doctor retrieves some leaflets and writes the number of the clinic in Leamington Spa on a piece of paper. Lou thanks him as he hands them to her.

Jen is already heading out of the door.

"Good luck," the doctor says empathetically as Jen escapes with Lou quickly following. Leaving the clinic and heading into the Manchester rain is a sliding doors moment for Jen. A real Gwyneth juncture.

Can we fix it? Yes we probably can!

But some things just don't need fixing, Bob.

They are fine just as they are.

Can we fix it?

Bob the Builder.

- 10 -
JEN: IT'S MY LIFE

3rd March 2000
Jen had stayed with Lou in Withington the night after the clinic. Kate was staying with Will in his student house and their other housemates were out, so they had the house to themselves for the majority of the evening.

Jen felt bad as Lou was still in some sort of shock from Eddie-twat-gate, but Lou insisted that it was the best thing. It was taking her mind off things, and she really really wanted to help and be a support to and for Jen. "We're in this together," she had proclaimed.

The two girls had talked and talked into the night. How had she not known? What about the way she had treated her body? The nights out, the drinking, the smoking. Has this damaged the baby? How would she tell her mum? What would her mum say? What would people say? How far along actually was she? What about her ex? What would the future look like? Would she be able to finish her degree? What would she say to the university? Would she ever get a job? How could she work with a baby? Where would she live? Endless questions, but few answers.

They banked the questions and Lou started making lists, practical lists. A list of questions and a list of potential actions. The action list was significantly less populated. "Remember Jen, it's your body and your decision. It's your life."

One thing Jen didn't discuss with Lou was her bulexia/anoremia. She had never told anyone about this. She worried whether that would have had an impact on the baby. She was worried about how on earth she was going to stop it. She was worried about so many things.

What she wasn't worried about was her decision. It was made. It had been made when she had seen Cherish in the shop window. No, in fact, it had been made in the toilet in Prague Five two nights earlier.

The consequences of her decision are unknown and uncertain. Her decision isn't.

The first thing she has to do is somehow tell her mum. After being unceremoniously dumped after twenty-five years of marriage for a rich widow with the same name as her, she knows this is going to hurt. She loves her mum very much and doesn't want to upset her any more than she already is. But she knows this is impossible. She knows her mum will be hugely worried for both of them. All three of them, in fact.

She also has to tell her much adored Grandpa. A devout Catholic, this is going to be a huge shock and difficult to digest. She will not even consider telling her ex until this is done and she understands a little more, until she has processed it further herself.

She had called her auntie; she had called her almost immediately after the clinic appointment. She, her mum's sister, knows everything. Unlike her sister, Jen's mum.

But that would all have to wait until later, both girls have to get to uni. Lou has practice and Jen has a decent degree to pull out of the baby bag. She is heading for a high 2:2 and hadn't really cared before. Hadn't really taken it too seriously. It now really mattered. She needed to be brewing at least a 2:1 for her and her little one. This was her life now.

"What are you doing here?" Jen's mum asks as she walks into the kitchen.

"That's nice isn't it. I do actually live here!" Jen teases her mum.

"But it's Friday night."

"I thought we could have a chippie tea and watch a movie?" Jen offers.

"Now I'm suspicious!" her mum says. "And it's a film, not a movie. We are not American."

"Come on, let's get some fish and chips – my treat. I can go and get a film too?" Jen feels guilty that she probably has not spent as much time with her mum as she should have since her father left. She is busy at work and has loads of friends there, but Jen knows her nights are as long as her weekends are lonely.

Hers is a generation where it appears you become a pariah to some of your friends once single. Instead of being wrapped up and looked after like friends should, and Jen thought hers would. Most of Jen's mum's friends were in couples. Some still called and made some sort of an effort, but it was a wary one for many. And for others, a choice between one or other of the crumbled couple. Not being part of a pair means an odd number at dinner parties or in restaurants, the wrong 'balance'. Invitations have slowly died away, especially on weekends. This is her life now.

"Ok, you go and get the food and the film. I'll carry on with a bit of packing here," her mum says, continuing to slowly pack up the semi in preparation for moving.

As Jen makes her way to the local Blockbuster, hoping there is a decent film left, she has a flashback. It was probably about eight or nine years earlier, but she couldn't accurately date it. Harrison Ford (much loved by the full Jones family from endless Star Wars and Indiana Jones viewings) was in a rare romcom, starring with Melanie Griffith, and Jen and her sister had pestered and pestered their mum to rent 'Working Girl' for them. Their mum had thought it was probably a little mature for her girls, but had relinquished to pester power - "but EVERYONE has seen it mum!" (lies) – and had booked the rental for that Saturday night.

The Blockbuster had not been open long and was a really exciting place. No longer the corner shop with a couple of dozen tapes on a metal wire shelf type thing which spun around (only one copy of any film of course), but a brilliant, big, shiny new store with hundreds of options and multiple copies of the latest and best releases. And the range of sweets and chocolate was amazingly. They called films 'movies' and the sweets 'candy', much to their mum's disdain. It all felt so American and cool.

Jen's mum went to pick up the pre-ordered, prized movie/film. She headed to the counter and gave her name for the booking list. "Here we are Mrs. Jones, I've got you'" the greasy-haired man-boy confirmed, giving her a wink.

Unsure what to do with said slightly weird wink, she checked it was the right film in the blue Blockbuster box (experience had taught people to do this in the Blockbuster era) and paid swiftly while he parroted "Back by tomorrow at 3pm. Be kind and rewind. If you're not kind and don't rewind, you'll be fined." He had added the last sentence to the corporate line and was clearly rather proud of himself. He hated having to check all the films when they came back in and rewind them himself (it took forever), and he hated it even more when people complained about having to rewind them at home before watching them because some heartless bastard had not been kind and one of his lazy Blockbuster colleagues had been clearly equally unkind, knowing he would not personally be fined.

At home Jen and her sister were excitedly waiting in the lounge in front of the big TV and the VHS player when their mum arrived back with the cherished little blue box. "Thank you mum!" both girls yelled, wrapping their arms around her.

Armed with two cups of Dandelion and Burdock poured from a glass Barr bottle and a Sherbet Dip Dab each, Jen's sister popped the tape into the VHS player. Some heartless bastard had not been kind.

Many minutes later it had fully rewound. Then, of course, they had to fast forward a proportion of the previous rewind to skip the trailers. Fast forward was rewind's ugly cousin. It was pretty much uncontrollable in its one speed, making it almost impossible to stop at the 20th Century Fox fanfare. Inevitably it would include another 'rewind' to prevent missing the start of the film. Like trying to stop/start write the lyrics of a song which unkindly didn't have the lyrics printed in the cassette sleeve. Exhausting!

They got to what they thought was the start of the film, having seemingly missed the 20thCentury Fox fanfare for the fourth time, and settled in as their mum washed up after tea in the kitchen where their father was reading 'The Independent' broadsheet.

No Harrison, Melanie or Sigourney from 'Alien' yet.

The girls waited and got a little confused. It hadn't started as they had expected, but they rolled with it as they Dip Dabbed and Dandelioned. A little while later, with lollies stuck halfway into their open mouths and sherbet dripping onto the patterned carpet, the girls realised that perhaps there was something amiss.

"Mum," Jen's sister yelled. "Mum, come in here a sec".

"Coming," their mum sang from the kitchen.

"We haven't seen Indiana yet," Jen said as their mum entered sporting her mandatory Marigolds. "And there's a naked man on a bed talking about his 'fantasy' to a girl."

"What the bloody hell is this?" she yelled. Mum rarely yelled. And she certainly never swore (bloody hell, Jesus, oh God and the like were definitely swear words in the Jones home).

She raced over to the VHS player and tried in vain to press the eject button with her soapy Marigold-ed fingers. She pressed pause by mistake and the screen froze at a highly inappropriate moment. "Girls, leave the room. Right now." Her tone did not invite questions or counters.

Jen and her sister giggled in the hall, not really sure what they had just witnessed – both on the screen and in their mum's reaction. But they knew that whatever they had witnessed, they shouldn't have. It felt grown up and cool. Their mum raced down the hall and out of the house with the now lesser prized little blue box bellowing, "This is never to be discussed! Do you hear me? Never ever!"

It wasn't until a good few years later that Jen asked her mum what had happened. "The stupid boy gave me the wrong tape. I gave him a piece of my mind, I'll tell you!" Jen knew what a piece of her mum's mind looked like and didn't envy the Blockbuster man-boy.

"But you always checked the tapes! What on earth did he give you?" Jen had chuckled.

"Working Girls," she had sheepishly replied. And it had all made sense. She had checked the tape. She had just not noticed the plural that made it a porn movie. The innocuous 's' that made it a sex tape.

"I assume it was from the little naughty section? He thought you were on for a porn night! You in your twin set and pearls," Jen couldn't stop laughing at how this incident, many years earlier, had left her mum with some form of PTSD.

"He kept saying I had requested Working Girls," her mum had said indignantly. "He made it out to be my mistake! And when he asked me if I had been kind and rewound, I told him that I'd rewind him." Her retort made absolutely no sense at all, but Jen, imagining her tone, knew Blockbuster man-boy didn't even attempt to give her a fine.

It was quite some time before the girls saw the non-porn Working Girl, simply because their mum gave Blockbuster a decidedly wide berth for a while.

The memory makes Jen smile and she experiences a wave of love for her mum.

Now, at the same Blockbuster, Jen chooses an Indiana Jones movie for posterity. She double checks the tape in case she had been given 'Raiders of the Lost Arse' or 'The Temple of Douche' by mistake. All good, she is safe.

The start of the transition to DVDs is happening, but video tapes still reign. "Be kind and rewind."

Jen picks up a fish for her mum, a cheese and onion pie for her and her bump, a portion of chips to share and a mandatory polystyrene pot of mushy peas.

She heads back home, not knowing at what point she is going to tell her mum her news.

There doesn't seem to be a good time for quite some time. For some reason she blurts it out in the rolling boulder in the cave scene when her mum is laughing and looking really quite happy.

Just after Indy says "Adios Señor," Jen says, "Mum, I'm pregnant."

Her mum continues to watch the screen but her expression is vacant.

Adios before.

Something changes in that moment between mother and daughter. It is a monumental shift. Almost a power shift, a tangible transition from then to now, from now to before.

"You're not thinking about keeping it?" was all her bereft, stunned mother can say.

"Yes, I am."

"Well, we will see about that Jennifer," her mum says to her twenty-year old child. "You will ruin your life."

"It's my life."

With that Jen races upstairs and promptly expels the barely eaten pie, chips and mushy peas as she wrestles with how to keep control of the situation.

"Some people care too much. I think it's called love," said Pooh.

Jen knows her mum only cares for what is best for her, she cares deeply.

But Lou's words ring resolutely in her ears as she wipes the seat and papers over it.

"Remember Jen, it's your body and your decision. It's your life."

It's my life.
Bon Jovi.

-11-
JEN: 7 DAYS

7th March 2000

Shrove Tuesday. Absolution following confession.

Pancake Day. The day of the feast. The feast before the fast.

It is randomly snowing.

It has been seven days since Lou realised what was going on with Jen (Tuesday), six days since the clinic (Wednesday), five days since the lists and the actions (Thursday), four days since Jen told her mum (Friday), the following two days had been difficult, and finally Jen chilled for a bit yesterday (Monday).

If only Craig David had met the girl on a Tuesday instead of a Monday, it would all have tied in nicely.

Lou had updated Kate and Em on the Friday. Em had selfishly kicked off about having not been involved earlier. Kate had kicked off at Em calling her a self-centred, spoilt brat. Lou had kicked off on them both.

Jen stayed upstairs in her bedroom for a while on the Friday after running upstairs and expelling her chippie tea. She got Cherish out of her box and just looked at her. Oddly nodded at her. Her ex had called her numerous times. She knew he couldn't possibly know, it was just his random obsessive behaviour.

Em had texted her:

Here if u nd to tlk. Yr Ex was here b4. Wnts 2 spk to u. Tld him f off.

Suddenly there was a thudding on the front door, the big original Victorian wooden door probably in place since the late 1800s when the house was built. It had been painted black a few years earlier. Jen had thought how smart it looked when she saw it. It had a lovely brass knocker and knob which her mum had always kept super shiny, and three well-trodden stone steps, which her mum had also kept immaculate. They didn't look quite as cared for since her father had last pulled the knob to close the door and bounced down the steps.

As the brass knocker was being over-stimulated and fists were clearly pounding the beautiful solid black panels and the bevelled glass, she knew immediately it was her ex. She checked the digital alarm clock on her bedside table. 21:13. She could not deal with him right now. But then she also knew her mum was probably in a worse state to do so than her. She had had enough of his antics over the last five months, and in many ways, the last five years.

She went downstairs and shouted at him through the door to leave her alone.

"I just want to talk to you," he shouted.

"I don't want to talk to you," Jen screamed. "Please just leave me alone."

"Just give me five minutes, then I promise I will leave you alone," he pleaded.

But Jen knew how this worked. How it had worked for quite some time now.

This went on for some time until Jen's mum appeared in the hall and screamed at the top of her lungs "LEAVE HER ALONE!!" and pulled Jen away from the door down the hall.

He started beating the door with force and within a split second the brass hinges gave way and the heavy Victorian mass fell into the hall. The glass splintering over the floor. Her ex looked stunned with his own strength, but even more flabbergasted when a police van sirened its way onto the drive.

Her mum never admitted to calling the police, but she could have. Or it could have been a neighbour.

Whoever it was, it didn't matter.

Her ex was handcuffed and escorted into the back of the van. Jen felt dreadful. She didn't hate him at all, she had loved him for years. It was so sad to witness. But she had been a witness for him numerous times in the past, had lied for him in court. Something she was not proud of. She had to remember all the things he had done to her or made her do over the years. She watched him being driven away, like his behaviour had driven her away.

A female police officer came in and sat Jen and her mum down in the lounge, followed by a male officer. The Indiana Jones closing credits rolled up the TV screen and 'The Raiders March' theme tune played joyfully. The police officer turned the TV off.

As the statement was being taken, Jen's phone started ringing. It was her ex. Jen's mum shouted, "Did you not take his bloody phone off him? He is even hounding her from the back of your police van!"

The rest was a blur for Jen. Yet again she was told she should write a diary for the next few months. Obviously the best first line of defence for the interception of stalkers.

"Dear Diary. It's day one and my front door has been kicked in," her mum said incredulously. "What are you wanting days two and three to be about? Or the seventh day?"

They brushed over her comment, probably knowing how ridiculous they were sounding. But not having any other line of defence in their armoury. They would caution him and the offence would be recorded. Did Jen's mum want to press charges for breaking and entering? But he had never entered. Then maybe for criminal damage? Jen just wanted them to go away. She had absolutely no confidence at all that they would be able to sort this, but she was also concentrating on what she knew that her ex didn't.

"Have you got somewhere you can go and stay for a few days, maybe a week?" the female officer asked. "Just to get yourself away for a short while. We will keep him in overnight, but by lunchtime tomorrow we will have to release him."

Jen thought that if this was their best strategy for the second line of defence, for her to keep herself safe rather than them actually doing their job of keeping her safe, then yes. She would go and stay somewhere. She was now not just keeping herself safe.

It was not far off 11:30pm by the time the police left and the man they had called had secured the property.

"I think it's time for bed, Jen," her mum said, totally shell shocked by the past three and a half hours. "Let's talk in the morning." She hugged her. Her mum wasn't really a big hugger, but that night she was. Jen was grateful that that night she was.

"A hug is always the right size," said Pooh.

The following day, the Saturday, Jen had tried to sleep in. She had not slept well – unsurprisingly. Her mum knocked on her door and told her to get up, that there were some people here to see her.

For fucks sake, Jen thought, thinking it was the police again. But it wasn't. Before she had gone to bed her mum had called her best work friend, a nurse, and asked for her help. She had come to the house first thing with another nurse friend to help Jen consider her options on 'fixing it'.

Jen could not believe it. That word again.

Railroaded, she sat in the same chair in the lounge where she had told her mum the night before, the same chair where she had sat when giving a statement to the useless police, the same chair she had watched porn whilst Dip Dabbing with her sister many years before.

Is that irony, Alanis?

As Jen had not had the chance to explain anything more than the fact of pregnancy, she went on to explain. Her mum and her mum's friends were lovely, caring people. The three of them listened.

It was 'decided' that Jen will go to the clinic in Leamington Spa to see whether 'fixing' is an option, and decide when she is there. Her mum will come with her.

Jen, exhausted, agreed to everything – apart from her mum coming. She said she needed to do it by herself. She promised her mum she would think very seriously over the next week or so, and that she would go to see what date the scan said. What her 'fix' options really were. She pinky promised. She pinky lied. She had absolutely no intention of going to any spa. Leamington, Bath or the local convenience store.

All three women looked relieved and pleased, or as pleased as they could be, with the outcome. Jen felt guilty that they clearly trusted her, especially that her mum trusted her. It reminded her of when she had just passed her driving test at seventeen and she had a little jeep with a big spare wheel protruding from the rear – about as high as Jen's inflating boobs. It was a white jeep with a windsurfing rhino on the side and a soft roof which had big press studs to take it on and off. It was very slow, needed the choke every time it got slightly cold, had just four gears and took all of Jen's strength to turn the wheel when stationary – but it was cool.

At the time her parents had owned a business and had an office with a small car park round the back. It was, again, a Victorian semi and the car park was enclosed by a very tall, beautiful Victorian brick wall. The car park was not visible from the office, or in fact from any other property, due to the location and especially due to the magnificent old brick wall.

One day Jen was in the car park trying to manoeuvre. Her three-point turns had always been crap, she just thanked her lucky stars the road she had done one on in her test had been huge and she had done it in her instructor's car, not the super heavy jeep. Compounded by a shocking lack of spatial awareness, it was an accident waiting to happen.

Of course the wall fell down. All one hundred years of it. As it started to crumble, she jabbed the gears into first and removed the arse of her jeep from said crumbling wall. Without looking back, she drove as quickly as the jeep would go out of the car park.

At home that evening she could hear her parents debating, or rather arguing, over the banjoed brick wall. They just could not understand it. How could a hundred-year-old wall fall down in the first place when there was no wind and none of the office staff's cars had any damage? Even more confusingly, how had only the portion higher than the first four feet fallen? They were frankly baffled. The only thing they could come up with was that it was a bin lorry or other vehicle with a tail gate at least four feet up from the ground. The following day the council were called and a complaint was made.

Jen remembers going outside to surreptitiously check the back of the jeep for any scratches or tell-tale signs. But the big, protruding, four feet off the ground rubber wheel had taken the strain and showed absolutely no signs of damage at all. Winner!

Jen had never told her parents. She never took any responsibility. Had let the argument with the council rumble on. The jeep/wall juxtaposition would never be revealed, and probably never be solved. As much as she knew her mum, and especially her dad, were intelligent, sometimes you never see the solution or the answer that is staring you in the face. Literally laughing at you from your drive. And in fairness, it had become far too funny as the conspiracy theories rumbled on.

She did feel a little guilty for quite a long time. But nowhere near as guilty as she did now. For promising she would do something she knew 100% she would not do.

It was a very different kind of guilt she had felt when her and her friends had gone out carol singing 'for the church', got invited into Christmas parties and dinner parties as entertainment, raised a small fortune – and then split it and kept it for themselves. Or the time they had taken some hardcore looking herbicide from one of their garages to the local bowling green late one night and created a rather impressive giant penis with equally substantial balls on the gloriously manicured green. It took a few days to reveal its full phallic features and many months to hide them. Or even the time she and her uni friends had rampaged around Manchester with a black marker pen adding an 'I' between the 'O' and the 'L' on numerous 'TO LET' signs. That was all passing guilt (sorry God, Grandpa, the keeper of the green and the multiple letting agents).

This was a guilt that was deep rooted, unlike the giant cock. She knew it would grow, bud, blossom, flower and last forever. She was in too deep.

But, unlike the Victorian car park wall, her house door, the bowling green and the TO LET signs - she did not need to be 'fixed'.

She just needed somewhere to hide out for a few days, to do the police's job for them. It needed to be somewhere her ex didn't know, so nobody local. She didn't have enough money for a hotel. If she went to stay with one of her own relatives or in one of her home friends' houses, she could be found. Lou's home was only down the M62, so a plan was hatched. Em promised she would make sure she went to every lecture, every seminar and tutorial to make sure Jen had all the work and notes she needed. She also promised she would illegally sign her in if a spot check happened.

On the Sunday, the three girls and a suitcase, with Cherish carefully wrapped up inside, shot west on the M62, Liverpool-bound in Em's Renault Clio. Jen couldn't face driving, and didn't want her car to give her away - even thirty three miles from her home.

Jen was settled into Lou's bedroom and Lou's mum fussed around them making them food and cups of tea. When it was time to leave, Jen gave Em and Lou a massive hug. Lou had to get back to uni. Lou didn't tell her mum about the pregnancy or her ex, had just said she needed some space for a few days. Lou's mum didn't question, just said she would be there for Jen if she needed her or wanted to talk.

She just left Jen to sleep on the Monday. "The girl is exhausted", she thought to herself. "Just let her chill".

And that takes us to Tuesday the 7th of March. Today.

Shrove Tuesday. Absolution following confession. Pancake Day. The feast before the fast.

God created the world in six days and used the seventh day to chill.

The special number seven.

There are seven Chakras. seven colours in a rainbow, seven musical notes, seven continents and seven wonders of the world.

And, of course, there are seven days in a week.

And what a week it has been.

7 Days.
Craig David.

-12-
JEN: THE TIME IS NOW

17th March 2000
St. Patrick's Day.
On a Friday - to the delight of Irish people all over the world, including the heavily Irish-rooted cities of Liverpool and Glasgow.

Jen's Leamington letter had come through far earlier than expected. It arrived on the 11th of March. As the letter had gone to her semi home address and Jen was still in Liverpool, her mum had opened it and called her with the details.

She was to attend the clinic on Wednesday 15th March at 11:30am. Her mum had worked out her route for her. Had clearly been to the local train station with a pen, a piece of paper and a clear purpose. She was to get the train from Liverpool Lime Street to Birmingham New Street at 7:08am, then the train from Birmingham to Leamington Spa at 9:03 getting in at 9:47. This gave her plenty of time to get to the clinic by 11:30. All sorted, all 'fixed'.

But she never caught the train, never went to Birmingham, never found out where Leamington Spa was and certainly never attended the clinic. She rang them to let them know she would not be attending, and asked them to not send any correspondence to her home address. She 'fixed' it.

She waited it out at Lou's. Being looked after by her mum, Len and her two sisters.

She had called her mum in the afternoon of the 15th from the Liverpool side of Leamington to give her the news. They had said she was over the twenty-three weeks and six days so they would not perform the termination.

Lou knew she would have to somehow work out the dates when she finally found exactly far along she was and got an actual due date, but at that stage she didn't care. The effort of the lie had been exhausting.

Her mum had sighed and just told her to come home. She waited three hours or so (to ensure the lie did not have any time or geography holes in it) and caught the train from Liverpool to

Manchester, then the tram back home. Her mum picked her up from the tram stop.

They drove the short drive home in silence.

At home, her mum said, "This is the rest of your life now, Jen. We need to make some plans, take some action."

She had clearly got over the initial shock and was starting to accept the inevitable – all in the four and a half hours it had taken Jen to get back from Liverpool Spa.

It was highly likely, in fact, that she had been on the phone to her sister to explain the awfulness of the situation, and her sister had had a good strong word with her and talked her round to focus on what needed to be done, rather than what had been done. Focus on the now. On what you can control.

It was late and Jen was exhausted. She just wanted to go to sleep.

"No, Jen, you need to face into your responsibilities. There is no time like the present. The time is now."

That was just two days ago and so much has been achieved.

With the help of her mum, Lou, Kate and Em – plus the combination of Lou's original list and the list Jen and her mum had written – Jen ticked off the following by 4pm:

- GP appointment booked and completed

- Hospital scan appointment booked

- University informed. First meeting completed. Special tutor assigned

- Grandpa informed (gently on the phone by Jen's auntie. Her mum couldn't quite face that job so gave it to her sister)

- Pregnancy and baby book bought by Em

- List written by Jen and Kate from said baby book as to all the things Jen and the baby would need

- List ripped up and rewritten by Jen's mum saying they were living in la la land

- Marks & Spencer and British Airways recruitment teams informed. Jen was not going to be moving to London or flying around the world any time soon

- Wardrobe assessed for what could and could clearly not be worn as Jen grew

The following, however, was not ticked off:

PAPER OVER IT

- Tell Jen's ex

Jen knows she has to tell her ex. It is only fair. He had always wanted a baby so she knows he would be over the moon.

Jen is on the phone to Em. "Jen, call him now. Tell him today. It will be another thing off your list. A really big thing," Em encourages. "Come on Jen, it's time. It's only fair."

Jen calls her ex at just gone five. As she had expected, he is over the moon. When he asks if it is definitely his, she privately laughs to herself that if she could have picked another she possibly would have. She says nothing.

What she does say, very firmly, is that he can have a part in the baby's life if (and only if) he now leaves her alone. She is not going to get back with him. She will have his baby but never him again. This was the only way it could or would work. She feels cruel and doesn't want to hurt him. Even after everything he has done, she still cares for him. Always will.

But she is quite brutal about it – and in his euphoria he just accepts it. This is the day things change, he changes. He is no longer her ex, he is going to be the father of her baby. Something snaps in him and he promises never to harass her again. She believes him.

What he also says is, "Thank you."

These two little words mean such a lot to Jen, but the one little word he says after means even more. "Sorry." Such a small word, such a huge relief to Jen. She knows by that one small word that things will be better.

"Sometimes the smallest things take up the most room in your heart," said Pooh.

Jen and her mum sit down that night to watch TV. Her mum promptly dozes off with her head back, snoring slightly. Jen finds the rhythm of it quite comforting. The girls are going to a big St. Patrick's Day party in Manchester and had encouraged her to go and have some fun, but Jen is not interested. She did say she would definitely go out the following week, but not tonight. Not now. She just wants to stay in, with her mum. She feels full of nervous energy, but strangely at peace.

As she sits there she feels the strangest sensation in her tummy. A flutter, like little bubbles. It takes her a few moments to realise what it is.

"We don't need to hide any more, little one," she says to her stomach. "You were hiding and so was I. No more. It's our time now."

The time is now.
Moloko.

-13-
JEN: DEEPER SHADE OF BLUE

2nd April 2000
Mother's Day.

Jen spends a nice day with her mum, knowing next year they will both be mums.

But the nicest thing about the day for Jen is a card through the letterbox with her name on the envelope.

'For you mum' is printed on the front of the card covered with flowers and butterflies. As she opens it, she immediately recognises the handwriting.

Thank you Mummy for looking after me and keeping me warm in your tummy. I'm doing fine and I know everything will be ok. So don't worry, because when you worry it only upsets me too.

I know that you will also be the best mummy ever and I love you more than anything or anyone in the whole wide world.

Thank you, and I will see you soon.

Love forever, Your baby xxxx

She reads it over and over, letting the words seep into her. It is such a lovely thing for her ex to do, to write. And so unexpected.

It makes her baby a little bit more real. Somehow, however silly she knows it is, it turns him or her into a proper little person with thoughts and feelings. She promises herself she will try and feel less worried and blue, for her baby's sake. She just needs the scan now.

Thank You she says simply in her text message to him. No SMS language this time.

NO THANK YOU he replies almost immediately. No SMS language in his either.

Just a bit shouty in its capital letters. And the absence of a comma makes it look rather like he is telling an unwanted front door knocker, touting gutter cleaning or the spiritual benefits of being a Witness of Jehovah, to basically fuck off.

3rd April 2000

73

Scan day.

Jen is terrified. Again.

She hasn't slept well for quite some time, but the last week has been particularly difficult.

Brutal, graphic and traumatic dreams have filled her subconscious. Blue, deformed babies fill her nightmares.

"But I didn't know," she screamed so loudly her mum raced into her bedroom.

She found her child wet with sweat, shaking, slightly blue, with wide, terrified eyes.

"Jen?" she murmured.

"No!" Jen screamed.

Her mum went into the bathroom and got a face flannel. She let the tap run for a few seconds so it was cold and soaked the cloth before wringing it.

Back in the bedroom she saw Jen's eyes had closed. She had fallen back to sleep. A troubled, twitching, unhappy sleep. She was sucking her thumb like she did as a child. She placed the cold flannel on her forehead and stayed for a few minutes until Jen calmed, got some colour back and her breathing took on a more rhythmical metronome.

Jen's mum cried silently watching her daughter's little body rise and fall. She had not been sleeping either. She is genuinely terrified of the future. For herself, her daughter and her grandchild. She just prays they will all rise, not fall.

Jen had not known she was pregnant. The moment she did, she had taken better care of herself. She was not a big drinker, but she had clearly drank alcohol when pregnant. She had smoked. She was not a big weed smoker at all, like a lot of her friends, but she had had the occasional spliff. The guilt was all-consuming.

The fact that she hadn't known she was pregnant did not make anything better. She was terrified that she had damaged her baby. That there would be something wrong with him or her. That it would be absolutely her fault.

She had been to the library a few days earlier and looked up books on pregnancy and substance abuse. There were lots of information on FAS, Foetal Alcohol Syndrome. It was horrific. She gagged when

PAPER OVER IT

she read about growth issues and lower than average intelligence, and saw pictures of the poor babies and children with deformed facial features. She ran to the toilet and was physically sick.

She hadn't spoken to anyone about it. She hadn't been able to bring herself to. And it wasn't just this, she was generally frightened that there would be other defects and abnormalities. That her bulexia/anoremia had caused complications. That the scan would show her baby had not developed properly. That he or she had heart issues or other organ problems, not enough toes and fingers, or too many. She felt a deep shade of blue in that moment, peppered with gruesome, blazing guilt. That she'd love her child was never in doubt, but that she may have caused a harder-than-it-should-be life for him or her was devastating.

She knows deep down that most mums probably had these blue thoughts, she was certainly in company. But most mums don't find out they are pregnant at five months. Most mums have their first scan at about twelve weeks. Know if there are any potential issues much earlier on. Most mums were better. Being in better mum company didn't help her sleep at night.

The clocks had leapt forward last Sunday, so the sun is starting to rise. She hears her mum's 6:30am alarm clock going off. She is due at work at 7:30am. It is about a twenty-minute drive to the hospital. She wears a uniform so normally gets ready really quickly and easily, no decisions to be made apart from which bra and knickers to wear.

Jen is to meet her at the maternity unit reception at 10:50am, ten minutes before her appointment. It is just downstairs from the neonatal unit. She has to have a full bladder and some cash for both the car park and the ultrasound pictures.

She hasn't told her ex she's having the scan. She'll update him after.

She gets up, goes downstairs and puts the kettle on. She makes two cups of tea and takes one up to her mum.

"All ok?" her mum asks.

"Yes, fine," Jen lies. She doesn't know about her mum's late night visits to her bedroom. Her mum thought it was best not to tell. Couldn't think of a positive reason to. She also doesn't know how blue her mum is also feeling.

"It will be fine," her mum assures her, unsure herself. "Why don't you go and have a nice bath?"

It makes Jen laugh when her mum, and other people, add 'nice' to things. It's so unnecessary. You wouldn't exactly go out of your way to have a bad bath, a crap cup of tea or a nasty nap.

And 'nice' is such a bland word. Like magnolia paint, vanilla ice cream, navy blue and ready salted crisps. But Jen actually really likes vanilla ice cream and ready salted crisps. She also rather likes navy blue. She does agree that magnolia paint is a little bland, however.

Right now, nice and bland are good. Jen craves nice and bland. She's had enough of drama.

She takes her nice cup of tea into the bijou yet bland magnolia bathroom and runs herself a nice bath.

"Bye Jen," her mum shouts ten minutes later. "See you in a bit."

"Bye mum," Jen yells back from her bath, made even nicer with bubbles. She closes her eyes and lies back, submerging her head into the warm vanilla fragranced froth. Nice and bland.

Her mum had told her that the maternity unit car park could get really busy so to give herself a bit of wiggle room in case she has to go to another car park and walk through the huge hospital. She decides to leave at 10am to give herself plenty of wiggle.

After washing her hair using the shower hose she attaches to the bath taps, she takes the plug out and stands up to groom her overgrown growler. The Immac stink makes her gag a little, and her little bump is stopping her seeing exactly what she is doing. She has no idea whether her fu-fu will be featured in her first scan but wants to try to look as immaculate as she can, just in case it does get a rare outing.

She has to wait for six minutes standing in the bath. The maximum time on the leaflet. She is confident her overgrown lawn will need this long. Bored, she decides to clear the hair from the sink plug hole with a pair of tweezers she finds on the side. It is disgusting, but weirdly satisfying - like going to the tip. She drags out what lies beneath - a huge beast of a hairball monster. It grows gruesomely the more she pulls. A bit like her sleep right now, monstrous beastly blue thoughts perpetually lying beneath. Gruesomely growing.

Fully released it resembles a wet, dead rodent. It makes her gag

PAPER OVER IT

even more than the acrid Immac. She reaches over and flops the creepy creature into the toilet and flushes it away.

She knows she should be revising, but she just can't focus, so she spends the next few hours clearing out her room. Getting it ready for the move. She needs to keep busy to stop the blue beast rising beneath. She creates a satisfying monster mountain of bin bags. She will go to the tip later.

She just loves going to the tip. She finds it cleansing. Like having a big poo in one, no pushing, and having no skid on the loo roll post wipe. She likes to check these monsters out before papering over them and flushing. She knows she is odd.

She arrives at the maternity unit car park a blundering bag of nerves. Cherish is carefully wrapped and in her bag. She is not sure why she felt the need so strongly to bring her, but she did. She immediately finds a parking spot for Honey, her sweetly named car. An easy spot. She is still shit at manoeuvring with little to no spatial awareness. She hopes this is a good omen.

As she walks to the reception, she braces herself. She knows she is very early but thinks she will find a drink machine, get herself a nice cup of tea, cop a spot and just wait.

Looking around the large waiting room, she is faced with couples. Dozens of couples. Happy couples. Laughing couples. Couples chatting to each other and to other couples, sharing their pregnancy joy stories.

She suddenly feels very small, she feels sad and alone. Blue. She notices the lady sat next to her looking openly at her empty ring finger. She feels her cheeks redden, knows she looks younger than her years, like a teenager in fact. She ignores the stare and hides her unadorned digit with her other hand. She makes a mental note to source a suitable ring, even if just a stainless-steel band. To make her feel less stained.

She is cross at herself for feeling like this, for being embarrassed of herself and her situation. She even thinks she should maybe have brought her ex. But then she thinks better of it.

She needs a wee and gets up to go to the loo, relieved to get away from Little Mrs. Judgy. In the toilet there is a sign reminding her she has to have a full bladder for the scan. For fuck's sake. She leaves the loo and decides having a nice cup of tea is probably not the best idea.

She picks up a well-thumbed home magazine. A Christmas edition. An article on the top ten artificial trees for Christmas 1999 keeps her busy. They all look crap to her.

"Hi Jen," her mum plonks herself on the chair next to her. "I was waiting for you in reception."

"Oh, sorry mum," she replies. "I just couldn't wait to choose which tree I could have bought five months ago," she laughs, showing her mum the shitly named article, 'Which trees are the bee's knees?'

"Is there a crossword in there?" her mum asks.

"My appointment is in five minutes," Jen says. "We'll barely have time to start it."

Her mum laughs, "Knowing this unit as I do, we will have finished it and started another by the time you're called." She takes a pen from her blue tunic pocket and gives it to Jen.

Jen leads the cryptic crossword and reads the questions out loud, followed by the number of letters. From experience she knows if she lets her mum lead, she will fill them all in straight away and Jen will just be ignored and get bored.

"A hive of joint excellence," Jen says. "One three letter word and two four letter words."

"Any clues?" her mum asks.

"Second word, second letter 'e'," Jen replies. "Third word, second letter 'n'."

"The bee's knees!" her mum shouts a little loudly. The pair laugh at the insect coincidence and Jen's mum's irritating excellence at crosswords. Jen has to cross her legs. She really really needs a wee now. Her knees are well and truly glued together like the two pieces of bread in a honey sandwich.

"Miss Jennifer Jones," a lady calls a while later. A midwife.

Did she really have to say 'Miss'? Was it necessary? Jen's mum makes a mental note to ask her later.

Jen and her mum stand up and walk towards the lady. "Right, let's get your scan done first as we need to try and date this baby, don't we?" she says brusquely. "Then we can focus on you."

"Why are they all so brusque?" Jen thinks to herself.

She leads them to the ultrasound room and says, "See you in a bit."

The cold gel on her filling tummy and full bladder shocks her. "Sorry," the sonographer says. "It can be a little chilly."

She gently presses the ultrasound device on Jen's stomach and moves it back and forward. She stops occasionally and looks at a screen they can't see. Clicking and tapping away at something. Stopping and starting. Like the Pure Shores CD. At one point she stops for what feels to Jen like a lifetime. Jen fears the worst, something must be wrong. "Is everything ok?" she asks.

"I'm just checking everything," the sonographer says, still staring at the screen, her concentration disturbed. "Give me a few minutes." This does not allay Jen's fears in any way.

After another long, frustrating delay, she says, "Can you hear that?"

A faint little double thumping sound is clearly coming from the machine. It is comforting in its rhythm.

"Does it sound ok?" Jen asks, almost begging for some positive information.

After another short while, her concentration is diverted to Jen. "Yes, everything is looking absolutely fine."

She holds the screen and asks, "Do you want to see?"

"Yes please," Jen replies, feeling her body de-tense. Her breathing slow. Her blue subdue.

"There's the heart," she points at the now turned screen. "It's a really good, strong beat," she confirms. "Everything looks perfect. I have taken some measurements and I would estimate you are around twenty nine to thirty weeks pregnant." She checks a calendar and adds, "I can give you a due date of the 14th June. But this is approximate. As we are so late scanning and dating you, I can't give you anything more accurate."

Jen isn't really listening. She is just absolutely thrilled that everything is ok. No, not thrilled. Overwhelmingly relieved. She just stares at the screen, enchanted. In a trance. This is unlike her previous delirious white wave trance. This is more N-Trance, setting her free. She is entranced.

"Ok, thank you," Jen's mum replies for them. "14th June," she writes it down in the little pad she has brought with her.

The sonographer then shows Jen and her mum the head, face,

arms and legs. "Everything looks exactly as it should do. On the small side, but you're petite too, so I'm not surprised. And look, you've got yourself a little thumb sucker."

"Awwww," Jen and Jen's mum say in unison, mesmerised by the image on the screen.

"Would you like to know what the sex is?" the lady asks.

Jen looks at her, slightly surprised. She had honestly not really thought about this. She had been so worried her baby would not be ok, she had genuinely not even cared about whether it was a boy or girl. She knows her mum secretly wants a boy after having two girls herself, but she hadn't cared herself. So much so she hadn't prepared herself for the question, or whether she actually wants to say yes to it.

"Can you tell what it is?" Jen asks her.

"Yes," she confirms, smiling. "I most certainly can."

"Well if you know, I need to know," Jen laughs. Decision made. "What is it?"

"It's a boy," she reveals.

Jen beams. She's not just having a baby, she's having a little man.

She looks over at her mum who has started to cry. "It's a boy," she repeats. "We're getting a boy, Jen."

They are getting blue, but in a really good way.

Deeper shade of blue.

Steps.

-14-
THE QUARTET: RISE

9th April 2000
Yet again Will has pulled the hat out of the proverbial bag.
"Who does he know?" Lou had asked Kate.
"Don't know, don't care."

The new Julia Roberts film 'Erin Brockovich' has just premiered and he has somehow got five tickets for the first Sunday night showing. He was not going to miss out on watching his beloved Pretty Woman on the big screen, so he is coming too. It is the 7:30pm showing.

It had been Jen's twenty-first birthday two days earlier so this was the perfect birthday treat for her – and a great Sunday escape from dissertations and revising for all.

Jen hadn't wanted anything for her birthday. Had asked her family and friends to save the money they were going to spend and wait until the baby was born. The only present she had wanted was the positive scan, and finding out she was having a little man, was getting blue, was the icing on the absent birthday cake. The girls had been thrilled when she told them the sex, as had her ex.

They agreed they will go on a proper bender for her twenty-first after the baby boy is born. Everyone is doing their finals in May and June, apart from Kate who is on a four-year course. It is starting to dawn on Kate she'll be in a very different place the following academic year, to panic and discombobulate her. She has friends on her course and at work, but they're just drinking friends, not friend friends. And of course there's Will. He will have finished too.

Jen is now spending most of her time at home in the semi, so this was also a great opportunity for the foursome to catch up properly. It is agreed that the girls will go for an early tea somewhere, and they would meet Will after at the Odeon.

Jen's due date of the 14th of June means she has a chance of completing her finals as her last exam is scheduled for the 12th of June. In her special circumstances she has been told she has to sit her penultimate exam on the 8th in order to get her degree, otherwise she will have to resit. That terrifies her. She desperately wants to be able to sit the 12th of June one as it is the part of the course she is best at. Could improve her scores the most. It is all very tight. Highly stressful.

She just has her head down working for her degree and trying to rise to everything she needs to do to prepare for her baby. Selling things to raise money, and helping her mum pack up the semi.

All the other girls have been keeping their heads down too.

Lou and Em facing into their finals, Kate helping Will relax a little while he revises for his finals.

"I don't swallow though," she told the girls. The general incredulous response was, "Who does?"

The consensus for early tea had been Pizza Express as a big treat, so they planned to meet at 5pm. All super excited for their quartet to be back together for the first time in what felt like an age, but had actually only been a few weeks.

"Jen!" Em shouts at Jen from over the road, nearly getting knocked over as she races over to her. "Oopsy daisy" falls out of her mouth, visibly annoying her as it does.

"For God's sake Em, watch out!" Jen scolds as she accepts the bear hug that Em folds her in.

"How are you? And you?" she points at Jen's eyes and Jen's stomach on each emphasised 'you'.

Even though Jen is still tiny, it's almost like the baby has released himself since Jen had told him not to hide any more. She has a gorgeous little bump.

"I ... sorry we... are all good," Jen smiles. "How are you?"

"Shit. Monumentally shit," Em sulks. "Dad's being a dick. Says I have to go home for Easter for 'family time'. Happy to see him and the bro, just can't bear her." Em is referring to her stepmother, Eve.

Kate and Lou sneak up on them and hug one each from behind. This quickly turns into a quartet squeeze.

"Wassup!" Lou says.

"Wassup!" the remaining trio respond.

"Right, I'm fucking starving. A big fat American Hot has my name all over it," Em nips the wassupping in the bud.

Sitting at their table, comfortable in their perfect quartet harmony, they all eat their different pizzas slightly differently. But their differences make their harmony. Otherwise they would just be one note, one loud long irritating note.

"The things that make me different are the things that make me me," said Piglet.

"How's little man?" Kate asks Jen, eating just the centre of her Margherita. Ignoring the crusts.

"Want to see him?" Jen replies, picking a pepperoni slice off her American and popping it in her mouth.

The three girls look back at her blank faced, completely confused.

"How can we see him?" Lou asks incredulously.

"Do you have a see-through stomach?" Kate adds, putting her folded slice of Fiorentina back on her plate.

Jen laughs, "No, you idiots, I've got the picture from the scan. Well the two pictures. He's too big to fit on one."

"Ohhh," they all reply, feeling like the idiots they are.

Jen gets the pictures from her bag and they pour over them while Jen pours herself a glass of water.

"He looks like you," Kate says excitedly. Jen finds it funny that she is the third person who has said this. She can see no resemblance at all. Apart from his thumb sucking which she hadn't done for years. She didn't think.

Jen points out where everything is as it's not clear over the two grainy black and white images.

"He's definitely a boy," Em exclaims.

"Trust you, Em," Jen laughs, putting the photos back in her bag. "Right, I need a wee. Again."

When she returns to the table, she hears Lou ask, "Want to talk about Easter, Em?"

"We were eavesdropping earlier," Kate adds honestly, for context.

"Honestly, she's such an absolute bitch. I fucking hate her," Em spouts sulkily. "She's a 29-year-old gold-digging bitch. She saw her apple and she fucking ate it. Bitch."

Her father is 47, her mother 46. They had gone through a very messy, bitter divorce which had started over six years earlier, when Em was fourteen. Not a standard divorce where the fight is about the kids and how the funds from the small house with a mortgage are split; a helicopter divorce where there is so much to fight for, so much to lose and gain for the lawyers and couple alike. So much hidden that the fight becomes totally toxic and the kids are frankly forgotten.

The fights had started many years earlier than the start of the divorce.

"Why do you hate her so much?" Kate asks. She knows Eve was not the cause of her family breakdown. Em always evades any real conversation about her stepmother Eve, forbidden like the fruit, so Kate expects Em to deflect.

True to form, Em counters with, "How's Will? Saw him the other day looking hot!"

Not surprised, Kate simply winks and says, "I'm a lucky girl.".

As her second line of defence, just in case anyone else asked a question about her outburst, Em asks, "How are you LiverLou?" It has been almost two months since Eddie-twat-gate.

"Well you know," says Lou. "I still can't quite believe we're through. But as my dad says, when he's not talking about the weather, time's a healer."

"It's gonna take time," Kate says remembering how horrendous Valentine's night was and how much she now genuinely hated Eddie after what he had done to her friend. "But I genuinely think you're better off without him. You'll get over him, I promise. It will be alright."

"We're going to make sure it's alright," Jen adds.

"He called me the other day just to see how I am," Lou says.

"Why?" Jen questions.

"I really don't know. We just chatted for a bit about what he was doing and my exams and stuff," Lou ponders. "No real reason."

"I hope you told him to fuck the fuck off?" Em fucks.

"I asked him what he wanted. He said just to hear my voice."

"He literally broke your heart, Lou! And he thinks he has the right to hear your voice?" Kate retorts furiously.

"This is Jen's birthday! Let's not get side-tracked by my ex," Lou deflects, Em-style, but privately loving and needing her friends' solidarity, firm words and unadulterated support. "How's your mum, Jen?"

"She's invited you all over next Saturday if you're free? You can stay over. What do you reckon?" Jen asks her friends. "Last time in the semi."

"Can we play pool in the cellar?" Lou asks.

"I've sold it," Jen says brightly. "No room in the new house – and I got enough money from it to buy a travel system."

"A what?" Lou asks, confused and gutted that the cool pool table has gone. Jen had been gifted it by her parents for her fifteenth birthday. An ex-pub one with a slate bed and the pay mechanism still working.

"Mum and I went to Mothercare. I'm going to get everything else second-hand, like the cot and all that, but we decided we could buy the travel system new as I made a small fortune on the pool table," Jen replies.

"We still have no idea what you're on about," Em says, popping the last piece of American Hot in her mouth.

"It's a buggy and a car seat all in one. So exciting. They are all the rage! I got it in navy blue tartan," she says, proud as a preening peacock.

"Oh my life, who are you?" asks Em, also confused. Unsure whether the thought of Jen getting so excited about a baby mover or the fact she had chosen navy blue tartan. Whether either fascinated or gutted her more.

The other two girls just look at Jen. Lou swelling with pride as to how far Jen has come, after having been the most involved in the situation. Kate starting to realise what is to come for Jen, how much responsibility she is taking on, how much she now has to cope with and plan for.

"I know, it's funny," Jen smiles at Em. "But I can't push a baby around in a pool table, can I?"

"I'm so proud of you Jen," Lou starts to well up. "It's all such an adventure."

"I'm not sure I'm proud of me, but I'm ok. Terrified but ok," Jen admits. "And I've got my mum. She's being amazing to be honest. Horrendously practical and opinionated as always, but amazing." Jen loves the word 'adventure'. It feels right, is so positive and exciting.

"We are all so proud of you, Jen," Em says while Kate nods. "I just wished I'd have been there and talked you out of blue tartan, though."

"What the hell is wrong with tartan?" Kate vents.

They all laugh at Kate's Celtic pride and tartan indignation.

"What the hell is right with tartan?" Em counters. "The only tart-on I would ever wear is a peekaboo babydoll."

"Bitch," both Kate and Jen say in unison. Both knowing Em would rock any peekaboo babydoll, tartan or not.

"You know me so well," Em sings whilst winking at her friends. Also knowing she would rock any tart-on outfit she chose to wear.

When you have a bitch in your midst, keep her close. Especially a bitch that loves you. They tend to be the absolute best of friends, will always rise for you. Whether you want them to or not. There for you forever, for life.

"So can you come next Saturday?" Jen cuts the momentary silence. "Just so I can let my mum know. We have a lot of the furniture being picked up by a house clearance company, so it's the last chance."

"I can," Em says. "Alright with you girls?"

"Absolutely! Wouldn't miss it for the world," Kate grins.

"I'm in," Lou completes the trio. "And we've got some little things for you, Jen."

"No! We don't do birthday pressies!"

"We have made an exception," Kate says. "It's only some odds and sods."

Lou hands her a bag full of little baby grows (one with a tractor, one a spaceship and the other a dinosaur), a pair of booties, a blanket and a hat and little mittens knitted by Lou's mum. Jen is overcome as she bites back tears. Her emotions are getting on top of her quite often, she can't control them.

She even cried in the car the other day when Randy Crawford 'One Day I'll Fly Away' played on the radio. It is one of her favourites, but she did have to have a strong word with her reflection in her rear-view mirror.

"Thank you," is all she can say.

"We've got you one more thing," Kate squeals.

"What is it?" Jen asks, intrigued by Kate's squeal.

They hand her a wrapped box. Inside there is an Ann Summers

Rampant Rabbit. A bright pink one. It's two little ears fucking her off through the box's plastic window. Its see-through stomach.

"What the hell am I going to do with this?" Jen is literally howling.

"We thought you might find it useful," Lou laughs back. "Post baby. We thought you may get a little bored, in on your own and all that."

"Well," Jen says. "I can honestly say I was not expecting this. But thank you."

"Shit, look at the time! We're going to be late," Kate shouts. And if Kate thinks it's late, it's late. "Jen, you've only eaten half your pizza."

"I'm not really very hungry," Jen lies. "Got a bit of indigestion."

"I only get indigestion when I swallow," Em announces loudly.

"Can we get the bill please?" Lou says, shaking her head at Em while apologising to the parents of the family that had sat at the table next to them just a few moments before.

After splitting the bill three ways to take care of Jen as a birthday treat, Em minesweeps the table. Making sure there is no alcohol wasted. She picks up Jen's drink and downs it. "Eughhhhh, what the fuck is that?"

"Water," Jen screams, holding her stomach through the laughter ache.

The quartet leave Pizza Express in an express fashion after the same parents that Lou had literally just apologised to shake their heads at them. Again.

They are on their way to meet Will at the Odeon cinema. Jen feeling happily overwhelmed by the kindness of the girls' gifts, Lou feeling strong from the female solidarity.

Two girls, regathering their hopes and dreams, bolstered by their besties. Ready to rise again.

Rise.
Gabrielle.

-15-
THE QUARTET: WARRIOR

15th April 2000

Erin Brockovich was somewhat mind-blowing.

The girls and Will were in complete awe of the true story of this amazing woman, this warrior. And of Julia Roberts for playing her so brilliantly.

'She brought a small town to its feet and a huge company to its knees.'

A David and Goliath story of grit and determination, good versus evil, big versus little, the little voice against the big voice. A real warrior story.

Each part of the quintet took something quite deep from the movie. Misogynism still rampantly reigns and being a single mum, even in the year 2000, is still socially unacceptable to a good proportion of bad people, so it's great to see a woman, especially a young, divorced, unemployed single mum like Erin, not allow herself to be taken advantage of. She is, of course, dismissed and belittled throughout the legal loopholes and lies. Standard territory. Made to look like a fool. Taken the piss out of by apparently more intelligent, certainly more educated and definitely more successful and wealthy people. Mainly men. But there is one man who believes in her from the start. Even though she monumentally pisses him off. Ed Masry. Her David turned Goliath. The fact she comes out on top, through her warrior grit and the support of Ed, is inspirational.

Jen's biggest out-take is the strength of Erin as a young single mum. Her warrior mum mentality. It really stirred something in her and somehow gives her strength too.

It got Kate really thinking about her path in life and sowed a seed of law as her future career. Law to help people, not fuck people. Law for the less advantaged people with smaller voices. Law for less privileged warriors.

Lou loved the drama of Erin. Her tenacity and how she used a balance of her looks and clear charms, alongside her intelligence and tenacity, to get her own way. To be a warrior and win, against all the odds.

Em was, and still is, deeply affected by the character that Julia Roberts has just played. More so than she thought she would be. Something very different from her classic roles in movies like Mystic Pizza, Steel Magnolias, Sleeping with the Enemy, Notting Hill and, of course, Pretty Woman. She is acutely fascinated by her ability to take on different roles. But always, rarely and significantly, her ability to also be herself. Be Julia.

And Will, well he just loves Julia even more than he did before, which he had not thought was possible.

"Thank you, Will," Jen said as she hugged him goodnight. "That was really amazing."

"You're very welcome," he smiled at her. Kissed her forehead like a dad might do to a daughter. Jen loved it. Made her feel safe, somehow. Felt the spot he kissed with her finger after his kind, comforting, supportive lips left.

"Thanks Will," the other girls chimed in too.

It's now the following Saturday and the girls are all at Jen's house. Her semi. Her soon-to-be ex-semi. Jen made a lasagne the night before, when her head was too full from revising. She promised Lou on the phone that she would like it, even though she didn't really like Italian. But also promised she would make her some pancakes if she didn't. Has eggs, flour and cheese on hand, just in case.

Jen really loves making lasagne and is actually pretty good at it. The process is calming, a welcome antonym to her crash course in revision and baby planning. She enjoys the prep of the ragu and always lets it bubble away for a good few hours to make it super rich, and for the red wine to really kick in and do its body building warrior job. She even more enjoys making the bechamel sauce and is always oddly proud when it gently bubbles to the correct thickness.

It reminds her of Christmas, many years back, at her auntie's house when her mum (an excellent cook in normal, less drunken circumstances) was making the brandy sauce for the Christmas pudding and had clearly started with the wrong balance of flour, butter and milk for the bechamel.

The brandy sauce just kept growing and growing, like an old man's ears.

Instead of sensibly starting again, she stoically, and rather stupidly, stuck with it and the rebellious brandy beast just kept thickening like lava spouting from an aggressively bubbling volcano. Said lava flowed nearly as much as the wine, the flow of which had probably caused the brandy beast to be born in the first place. Pint after pint of milk (and subsequent brandy) were sloshed into the mix as Jen's mum tried to un-thicken the beast, shouting to her sister, "Another pan, we need another pan!"

Jen, Jen's sister and their cousins found this whole event hilarious as Jen's mum and her sister, alongside their step-mum, danced pissed around the kitchen, Morecambe and Wise-style (though definitely not looking that wise). Sharing bottles of milk, the quickly depleting bottle of brandy, the rebellious brandy beast, multiple pans, bottles of wine and then other receptacles once all the clean pans had been used (or to be more specific, abused).

Jen's mum was never allowed to make the brandy sauce at Christmas again.

With lasagne bound bechamel sauce, excellently made with the perfect consistency, Jen began the highly satisfying layering stage. Ragu, bechamel sauce, sheet pasta, ragu, bechamel sauce, sprinkle of parmesan, sheet pasta, ragu, bechamel sauce, a few knobs of butter, sheet pasta, ragu, bechamel sauce, sprinkle of parmesan, sheet pasta, bechamel sauce, good layer of parmesan and grated cheddar. Many knobs of butter.

Always the same – it had to be in this order to make the perfect layers, and the ideal slightly crusty top. Jen makes a banging lasagne.

She remembers having to explain to Em what 'banging (or bangin')' meant, rather like the 'hangin'' incident.

"It means really good. Excellent," Jen had explained. "Opposite to hangin'."

"Just like me then!" Em had responded with an overzealous wink. "I bang." Jen wasn't sure the adjective transferred this way and knew how often Em liked to bang, but didn't care. It was funny.

Em goes to pick up Lou and Kate from Withington just after lunch. Kate is late.

"Why have Dolcis not sacked you?" Em asks Kate when she finally bangs her front door shut and Em manages to grind her Clio into

PAPER OVER IT

first gear.

"Why can't you drive?" Kate retorts, trying to emulate Em's haughtiness, but failing epically. Knowing she can't drive herself. And is shit at haughty.

"If you can't find 'em, grind 'em," Em laughs, parroting a phrase she heard Jen's ex say a few years back. "And you can't actually drive anyway, you prick," she can't help adding.

The trio arrive thirty minutes late, due to the perpetually late Kate. It's a beautiful day, the first real day of spring, so they spend the afternoon in Jen's garden. Putting the world to rights.

A little later they move into the kitchen. The table is surrounded by two reconditioned church pews and two large pine chairs, plenty of space for the five of them. The quartet and Jen's mum tuck into the perfectly bechamel-ed lasagne. Lou lapping it up like she likes it.

"How's work?" Em asks Jen's mum.

"Oh no, don't ask her!" Jen eyerolls. "She's bound to have a story."

Working in the neonatal unit at the local hospital, she always has stories, both happy and sad. Like the time two babies came into the unit on the same day with the same dad - and they weren't twins. The time a very young mum told Jen's mum she was going to call her daughter Clisoris - and took some convincing as to why this possibly wasn't a great idea. The women in labour who came in from the local prison in handcuffs. Many told Jen's mum they were doing time for their partners or husbands. And the sad story of a university student whose parents were living abroad, who had her baby and immediately gave her up for adoption without telling her parents. The last one had really got to Jen's mum and the whole unit. Which was ironic, really, when Jen thought about their initial and immediate response to her own news.

Is that irony, Alanis?

Jen's mum is great at stories, but you had to settle in. They could take some time. And there could be some poetic licence, in fact a whole lot of poetic licence. Sometimes barefaced make believe.

"I do have a story," Jen's mum announces. "I never told you, Jen. Although I'm not really sure I should tell it."

"Go on!" Lou pushes, while pushing the fifth fork-load of previously hated lasagne into her mouth.

"Please," Kate urges.

91

"Oh my days," Jen says, head in hands.

Jen's mum explains that a baby boy had come into the neonatal unit about a month earlier. "He was the eighth child of a Mr. and Mrs. Woof," she explains.

"Oh come on, mum," Jen rolls her eyes again. "Are you making bits up already?" The other girls start laughing. It's like the lights have been turned on in her mum recently, like the sun has come out. It is a joy to witness.

"It never hurts to keep looking for sunshine", said Eeyore.

"No, I am not," her mum says indignantly. "It gets much better… or worse," she promises. "I met the Woofs when they told me the child's name so I could set him up on the system." Jen's mum starts to laugh a little and pauses.

"Go on," Lou encourages.

"They named him Conrad Octavius Woof," she splurts. "Octavius for the eighth child." At this point tears start to fall from her eyes as she tries to stop laughing to carry on her story. "When I wrote his initials, as I had to do, it spelt C. O. W. – it spelt COW." At this point she is spurting her words out with laughing. "All I could think of was that cows go moo not woof."

As all four girls start to lose it laughing, not just at the story, but at how much Jen's mum is losing control telling the story. Tears now running down her cheeks.

"That's hilarious," says Kate, still laughing.

"No, no – that's not the worst bit," Jen's mum blurts. "It gets worse."

"Oh god mum, what did you say?" asks Jen, head in hands again.

"It wasn't me – I kept my cows, moos and woofs very much to myself and was highly professional." she promises. "It was Jane."

Jane is one of the neonatal nurses, a lovely lady with a great bedside manner and a wonderful technician.

"Bear in mind, like I said before, all babies are now absolutely fine and doing really well," Jen's mum repeats.

"What did Jane do?" asks Em, wide eyed.

"Well, she had been on holiday for a week, her first day back, and one of the incubator babies had taken a slight turn and needed some new treatment. It was unfortunately Conrad Octavius Woof,"

Jen's mum explains.

"So she went into the parent's room and said to the lady half asleep on one of the chairs, "Are you Mrs. Woof?" The lady nodded and said, "Yes". Jen's mum continues. "Jane then had to explain to her that her baby was going through some small complications and they were doing everything to make sure he was ok."

The girls stop laughing as the story seemingly takes a turn. All heads lean slightly more into Jen's mum waiting to hear the rest of the story, lasagne forks in hand.

"The lady started to get naturally very upset and started crying, "But my baby was absolutely fine! I was about to take him home. I don't understand. What have you done?" So Jane tried to calm her down and took her gently over to Conrad to show her the new treatments they were giving him."

Jen's mum took a moment to take a breath.

"'That's not my baby,' she yelled at Jane as they arrived at the incubator. And Jane said, "But you are Mrs. Woof?" And the lady responded, "No I'm Mrs. Taylor"."

At this point Jen's mum has to stop. She knows she shouldn't be laughing at all, never mind so uncontrollably.

"Come up mum, you can't stop there," Jen exclaims.

Gathering herself, Jen's mum continues, "So Jane said, "But I asked you if you were Mrs. Woof", and the lady said, "I thought you asked me if I was feeling rough"."

At this stage Jen's mum literally can't speak and all four girls are shrieking with laughter.

"I know it shouldn't be funny," she blurts. "But it just is. Jane was mortified as the lady blasted back to her that she had said 'yes' because she was feeling rough. And if she hadn't been feeling rough before, she certainly would be now!"

Still laughing, and very pleased that no babies were harmed in the making of the story, the girls ask what had happened next.

Jen's mum explains that the correct Mrs. Woof had been informed (she had unfortunately been in the toilet when Jane had entered the parents room) and there were obviously a lot of apologies and conversations. They are still unsure whether there will be a complaint made about Jane but that Mrs. Taylor had taken her healthy baby home a few days later, so was feeling a lot better about the 'rough Woof' situation. And that Conrad Octavious had been taken home by the Woofs, happy and healthy, a week or so after.

All three girls are in awe of Jen's mum. She tells ridiculously funny stories. Jen knows her mum loves the attention.

After being hurt so much after the twenty-five marriage breakdown, and having lived in collective disappointment with her husband for many years prior, she has been a diminished version of her former younger self. A mouse, a worm even. But her worm is slowly turning. Her confidence growing. It is really great to see her become stronger, and lighter.

She has been papering over it for far too many years, and she is starting to get her warrior on. For herself, her daughter and their impending baby.

Its like her sun is ready to come out, ready to shine now.

Warrior.
Warrior.

-16-
THE QUARTET: BEAUTIFUL DAY

15th April 2000 – continued
"What are you up to for Easter, girls?" Jen's mum asks, once she had been upstairs to sort her mascara.

Yet another bottle of wine has been liberated from the wine cellar (a cupboard in the cellar that Jen's mum always pretentiously called 'the wine cellar' and had a lock put on it at some point in Jen's teens) by Em, along with some random half-drunk bottles of Cointreau and Campari. Coupled with an old soda syphon with a big lever on the side. Jen's mum told Em just to bring up whatever she wanted, it all had to go anyway.

Jen has been upstairs for a small while too, not fixing her make-up. Papering over it. She just can't manage to stop. She is appalled with herself, but seems completely stuck with her bulexia/anoremia both mentally and physically. Its not moving anywhere. She has to find a way of moving on from it.

She comes down just in time for the answers to her mum's Easter question.

"I'm at home," Lou says, gulping her wine. "Kate's coming to mine."

Kate is upset to not be going home, but it's a long way to Glasgow and costs a lot of money. So she accepted Lou's offer of Easter in Liverpool. Will is going skiing for a few days with his brother and their parents, to a chalet in Verbier. He had invited her, as he had last year, but having never skied she didn't fancy being 'Bambi-nursery-slopes' in front of his family. As much as she actually really likes Will's family, and they seem to really like her back. They are a close-knit family of piss takers and she doesn't want to be the complete butt of all Bambi jokes. Or spend the week by herself in 'school'.

"And you, Em?" Jen's mum questions.

The girls unconsciously cock their heads and look at Em. They hadn't managed to get any more out of her after her outburst outside Pizza Express last Sunday.

"I'm going home," she says, not wanting to be rude to an old person of fifty-one.

"That's nice," Jen's mum nods. "Where's home again?"

"Hertfordshire."

"Is that your dad or your mum?" Jen's mum asks.

The other girls are now literally doing a Wimbledon with their head swings, knowing Jen's mum will probably get more out of Em than they ever have on the subject. Em is not going to tell Jen's mum to fuck off and pull an Em deflection.

"My dad," Em replies. "My dad and my brother."

"Isn't your dad recently married?" Jen's mum asks, just curious. Sipping a recently poured Campari and soda from the old syphon. It's a little flat. "Cam-pour-me?" she had asked Em, to the hilarity of everyone but Jen. Who just rolled her eyes.

"Yes," Em replies, walls broken by Cointreau and questions. "To a complete bitch."

Jen's mum's mouth unconsciously creates a great big O, quickly followed by an equally unconscious great big "Ohhh" from her mouth. She isn't aware she is stepping on a virtual land mine. Boom.

Seeing her action, Em says, "Oops, sorry. Don't mean to be rude. But she made me wear the most horrific green bridesmaid dress at the wedding. To make herself look better," Em pouts furiously. "Daddy said if I didn't wear it and smile, he would take away my car. He made me promise not to do or say anything that might make it anything but a beautiful day for her, the bitch."

The girls had never heard this before. When asked about her father's wedding in Barbados early the previous year, she had just shrugged and said it was fine.

With her pout further extended, she continues to theatrically say, "I looked like a fucking Teenage Mutant Ninja Turtle." At this point Jen starts to wobble, like the Millennium Bridge. Jen's mum swallows another gulp of Campari and flat soda. The rest keep it together until Em says, "And it had a orange sash so I looked like fucking Donatello."

Jen's mum is genuinely not used to this sort of language, but a repressed giggle wins over her slight horror, mainly due to Em's dramatic indignation.

Jen cracks and starts to giggle. "Sorry Em, I know it's not funny."

While Lou starts to crumble, in no way hiding the snort that just snuck out.

Fully knowledgeable about turtles, Kate shouts, "Michelangelo! Not Donatello. Donatello is purple," correcting her friend's Ninja-blunder. Trying desperately to keep her howl within. She knows them all very well, they are all over her bedroom at home.

"Is that what you take out of my green nightmare?" Em yells back at Kate. "Me mixing my Sistine Chapels with my bronze Davids?" Her private education had filled her with countless fairly useless things, including art history, Latin and an amazing knowledge of capital cities and world flags.

The girls and Jen's mum can't hold it in much longer.

Em is starting to break a little, faced with four full melting pots all desperately trying to keep their lids on, ready to explode. She appreciates their efforts, however futile.

"A day without a friend is like a pot without a single drop of honey inside," said Pooh.

"Ok, ok," Em scolds while rolling her eyes. "You can laugh at me now if you must. I am clearly a hopeless case." Em hates people laughing at her, but she bravely concedes, "Go, Ninjas, go".

Melting pots all instantly de-lidded, Em joins in with the hilarity of her turtle trauma.

Although Jen can see that Em sees the funny side, she can also see that deep down she is not happy at all. Not ok. She is papering over it it too. For the first time Jen sees real cracks in Em, cracks she knows she will quickly deflect. But deep cracks, nonetheless.

She knows Em doesn't like her stepmother, but not to this level. Her green dress is clearly an analogy for the deep envy and jealousy she feels inside. The turtle a personification of her teenage trauma and subsequent mutant adult malice towards Eve.

At this stage Jen's mum bids them goodnight. It has been a rare, beautiful day and she doesn't want to get so drunk she let's it get away. "I am going up to Hertfordshire," she malaprops Bridget Jones, confusing her home counties. Although Bedfordshire is also confused as to whether it actually is a home county or not as it doesn't actually border London.

"Bedfordshire!" Jen eyerolls yet again, still chortling from turtle-gate. "You're going up to Bedfordshire." Jen and the girls had just loved the Helen Fielding classic, written just a few years back. 1996, she thinks. The same year as the Manchester IRA bomb, The Spice Girls telling us what they want, what they really really want, the birth of the cloned Dolly the Sheep, Baddiel and Skinner assuring us 'It's Coming Home' (it didn't) and the divorces of both Fergie and Diana.

The girls were all alive for both weddings, but have no recollection of Diana's in 1981. Were too little. They do, however, remember the grinning Sarah Ferguson as a bride in 1986. With her cheekiness on the Buckingham Palace balcony, her clear joy at the occasion and her bouncy red curls. They had all fallen in love with her whilst watching the pomp and ceremony on the Tuesday on tank like, fake wood school televisions which were wheeled on precarious trolleys into halls and classrooms across the UK. Lou had especially fallen for her and her auburn mane.

The girls were all totally shocked and shattered when Diana tragically died just over a year after her decree absolute. They all mourned with the shocked nation, and the world. Over two and a half years ago now. August 31st 1997. RIP.

"Night night, don't let the bed bugs bite," Jen's mum mothers and climbs the semi stairs.

"Night night," the girls echo, each loving the mothering.

As the girls sit chatting about Jen's baby and what vegetable he is now - as per Emma's, not Bridget's, Diary - Jen sits back. She isn't sure how appropriate comparing a baby to a vegetable is, but goes with it.

She feels content sitting with her friends. She no longer has that overwhelming, incessant feeling of wanting to be taken to another place now she knows her baby is doing well from the initial scan twelve days ago and the one last week. She is very much starting to feel less of a hopeless case.

"How many weeks are you now, Jen?" asks a slightly wonkey-eyed Kate, flicking through Jen's Emma's Diary.

"They think about thirty-one weeks, but not one hundred percent sure," Jen replies. "As he's so small, I'm having to go for weekly check-ups and scans." These scans are an absolute blessing to Jen, as she is still worried about her baby. It is a weekly reassurance that he is absolutely fine.

PAPER OVER IT

At the second scan she had finally spoken very openly to the midwife who did her check-up. She had gone to the appointment by herself even though her mum had offered to pop down.

She was the same rather brusque midwife that Jen had met on her first scan. Sensible and no-nonsense. Quite old, Jen thought. Probably in her mid-forties. It was the first time Jen had told anyone about her bulexia/anoremia. She has been battling to stop, but the sense of control it offers her is needed now more than ever. It is a difficult and devastating daily struggle.

The midwife had kindly, and very unexpectedly, taken Jen's hands while taking a practical but sympathetic tone. Less brusque.

"Your baby is basically a leech. It will take everything it needs from you and, if necessary, leave you with nothing. It will suck all the goodness you have in you to make sure it's getting what it needs to develop and grow."

Jen, yet again in this whole adventure, was wide eyed and wide mouthed. Still holding her hands, the kind midwife went on to say, "You're young, your body will cope. Just make sure you leave enough in there for your baby to cope too. It will need about three to four hundred calories a day. Try and eat some protein, carbs, fruit and vegetables every day if you can. Eat little and often if that helps."

This practical, no nonsense, medically accurate advice sent a surge of relief through Jen. She hugged the kind lady, much to both of their surprise.

She took her hand again when the awkward hug had ended, and said in a friendly soothing way, "Take care of yourself, Jennifer. And of him. It is all going to be fine. I'll see you next week."

Jen replied simply, "Thank you." She was pleased she had opened up to her. And that this kind lady was going to be with her on her adventure. She feels she has found a kind of friend in this place.

Jen promised herself she would continue with her battle, and make sure her baby leech got what he needed. Every day. Even if she was left with nothing.

A baby leech, as inappropriate as the baby vegetable that the girls had found in the diary. "He's a coconut!" Kate shouts, grinning.

Is a coconut a vegetable?

"Do you think he's shy?" Lou quips, rather proud of her funfair metaphor.

"Well he was bloody well shy for his first five months, wasn't he?" Em laughs, back on form.

"The little nut isn't bloody shy now," Jen winces as his kick causes her to flinch. "Want a feel?"

All the girls pounce on her, desperate to feel their little coconut.

"On my fucking god, it's like bloody Alien!" Em is fascinated and slightly repelled.

"Vegetables, leeches, aliens - anything else you want to compare him to?" Jen smiles through her scolding.

"Leeches?" Kate asks, confused. "What are you on about?"

"It's a long story," Jen quickly back tracks. "Let's get some ice cream," she deflects, Em-style.

Em liberates the ice-cream from the chest freezer in the cellar where it has been merrily mingling with escaped frozen peas and fish fingers, never used ice packs, five year old orange pyramid lollies from Iceland, grey sausages, an unopened pack of Wall's Funny Feet, a hunk of undisclosed meat, a long forgotten school woollen jumper with chewing gum stuck on it and countless (again long forgotten) batch-cooked frozen chillis, spag bols and unrecognisable browny beige lumpy concoctions.

Em scoops out an equal amount each into the stainless-steel ice cream bowls with the funny skirts, and then discreetly gives herself one scoop more. "That's enough now!"

"But you've got one scoop more!" Kate accuses.

"I have not, you cow," feeling no guilt at all. "Got any Ice Magic, Jen?"

An absolute stalwart of the girls' youths, apart from Em's. She had been blown away when Jen introduced her to this Bird's Eye classic a few years back. A classic which magically metamorphoses from liquid chocolate to an amazing hard chocolate shell on contact with the cold ice cream. Magic! Or simple viscous science?

Two mountain shaped cone bottles with fake snow lids, one brown for 'original chocolate' and other one green for 'mint chocolate', are retrieved from the cupboard.

"Plain chocolate or mint chocolate?" Jen asks.

"Mint all the way for me," as Em grabs the green topped bottle.

The contents of the green bottle are running low so Jen grabs it back and holds it under the hot tap for a minute, just to make sure the minty magic marvel pours proficiently. This is a learned trick by every eighties child.

As Em liberates her minty green onto her ice-cream she is blissfully unaware that her personal green will be tested very soon. That it will be challenged to metamorphose, worse than anything in the maze of her imagination.

The calm before the storm. Manchester's empty Arndale before the bomb.

But for now, the girls sit contently eating their ice cream; three pissed, one sober. In a ice-magic maze of imagination.

All thinking what a great, beautiful day it has genuinely been.

Beautiful Day.
U2.

-17-
EM: BETTER THE DEVIL YOU KNOW

21st April 2000
Good Friday.
Why is it called this? The day Jesus was crucified. Surely this was a bad day?
It should undoubtedly be called Bad Friday.
Jen resolves to ask her Grandpa on Sunday why it is called Good Friday not Bad Friday, or even Bloody Awful Friday.
And you have to eat fish. Jen doesn't really like fish. The only fish they had been given growing up was chippie fish, pilchards in a can and fish fingers.

Jen doesn't like the batter on chippie fish so tends to always choose a cheese and onion pie, and she absolutely hates canned fish (nearly as hangin' as liver or tongue). So fish fingers were and are always freed from the chest freezer on Good/Bad/Bloody Awful Friday.

She remembers one year she, her mum and her dad had spent Good/Bad/Bloody Awful Friday with her sister in the Priory. She had been admitted the week before and was hating it. Jen hated seeing her in there, so sad and so trapped.

Jen detested the smell of dying lilies which pervaded the place, symbolising the fading fire and frame of mind of many young patients/prisoners.

The biggest things Jen learned from her time visiting her sister in The Priory were that depression and disorders can't be just 'fixed'. 'Snap out of it' is not a useful phrase. As useful as 'Get over it', 'Buck up' and 'Sort yourself out'. 'Think about what you have rather than what you don't have' does not help a person in such a hole they end up in a place like The Priory. Family counselling sessions tend to end up a game of blame. And to never, ever let on you have an eating disorder. Just in case you find yourself 'loved' away, to a place like this.

She thought their treatment of people with eating disorders was brutal. It was not really understood then, and is still not now based on Jen's unnamed bulexia/anoremia, so they are treated with force.

Open toilets and closed eating.

"You will eat everything on your plate, or you can't leave", Jen recalls one member of staff in a white coat saying to a 'patient'. Not in a Little Chef 'you'll get a lolly' encouraging way, but in a 'we will sit here and watch you for as long as it takes – and when you do leave, we will follow you' sinister way. The worst things you can ever do to a person with a disorder like this, in Jen's personal opinion. The most private of people. Especially minors. Children who have managed to effectively shadow a huge part of their lives so no-one notices. Kids who have learned to lie and deceive, for years. To put them in a place they can not escape from, and to give them no choices, is inhuman and brutally savage in Jen's eyes.

But this Good Friday is genuinely a Good Friday for Jen. Her sister is on her way home from university in Scotland for the weekend and is really excited to see Jen and her growing bump. She just can't wait to be an auntie.

Although Jen is two years younger, they are both in their final year at uni and have spent lots of time recently on the phone talking exams and babies. Jen is really looking forward to seeing her sister.

Kate and Lou had got off the train at Liverpool Lime Street a few hours before. They were met by Lou's sisters, who promptly dragged them and their respective backpacks off to Concert Square 'for some Good Friday bevvies'. Neither Lou nor Kate put up any form of protest. The four girls literally bounced the last few metres down Wood Street.

Will is on the Swiss slopes already heading down a Verbier black run.

Em is about ten miles from home. 'Toca's Miracle' by Fragma blasting from the Now 45 CD she bought the day before from Our Price for the journey. She is bracing herself for the weekend.

Her brother Charlie is just one year older than Em. He lives in London and works in the city. He is unusually good looking, and knows it. Very talented at sports, especially rugby, and knows it. Life has been easy for her brother, Em thinks. Loved by everyone he meets, including her. Preferred (she thinks) by both their mum, dad and, having totally and annoyingly accepted her into his life, bitch stepmother Eve.

"Better the devil you know, sis," he had said to Em when she had accused him of being unfaithful to their mother by being nice to Eve, and for being 'dad's tart'.

'Golden Balls' she had pet-named him a few years earlier. She loves him to bits and they had been really close when they were younger, especially through the difficult, destructive mess of their parents' relationship and their ultimate divorce. They had been partners in crime, or rather comrades in pain. But he didn't really seem to notice her or be interested in her anymore. Had swerved her in many ways. It had been going on for the last few years and Em really couldn't understand it. If there was anything that Em couldn't bear, it was being ignored. Not being noticed.

Arriving at her large Hertfordshire home, she notices the gates are open.

Charlie is getting out of his new VW Golf, all broad shoulders and floppy hair with highlights of arrogance. He radiates a special self-belief that exudes from Em too. But his personal assurance comes totally naturally, while Em's outer confidence is constantly being curated in a calculated way from the depths of her inner insecurities. But she never lets anyone know, most of all him. Being the younger sibling, she is desperate for his attention and affirmation.

"Hey big bro!" she shouts out of her open window.

"Sis! How are you?" he replies, giving her a wide smile and a wink. "Come here."

"What the hell is going on? Why the fuck have we been summoned?" she asks him after they hug it out. "What has that bitch got to say now?"

"No idea," he replies. "But Em, honestly, give it up. Please don't be an idiot. What has she actually ever done to you? I don't understand. They've been married for well over a year now. You just have to get over it. She's going nowhere fast." And just to wind Em up even more, he adds, "She's actually really nice. It could be worse. Remember, better the devil you know sometimes, Emster."

"She is the devil" Em replies. Eyes down, hackles up.

Em had just turned seventeen when her father had introduced Eve. At twenty-five she had looked about five years younger. Em had immediately and tempestuously hated her. Had not given her a shred of a chance.

Unlike the biblical Eve, who had been sentenced to a life of sorrow under the power of her husband, Em witnessed her being gifted the love of her father, a beautiful place to live, her place, holidays to Barbados and beyond, a gorgeous new racing green Audi TT convertible roadster and a general life of joy. Envy tore through Em like Concorde tears through the sound barrier.

Is the racing green ironic, Alanis?

Throughout the discord of their family life, Em's dad had always loved her. She had been his princess and had called her 'his little star'. But her crown had been stolen. He even called the bitch 'princess'. And her dad had not called her his star for quite some time now. She could not see, in any way, that her behaviour could have led to this. That she was what was causing her star wings to be clipped. That there was room in her dad's heart for a princess and a star. And in his wallet for two crowns.

There were times, especially when she found out they were getting married, that Em genuinely thought about ways of killing Eve.

"Greetings offspring," her dad bellows as he makes his way across the copious front lawn sandwiched by Joey and Chandler, the two black labrador puppies she has never met. Em had wanted to hate the two little brothers because they are Eve's, but they are just adorable - and in fairness she thinks they are adorably named too (but obviously doesn't say, even to her friends).

Em loves animals. As a kid she had various ponies, two cats, a dog, chickens and rabbits. She adored each and every one of them, treated them like her babies. Spoke to them often about how she was feeling, like she never spoke to a human. Sang to them to block out the incessant arguing. Regularly dressed them up. One of her favourite TV programs as a kid was 'All Creatures Great and Small' about the Yorkshire vet James Herriot. She had loved the books too, as much as she had loved 'The Animals of Farthing Wood' by Colin Dann.

The puppies fly into Em's arms as she crouches down to meet and greet them for the first time. They are absolutely delectable. She breathes in their deliciously malty, fresh cut hay smell.

Her father is a very attractive man for an old man of 47, Em thinks while being lovingly licked by two over-zealous, slobbery tongues. He's a real silver fox.

"Great to see you both!" he says fondly.

He shakes his son's hand and puts his other hand across his shoulders in a kind of half handshake / half hug as people like him do, saying, "Those shoulders are getting mighty big, son."

He kisses his daughter on both cheeks after she has extracted herself from the little licky brothers, then holds both her shoulders and asks her if she is looking after herself as she looks tired.

"What's going on dad?" she asks, annoyed at his remark. "Why are we both here?"

"Do I have to have a reason to ask my children to join me for Easter?" he berates. "You have the devil in you sometimes, child, just like your mother."

"Let's go inside," Charlie interjects. Disinterested in Em's drama, he's had enough of it over the past couple of years. He's steered clear of her recently, wanting his partner in crime back instead of this petulant, angry person he doesn't recognise. He is also annoyed at his father's slur on his much-loved mother. Yet again, he is just trying to keep the peace.

Eve is inside, busying herself in the huge kitchen, leaving her husband to greet his children. Ten years ahead of its time, it has an island and space for both a huge table and a comfy seating area. It also has big glass doors opening out to the immaculate, expansive garden, the swimming lake with the little rowing boat (named Bob) merrily bobbing, the renovated out-buildings, the stables and the fields beyond.

Eve is bracing herself to see Em. The girl hated her from the moment they met. She had understood and had been patient. As a maths teacher at the local high school, she is used to handling troublesome teens and petulant pupils. But Em is no longer a child. Eve had tried so hard to crack her. Had used all the tools in her teacher kit, had naively thought they could be friends. She had had absolutely nothing to do with her parent's divorce. But her patience had gradually ebbed as Em's sabotage fully flowed. Her snide actions and spoiled, selfish behaviour disguised the bruised child she was. Eve was possibly too young herself to really understand the full picture, how she had been affected by the chaos and carnage of her troubled younger life.

Em had gone to the local prestigious private school and lived

PAPER OVER IT

at home whilst her brother had gone to Eton boarding school at thirteen. Em had missed him desperately when he went, she had been just twelve. She missed him dreadfully every time he went. Each and every term. Had always felt there was something missing in her life before the age of twelve, but when Charlie left she was simply bereft.

She had witnessed so much more, and had had to face it alone in term time. She had learned to paper over it and created a parallel universe of her home life to her friends at school. Her animals were her real friends. The ones that really knew her. Her solace. They knew everything. She told them everything.

Eve could not see the young personification of a punching bag between mother and father, wife and husband, lawyer and lawyer. The victim of years of hidden dark distress and very visible devil divorce. Eve now just sees the devil in her.

"Charlie!" Eve grins as she spots her stepson in the hall.

"Hello stepmother," he says as he envelops her in a bear hug. "Sure you don't want a younger version of your old man?" he teases.

"Give me a few years when he's really old and wrinkly," she teases back, grinning at her husband while he blows a kiss to her and confidently smiles back.

Em almost retches at this triple display of affection, and the ever so slight sexual tension between her brother and stepmother.

"Hi Em," Eve offers. "You're looking well."

"Thanks," Em replies. "You're looking a bit tired," batting her father's recent cutting remark over to Eve. In fact Em is highly pissed off by how good Eve looks. Her annoyingly beautiful brown skin is positively glowing as are her deep, dark eyes. Her gorgeous corkscrew curls are irritatingly shiny. Bitch.

"Are you thirsty?" Eve asks, papering over Em's bitchiness. "There's some nice cold bottles of water and cans of coke in the drinks fridge in the utility room through there," she points.

"I know where my drinks fridge is thank you, Eve," Em spits, unkindly. "And where my utility room is."

"Ok," she says, not rising. "Well, let's get you both upstairs and settled in," she changes the subject. "Drinks in the garden in an hour."

"You're allowing me to go upstairs to my own bedroom in my own house?" Em spits. "Thank you."

"Behave, Em. I'll not ask you again," her dad warns her.

"Come on Emster, let's go," Charlie takes his sister's hand and pulls her into the hall and up the stairs.

An hour later, they are all outside in the garden sitting by the swimming lake. It is unusually warm for April. Em had called Lou from her childhood bedroom. It is pissing it down in Liverpool. She had then called Jen. It is pissing it down in Manchester. She desperately wanted it to be pissing it down in Hertfordshire. To match her miserable, bitter mood. She flashes back to her GCSE English Literature. A 'pathetic fallacy' she recalls. When the weather perfectly matches the mood.

She can't see it, but the only pathetic thing in Hertfordshire is her own miserable self.

A bottle of Champagne has been placed on the table, alongside four beautiful, bejewelled flutes. Em doesn't recognise them. She thought they must have been on Eve's crazy Harrods wedding list.

"So I have my three favourite people here in the world," Em and Charlie's dad announces. "Sorry, and you two too," he apologises, fussing Joey and Chandler as they puppy bark for his attention.

"Oh fuck, what's going on dad?" Em cuts him short, rising to her feet.

"Emily, can you please just give me a minute?" her dad asks her kindly but sternly, using her full name.

"Emster, let him talk," Charlie forces her back to a seated position through his stare.

"I, well we, have an announcement to make. We needed you two to hear it from us first."

It was like a sucker punch to the heart. It was not expected. She had not seen it coming. How had she not seen it coming? Of course the bitch Eve would want to fill her womb with her father's seed. Of course she would want to stake her devil claim on him even further than she had - through semen and blood.

"We are going to have a baby aren't we, princess?" Em and Charlie's dad confirms Em's fears, clearly very proud and excited. He pulls his beautiful, pregnant wife into his embrace and kisses the top of her head. Like he had done to Em many times before, when she was his little star.

PAPER OVER IT

Em's green can't cope. Her terrified teenage turtle is unleashed. Her mutant maddened.

"What the absolute fuck, dad?" she screams. "What the fuck? Can you not see what the bitch is doing?"

Eve recoils from her husband's embrace, having fully expected the outburst. Having told her husband this would happen when he had been convinced it wouldn't.

"Emily, have some respect!" her dad orders, pulling his wife back into him by her nearest hand.

"You bitch," Em now focuses her attention, her venom, on Eve. "How dare you!"

"Em, please just stop," Charlie pleads, pulling his sister away by her shoulders.

"That's enough, Emily," her dad shouts. "I have been patient with you but this is not acceptable. I am not papering over it anymore. I thought you would have grown up a little by now. I have given you everything you need and want to help you grow up. It will be very different from now on, young lady." Her dad is absolutely furious.

"Dad, can you not see?" Em pleads.

"No, Emily. I can't" he says with a calmness which is hugely unsettling for Em. "This is it, now. I've had enough. Your petulance is futile. I do not want to even look at you. You and your behaviour disgust me. I will pay for everything I do until the end of the summer, and then it stops. You're on your own. I have had enough."

"But dad," Em pleads for her dad to understand. She weeps, trying to resurrect the dad she used to know. The dad she could wrap around her little finger. The dad who had called her his little star.

"No more excuses Emily, I've heard it all before. A million times," her dad cuts her short. "I am just not interested. We have given you countless chances. I have excused your behaviour more times than I can even remember. You are not a little girl anymore, you're a twenty-one-year-old woman who is completely wrapped up in herself. Utterly selfish and frankly bloody unpleasant. You've made your bed, now you lie in it."

Em races upstairs to her childhood room, no control over the devil in her. Back to that feeling of hopelessness when her parents fought and fought. Back to that feeling of isolation and sadness when her brother was away. Back to creating a fantasy world. Back to green and therefore back to black.

"I'm not lost for I know where I am. But however, where I am may be lost," said Pooh.

When you cannot see and do not know, therefore have no control over, your devil within. That's the ultimate devil.

Better the devil you know.

Steps.

-18-
THE QUARTET: LUCKY

23rd April 2000
Easter Sunday.
 Jen has been really looking forward to a day with her sister, mum, Grandpa and step-grandma. The first Sunday in their new little cottage. No longer living with the ghosts of her semi world. She has loved spending the last few days in the cottage with her sister. Catching up and chatting until the small hours about Jen's adventure and her sister's plans. Jen feels really lucky.
 Jen and her mum had moved a little further out of Manchester, towards the plains of Cheshire. A little further from any form of life, as Jen saw it, but didn't say it. Jen had no choice, she was fucked. Had nowhere else to live. She realised quickly she was actually really lucky to have somewhere lovely to ride out her adventure and to live with her baby.
 Jen's mum is liberated by the little cottage. It is beamed and beautiful, cute and cosy, handsome and homely. She feels lucky for the first time in a long time.
 They arrived with barely any furniture. Are sleeping on mattresses on the floor. They sold most things before they moved, including Jen's piano and pool table. They had been a great team. Just got rid, not wanting to hang on to any form of the past. Big mahogany dining tables and large, ornate chests of drawers had no place in the little cottage. They left the big chest freezer for the new occupants, whether they wanted it or not. Out with the old and in with the new, when they could afford it. Jen's ex had borrowed a van and helped them on moving day. Although Jen was absolutely exhausted by the end of the day, between the three of them they had made a great team.
 The van reminded Jen of her first date with her ex, before he had bought the black Ford Fiesta XR2 with the rampant roaring exhaust. He had picked her up on a Saturday night in an old red Ford Escort van, to the horror of Jen's mother.
 As she climbed into the passenger seat, she knocked something by mistake and her ex said, "Bloody hell, you'll have to hold it

now or we'll be late." He handed her a thick piece of string or a thin piece of rope. She wasn't sure. As she tugged it she realised it was keeping the back door of the van shut. "Are you joking?" she laughed. "You knocked it off," he laughed back.

Jen had never been in a van before, had certainly never been in a van before which needed a piece of rope string to keep the door shut. She smiled at the newness of it all. The excitement. The adventure.

As her ex started the engine, the van filled with the biggest noise she had ever heard. She could almost feel her mum's disdain through the big old Victorian front door. 'When a man named Al Capone' permeated every panel. Looking backwards to check that the doors hadn't been blown off by the din, she saw two enormous mahogany speakers with wires leading to the tape deck in front of her. "What the hell are they?" she yelled over the racket, wide mouthed. "My mum's lounge speakers. I borrowed them for the day. She'll never notice," he yelled back.

And with that Jen looked forward again, held on tight to her piece of rope string and was introduced to the rest of Black Lace's 'The night Chicago died' followed by the Drifters 'Kissin in the back row of the movies on a Saturday night with you.'

She loved every minute of the movie and the rest of that Saturday night.

"Hi, Grandpa," Jen and her sister collectively greet him. "Happy Easter."

"Hi girls," he lovingly responds, as his wife walks in behind him with a cake on a fancy cake stand covered with a doily. "Hi girls," she says as they hug her, nearly toppling the cake.

"How was midnight mass?" Jen asks. As a practising, devout Catholic, her Grandpa never misses mass. His faith is a beautiful thing to witness, and he is heavily involved in his church.

The girls had gone to Sunday school and mass as kids, but had started to question their faith when their Grandpa had told them that dinosaurs never existed, that Mary genuinely got pregnant without having sex and that Darwin was a lying crook.

By hook or by crook, Jen and her mum had, that week, sourced a fabulous second-hand kitchen table, made from old railway sleepers. Perfectly fitting for the cottage kitchen. They had wanted to make the first Easter in the cottage a lovely event - and eating a lamb roast (or any plate of food) on your knee on the floor is not the way her mum rolls. An eclectic mix of garden chairs and old stools surround the railway sleepers, for now.

The first few nights in the cottage, on her mattress on the floor, had strangely been the best night's sleep Jen had had for a long time. For the first time in a long time she realised there was nothing really missing in her life, she was on an adventure. So she understood why the tears, for the first time in a while, did not come at night.

After the lamb lunch and exchange of Easter eggs, Jen's Grandpa asks, "What are we going to call this baby, then?"

After the initial shock and realisation that this was not an immaculate conception. That his much-loved Granddaughter had clearly had sex (in his mind she was still about 12). He had come to terms with the out-of-generation special surprise. He was really looking forward to the adventure of being a Great-Grandpa.

"Well, as you know it's a boy," Jen replies. "What do you think we should call him, Grandpa?"

"What about choosing a name from the bible?" he suggests.

Eeek. Jen freezes for a moment. All names on her mental shortlist now being metaphorically tippexed.

"What about Joseph?" Jen's sister asks.

"Perfect," their Grandpa says. "It means 'God shall give'."

"Perfect," Jen repeats, thinking she bloody hopes he will give her some luck.

So it was done. Simple as that. Perfectly done. 'Joseph'.

Thirty-five miles west, Lou and Kate are having a great Easter Sunday with Lou's extended family and her auntie's dog Fu-Fu.

She had initially been named Honour by Lou's auntie, but while trying to train her in the local park with other dog owners, families and kids in earshot, Jen's uncle fairly quickly realised that the phrases he was bellowing out were not ideal. "Lie, Honour", "Sit, Honour" and "Come, Honour" to name just a few.

She was promptly renamed Fu-Fu as a shortened version of the profanities he bellowed to his bemused wife when he got home. He had no idea what he was now bellowing at the park.

They are now all playing charades in the front room. All adults suitably pissed.

The jollity and family madness reminds Kate of home and for a moment she feels very homesick until she realises how lucky she is to be there.

It's the first time Lou has been back home since Eddie-twat-gate and she realises how much better she feels. How she doesn't often feel any more there is Eddie-shaped something missing in her life. She feels lucky.

Halfway through pissed charades, Lou's uncle tries to act out a daffodil and ends up looking like a creepy old witch with crippled hands reaching for the sky for some heavenly message from God. After standing on one leg and pointing at his gold wedding band, to help his team understand he is a daffodil, he falls over onto the floor and the drunken onlookers all fall about laughing.

"What the hell was that?" Lou's dad asks his big brother, crying with laughter.

"A bloody daffodil, what did you think it was?" he replies, still on the floor bent over with laughing.

"Why are you even doing a daffodil, dad?" asks Lou's cousin taking the card off his dad, half crippled with laughter and Lambrini. "It says Damon Hill."

Lou's mum has to hold her crotch as she speeds, like the Formula 1 racing driver Damon, to the loo. Her menopausal pelvic floor incapable of coping any more.

"I've lost my glasses," Lou's uncle says indignantly to the uncontrollably laughing crowd. By way of an excuse.

"You've lost your bloody marbles, more like," his wife shrieks affectionately. "Bloody daffodil! Sometimes I have to pinch myself to realise how lucky I am," she teases him, fondly.

One hundred and sixty miles south, it is a completely different story.

Em is wandering lonely as a cloud. There is no raucous crowd, nor a host laughing at his brother's golden daffodils.

She had stormed out of her house on Friday afternoon and gone to stay with an old friend who lives down the road. She said nothing of the reason she had asked to stay at Easter, and her friend hadn't pushed her, knowing Em rarely shared anything really important. With her parents being away, the two girls spent Easter Saturday and Sunday slowly making their way through the well stocked bar.

Her big brother Charlie, her Charliebobs, had come into her room an hour after the horrendous argument and tried to make her see sense, tried to make her go downstairs and apologise. To see how lucky she really is. But Em wouldn't, she just couldn't. Couldn't bear the thought of her beloved father with Eve, never mind Eve's baby. She was eaten up with jealousy. Living in a greenhouse of her own making. Not a sanctuary of calm and plant life like Len's. A stifling greenhouse with no door and no air. She was trapped. Suffocating. She had trapped herself. Her green devil raging within.

After ten minutes of trying to coax her, Charlie gave up. He had had enough of her too.

Her star is fading, in fact it has been fading for some time now. It was her fault. Her spoiled, selfish fault, Charlie had told her. It stung Em like a hornet, but she didn't react. She acted like she'd not heard him and turned over in her bed so he couldn't see her. He admitted defeat and left her alone to wallow in her sea of green. She didn't know how lucky she was, he repeated to her as he left. But she just couldn't see it.

Lying alone crying in bed at her friend's house on Easter Sunday night, filled to the brim with alcohol, tears, her devil, her lonely heart and her green, she listens to Britney and feels anything but lucky. Anything but a little star.

She scratches her right wrist until it bleeds.

Lucky.
Britney Spears.

-19-
KATE: BREATHLESS

1st May 2000
The first May Bank Holiday Monday.

Ten days since Em's Bad Friday, eight days since Joseph was named and seven days since Lou answered a call from Will's brother, a devastating call.

That number again, seven.

It had been Easter Monday. Lou and Kate were nursing hangovers from hell having gone out into Liverpool with Lou's sisters after Easter Sunday golden daffodil charades had got so wild and rude it had to be stopped by Lou's mum and her sister-in-law. The girls hit the town already half cut and proceeded to fill the other half.

Lying on Lou's single bed at just before nine in the morning, head to toe, Lou's phone rang. She reached across Kate's legs to grab it. It was Will. Kate still doesn't have a phone.

"Hey Will," Lou groaned. "What time do you call this? It's a bloody bank holiday, you twat!"

"It's not Will. It's his brother," he said a little breathlessly.

He is just one year older than Will, and the two are very close. They had gone to the same boarding school when each was thirteen. Will had missed his big brother desperately when he had gone first. Had also missed him when he had gone to work in London, which is where he still lives.

Instantly sobered, Lou sat up, turned her lamp on and demanded, "What is it? What's happened?"

"There's been an accident. On Saturday. He's in the hospital," He said slightly breathlessly. The line was bad so Lou just about heard 'accident' and 'hospital'.

"Accident? Hospital?" she repeated loudly, waking Kate.

"What's going on?" Kate winced through half shut eyes. "Bright light! Bright light," she gremlin-ed. "Turn it off." And immediately fell back to sleep.

"Kate," Lou said quietly but purposefully, nudging her gently. "Wake up. It's Will's brother."

Like lightning, Kate bolted upright with her head immediately demisted. She took the phone from Lou.

"It's Kate. What's happened?"

Lou only heard half of the conversation but from the half she heard, it was clearly serious. The line was still really bad.

Will's family met Kate just over a year and a half ago, and had absolutely loved her. Will had been slightly concerned she wasn't the 'type' of girl he thought his parents thought should be his girlfriend. But he couldn't have been more wrong. He had berated himself after, like he had when he first met Kate in Dolcis.

The first time he took her home was overtaken with his dad and Kate, totally politically opposed, talking politics and social theories. Kate's clear intelligence, warmth and wine-filled sass, with a side of 'left' and a twist of Scottish Labour, was enjoyed enormously by his Conservative voting dad. He was mesmerised by her Arabian looks, gifted from her Lebanese father, and the strong phonation of her Scottish tongue, gifted from her Glaswegian mother.

"You don't look like you're from Scotland," he had said, after they had had a heated debate over the merits and de-merits of Marxism.

"Where do I look like I'm from?" she had asked inquisitively, irritatingly used to people asking her where she was 'from'.

"Somewhere exotic," he had responded.

"Lebanon and Scotland," she responded. "The exotic combination of Beirut and Glasgow, to be more precise. And you do look like you vote Conservative."

Will's dad had laughed out loud, taken off guard by her answer and her bold political response and assumptions. He asked her what she meant by the Conservative comment. She had responded by asking if he did vote blue. He had said yes, he was blue through and through.

"So I'm right," she had smiled cheekily. He couldn't help but smile back at this gorgeous, bright, warm, slightly sassy girl.

He had winked at Will later, "Got yourself a keeper there, son."

Will had winked back, "Just hope I can keep her, dad." He had fallen head over heels for Kate, had never felt as seriously about anyone. Had lost the will to try and hide from or deny it. Had previously been as good a player with girls as he was with a rugby ball.

And for Kate, Will's dad was a revelation.

She had thought she would hate the man, hate everything about his pre-assumed bourgeois behaviour, ballast and bollocks. But she found him fascinating. The pair sat up talking (or rather, loudly debating) way into the night.

And as for Will's mum, who had lived in a male world for so long and had never had either of her sons bring a girl home that she liked, Kate was just perfect. All bright-eyed cheek, clear intelligence, warmth and Arabian beauty. She was not expecting a hug when they first met, but Kate had gone in for one. Will's mum had, quite frankly, fallen in love with her at that moment. And Will's brother, well he fell in love with her immediately too. Awkwardly.

They didn't behave or speak like Kate was expecting either. They seemed totally normal. Not posh and slightly affected like Will and his brother. But above all, they seemed to really love each other. Have a huge respect for each other, and make each other laugh. A lot. They seemed like a real team. It made for a very happy home.

From the first moment she went to Chester, Kate was always welcomed warmly into Will's beautiful, gated home. Just forty miles down the M56 or on the train from Manchester. She loved going. Went often with Will.

Kate explained to Lou, when she put the phone down, that she had made out that Will had fallen badly on a black run, been airlifted to the hospital and been put into an induced coma with potential brain damage. She was remarkably calm. It was the adrenaline. The shock.

All she could think about was getting to him. She had no idea where Verbier was, what country it was in. What country he was in. She was completely terrified and crushed.

Lou's father was in his greenhouse. "Dad," Lou called him in. "We need your help."

Len found out, from his atlas, that Verbier was in Switzerland and the local airport to Verbier was Sion.

Ten minutes on Teletext confirmed that there were no direct flights from either Manchester or Liverpool to Sion. Consulting his atlas again, Len saw that Verbier was not that far from Geneva, so Teletext was consulted again. There was a flight to Geneva on the Wednesday from Manchester. They would work out how Kate would get from Geneva to Verbier at some point, but the flight was booked. A one-way flight.

"But I don't have the money," Kate said, panicking. Breathless.

"We will work it out, love. Just pay us back when you can," Lou's mum had mothered.

"Thank you," Kate had cried while being hugged by Lou's mum.

It turned out that Will had actually been airlifted to a hospital in Geneva so it was a highly successful unplanned plan.

A week on, the early May Bank Holiday, Kate is still in Geneva with Will and his family. His injuries are not as bad as initially thought, and Will is now conscious. He is definitely not in any fit state to walk yet, never mind do his imminent finals or finish his final year at uni. He is, however, able to be flown home and be treated in the UK. He is desperate to go home, as are they all.

Kate is in the third year of her four-year course, so does not have finals to contend with. The university has been informed for both Will and Kate, and Kate has rung her manager at Dolcis.

Lou went back to Manchester on the Tuesday. Jen went to pick her up. The girls have not heard from Em at all. She has been ignoring their calls and messages.

Jen spent the week revising, head down. But she had not felt well at all. On the Friday, at her weekly scan, she had been told to slow down. She had been getting headaches and her blood pressure was on the high side. Was told again, by the kind, friendly midwife, that she needed to look after herself for the baby's sake. But she also needed to get her degree for her baby's sake. It was a difficult dichotomy.

Jen and Em's finals start on the 15th of May. Just two weeks away. Lou is working really hard on finalising her independent performance showcase project, which will make up a large part of her degree.

She has also spent a lot of time over the past few months honing her audition technique and pulling together a portfolio, all in preparation for a professional career. As one of the most talented people on her course, she is being helped by the university to find an agent.

Everything is starting to feel very imminent and scarily real for the final year students.

"Em," Jen asks when she finally gets hold of her today. "Are you ok?"

"I'm fine," she says simply. And stops there.

She had been absolutely horrified when she woke up on Easter Monday at her friend's house.

The first thing that hit her was the pounding headache, then a split second later the burning sensation on her right wrist. She looked down at the multiple deep scratch marks - each nearly two inches long. Deep, angry, raw and bleeding. She couldn't believe what she had done to herself. It really hurt and looked dreadful. She immediately got up, left her friend a note and somehow drove up to Manchester. To be alone in her flat. To block out the world. She couldn't get away from herself unfortunately, but at least she could remove her mortified self from other people.

"What's going on? You have been incommunicado for over a week. We're worried about you," Jen pushes. "Do you know about Will?"

"Honestly I'm fine. Don't worry," she looks at the scabbing, yet still weeping and pulsating, wounds on her wrist. "What about Will?"

Jen proceeds to explain the horrendous situation and Em feels dreadful for being so wrapped up in her own frantic forlorn feelings and horrendous self-harm.

"Oh fuck. I'm so, so sorry," she says. "What can I do to help? What can I do?"

"Kate's coming home in a few days with Will so there's nothing you can do there," she confirms. "But totally selfishly, I could do with a friend. Can I come and stay at yours for a few nights? It's so hot in the cottage. I need your air con. I don't feel great and I need help with revision. It's two weeks today."

Then she adds, quietly, "I'm scared, Em."

"Oh my god, yes," Em replies immediately. "I'm so sorry Jen. I've been such a shit friend. Get your shit together right now. I am literally getting in the car in five to come and pick you up."

"Thank you," Jen is very grateful to her friend. She is drowning, not able to concentrate. Feeling dizzy and disorientated. She needs her friend. She needs Em. She also needs Em's brain and course notes.

By the time Em arrives to pick her up, she has gathered up all her books and notes and packed everything else she needs for her stay. Including the carefully wrapped Cherish.

By the time she says goodbye to her mum, who is enjoying the bright and very warm bank holiday sunshine in the courtyard, she feels lightheaded and slightly breathless. Struggling for air in the heat.

Breathless.
The Corrs.

-20-
THE QUARTET: DON'T GIVE UP

2nd May 2000
Jen's mum had not wanted her to go to Em's yesterday, but understood why she wanted to. She had given up trying to convince her otherwise.

She had given Em very clear instructions to look after her daughter. To feed her, water her and watch her. Em had promised that she would wrap Jen in proverbial cotton wool, while thinking what a worrier Jen's mum is. Jen isn't bloody Steve the Cheese.

Just before Jen said she was tired and wanted to go to bed, she spotted Em's right wrist as she pulled up the sleeves on her jumper absent-mindedly. Having purposefully kept them pulled down since she picked Jen up earlier. The first person she has spoken to all week other than the man in the off-licence.

"What's that?" Jen asked wearily. "It looks sore."

"It's nothing," Em papered over it, pulling her sleeves down. Steering Jen into her bedroom where they will share her bed. "I think I've had an allergic reaction to something."

Jen mumbled something about her changing her washing powder as she passed out. Exhausted.

Jen had not told her mum or Em she had been feeling a little unwell. Had not wanted to worry them. But today Jen takes a turn.

Her vision blurs and she feels sharp pains just below her ribs. She is confused and disorientated. Em is terrified. She calls Jen's mum and then takes her straight to hospital. Where her mum already is.

Jen is diagnosed with preeclampsia. Is told to rest and keep her feet in the air, higher than her heart, at all times. Em and Jen's mum are told that this instruction is vital for the health of both Jen and Joseph. It's life threatening to both.

She is allowed out of hospital and she goes home with her mum. Em is far too frightened to be responsible for not only her friend, but her friend's baby too. Em will get her things from the flat and come over later with them. She will come every day after and they will revise together. If necessary, Em will stay over.

That evening at home in their cottage, Jen's mum asks, "Why

PAPER OVER IT

didn't you tell me you weren't feeling well?"

"I'm sorry," the exhausted Jen replies before she falls asleep, too tired for any conversation. Too overwhelmed. Too terrified. Too scared that her body is going to give up.

In and out of sleep, sweating and dizzy, Jen dreams dazed, confused and delirious dreams.

She remembers her first transvestite encounter in the toilets of Via Fossa. How she got pissed with Marilyn, and her and an old school friend had 'all the questions'. They hid their heads in their own shame the following morning for being so rude and inquisitive.

She remembers her Grandpa's wedding when she and her sister wore matching berets and smart outfits from the posh kids shop 'Young Cheshire' in Altrincham. Has flashbacks to her sister and the dying lilies in The Priory.

She remembers the Christmas years back at her aunties in Lincolnshire, her happy place, when it kicked off royally over a game of Monopoly and her dad had upended the board and stormed off. Drove home pissed over the Pennines. Park Lane hotels and Utilities cards were strewn everywhere. She remembered the water works that followed in the kitchen between her mum and her auntie.

Jen, her sister, her mum and her mum's pride had to take the slow route home in her Grandpa's stoic Volvo with his lovely wife, a tartan blanket on the back seat, a 1994 AA large scale road atlas of Britain in the seat pocket behind the passenger seat, a black 'man-size' pack of Kleenex and his black wooden handled umbrella on the back shelf, and the smell of his pipe. "Do men have much bigger noses than women?" she remembers asking.

She recollects his stories of Dunkirk, Egypt, Tobruk, India and Burma. The diaries he had written in the second world war which he had talked her through so patiently and vividly at his kitchen table. His stamp collection, so carefully collected and curated.

Jen just loves the smell of his pipe. It's peaceful somehow. As is the gentle tapping of it into his ashtray, his rhythmic sucking of it and the way he stuffs the tobacco in so carefully and precisely from the little brown leather pouch. She can somehow smell and hear it quite vividly.

Kate also can't sleep alone in her huge hotel bed. Her mind

races, jumping around. They are going home tomorrow. Geneva to Manchester. A special transit that Will's parents have organised to get Will safely back to the UK. She picks up a book, giving up on sleep.

Em can't sleep either. The hospital and Jen's scare the day before had really upset her. In fact it had terrified her. Had made her think a lot. Every day had been an uphill climb since Bad Friday. She had felt like giving up. Hadn't wanted to see or speak to anyone, especially after she realised how much she had hurt herself. Ignored everyone. But the fact she had known nothing about Will, nothing about her friend's trauma, and had not been there for Jen when she had clearly needed her, was unforgivable. They had needed her, to see and speak to her. She is so selfish. Such a selfish, self-absorbed, self-harming, shit person.

She thinks about her dad and her brother. About Eve. About her impending half sibling. About everything. Em hasn't slept well for ages, but alcohol had comatosed her each night for the past week so she hadn't really dreamed. Certainly hadn't been lucid enough to know or remember any, anyway. At least she hadn't hurt herself again. This was the first night for over a week, apart from the night before in the hospital, that she was aware. Her lucidity terrifies her. Leaves her breathless.

She remembers something Charlie had said to her years ago when he was, yet again, whipping her at chess. "Life is like a game of chess, Emmie. You can't undo a move but you can focus on making the next one better,' he said. "Fuck off, fuckster," she had so eloquently responded while unwittingly manoeuvring herself into checkmate. She felt she was now in metaphorical check, she just needed to work out how to not allow herself to move into checkmate. She couldn't give up. Couldn't lose like she always did at chess. But she is still thinking about 'winning' and 'losing'.

This chess memory also got her thinking about the fun she used to have at home with Charlie. The daft games they had played on one or other of their bedroom floors. Sometimes just because they wanted to, and other times to help drown out the incessant arguments below.

Ludo was her favourite. They used to have two or three colours each racing around the board, and the stakes were always high.

"Whoever wins tidies the other's bedroom," or some other equally juvenile high-stake challenge.

They had both liked Scrabble, but had a love-hate relationship with Mousetrap. It took them longer to set it up than to actually play it. And more often than not the bloody boot wouldn't be lined up to kick the bastard bucket so the little steel ball didn't roll down the blue zig zag stairs. And the crimson dome shaped cage would invariably randomly drop in the middle of the game, trapping absolutely no mice whatsoever. At that stage they would normally give up, wondering why they had bothered building the stupid thing in the first place.

Charlie liked Operation. His annoyingly steady hands always fished out the Adam's apple, funny bone or spare rib without initiating the irritating alarm and the gleaming red glow nose. Right now all Em can think of is that if she had a wishbone, she would wish that Charlie could tweezer out her cold, green heart and help fix her. She misses him so much.

In this self-absorption, she promises herself to try and be less selfish, less self-absorbed.

Is that irony, Alanis?

She knows deep down she's made a really wrong move, like in chess, and needs to decide what her next one is. However consumed by her green she is. She knows she has to have a long hard look at herself in the mirror, Michael Jackson style. Needs to somehow change her ways. Charlie's hornet sting still hurts deeply like her wrist, but somehow she still can't really accept that it is her who is in the wrong.

So the venom remains, silently circulating inside her. Feeding and further poisoning her green.

Lou hasn't slept either, worrying about her friends. She's been in contact with Kate through Will's brother. Had finally got in touch with Em who updated her on Jen's scare. She suspected something bad had happened to Em, but had not pushed it.

What is going on? Her three friends in such a bad way. She misses them. Especially Kate. Her other flatmates are great, but they aren't her kind Kate.

She has a moment with Hairy Potter to try and summon absent sleep.

Don't give up.
Chicane.

-21-
JEN & EM: A LITTLE BIT OF LUCK

15th May 2000

Monday. The first final exam for Em and Jen. They have done all they can, now they just need a little bit of luck.

They have both worked so hard over the last few weeks. Jen at home on the newly bought sofa, second hand from Buy and Sell magazine, with her feet in the air, higher than her heart. Dirtying her mum's cottage wall. "Will you either clean your filthy feet or take them off the wall?" her mother had demanded, overwhelmed by the situation and the newly grubby wall.

After a few days of keeping her legs in the air while revising, Jen was feeling a lot better. The irony that having her legs in the air was what had got her in this situation in the first place was not lost on Jen.

Is that irony, Alanis?

Her blood pressure had come down and the dizziness was diminishing. She was finally getting a bit of good luck. She had only had one highly hormonal moment where she smashed her plate of grilled tomatoes on toast on the floor. She had absolutely no idea why she had done it.

With no tomatoes left, she had popped, or rather roughly thrust, the last two pieces of bread into the Russell Hobbs toaster. Had spread a big spoonful of raspberry jam and spread it on the toast out of flavour desperation. She wasn't a fan of raspberry jam as she didn't like the seeds, but there was nothing else in. The Robertson's label told her it had gone out of date in July 1996, just after the mould informed her this was probably the case.

"Why the hell did you bring this with us mum? We brought no beds, no sofas and no chairs, but we brought some shitty, mouldy, seedy, rancid four-year-old raspberry jam?" Jen hollered hormonally.

With no bread left and the tomatoes on the floor silently swimming in olive oil and their own juices, infested with sharp toothed ceramic plate sharks, Jen gave up. Grabbed a slightly soft, blackening banana and stomped upstairs. At least she wouldn't have the control conundrum, she thought positively. Right now, Lady Luck was as much her ally as her hormones.

Her mum had just watched this all play out, retrieved some kitchen paper from under the sink and cleaned up the front-crawling tomatoes and the sharp circling sharks. She eye-rolled and sighed as she felt a ceramic shark splinter infest her finger.

"Give me strength," she said to no-one in the ceiling while sucking her slightly bleeding, splintered digit. "Or just a little bit of luck, please."

Em had been bouncing between her flat and the cottage. Grateful for the distraction of the exams and Jen.

Jen had asked her if she wanted to talk, knowing something had happened over Easter. Em had just deflected, Em style. Papered over it by diverting the attention to her paper course notes.

Jen had been granted special privileges going into the exams, being the only pregnant person in the whole of Manchester Uni. Ouch. Being the only so heavily pregnant person doing their finals ever at Manchester Uni. Double ouch. She is to be at the front of the room for all exams, meaning easy access to the toilets, if needed. She is to have fifteen minutes longer than everyone else, if needed. She has a special tutor available at all times. And she had been told that the Manchester Evening News were on alert in case she went into labour during an exam. Triple ouch. She is mortified and highly embarrassed at all the attention.

The girls have seven exams in total, a very tough few weeks. The university had said that if Jen managed to complete six of the seven exams, they would mark her based on her previous work and the six exams. If she didn't, she would have to re-sit.

"With a little bit of luck, we can make it through alright," her tutor had said kindly.

Jen had wondered where the 'we' had come from. Was he going to take the exams for her in this blistering heat with a now fully formed baby bouncing between sitting on her bladder and climbing into her ribs? But then she realised she was being a venomous, hormonal hornet to this kind, slightly awkward man. So she thanked him and held up a pair of crossed fingers.

With the penultimate exam on Friday the 9th June and the final exam scheduled for Monday the 12th June, and Jen's due date

PAPER OVER IT

being Wednesday 14th June, it is tighter than a haemorrhoid suffering duck's arse. She just hopes her pelvic floor has the same strength and tightness as the duck, otherwise she's fucked.

She was only sick three times last week. The desperation for control is still overwhelming, but she controlled it four out of the seven days. The majority. When control controls you in your desperation for control, it's hard to control. She knew what she had eaten, or kept down, was enough for her little leech to be ok. It was confirmed by her Friday scan. Joseph is progressing beautifully, apparently.

Will has been home over a week now and is doing well, amazingly well. He has been very lucky. Kate has been staying at his house in Chester while he was still in hospital. Lovingly treated like a member of the family. His mum fussing over her nearly as much as she fussed over Will. She was studying for her end of year exams as much as she could, but her mind was obviously pre-occupied.

Will's mum had come home one day from a quick trip into Chester with Will's dad and presented Kate with a brand-new mobile phone - a Nokia 3210 just like Lou and Kate's. She couldn't believe it, was totally overwhelmed by the generosity. She was so lucky.

"So you can keep in touch with Will and us when you go back to uni," Will's mum had said practically, batting away Kate's "I can't accept it."

Will had told her to just accept it, that his mum had always yearned for a girl. That in fact it was a family joke that she was so sure that Will was going to be a girl, she had bought everything in pink and even had the nursery painted in rosy tones. She presumptuously named him Winifred after her beloved grandmother, Winnie for short. When she had eventually accepted there were to be no pretty pink tights or cute bouncing hair bunches, she had called him William Frederick. Not the largest of leaps from Winifred. Luckily Will was not called Willie for short and he always saw the funny side each and every time the story was told. Called it his 'feminine side'.

Jen and Em walk into the expansive exam hall. Arms linked, armours chinked.

"We've got this," Em winks, squeezing Jen's hand to help arm her with the confidence she needs, to remove some of her chinks. "All three of us."

"Thank you," Jen says, unconsciously touching her stomach. "Let's do this my Em," she squeezes her friend's hand back, arming her too. Trying to remove some of the vulnerability Jen has spotted in her recently. Her chinks, her green/blue Stilton cracks.

Performing well is undeniably hugely important to Jen. Em wants to do well because she dislikes failing, rather than really caring about the course and the resulting degree. They both sit, one at the front and one at the back of the room. Both raise their hands and ask for more paper, please. Jen on a monumental mission to get everything down she can, Em just an annoyingly fast writer.

After the exam, Em and Jen go to the Trafford Centre to buy a few items of clothing to get Jen through the last few weeks of pregnancy and her first few months after. They have three more days until their next exam, so a break for a few hours is deemed highly acceptable. It is sweltering for May, and June is promised to be even hotter. Michael Fish said so. So it must be true, right? Just what you need as a heavily pregnant, over-heating, highly hormonal girl in the middle of her finals. A heat wave.

The Trafford Centre, about five miles west of Manchester and 30 miles east of Liverpool, just off the M60, opened in September 1998 to much excitement. Over twelve years after its initial proposal and two years after the Manchester IRA bomb, Manchester city centre businesses were terrified it would take footfall and trade away from the city centre as the bomb had. It did, as it did Liverpool. They vowed, as a business community, to never let the then six-year-old Metrolink network go to the Trafford Centre.

A huge indoor shopping centre and entertainment complex of epic scale with an eclectic, slightly bonkers mix of neo-classical maroon and cream marble, fanciful fountains, towering palm trees and a heady mix of Venetian and Vatican vibes. Eating in the largest food court in Europe, The Orient, feels like you are on a 1930s ocean liner.

Jen has most of the things she needs for the baby. Her ex's sister kindly donated a gorgeous Winnie the Pooh wooden cot and her ex had bought a new mattress from Mothercare for it. She has bought a moses basket, some baby bottles, a steriliser, a bouncer and a pile of baby clothes from a lovely second-hand shop in the little town where she now lives. The pool table funded navy-blue tartan travel system is proudly placed in the porch. She had sourced some muslins (although she had no idea at the time why her mum had said she needed some Muslims) and her mum's friend had knitted her a beautiful patchwork blanket.

They are going to go to a pub for a quick drink after shopping. Jen said she would drive so Em could have a drink. She has a ten-year-old white Fiesta XR2i bought the previous year from the proceeds of spending the summer temping on reception at BUPA corporate in Trafford Park and selling her old Fiat. She loves her little car. It has balls, 'i' balls, 'injection' balls. Unlike the rampant roaring, non i'd, virginity-stealing XR2. She calls her Honey, as the number plate is randomly H101 NNY.

Having been cooled down somewhat by the Trafford Centre air conditioning, and the fanciful wishing fountain Jen smashed her face in to cool herself further, much to the hilarity of a group of young teens, the pair proceed to systematically source the things Jen needs. Elasticated shorts, a few t-shirts, lightweight tracksuit bottoms, some Bridget Jones knickers and a couple of little floaty dresses. It is quite the challenge buying non-maternity maternity wear. Jen is too small for actual maternity wear and it is far too expensive anyway. Under budget and in under two hours, they are done. Have smashed it!

Positively thrilled at their haul, they make their way back to Jen's little Honey, which is parked by the Selfridges rear entrance. Em opens the boot to find it full of crap, like the rest of her car, and clothes. Including Jen's cherished sheepskin aviator jacket her parents bought her from Lakeland a few Christmases before and her prized Prince tennis racket. "Why the fuck have you got a sheep in your boot in May?" Em laughs, wiping sweat from her forehead, shutting the boot and putting the haul on the back seats. The rest of Honey is equally as squalid. "You're a tramp," Em says.

"Why have you got a long-sleeved jumper on?" Jen retorts. "It's bloody boiling."

"Stop deflecting from your rampant trampy-ness," Em quickly replies, pulling her cuff down further over her hidden large scabs. Jen doesn't notice and just laughs.

Sitting in the pub with Em nursing a pint and Jen sipping a lemonade and lime, the girls look over the shopping list they had made and ticked off, feeling rather proud of themselves. They also discuss their revision plans for the next few days, writing them on the back of the shopping list with a little blue Argos pen Em finds in her bag. A car alarm annoyingly blasts outside.

As they make their way to the car park, Em asks Jen why her boot is open. As they get closer to Honey, they realise the passenger door is also open.

"Are you fucking joking?" Em shouts to the sky over the screeching car alarm as they realise their haul, the sheepskin and the tennis racket have all been stolen. "All she fucking needs is a little bit of luck, God!"

On the brink of tears, Jen simply says, "Are you there God? It's me, Jennifer."

Em half smiles at her friend's Judy Blume, and shakes her head. Heartbroken for her. "I'm so sorry Jen. If I hadn't put all the bags on the back seat so they could be seen, it probably wouldn't have happened."

"Don't be ridiculous Em, this is in no way your fault. It's just my luck at the minute. I am definitely banking some of the good stuff," she says, "And it's just things, just stuff. It's not important" she adds bravely, biting back tears.

"Shall we Judy Bloom?" Em offers, trying to lighten the lousy situation.

"Ok, let's do it," Em nods, wiping her eyes.

What a picture it is if anyone is watching. One screeching, invaded Honey and two girls doing what looks like the chicken dance, singing "We must! We must! We must increase our bust!" then falling about laughing before falling into each other's arms.

Jen weeps on Em's shoulder for quite some time, her emotions totally getting the better of her. Her hormones raging nearly as much Em's internal rage at the unfairness of what has just happened, the outrage of it.

"Tiggers never go on being sad," said Rabbit.

What the fuck does Rabbit know?

The movie Gladiator had just premiered with Russell Crowe. Em silently vowed to be Jen's Gladiator, determined to avenge the injustice.

A little bit of luck is what she now needs, and Em promises herself that she will do everything and anything she can to help her make it through alright.

A little bit of luck.
DJ Luck & MC Neat.

-22-
LOU: HE WASN'T MAN ENOUGH

17th May 2000

Kate returns to Manchester just in time to start her end of year exams. Will's mum gets up early with her and gives her a lift from Chester.

She knows she won't perform as well as she should or could, but she also knows she has another whole year to pull up her grades. She definitely now knows she wants to become a lawyer. Had spoken about it with Will's dad at length. Her ultimate goal is to be a barrister, to take the bar for the underdog.

Will's dad is a founding partner in a big law firm with offices in Chester and London. He has offered her work experience over the summer in the Chester office. Has told her to carry on with her politics degree and get the best grades possible, then apply to some big law firms as a graduate.

Kate desperately wants to go home for the summer, and she also needs to earn money. She has already sorted a job at Dolcis Renfield Street in Glasgow, and knows she can pick up shifts at the pub she worked at on and off for a few years. She also needs to work out where she is going to live after the summer, for her final year. Lou and her other housemates are graduating so the house in Withington either needs filling with three other students, or she needs to hand the keys back. She is now conflicted about summer. But her conflict isn't going to help complete these exams, so it is temporarily repressed.

Kate returns to Manchester also just in time to see Eddie-twat sitting in his car outside their house in Withington.

"What the hell are you doing here?" she demands. "It's eight in the morning."

"I've made a big mistake, Kate," he pleads. "I just want to see her."

"Does she know you're here?" Kate interrogates.

"No," he admits. "I've been here over an hour trying to psych myself up to knock on. She's stopped taking my phone calls. Doesn't answer my texts. I'll do anything. I'll beg her to stay with me."

"You broke her heart, Eddie. And she can't stay with you, she's not with you, you absolute nob!" she replies. "And yes you made a big mistake, huge! You weren't a real man at all."

"Please just go and see if she'll speak to me, please Kate?" he begs, pathetically.

"Stay here!" she commands.

She lets herself into the house, calling Lou to see if she is in while depositing her heavy rucksack on the hall floor.

"Kate!" Lou screams as she races down the stairs and into the hall, wrapping her arms around her friend. "Tell me everything! How's Will? How are you?"

"I will. But listen, Lou, do you know Eddie has been outside for over an hour?"

"Really?" She leans round the corner into the lounge and looks out the window. "Why?"

"He said you weren't taking his calls," she explains, pulling her back round the corner. "He says he just wants to talk."

Lou very recently turned a significant metaphorical corner. She also turned a physical corner in the library and bumped into someone yesterday. She had clocked him clocking her a short while earlier, and had been certain the accidental physical meeting had not been a complete accident. He wasn't really her type, but 'her type' had proved to be as reliable and attractive as an oily, wet trout. So she thought she would finally go fishing again. And what a catch he had been! He did things to her Eddie would never have dreamed of, the library blowfish boy completely blew her mind.

There was a slight misunderstanding when he asked her if she liked water sports, and she said 'yes', wondering why he was asking her whether she liked swimming or other water based activities when they were doing the six and nine. But apart from that (he somehow caught himself and raced to the loo) it was a highly successful first post-Eddie fishing sesh. He had only left the house about ten minutes earlier, floating out as un-coy as a very confident, non-conforming carp.

"I don't want to talk to him, Kate," Lou says simply. "Will you please tell him to go away? I need to concentrate on fishing this year. I don't want to see him. Please make him leave." Lou vows to update Kate on the library lust and recently exited sexpert, but for now she is tired and just wants Eddie off her street, out of Manchester and out of her life. Time and recent rampant house guest have collectively branded him slightly pathetic, unattractive. Slippery and weedy like an eel. She sees through him now. Sees him for the real slim shady he is. She finally realises he simply isn't man enough for her.

"Ok lovely, leave it with me," Kate replies, assuming she meant to say that she needed to concentrate on finishing the year, not fishing. She is so tired, she must have misheard.

Kate opens the front door and proceeds to rid Eddie from Lou's life, to make him leave. She is exhausted from the past few weeks, doesn't have the energy or patience for Eddie and his self-pity. Normally so kind and warm, but his tears do nothing for her as she remembers Kate's heartbreak on Valentine's Day and her own heartbreak when she had found out that Will was so poorly. Eddie doesn't even have the balls or passion to even try and get into the house like Jen's ex had, as awful as that had been. He really is rather pathetic.

He stays outside in his car for another half an hour before he drives off, grinding his gears. Lou and Kate watch him from behind Kate's bedroom curtains. And that was the end of Eddie. "Good riddance! You can now be a bird of prey." Kate says hugging her relieved friend. "He is so not man enough for my Lou! Never was."

Lou nods slightly guiltily, still rather moist and chafed from being a bird of prey just yesterday and having had a man enough all night and this morning.

Kate is going to be late for her exam if she doesn't get a wriggle on. Hadn't planned Eddie-twat-slim-shady-cry-gate into her tight schedule for the day. So she gives Lou a hug and promises her they will catch-up properly on everything later. That everything is ok, well much better than it could have been.

"You'll never guess what, I've only gone and got a bloody phone!" she shouts as she races out of the house to the bus stop and her first exam.

Lou mishears her, thinking she says, "I've only gone and got a muddy bone."

"A muddy bone? What the hell is that?" she yells at her down the street, but she's gone. No chance of contacting her until she is home to ask her.

"She really needs to get a bloody phone," Lou says to her herself. "And a shag."

He wasn't man enough.
Toni Braxton.

-23-
THE QUARTET: BAG IT UP

28th May 2000
The Sunday before the late May Bank Holiday Monday.

All the girls are in the middle of their exams, Jen is still revising upside down. Eating lots of apples as she read that they reduce blood pressure and protect your brain. Hoping her head being lower than her legs will somehow help her through gravity bagging up knowledge and sending it down, Isaac Newton-style, to her brain. She is fully aware this is stupid, but anything that will help right now is to be considered. Even apples and gravity.

Em and Jen have spent a lot of time together recently, but all focus has been on revision and the impending baby Joseph. Em hasn't spoken about Easter once, but has promised Jen she will. As soon as she is ready. She has become a softer, more considerate and more openly kind Em recently. Jen knows her friend is hurting, that something awful has happened, and she just wants to help her. Like she is helping Jen.

Living together, Kate and Lou have obviously seen each other loads - although no real quality time. Kate had howled when Lou updated her on the library blowfish and water sports confusion, so much so she almost had unintended water sports herself.

Kate has finally got to grips with her new phone and is now in daily contact with Will, who is progressing excellently, although still poorly and with months of treatment and rehab planned for his head injury, brain bleed, broken ribs, lung damage and knee fracture.

But the four girls have not been together for what feels like an age. Em has invited them all over to hers for a few hours' break. Sunday afternoon. She has got pizzas, beers and wine in. Plus a couple of bottles of MD 20/20 for posterity.

"Mad Dog!" Kate screams when she sees it.

"It's not actually Mad Dog," Em educates. "MD stands for Mogen David. Its producer."

"Shut up Em, you bore! Gonna treat us to some Latin too? Maybe some art history? A few flags?" Lou teases. "Got a straw?"

MD 20/20 is a frankly disgusting fortified wine drink that paved the way for the alcopop likes of Moscow Mule, Bacardi Breezer and Hooch. The Orange Jubilee, Blue Raspberry and Banana Red flavour colours make it look like Acid House has snotted all over its neon self.

Any self-respecting, park-going teen of the 1990s had a handy bottle of 20/20 and a straw tucked in their coat pocket. The perfect sized bottle for hiding from your parents on the way out. It reminds Jen of illegally doctoring her twelve-month temporary paper passport from her birth year of 1979 to 1973. A simple scratch of the flimsy card removed the curve off the top left of the handwritten 9 to reveal a 3. Magic! At fifteen, with absolutely no curves, she was suddenly twenty-one. The fact she was believed, and served, in pubs and bars sporting mouth braces and slight acne, was an absolute sign of the times.

You could pick up a twelve-month passport (BVP - British Visitor's Passport) from the Post Office last minute for just £12. Only needing to show one proof of identity like your old 12 month passport or student ID. Which of course could both be easily doctored. Clearly no issues with security or opportunity for fraud or deceit there. No wonder they were abolished a few years later in 1996.

At just turned fifteen, Jen's parents had thought she was in Altrincham at Spud-u-Like or Wimpy, ordering a cheesy bean jacket potato or a strawberry milkshake. She was actually in Canal Bar in Manchester ordering a Hooch or a Reef.

Jen also remembers a night at her friend's house a few years earlier. She thinks they were about 13, but not sure. Her friend's mum was recently separated and had allowed the pile of girls to pitch a large tent in her equally large garden for a sleepover. She was one of the more chilled mums. Jen would never have asked her parents to do this. It had trouble written all over it. If she remembers rightly it was her dad's tent from his Scouting youth and there were about eight girls. But again it is a bit blurry - a bit like the night.

They had all colluded at school to bring something alcoholic to the tent party, and to hide it in their sleeping bags, not in their actual bags, in case of a spot check. This was before they had faked their

IDs so robbery was the only option. The girls, mainly from semi-detached and detached 1990s dinner party type houses, didn't find less dangerous beer, alcopops or cider in their parents' drinks cupboards. Or cupboards in the cellar. They only found the hard stuff.

One came with an almost full bottle of Campari, another a bottle of port. There was half a bottle of Cinzano, three quarters of a bottle of Mateus Rose, a rather dusty old bottle of red wine 'it was right at the back, been kept there for years so is probably a rubbish one', a flask with Martini in it, another flask filled with Sambuca and a random bottle of Newcastle Brown Ale.

No mixers. No glasses or straws had been considered either.

The girls got absolutely hammered drinking neat from the bottles and flasks, and danced around the garden singing Madonna's Immaculate Collection at the top of their voices. When the mum finally came out to tell them to be quiet and was faced with the sozzled scene, she yelled, "Go to sleep now or I will call your parents! And next time, bring your own Gripe Water!"

They had absolutely no idea what she was on about and of course found the whole thing hilarious in their stupor. It was funny until one of the girls started being sick in the entrance of the tent. She had clearly had macaroni cheese for tea, or some sort of creamy pasta. This mixed with strong red port made a frankly disgusting puce pile of lumpy puke. Other girls started heaving too at the sight of the crimson chunks. One started to cry, another consoled her - and then puked over her shoulder. If the mum was checking out of the window (which Jen imagines she was, making sure they weren't dying), she would have probably been laughing out loud at the outright carnage.

The following morning they all had to go, dehydrated tails between their hungover teenage legs, and apologise one by one in the kitchen. With stonking headaches, each had to face the mum, who was sitting next to the phone with her telephone number book out and a pen in hand. Looking very much like action was about to be taken.

She never actually phoned anyone's mum, and the girls certainly never did it to her again. Teenage gratitude at its best. Or at least never did it again in anyone's house or garden when a parent was actually in residence. They had learned their lesson well.

"How's Will, Kate?" Em asks, handing her a straw for her misnamed Mad Dog.

"He's doing so much better," she grins, sucking the neon filth. "They think he might make a good, if not full, recovery, but it will take time. He has to be patient - which he's not being very good at."

"What actually happened?" Jen asks curiously. Then quickly adds, "Only if you want to say."

"It's absolutely fine, it could have been so much worse," she assures and proceeds to tell the girls the full story of the fall, the head injury and brain bleed, the broken bones and lung puncture, the emergency airlift, the panic in the hospital, the induced coma, the surgery and his amazing improvement, which meant he could come home far sooner than initially anticipated. "He has a long way to go, but he is getting the best care."

"So relieved for you, Kate," Em says feelingly, still very upset at herself for not having had a clue about the accident while she was pruning her green, feeding her devil. She gives Kate a big hug and holds her a little longer than she would normally do.

"Are you ok, Em?" Kate asks, pushing her friend back and forcing her to face her, her hands on her friend's shoulders.

"Yeah, fine," she says, slurring her words slightly. "Bitch Eve is having a baby."

"Oh fuck," Lou says.

"Shit," Kate says.

"Jesus," Jen says.

All in unison, a perfectly synchronised trio of shocked profanity. Followed by an equally harmonious silence, all waiting for Em to continue, but knowing she won't.

"When is she due?" Jen finally asks, not really knowing what else to say. But desperate to fill the awkward silence.

"I've forgotten. It's not important. Let's talk about this little man!" she deflects, pointing at Jen's bump.

"But it's your brother or sister, Em," Kate encourages, putting her arm around her friend. "And you just dropped an absolute bomb. We can't ignore it." Knowing how deeply this is affecting Em, but not really one hundred percent understanding why.

"Honestly, I don't want to talk about it. It's not important," Em says abruptly, papering over it yet again. "Stop fishing, will you?"

"Ok," Kate concedes, slightly annoyed with her friend. She brought it up, opened Pandora's Box. And they aren't fishing, they are just concerned. But she lets it go, for now. "We may as well all hear about Lou's fishing trip then."

"What fishing trip?" Jen asks, nursing her one glass of white wine with the ice that Em had brought for her in a little plastic bag from the freezer.

"Oh lord, do I have to?" Lou cringes.

"Yes, you do!" Kate confirms. "And we want the full graphic details."

"Graphic details of a fishing trip?" Em questions, now calm and collected again. "What on earth happened on the fishing trip?"

Lou proceeds to tell her story, adding more details about her watergate scandal and adding in teabagging. She also adds that the whole thing was a revelation as she now realises how comparatively dull her and Eddie's sex life had been. "Sometimes I'd just roll over on my front and tell him to crack on and I'd read a magazine or watch the tv. Never pornos. And always just the front door. He slipped in the back door once, by mistake. It was like space invaders on stinging speed."

"Can't believe he ever made you wet enough for an accidental slip and slide," Em adds, sexualising the frankly dangerous 1980s kid's garden game of a long sheet of polythene plastic and a hosepipe.

Lou laughs out loud in agreement and finishes her fishing story. Jen asks, wide eyed, "What the hell is teabagging?"

Lou and Em proceed to demonstrate teabagging using Jen's little bag of ice as a scrotum prop, Lou underneath and Em squatting on top.

"Are you actually joking?" Jen nearly swallows an ice cube. "But… why?" she asks. Half choking, half laughing.

While Kate claps Jen on her back to help her swallow her non-scrotum prop ice cube, Lou says, from underneath Em and her dangling ice-cube scrotum, "I have absolutely no idea. He just kept dipping, like he was doing squats at the gym. I just lay there with my mouth wide open like Big Mouth Billy Bass."

PAPER OVER IT

Big Mouth Billy Bass had been the surprise hit of last Christmas. Who doesn't want a plastic large-mouthed bass fish mounted on a plastic fake wood plaque which, when he detects motion or has his red button pressed, flaps his tail, turns his head to face you and very loudly sings 'Take me to the river' by Al Green, or 'Don't worry be happy' by Bobby McFerrin? Many a grandparent had thankfully just about dodged a heart attack on Christmas Day when terrified by the reggae jazz pop-singing, frolicking fish. Big Mouth Billy Bass - as essential yet frankly useless and farcical as the Rock 'n Flowers dancing flowers of the 1980s

"Big Mouth Billy Bass!" Em shrieks. "You're killing me!"

"You're killing me with your scrotum squatting," Lou shrieks back, pushing her friend off as the ice bag splits, spilling half defrosted ice cubes all over her face.

"And then came the water sports," Kate howls with laughter as Lou wipes the liquid from her eyes, nose and mouth, also in stitches from laughing. She starts to bag up the remaining cubes back into the little bag.

"You're going to break my bloody waters if you don't stop," Jen pleads, tears flowing down her face as she shrieks with laughter. "I'm going to have to wee," she fast-waddles to Em's loo like a speedy penguin, cupping her crotch as if she is trying not to drop the baby.

"That was how I was walking when he had finished with me," Lou lolls, wiping down Steve the Cheese's leaves, which had also been sprayed during the action.

"Was it that good?" Em asks, laughing mischievously.

"It was very good, and very long!" Lou laughs back.

"How long?" Jen questions from the loo, eyes widening, having only ever experienced one length.

"All bloody night and well into the morning!" Lou replies. "And he didn't cum too early once."

"Ha! I'm fairly confident that's not what Jen was asking," Kate grins.

"Cum," Em cringes, a bit like Jen had done with Kate's 'minge' months earlier. "What an awful word."

"Are we on this again? You and Jen and your issues with words,"

Kate counters. "What, may we ask you, your highness, do you call Sir Semen?" she asks Em in her best Queen's English.

"Spunk," she replies. "And if he likes to do one often, he shall be knighted Sir Spunkalot."

"Why do we always have to end up talking filth?" Jen asks, returning from the toilet to the phallic frivolity, the jizzy jollity.

"That's exactly what I call it!" Kate spouts, sucking the end of her second 20/20 through her straw.

"What?" Jen asks. "Will's filth? Are you joking?"

"Yes! My juicy lips and his filth," Kate admits rather proudly. "Men are from Venus and girls are from Mars."

"You've confused your John Gray there, Katie-Pie," Em annoyingly educates Kate on the classic relationship self-help book.

"No, you've confused your Geri Halliwell there, Emsie-sly," she bites back, referring to the ex-Spice Girl's recent hit about girl power, sex and confidently asserting yourself over the male species.

"Well, he definitely pleased me and chased me, right round the bloody house," Lou grins, diffusing the pissed planet-off with some stomping Geri lyrics.

"Are you going to see him again?" Jen sensibly asks Lou, fascinated by her story. And also stone cold sober.

"Not sure. I may just call him when I fancy another long one," she says saucily.

"Look who's wearing the trousers now," Kate smiles proudly at her friend.

Jen can't help another practical inquiry. "Did you use a condom?"

"Absolutely!" Lou confirms. "We bagged it up, every single time."

"Oh Lou," Em protests. "Bag it up? Really?"

"Shut up, Em," all three girls holler, as they prevent another conversation about what Em does and doesn't like things being called. If they didn't love her so much, they would have probably bagged her up by now. And thrown her in the bin.

Jen leaves shortly after, feeling very happy but extremely tired. The rest go out, even though they had promised each other they wouldn't earlier in the day.

But Kate needs a blow out, and Em now sees in Lou a partner in

crime.
 A fellow bird of prey to help her bag a man.

Bag it up.
Geri Halliwell.

-24-
THE QUARTET: LIFE IS A ROLLERCOASTER

10th June 2000

Saturday night and the Euros have kicked off.

There are high hopes for Kevin Keegan's England squad of Beckham, the Neville brothers, Ince, Gerard, Fowler, Shearer, Southgate, Owen and Seaman, to name a few top quality, world-class players.

It's coming home! Four years after Baddiel, Skinner and the Lightening Seeds said it would, it most certainly is!

After thirty-four years of riding a rollercoaster of bare chested, lion trio tattooed disappointment and hurt, it is totally coming home. 'The Sun' and 'The Mirror' said so. Even 'The Daily Express' had swerved the weather for a day and said it was. Thirty-four years - the same number of years Adams, Keown and Wise have been alive. It has been a long time coming. Don't fight it. It is definitely coming home!

England flags and banners adorn houses and car windows. Office sweepstakes are in the bag. Supermarket owners and shareholders are rubbing their hands waiting for the best summer ever, as are pubs and bars. 'Campione' by E-Type is blasting out wherever you go. Streets are puked with red and white looking like massive barber shop poles.

Scotland, Wales and Northern Ireland had not qualified so nearly twenty percent of the population do not give two shits and don't want the St. George's Cross anywhere near them.

The first England match is in two days v. Portugal, on the 12th of June. What could possibly go wrong?

Kate has finished her exams and is at Will's house working out what to do over summer. He is doing really well and can go out in the garden and hop slowly and painfully on crutches, but he gets tired and the headaches are at times quite overwhelming. He had told Kate on the phone to just go and have some fun, to enjoy her post-exam weekend. But she is very happy drinking fine wine in the afternoon sunshine with Will and his parents in Chester.

She removed Charles Hetherington-Smythe from his Fab lolly-sticked, sellotaped, blue-tacked berth on the lounge wall at No. 52 yesterday at the request of Will. God knows why. He said it would be a shame to just chuck him out. The house needs to be vacated in a few weeks. She will work out what to do with Hairy Potter when she gets back. Before the landlord does his end of tenancy deposit checks.

Charles's tweed and salubrious, not-so-sexy stare caused much hilarity on the train yesterday afternoon as he was given his own seat in the half full carriage. A pile of girls, dressed as naughty schoolgirls (some had clearly not seen a school uniform in their wardrobes since before England had won the World Cup) and donned in 'bride to be' and 'bridesmaid' clobber, got on the train at Altrincham, drinks in hands. They offered her money for Charles. Wanted to take him on their hen night. Kate, always one for a deal, did consider it - but then she shuddered at what she thought they may do to Charles. She had become rather fond of him and didn't want him bent in the middle, or worse.

By the time the girls got off the train at Knutsford, Charles had been licked by more alcopop-ed tongues, stridden by more 'school girls' and snapped by more Coolpixes than he could have ever imagined in his wildest dreams. He had not been riding the slow train to Chester, he had been riding the rollercoaster of his latent life. Kate felt sure his eyes were twinkling.

"You're safe now," Kate assured Charles as the girls bounced off the train.

On the station, one older hen said to another younger one, "Kelly, you're showing your knickers. Pull that skirt down. You look like a bloody slut!"

"Oops," she laughed cheekily, pulling her tiny skirt up higher, full-on flashing her frilly Bridget Jones panties. "I did it again," winking at her long-suffering mother.

Kate laughed as all the other young hens did exactly the same, brandishing their matching pink frilly Bridgets. Shocking, or exciting, the open-mouthed commuters on the small town station.

"Watch out, Knutsford," Kate said laughingly to Charles, being looked at strangely by a couple of student teens who had just entered the carriage and sat opposite her. She smiled at them and simply said, "I'm taking him home for my boyfriend." She laughed at their awkward reactions and their brisk donning of their headphones.

Em and Jen's final exam is in two days, Monday the 12th June, so they are both desperately cramming. Jen is simultaneously and desperately exercising her pelvic floor, willing her baby to stay in. Her efforts to cram him in through perpetual pulsations of her pubococcygeus must be making him feel like he is on a never-ending rough and tumble rollercoaster. Making the poor little thing desperate to come out, not stay in as Jen intends.

She was thrilled to have completed her penultimate exam the day before, Friday the 9th, so she knows she will get her degree. But the one on Monday is the one she knows she is really good at. Is highly likely to lift her end grade. She really doesn't want an average of what she has completed to date. She wants, needs, to make it to the Monday exam. She can't get off this specific rollercoaster quite yet.

Lou smashed her showcase yesterday. It was an epic performance showing off not only her dazzling dancing skills but also her accomplished choreography credentials too. She really is the full package. Her tutors are confident she will find an agent very soon. She just needs to make up her mind what she wants to do, and more importantly where she wants to go. Everyone is very proud of her. Especially Len.

12th June 2000

After days of critical cramming and clunch clenching, Jen has made it into the exam hall for her final final.

As before, she is placed in the front by the exit to the loos.

"Deep breaths," Em had said to her when they walked in together and everyone on her course, including her tutor who came to see her, wished her luck. "Remember, it's just part of the adventure," Em adds. Even if she starts panting in this hall, she is going to get this done.

Having to sit in the sweltering old Victorian room with her baby doing the Macarena between her ribs and pelvis is painful and frankly exhausting. But she finishes. She finishes early. She checks it twice, but knows there is no more she can do. And she has to get out of the room, has to stand up to give her ribs and pelvis more room for the Agadoo.

Waiting outside for Em, she desperately wants a cigarette, but doesn't. She had a few in the early days after the midwife had said if there was damage to be done, it had already been done. But in these later weeks it had felt so wrong. She breathes in the sticky air and walks around, trying to get comfortable. She had borrowed some clothes off her slightly larger friends to get her through the weeks since her Trafford Centre haul had been so cruelly taken, but nothing feels right or comfy. She is absolutely exhausted emotionally and physically. Feels totally and overwhelmingly relieved to finally come off the relentless revision and exam rollercoaster ride of the last few months.

"It's over!" Em and a few other people from their course race out of the big university door onto the street. Spotting Jen, Em yells, "Jen, we're done, we've done it! You've done it!"

She wraps her arms around Jen and dances her round. But all Jen can say is, "Please Em, can you take me home?"

A while later Jen is sat at home with her mum in their little snug, tele on. Em drove her home and by the time they had arrived at the cottage, Jen was fast asleep. Em helped her in. Her mum had not yet got back from work so she found Jen's key in her bag. She settled her onto the sofa and placed her feet up high, then just sat and watched her sleeping, totally spent friend for a while. In a complete trance. She watched her bump rising and falling with the slow, deep breaths Jen was taking. She thought about her little brother or sister, she thought about her dad and she thought about Charlie. Her absent Charliebobs. She also thought about Eve. She thought a lot about Eve.

"Why are you crying, Em?" Jen's mum asks as she entered the snug dressed in her uniform and NHS lanyard, "What's the matter?"

"Am I crying?" Em dances out of her trance and wipes away the tears she didn't realise are there. "I'm fine, honestly. Sorry, I'm just tired and relieved it's all over."

"Well done Em, and thank you for bringing her home," she gives Em a hug. "If you ever want to talk, you know I'm always here." Jen's mum sees a darkness in Em, demons. She also sees a sad little girl in a bold, brazen body. She has got to know Em quite well over the past few months and has become very fond of her, but has never cracked her. Ever since her outburst a few months ago in the semi, she had been worried about her daughter's feisty friend.

"Thank you, but honestly I'm fine," Em replies, hugging her back. "Keep me updated will you?"

"I will," promises Jen's mum.

Most people in England, including Em, Lou and Kate, are just about to watch, with excitement and expectation, the first England Euro match v. Portugal. The trio have braved the city centre where there is a big screen in a fan zone. 8:45pm from Eindhoven in the Netherlands, St. George's crosses wave wildly with anticipation across the nation. Kate is just going for the craic. And there are definitely lots of cracks on show tonight, unfortunately2|". Having got to the group stages four years earlier, Scotland had not qualified for the 2000 UEFA European Championships. Kate doesn't really like football that much anyway.

Jen wakes up just about in time for the match to kick off, but falls asleep twenty minutes later, contently comfortable that they are 2-0 up. Scholes at three minutes and McManaman at eighteen.

If was awake she would hear the despondent, head-in-hand gasps and groans from homes, bars and pubs across the country as Figo, Pinto and Gomes tap in a trio of torment and torture. The thrilling threesome break English hearts.

It finishes 3-2 to Portugal.

But…. it is obviously still coming home! Just a blip in the thirty-four-year perpetual positivity for its three lions. It isn't like Germany is in their group as well. Oh, wait, yes they are.

That's next Saturday's rollercoaster of nail-biting 'fun'.

Em and Lou want to stay out commiserating. Kate isn't too sure. Manchester is rammed full of sweaty men confidently still singing 'It's coming home'. Tops off. Cracks out. Remnants of red and white painted crosses on their beer filled, bulging bellies. A delight for any girl to witness.

They beg her to stay out and after a few minutes of saying na, na, na, na, na… she doesn't fight it.

Life is a rollercoaster.
Ronan Keating.

-25-
JEN: BORN TO MAKE YOU HAPPY

14th June 2000

Kate goes home to Glasgow, desperate to see her family. Three and a half hours on the train from Chester. She promises Jen she will come straight back down as soon as there is any baby news.

She hasn't seen her family since Christmas. Her dad and little ten-year-old sister are waiting for her on the platform wielding a yellow 'Welcome Home Kate' banner her sister has clearly spent ages making for her. At home the rest of her family have put on a party for them and their extended family. Kate is buzzing.

Em goes to stay with Lou in Liverpool, not wanting to go home to Hertfordshire. In fact not knowing if she has a home to go to anymore anyway. Barbados summer plans, and her thoughts of inviting Jen, a distant pure shore dream. Lou is having a ball with her sisters and Liverpool mates, Em is pretending she is having a ball. Kate had asked Em to go up to Scotland with her, but Em didn't want to be too far away from Jen after her personal promise to be there for her.

Jen is at home with her mum.

"Grilled tomatoes on toast?" her mum asks her. Standard.

"Yeah, fine," Jen responds, a little sick of the round red boys especially after the shark incident a few weeks before, but grateful for the offer. Money is tight and is only going to get tighter. "Thanks mum."

Jen and her mum sit in the snug watching Coronation Street, synchronically eating tomatoes on toast, when suddenly Jen stands up.

"What?" Jen's mum asks, mid mouthful.

"I don't know," Jen responds, just before a gush answers for her.

"Right!" Jen's mum says slowly, looking at the puddle on the carpet and the grilled tomatoes spilt on the sofa. "No need to panic, it'll be a long time yet. Just settle back down and let me clear this up."

Most women go into natural labour around twelve hours after their waters break. But Jen is not most women, Jen is Tigger. Within about thirty minutes her contractions have started with gusto. Jen's mum rings one of her nurse friends and they advise to take Jen in, that the labour seems to be accelerating quite fast.

She tells Jen to head out to the car and retrieves the hospital bag from the inside porch where it has been waiting patiently on top of the buggy part of the tartan travel system. She is just about to close the cottage door behind her when she stops, knowing she has forgotten something. She goes back inside and grabs the car seat part of the tartan travel system remembering they are going to be bringing a baby home. Shit, they are going to be bringing a baby home. She locks the cottage door, helps Jen into the car and heads to the hospital.

The hospital bag contains a carefully wrapped Cherish. Jen's still not really sure why she feels the need to bring her to everything important to do with her baby. She's not superstitious, apart from saluting at magpies. But her presence is important, somehow.

The hospital bag does not, however, contain the onesie Jen's mum had 'thoughtfully' bought a few weeks back for her to take into hospital. The onesie is a new phenomenon, an excellent addition to anyone's pyjama drawer. But is possibly the most ridiculous thing you could take into a maternity unit when fu-fu access is required at all times. "Yes, you're probably right," her mum had said laughing when Jen questioned the highly impractical, frankly potty purchase. "I didn't really think that one through, did I?"

It's just before 9pm when Jen and her mum check into the maternity unit with one maternity bag and zero onesies. Jen's labour is progressing faster than initially thought, a bit like Concorde beating all time zones the previous Millennium New Year.

Jen is taken straight into a labour room and has a heart monitor strapped to her stomach. By 9:30pm she is six centimetres dilated, far too progressed to have the epidural she wanted. The contractions are overwhelmingly painful, Jen is not prepared for the incessant agony. Once one finishes, another starts with gusto. There is no relief. She begs for help. She is given a pethidine injection in her thigh.

At 11:40pm Jen is really screaming, gripping her mum's hand. The two hours of sheer agony not really touched by the opioid, apart from the three times she is violently sick. Grilled tomatoes. Piles of

PAPER OVER IT

puce puke reminiscent of the comedy camping chunder many years earlier.

"It hurts, mum!" Jen screams. "It really fucking hurts. Get it out."

"It's ok Jen, it's ok," she tries to calm her. "You'll be ok." She goes to find a midwife, seeing that the contractions are now coming even thicker and faster.

"Right," the midwife says coolly while inserting her cold, lubed fingers inside Jen. "You're ten centimetres, let's get this show on the road. It's time to push ,Jen."

Jen pushes through the pain, almost silently screaming, hurting her mum's hand. She wants to be on all fours, but the midwife says she needs to stay on her back as the heart monitor needs to stay in place for her baby.

"Here's another big one coming," the midwife says. "Push, Jen, push!" she encourages energetically but empathetically.

Jen smells a distinct whiff of shit, but it quickly passes. Nothing happens, contraction after contraction, nothing progresses.

The midwife looks at the baby heart monitor read, a hint of concern builds on her brow.

Jen's mum sees her press the big red button. Within moments the room fills with medical staff and they zip into action, like a well lubed machine.

"We need to get this baby out, now," someone says calmly but crucially.

Just before midnight, Jen is slashed. They try ventouse first (a suction cap inserted and placed on the baby's head) and then, when that fails, forceps.

"It's back to back," Jen vaguely hears someone say, not having a clue what that means or what was going on. "Push, Jen, push!"

15th June 2000

At seven minutes past midnight, Joseph is born and immediately whisked away. A bit like Jen's little accident earlier.

Jen is in a delirious state, but the pain has subsided so she feels her body relax slightly. Until... what the fuck is this, another contraction?

"I'm having another one!" she screams.

"Calm down Jen, it's just the afterbirth. The placenta," the midwife explains.

"Where's my baby?" Jen pleads whilst panting through the pain of giving birth to the uterus baby she had no idea she was going to have. "Why isn't he crying?"

"We are just checking him over," she assures. "He's been through quite a trauma too." As she says this, Jen hears a little cry from the corner of the room.

"I just need to give you this. Roll over and then we can get you stitched up," the midwife says. "It's an anti-D immunoglobulin."

"What the fuck is that?" Jen screams as the biggest needle she has ever is introduced into the bloodied trauma.

As the needle is jabbed into her arse and Jen yelps, her mum explains something about the danger of mixing blood types between baby and mother. It's just garble to Jen, like Kate's muddy bone had been to Lou a month earlier.

Exhausted and glad it's all over, in agony still but slowly starting to breathe normally, Jen feels her whole body slump.

"Just a little scratch," the midwife says as Jen feels another sharp jab in her thigh. "A little top-up of pethidine to get you through."

"Get me through what?" asks Jen, watching a big medical lamp roll over and shine on her. "I thought it was all done?"

"We will just give this a while to take effect and then we will get you fixed," the midwife calmingly explains. "You have had quite a significant tear and a rather large episiotomy."

"What's an opeesotoomy," Jen asks the shining lamp as she starts to see little fairies dance in the glow, the opioid suddenly taking effect like it hadn't earlier. "Where's my baaaybee?"

The back of her bed is raised a little so she is half sat up and both of her feet are put into stirrups. After a few minutes a man in blue scrubs rearranges the lamp and sits facing her, looking straight into her fu-fu growler. She had not had the time, energy or inclination to mow her lawn. The man is beautiful looking. "Helloooo," Jen slurs suggestively. "Youu're love-ely. What's youuur name? What you dooing donight?"

Not in any way a natural flirt, much more a tom boy, this is highly out of character for Jen and makes Jen's mum half laugh and half cringe.

"I'm Doctor Foster and I'm just going to get you sorted down here," he explains calmly and professionally, but with a slight laughing twinkle in his eyes. "You have had quite a traumatic birth and we had to perform an episiotomy to make sure we got your baby out. You also have quite a significant tear," he repeats what the midwife had explained before he entered the room.

"Just a little scratch," he says as he injects her ripped perineum with anaesthesia.

"How many dimes do y'aaall wan doo preeck mee?" Jen garbles, staring into his eyes. The pethidine had taken complete hold, unlike its inaction in the actual labour. She feels the sharp, tortuous pain of the injection, but somehow manages to displace it. She places it up in the lamp with the dancing fairies. She watches the torture tango with the Tinkerbells.

"Just relax and I'll get this done as quickly as I can," Dr. Foster says quite forcefully. "It's a bit of a mess right now so I want to make sure this is as neat as possible, so try not to make any movements."

Jen does what she is told, like a good girl should. Just like when she had 'jumped' up on the awful red fake leather bed underneath the humming fluorescent strip light in the dreadful Manchester clinic.

Jen is totally exhausted. The fairies vacate the lamp and are replaced by naughty nymphs wagging their fingers at Jen, laughing villainously and shaking their hellish heads. "What have I done wrong?" she asks them half way through the procedure.

"You've done nothing wrong, Jen," her mum replies soothingly, having no knowledge of the noxious nymphs. "They will be finished soon, I promise." Jen's mum was horrified by the savagery of the last few hours and had found it incredibly difficult to watch her daughter endure what she had. She had always thought a quick birth would be easy compared to a longer, drawn out labour. But this had made her think again. It had been brutal, bloody and barbarous.

Over thirty stitches later, both internally and externally, Jen is apparently 'fixed'.

Finally, numb and knackered, Jen gets to meet her baby. "He is perfectly healthy, but he's very small. Just four pounds eleven. He is showing signs of jaundice and we want to check his blood sugar levels. So a quick cuddle and then we are going to take him off just to give him a little bit of help," the midwife says as she places the little blanketed bundle with a tiny hat on his head on to Jen. "Don't worry, he'll be back with you soon," she assures Jen and her mum.

She looks down at him through exhausted eyes, and falls in love instantly. Tears roll down her cheeks as she kisses his tiny hatted head then looks up at her mum. She is also crying, the emotion having finally got to her, the shock of the past few hours eventually overwhelming her. It's also pride welling in her eyes, and instantaneous adoration of the little man. Her little man.

"Hello Joseph," she says lovingly, as his tiny fingers wrap around her little finger. In many ways, in the worst year of her life, he was born to make her happy. Make Jen happy. Make countless other people happy.

He is an unexpected, much adored, slightly out of generational gift. Suddenly 'God shall give' makes sense, the name Joseph makes perfect sense. God has given them something very precious, something to be treasured and cherished.

"I'd do anything for you," Jen promises her tiny son as he is taken from her. "I promise to try and always make you happy."

As Jen falls asleep whilst being pushed onto a ward, she flits in and out of a dream. A fantasy of hopes, fairies, happiness and fears.

Born to make you happy.
Britney Spears.

-26-
JEN: NEVER HAD A DREAM COME TRUE

15th June 2000 – continued

Jen's ex has been waiting all night.

He's been waiting patiently. A new skill for him. He has totally rocked it.

Jen's mum had called him from the hospital last night. He had wanted to be at the birth, but Jen had said no. Rightly or wrongly. So her mum had said no.

He was so excited to meet his son, so pleased that Jen was giving him a chance, that he didn't even try to argue. For him it was a dream come true.

When Jen wakes up, she is faced with her ex sitting on a chair next to her bed, holding the baby. Holding Joseph. Her son. Their son.

She watches for a while. He is in a complete trance staring at his son, totally in awe. His face is full of love and fascination. He kisses the top of his tiny hatted head.

After a while, Jen says, "Hey you."

Her ex looks up and smiles. She realises he is crying. "He's perfect isn't he?" He looks back at his son and, with a look of complete and utter disbelief, simply says, "Thank you."

Jen isn't sure whether he is thanking her, Joseph or a higher being. But it doesn't matter.

She knows, in that moment, that whatever her ex had done, this is a gift she has given him which is the best thing anyone could ever do for him. That his son now filled a hole that had been burning through him for years. She knows that she is no longer his world, she no longer needs to fill the burning hole. There is a new kid on the block and, to be totally honest, rightly or wrongly, she is relieved.

"Is he ok?" Jen asks, concerned. The last she knew he had been whisked away from her in the delivery room.

"Yes he's absolutely fine. In fact they said he's perfect," he says, not looking up at Jen. Transfixed by his son. "They brought him in in that cot thing next to you," he nods without looking up. "They said they monitored him for a few hours and he's doing really well.

He's a dream come true, isn't he?"

"Can I hold him?" Jen asks, not answering his question. Just overwhelmingly relieved that he is ok. That she hasn't caused him any harm. That she hasn't hurt him with her behaviour.

Her ex stands up carefully and takes the few short steps to Jen's bed, making sure his head is meticulously held and safe throughout the short manoeuvre.

As Jen tries to sit up, she winces with pain. The agony stabs her. She feels like someone is taking a machete to her fu-fu growler. "Fuck," is all she can say.

"I'll get someone," her ex says, panicking at the palpable pain his tomboy, tough Tigger ex is clearly experiencing.

"No, I'm fine," she finds the comfiest position she can, putting her weight on one bum cheek. "Give him here."

As she takes her baby in her arms, not a natural yet but seemingly to naturally know what to do, the midwife comes in.

"What happened?" Jen asks. "Why was he so difficult to get out?"

"He was what you call 'back-to-back'," the midwife answers. "Which means his head was down but he hadn't turned so the back of his head and spine was against your spine."

"I don't understand," Jen says. "Why does that make it harder?"

"Well, if you think about putting on a polo neck jumper," she starts to explain. "You normally put your head down and push into it to get it on. Your baby had his head up and the wrong way round, so try and imagine getting your jumper on like that? Especially if your polo neck is new and the neck is tight. As in has never been worn before."

"Ahhh," Jen and her ex say, super fascinated and slightly floored. Jen's polo neck has clearly been worn before. That's exactly why they are here. It isn't the immaculate conception her Grandpa had hoped it was.

"When a baby is born 'normally' with its head and face down, it means the smallest part of its head leads the way down the birth canal," she continues to explain. "In your case, the largest part of his head was trying to open your canal. And your canal has never been opened before, being your first baby, so your muscles are very strong. It's a bit like a big fist trying to get into what a little finger should."

PAPER OVER IT

Jen and her ex-glance at each other at this analogy, trying desperately not to smirk. Failing epically. Wondering where on earth she was going next with this. Tight necks, virgin canals, big fists, little fingers?

Totally unaware of the hilarity of her analogies, the midwife cracks on undeterred. "Less than five percent of babies are born this way. We tried to manipulate him round but he wasn't budging. That's why we had to intervene with the ventouse and then the forceps. That's why you tore and had to have the episiotomy."

"Thank you. That makes perfect sense now." Jen has collected herself and buried her giggles. Saying it makes perfect sense when it doesn't prevents any further explanation. "Can I take his hat off?"

"Yes, but as I said he is a ventouse and forceps baby so his head has been slightly affected. Is currently a little deformed. It will go back to normal very soon, but baby's heads are so soft when they are newborn, to help them get through the birth canal and out, that any undue pressure put on them makes a difference," she explains. "Don't be worried, he will look perfectly normal soon."

Jen braces herself for the de-hatting, having no clue what she is about to see. Deformed? Still slightly affected by the opioid so all sorts of nightmares immediately fill her mind.

"He looks like a cone head!" she cries when faced with the shape of her baby's head, thinking about the ridiculous 1993 sci-fi 'Cone Head' comedy. The ventouse suction device had caused his little head to be shaped exactly like a cone. And the forceps had caused little rivets on either side of his cone.

"My baby has a cone head," Jen panics.

"And that's why we put this little hat on, just for a few days," the midwife says, swiftly popping the little white hat back on his little pointy head. Well used to this shocked reaction. "I promise you that in a few days his head will look perfectly normal," she assures the two young, wide-eyed, cone-phobic parents.

Jen thinks about her own head, knowing she was a forceps baby herself. She thinks maybe that's why she has a Star Trek Spock ear. Maybe she was dragged out by her ear?

She wonders about whether to ask the midwife about this, but thankfully she decides not to. It would be very funny but frankly daft. A bit like the 1987 Star Trekkin' No. 1 hit. 'There's Klingons on the starboard bow, starboard bow, Jim'.

"Now, how about feeding him?" the midwife asks. "He has had a bottle already, but would you like to try to feed him yourself? On your breast?"

"No," Jen says, shaking her head. Trying to remove all Vulcans, Spocks and Borgs from her mind.

With no counteraction or pressure at all, the midwife says, "No problem at all. Let me get a bottle of milk and you can feed him if you like? Is that ok?"

"Yes please," Jen replies, having forgotten she needs to feed him. "What a shit mum I'm going to be," she thinks to herself, still trying to mentally cope with the cone head, the Klingons and the agony consuming her fu-fu growler.

As she settles herself into the least painful position she can find, she feeds her beautiful boy for the first time and feels a peace she has never felt before. As much as breast is best, bottle means you can look them in their eyes. And they can look at you in yours.

He sucks rhythmically whilst staring into her soul. He barely blinks. And when he does, it is controlled, quite slow, and he immediately finds her eyes again every time. How does he instinctively know to look into her eyes? It is just amazing.

It reminds her of the metronome of her piano playing days, his sucking and his eyes controlling the rhythm, conducting the orchestra. It intoxicates her. She knows this adventure is not going to be easy, has no idea how she is going to make it all work, but she knows she can, and she will.

She has never felt so clear, focused, content and happy in her life.

"I've always loved you, you know," Jen's ex says.

"Funny way of showing it, dickhead," Jen laughs.

"If I could turn back time, I would."

"Are you fucking Cher?" Jen asks, but with a joy to her voice.

"You know I'll always be a part of you, and you'll always be a part of me now," he says, knowingly. "Whatever happens, I promise I will always take care of you and him."

Jen seriously doubts this, but chooses to nod. She is too tired to do anything else.

As Jen doses off with Joseph bubbling, overloaded with milk, his dad gently takes him off her.

As he sits down with his son, Jen's mum comes into the room.

"Hi," she says.

"Hello," he responds cagily. Not looking up.

"This is it now. One more chance," she says. "Don't fuck it up."

"I won't," he promises, never having heard Jen's mum say 'fuck'. He promises with no real idea what he is promising. He still doesn't look up.

"The decisions will be hers. Is that clear?" Jen's mum iterates strongly. "Otherwise you won't be going anywhere near either of them. Is that clear?" she repeats with a strength she doesn't know she has.

"Yes, absolutely fine," he responds, still gazing down at his son. Understanding that Jen and Jen's mum are in complete control. And totally accepting it.

"Do you know what she's decided on his other names?" he finally looks up at her.

"He will have our surname," she confirms. "But his middle is going to be William."

Jens' ex smiles.

He could kick-off about the first name he had no voice or choice in and the surname that isn't his. His standard modus operandi. But he doesn't. He just smiles. He's happy with the middle name.

"William. That's lovely. Thank you." He looks back down at his son as he starts to fall asleep. "Thank you. This is genuinely a dream come true for me."

"And you'll leave her alone now, right?" Jen's mum questions.

"Yes, I will," he says.

Jen is listening, she hears everything. Her eyes are shut but her ears aren't.

"Thanks mum," she thinks to herself as she lets herself succumb to a very deep, calm, dream filled sleep.

Never had a dream come true.

S Club 7.

-27-
THE QUARTET: DAY AND NIGHT

20th June 2000
Final match of the Euros group stages.

England had finally overcome their footballing nemesis and beat Germany 1-0 three days ago on the 17th June. Shearer had headed in Beckham's fizzing free kick at fifty-three minutes to the elation of all England fans. All they have to do to go through to the quarter finals is draw with Romania. No drama there.

Jen and Joseph spent two nights in hospital and have been at home for three nights. At just five days old, even Joseph knows it's coming home.

Jen has spent the last few days doing her very best, but in complete agony. Her huge episiotomy has completely de-bounced her. She knows she needs a poo, but can't let her bowel release it. Every time she tries, or in fact even when she isn't trying, her episiotomy stitches jab her like evil nymphs dancing a tiny machete dance around a campfire on her fu-fu growler. It literally burns. It stabs and it burns.

20th June - Day

She tries a nice warm bath. It is a momentary release. The milk from her swollen, unused boobs drips into the warm water causing little cream clouds. She swirls them into the water and they dissipate. She is horrified when she feels that the small swollen mass coming out of her anus has grown, she has absolutely no idea what it is. Has been there for a day or so now. Hadn't wanted to ask her mum. It is painful and itches dreadfully.

When she gets out of the bath, the minute machetes stab her again and again. As she tries to gently, cautiously dry herself with a cream towel, she doesn't know if it is the gruesome growth on her bum or the excruciating episiotomy that's bleeding.

The midwife is in the kitchen when she comes down, slightly early for the 2pm appointment. She is talking to her mum whilst holding Joseph, drinking a cup of tea. Her mum has taken the week off work.

"How is everything going Jen?" she asks. She is a lovely rather round lady,. Older. probably in her late thirties This is her second visit.

"Ok thank you," Jen forces a smile. "How are you?" She sits on the kitchen chair and unwittingly winces.

The midwife hands Joseph to Jen's mum. "Come on, let's take a look at you first," she says kindly, knowing from her last visit where the snug is.

She shuts the curtains and says, "Lie down," patting the sofa. "Let me have a look at you."

Lying on her back, with her huge pants and even huger attached sanitary towel removed, she lets it all flood out. "It's just so painful, it's like daggers stabbing me. It burns. I can barely sit to feed him. I can't sleep. I can't drive. And I have this funny thing on my bum. And something keeps bleeding down there. And my boobs are hot and red and really sore. And I still can't do a poo." Jen starts to cry. She doesn't want to look like she's not coping, she's coping really well with Joseph. She's just not coping very well with herself.

"But apart from all that, you're absolutely fine, right?" she laughs gently, winking at Jen. Having seen it all before, but knowing Jen's episiotomy is really rather large. "Let's see what we can do."

"Thank you," Jen smiles back at her, relieved and very pleased she's there.

"Ok, so I am now going to release a few of these external stitches. They are absorbable so don't need removing, they should dissolve within about a week or so, but I can see that some of them are really tight which is probably what is causing you so much pain."

Although the little scissor snips are in themselves uncomfortable, the release from the incessant pain is almost immediate. Jen literally exhales.

"Your haemorrhoids are really common postpartum. They are caused by excessive pressure on the veins in your rectum. So pushing in labour is the likely reason, but you've also probably been trying to push to empty your bowels but the pain from the stitches is causing you to stop. Putting off bowel movements can worsen constipation and aggravate the haemorrhoids."

"Haemorrhoids?" Jen had genuinely never heard of them.

"They are also called piles," the midwife explains. Jen nods, she's heard of those.

"What do I do with them?"

"They will go by themselves but you can get some hydrocortisone cream from the pharmacy to help. And to relieve the pain you can also put some ice on them, or an ice pack. That may be good for your episiotomy too," she explains helpfully.

"What about doing a poo?" Jen asks.

"It's probably a mix of constipation and you not wanting to push because of the stitches," she advises. "Drink lots of water and eat plenty of fibre. You could take some laxatives, but I think with these stitches cut and you treating the haemorrhoids, you should be back to normal really soon."

"Ok, thank you," Jen says, feeling better already.

"And finally your breasts," the midwife says. "This will pass really quickly. Don't try to express any milk, your body will think you're breastfeeding and will naturally create more milk which will exacerbate the issue. Give it a few more days and your body will work out the milk is not needed and it will settle down. Ice or ice packs can help with that pain too. And some paracetamol helps for all pain."

Jen nods as she pulls her behemothic briefs back on. "Thank you so much," she says. "I massively appreciate it. I thought you were here more for Joseph?"

"I'm here for you both," she says tenderly. "Now let's go and take a look at your little man, shall we? You find your little red book while I have a quick wee."

At just five days old Joseph is doing brilliantly apparently. He has put on six ounces and is now five pounds five. He has also grown a little so is heading towards the average length shading on the graph in the red book. His head circumference is within the average range and his cone head is de-coning. "He is progressing very nicely," the midwife says. "You're clearly doing an excellent job," she praises Jen as she hands him back to her.

She continues as Jen smiles, "I will come back on Thursday for another check in. Same time if ok?"

"Perfect," Jen says. She is signing on the dole on Thursday at 10:30 but should be well back for 2pm. "Thank you."

"And the health visitor will be in touch soon to arrange a meeting next week," she adds, packing up her bag. "If you need anything in the meantime, you've got my number."

"Thank you," Jen and her mum say in unison.

"Cup of tea?" Jen's mum asks her after the back door closes.

"Yes please mum," she replies, "That would be lovely. Can you fill the kettle a bit more? He needs a feed."

She gets Joseph's already made-up bottle from the fridge and puts it in a jug of boiling water for a little while. She then squirts a bit out onto her wrist to check the temperature, to check it isn't too hot. She takes the bottle and her baby into the snug.

For the first time she can sit fairly comfortably to feed him. Her fu-fu growler already feels better. Less growling, less burning, less on fire. Her spirit is very much lifted, her internal fire is sparked and is starting to burn again.

She lovingly looks down at him and he unblinkingly stares up at her, rhythmically sucking and folding his tiny fingers around her little finger. She settles in for the next fifteen minutes or so, her brew balanced on the little table next to them, her baby blissfully sucking the bottle. She feels at peace.

It has actually turned out to be a really rather good day.

Not just fu-fu wise.

20th June - Night

Em and Lou had driven over from Liverpool on Friday for a few hours to see Jen in hospital and to meet Joseph. They came with balloons and cards, a big teddy from Lou's mum and dad, four bottles of Babycham from Lou's sisters, and the most adorable fluffy bee rug from them and Kate. They know how much Jen loves Manchester and its bees.

Kate has yet to meet Joseph but had jumped on the train from Glasgow, Manchester bound, earlier today.

All three girls are coming over to the cottage to watch the England match, to watch them hammer Romania and go through to the quarter finals. Jen's mum is going out with a girlfriend, both decidedly disinterested in football.

It's going to be gold this time! Keegan and his crew are definitely getting gold medals put round their necks. We have the golden

David Beckham, our biggest showman. Named Golden Balls after the World Cup two years ago and runner up to Rivaldo for the Ballon D'Or last year. And we have the incredible Kylie adopting England as her home with her first-class comeback spinning around the nation in her sizzling gold hot pants, spreading sexy gilded glee. Gold all the way.

It's coming home! It's coming home! Football's coming home!

Looking out of the cottage's kitchen window, Joseph fast asleep in his moses basket, Jen sees the Renault Clio pull in. Two little white and red St. George's Cross flags flying from each back window.

"Well you didn't tell me not to open the bloody window," Kate shouts at Em as she opens the passenger door.

"Well I didn't say you could," Em barks back. "Who opens their window on the fucking motorway?"

"It's just two flags, Em," Lou laughs, climbing out from the back.

"But I want one on every window. Like you have one on each corner on a pitch. I bought four. Every match needs four. Now I've only got two," Em pouts indignantly. "It's going to be bad luck now. It's an omen."

"Do you want to wake up Joseph and every other sleeping baby in the North West of England?" Jen cajoles, opening the blue gate to the cute little cottage courtyard.

"Em!" Kate screams as she launches herself at her friend, the only one who hasn't seen her since Joseph was born. She had spoken to her on her new mobile phone a number of times. And had played hours of 'Snake'. Sneakily addictive.

"Careful," Jen says as her bruised swollen dripping boobs are Scot-squished.

"I'm so sorry," Kate says, pulling away concerned. "Oh god, it's your breasticles isn't it?"

Jen laughs at Kate's mammary terminology. "I'm fine, honestly. Just still a bit sore," she assures Kate. "What's going on with the flags?"

"Don't bloody ask," Kate laughs. "She has literally been banging on about it since we were on the bloody motorway. I just needed some air, it's really hot. And 'wham' the flag flies off and hits a white van. The white van man proper beeps and pulls alongside us shouting at Em through his open window." Kate is now giggling so much Jen can't help but laugh, knowing how cross Em would have been and how much Kate and Lou would have been laughing at her in the car.

Lou, listening to the frolicking flag tale, picks up where Kate had left off. "Em then flips her middle finger at him before opening her window to give him a piece of her mind and 'wham' her flag goes flying too. Right into the side of the same white van."

All three girls are now laughing. Two at the memory of it, one at the thought of it. All three at Em.

"Oh Em," Jen says sympathetically, seeing she is not laughing with them, yet. "You've still got two."

"I want four!" Em replies, having softened at the sight of her three friends finding her flag farce so funny. "But at least there's four of us," she laughs, pulling the quartet into a circular hug.

"Get your stuff and let's get inside," Jen says, smiling.

After much coo cooing and baby hugging, crisps put in bowls and pizza cutting, catching up and Babycham supping, four girls and a baby, a quintet, sit down in the snug.

8:45pm from Charleroi, Belgium.

No need any more to think about her calorie intake, Jen nips upstairs for a few minutes post pizza. She is in control again as she papers over it. She is out of control again.

Only one point needed, just a draw. With Romania. Surely? We are going for gold! And who cares about a superstitious flag omen when you have a pitch packed with such quality showmen.

The already booked Chivu scores for Romania at 22 minutes with a cross they are not sure was actually intended to be a shot on goal. It's fine. 68 minutes left. At 41 minutes Ince is brought down in the area. Penalty! Shearer equalises from the spot to make it 1-1. Phew. On the cusp of the half time whistle, Scholes makes it 2-1 to England. The whistle blows.

"Thank god for that," Lou says, sipping her drink. She is the biggest football fan of the quartet.

"Why do they have to make it so difficult for us to watch?" Em adds.

"Because you only have two flags," Jen replies naughtily. Her pain almost forgotten for a while.

"I'd forgotten for a minute about my flags," Em gets irate again.

"Will you stop banging on about your bloody flags," Kate says, coming back in from the loo. Not particularly interested in the England match. Drinking slightly more than the others through sheer boredom.

Joseph has nothing to add about either flags or football. He is fast asleep in his moses basket in the corner of the room.

The second half begins. At 48 minutes England are all over the place at the back, a bit like Em's flags are all the M56. Munteanu strikes and scores. 2-2.

"It's the flags, I'm telling you," Em says, on the edge of her seat. "It's the flags."

At 64 minutes Shearer is booked for diving. And he really does. Like a penguin who has just won gold at the annual South Pole diving competition. At 87 minutes they are all, but Kate, holding their breath for the full-time whistle to come and the extra time relief. It's still coming home.

A minute later, the P of the Nevilles brings down Moldovan in the box. The P now stands for penalty. Ganea puts it in the back of the net. 3-2 to Romania.

"Do you think Moldovan is from Moldova?" Kate ruminates in her slightly hazy state.

"No. He's clearly from Romania, you idiot. We're playing Romania," Em replies.

"Oh, yes," Kate says. "Stupid of me."

Lou and Jen giggle.

It's all fine. There's still two minutes plus stoppage time. It's still going to come home!

But it doesn't come home. A bit like two of Em's flags. 3-2 to Romania at the final whistle. England don't even make it past the group stage. Embarrassing. The P now stands for purgatory. Thirty four bloody long years of it.

"For fuck's sake," Lou says. "Romania? We beat Germany and we can't even beat Romania. Where the hell is it anyway?"

"North of Bulgaria and south of Ukraine and Moldova," Em educates them. "Home of Dracula. Nice blue, yellow and red flag."

"Shut up, Em," Jen and Lou shout. They both know Lou wasn't really asking a question.

"She's back on her flippin' flags," Kate adds. Then asks, "So he could be from Moldova?"

"He's Romanian," they all shout.

One thing which is coming home is the throng of gutted fans, no longer singing their song.

Tickets home from Belgium are currently being bought, for players and by fans alike. No heroes' welcome at Heathrow. No open top bus putting on a show. No flag waving and fanfare. No proud speech from Tony Blair. No gold. Not a gilded gust of it. Not even a Kylie hot-panted whiff of it. Just the whiff of embarrassment and failure.

With seventy five percent of them sloshed, the quartet head out of the cottage and remove the remaining fifty percent of the red and white flags from the Clio.

"Doesn't matter now, right Em?" Kate says, flagging the now fruitlessness of the flags.

"Yeah, fuck the flags," Em replies, running around the courtyard garden streaming one of the remaining flags, Lou racing around flying the other.

Jen and Kate watch in amusement as their two friends chant "Fuck the flags, fuck the flags," until Jen's mum arrives back a few minutes later from her night out.

"I think it might be time to go inside, girls?" she says in good humour, noticing a few twitches of curtains, before heading up to bed.

The flags are unceremoniously dumped in the black bin, and the quartet go inside. Giggling.

"Trivial Pursuits?" Jen asks, after checking on Joseph.

"Yes," say the rest, the idea blessed.

"It is not plural, it's 'Pursuit'," Em educates, full on Babychammed. "Trivial Pursuit."

"Fuck off, Em," the others reply before smashing into the navy blue, orange-yellow bordered box and picking a pie piece holder each. Kate regaling how much it reminded her of her favourite Laughing Cow cheese whilst choosing her favourite colour, yellow. Lou's competitiveness ensures she nabs the blue one. Her football team.

After a raucous, hilarious game where each has different versions of how you actually win so the instructions have to be consulted, Em wins.

"It's only because of your ridiculous brain bank of useless information," Lou pouts.

"Not so useless now, is it," Em beams back at her making a W with her two thumbs and forefingers, then an L with one set.

Afterwards the girls talk into the night. Loving each other's company. Making each other feel good, feel special. Listening, confiding, advising and guiding. Well, all but Em on the second one.

Jen has had the best time with her friends. It has actually turned out to be a really rather good night for all.

Just not football wise.

Day and Night.
Billie Piper.

-28-
JEN: I TURN TO YOU

27th June 2000

It has been a week since England were unceremoniously dumped out of the Euros by Romania and the Romanian Moldovan.

Jen opens the door to the health visitor.

"So Jennifer, how is it going?" she asks.

Everyone asks her this. What is 'it'? And where is 'it' meant to be going?

"Really good, thank you," Jen replies. "Call me Jen." Her mum is back at work so she's home alone with Joseph. She doesn't warm to her new house guest.

"Okay," the health visitor says bluntly, ignoring her request. "I'm going to ask you some questions. Is that alright, Jennifer?"

"Fine," Jen responds, equally as blunt.

"How are you coping mentally? Are you having any suicidal thoughts?"

What the actual fuck?

"I'm fine, thank you. I am not planning on killing myself any time soon."

"Right, that's good," she replies, her pen ticking away. "Do you have any negative feelings towards your new baby?"

Again, what the absolute fuck?

"No, no I don't," Jen replies. "I love him."

"Is he making you stressed in any way?"

Jen takes a moment. Of course she's stressed. Is that not normal? Is it him, her, her situation, her fu-fu, her piles, her sore boobs, her finances, her unemployment, her 'dole' status, her future, her mattress on the floor, her lack of sleep, her terrible roots, the new weeping cold sore on her lip, the huge new spot on her nose or the bitch in front of her that's making her stressed? Or all of the above?

"No, not at all," she responds, smiling through gritted teeth.

"Good," the health visitor clips, ticking more things on the piece of paper clipped to her crimson clipboard.

"So you have chosen to not breastfeed your child, is that right?"

"Yes," Jen replies.

"You do know that breast is best, don't you?"

"Yes, I am aware of the rhyme, thank you."

"Hmmmm," the health visitor slightly shakes her head whilst purposefully ticking another box. "And money?"

"Money?"

"Can you support the child, financially?"

Jen wants to say, "He's called Joseph," but she bites the painful herpes on her lip, winces and proceeds to tell her she is planning on getting a job. She has a degree (she hopes, but she doesn't say this), had signed on the dole last Thursday, is getting milk vouchers for 'Joseph' and she is to collect her dole money from the Post Office every Thursday. Her mum is gifting them both a home. So yes, she can financially support him. Thank you.

"Let me take a look around the house, then."

"Why?"

"Just to check it is an appropriate home for a baby."

"You can see it's an appropriate home for a baby," Jen says, seething but trying to remain controlled. She needs to be in control. She wishes her mum is here.

"You are a young single mother with no husband, no job, no income apart from 'the dole', as you call it, and no current means," the clipboard bitch responds. "It is my job to check on the welfare of your baby, Jennifer."

"Look away then, check away," Jen reacts, hearing Joseph stir in his moses basket in the corner. "I will check on my baby."

Jen puts the kettle on for the hot water to heat his bottle, on the verge of tears. The fun night with her friends just a week ago is a distant memory.

She has never felt so shit in her life. So vulnerable, so marginalised, so small, so judged. She just wants her mum.

"Everything looks ok," bitch says after nearly ten minutes of absence. "I will be back next week to check on you both."

"Fuck you, fuck you," Jen says under her breath as she watches the grey Ford Mondeo estate drive off. "Fuck you," as she blinks away tears of frustration, pain, fear, indignation and lack of sleep. "I'll show you, you bitch."

After she feeds her son and puts him safely back in his moses basket, she goes upstairs and expels nothing. Just bile. She has eaten nothing. But she is in control. She is in control of something.

Her mum comes back from work a few hours later to find her daughter in tears hugging her grandson in the snug.

As Jen turns to her, her mum takes her in her arms and just holds her.

"Let's get away for a few days, Jen," she says, stroking her hair. "The three of us. I'll call work and take a few more days off. Let's just get away."

"Yes please, mum," Jen replies, weakly. "Yes please."

I turn to you.
Mel C.

-29-
JEN: FILL ME IN

30th June 2000

By 4:30pm Jen, Joseph and their XR2i Honey are ready. One back seat down, broken locks fixed thanks to her ex, her slightly dodgy exhaust patched - again, thanks to her ex.

In fact he had got a decent exhaust from who knows and had put it on Honey so she passed her MOT. He then took the 'borrowed' decent one back off, gave it back to 'who knows' then put the old dodgy one back on and patched it up. Filled the holes in. Marvellous. What could go wrong?

She has filled Honey with the blue tartan travel system (cleaned up after a bird shit incident earlier that day), moses basket, travel cot, bouncer, nappies, changing mat, bottles, baby milk, all other baby paraphernalia. All tucked in somehow. And of course a baby. She ponders how small Joseph is compared to all his shit.

Jen has not packed a lot for herself. She knows she doesn't need much, apart from her ridiculously big sanitary towels and equally prodigious pants. Where she is going she knows that she won't see a soul apart from her mum, her auntie and her uncle. Some horses, dogs, geese, chickens, cats and ducks. And potentially a cousin or two. None of who or which require a bra, any form of decent clothing or makeup. It isn't like she is going to meet anyone new, anyone important to meet.

Cherish is left pride of place on her bedroom shelf. She watches over Joseph at night, but now that Jen actually has Joseph, she doesn't feel the need to take her figurative figurine everywhere with her anymore.

Her mum had offered to drive over the Pennines to Lincolnshire, but Jen's fu-fu has growled a lot less over the last few days. She is happy to drive over the M62, she wants to drive.

Her mum gets home from work at 4:45pm and they get on the road straight away. Jen has already inserted 'Barbara Streisand: Duets' into the CD player. Joseph has been filled with milk, changed and is sleeping in his car seat belted into the upright back seat. Tucked into the madness somehow.

Mum and daughter spend the following forty-five minutes dueting 'You don't bring me flowers', 'Tell him', 'Make no mistake, he's mine', 'Guilty' and their absolute fave 'No more tears (enough is enough)'. Poor Joseph sleeps through the cacophony. He is used to the noise from the cottage.

They have passed the nutty, notorious Stott Hill Farm in the middle of the motorway. Like a vast vehicle vagina with motorway lane labias, a big bush surrounded by a bevy of bushy sheep and a cottage clitoris. Urban myths said the farmer in the 1960s, Ken Wild, had refused to move from his farmhouse cottage so the M62 builders had to split the west and east bound carriageways and snake the two sets of labia lanes around it. However, Ken told a documentary many years later that this was a wild tale and he was not the road rebel he had been branded. A geological fault had meant it was easier and cheaper for the engineers to work around the cottage clitoris and construct the ginormous genitals.

They fly under the iconic Scammonden Bridge (Brown Cow Bridge to the locals of West Yorkshire) which, on opening in 1970, was the largest concrete arch bridge in the UK. In the middle of 'enough is enough' and after the sign that tells them they are very high up at Windy Hill 'M62 Summit: Highest motorway in England 372m (1221 feet)', Honey starts to splutter.

It is absolutely pissing it down. Putting her foot down, Jen gets nothing.

Jen points Honey towards the hard shoulder. She understands why it is called a 'shoulder', but why is it 'hard'? Should it not be 'hell shoulder'? She thinks she will ask her uncle to fill her in later.

Stationary, Jen's mum fills her in that she is still in the AA. Relieved, Jen finds her phone. She knows it is the person that is the member, not the car, so they will be ok.

There's no signal.

Fuck.

"Give me your AA card," Jen says to her mum, checking Joseph is still asleep. "Wait here, I'll go to an emergency phone."

Jen braves the elements, not clothed for the savage summer high altitude storm. She looks at the arrows on the signs on the marker posts. They tell her to go east to the nearest telephone. As she walks rather wonkily, battered by the rain and wind, she notices the sheer drop on the other side of the small metal barrier. She looks forward. After a while she reaches the orange SOS telephone.

Back in the car, Jen tells her mum it's fine. Not knowing if it is fine. Barbara can't tell them to 'Get Happy'. She has been muted. There's no power. But it's fine.

Forty five minutes later a bright yellow van is reversing towards them on the hell shoulder. AA. 'Arse and fucking Arse', Jen thinks, still soaked to her non bra-ed daisy cow tits and bat-shit big sanitary towel and pants.

"You should be ok, now," their Arse and Arse superb yet sodden rescuer fills them in. "It was your battery. It must have flooded. You should be fine now to get going."

"So nothing to do with my exhaust?"

"Nope. That's fine."

"Thank you," Jen says, a little stunned, but genuinely meaning it. Further stunned that Joseph is still amazingly asleep. The noise training in the cottage (as in as much noise as possible) is clearly paying off.

"I will follow you for the next mile or so to make sure you're ok," he offers. "Until the next junction. Until Bradford."

"Perfect," Jen's mum says. "Thank you."

"For God's sake," Jen laughs, forcing Honey into fifth in the fast lane. Just past Bradford. "Get Barbara back on, mum."

'Enough is enough' smashes back on. They collectively yell about not being able to go on any longer on their way to Leeds.

As the copious piles of the Pennines give way to the winding Wolds then flat plains of Lincolnshire, the rain stops. The sky is being dusted with dusk.

They turn off the main Grimsby Road and then down the tree lined, gravelled drive. Both driver and adult passenger exhaling involuntarily, both instantly and visibly relaxed and relieved. Jen's happy place.

"Right, let's get you all in," Jen's auntie says after hugging it out with Jen and asking why they are so late. And why she is so wet. She has somehow retrieved her new and newly met great nephew Joseph from his cosy incarceration too.

Her uncle helps bring the paraphernalia into the house.

PAPER OVER IT

As they enter the farmhouse kitchen, they hear Barbara Streisand and her duets playing from the tape deck in the corner.

Spirits and kindred come to mind. Wine comes to hands. Chicken curry comes to the table.

After eating the delicious curry Jen's uncle has made for them, and his wicked dahl, Jen excuses herself. Joseph is happily smiling in his bouncer.

She goes into the downstairs loo, locks the door and goes through the motions. There are two doors between her and her family and the music is still playing so noise is not too much of a problem, but what she has learnt from countless visits to this toilet over the years is that the plumbing system doesn't work as well as in suburbia.

The house, being in the country, has a septic tank for sewerage and waste. She knows it can block quite easily (her or her sister's tampons and her cousin's condoms had caused previous passage problems) so she always stops halfway to not overload a single flush. She then flushes, carries on with the second serving and then flushes again.

Two courses. Like a starter and a main, or a main and a pudding.

She knows that a double flush is a potentially suspicious necessity when the drains aren't connected to the mains. But she has no choice.

She papers over it and returns happily in control to the noise and joviality of the kitchen. Her mum is feeding Joseph.

1st July 2000

Jen is in the kitchen with Joseph, a brew in one hand and his just warmed bottle in the other. It is just past seven on Saturday morning.

"You ok?" Jen's auntie asks her as she walks in.

"Yeah, you?" Jen responds. Her auntie has never really asked her if she's ok she doesn't think. She's not that kind of person. They had all just drunk wine and danced Joseph and the dogs around the kitchen to Barbara last night.

"The horses need feeding, watering, putting out and mucking out."

"Would you feed him for me?" Jen asks, nodding at Joseph in his bouncer.

"Yes, of course," her auntie knows Jen could do with some time outside in her special place, and actually looking forward to some one-on-one time with 'the little bird' as she christened him last night.

Jen is liberated. She knows exactly what to do. Has loved this place forever, has wanted to live here since she can remember.

She gets going with the horses. Knows the water, the water buckets, the feed, the feed buckets, the head collars, the hay, the wooden farm gates, the shovels, the wheelbarrows, the brushes, the horse shit, the straw, the straw shit mountain waiting to be lit. She knows everything. She sorts everything.

It's a beautiful day.

She sits on the fence by the stables, looking out over the fields, listening to the geese soundtrack.

After a while, she jumps down and starts to re-brush the sparkling yard.

"You ok?" she hears from behind her.

"Of course I'm ok," she responds, emboldened, carrying on brushing. "When did you ever ask me if I'm ok?"

"I'm asking now."

"I'm fine."

"You're not."

"I fucking am," Jen says, turning to face her. Brush in hand. Surprised at the language which has flooded from her.

"You are fucking not," her auntie confirms with conviction. "How can I help you?"

"I don't know."

"You need to fill me in. I need to know everything."

The pair continue to brush the spotless yard together, her auntie finding the second brush. They talk. Or rather, Jen talks. She fills her in about everything other than her bulexia/anoremia.

"It's going to be ok," Jen's auntie says after a while. "It really is."

"I'm not sure it is," Jen responds. "Who's looking after Joseph?"

"Your mum's up," she replies. "Let's go and get a brew?"

"Ok."

Back in the house, with Jen's mum entertained in the lounge by her brother-in-law and 'the little bird', Jen and her auntie pour over a newly opened Wasgij jigsaw on the kitchen table.

A traditional type jigsaw, but the scene on the front is seen from a different perspective than the picture on the jigsaw. You have to work it out.

As Jen finds the corner pieces and her auntie corners all the edge pieces, she starts to speak to Jen. Gives her perspective on everything Jen has shared, has filled her in on. A different perspective. A more positive one.

Jen listens with open ears and diminishing fears.

"It's going to be ok, Jen. I promise," she says as they start to fill in the middle pieces inside the completed outer frame.

Fill me in.
Craig David.

-30-
JEN: BLACK COFFEE

4th July 2000

After a lovely few days enjoying beautiful beaches on the east coast, loving the great big blue sky, the sunshine, the beach walking, the stars, the night swimming, the company, the conversation and, in a big way, the countryside silence, Jen has only one more day left before she has to drive back west to get her mum home ready for work tomorrow.

They plan to leave at 5am to miss the traffic. They will get all packed up tonight, apart from the travel cot and a few odds and sods.

Sitting at the kitchen table at lunchtime, Jen's auntie tells them she has a client coming over from Leeds (she thinks) for a bridesmaid dress fitting.

"That's a trek," Jen says, still in her baby milk-stained onesie, which she has become rather fond of, her cold sore now very attractively scabbing over and dirty hair slicked back into a greasy ponytail.

"It's the wedding in Leeds you recommended me for, Jen," she explains. "The bride is definitely in Leeds. It's your friend's friend. Remember? But I'm not exactly sure where this bridesmaid is coming from."

"Ah right, yes of course!" Jen had forgotten all about this after the rollercoaster adventure of the last few months. "So you're doing all the dresses?"

"Yes, and the men's waistcoats and some other things, I think," her auntie answers. "I need to check my notes. Oh, she's here," watching a car pull down the drive. "See you in a bit," as she heads to the back door and into her sewing workroom.

Jen and her mum sit chatting for a while over yet another brew, Jen's mum holding Joseph. Jen is still exhausted, as is her mum to be fair, but this has been exactly what she needed. Exactly what they needed. In exactly the right place, Jen's special, happy place. She wouldn't want to be anywhere else but here right now. She wouldn't want to change anything at all.

After about forty minutes, Jen's auntie comes into the kitchen followed by a lady. She looks about in her late twenties, Jen thinks. She also looks really smiley and nice, pretty and bubbly. Just slightly taller than Jen. Jen feels like a tramp, Jen knows she looks like a tired, greasy, dirty tramp sporting lip herpes.

"I'm Carla," she says. Jen immediately warms to her. "I don't mean to disturb you. I just need a black coffee for the drive home. Then I'll get out of your hair."

"I'm Jen," Jen replies, thinking that no-one would want to be anywhere near her hair right now, never mind in it. "And this is my mum."

"And who's this?" she asks.

"This is Joseph," Jen's auntie says. "He's just over two weeks old. I just have instant coffee. Is that ok?"

"Yes, of course. And he's just adorable!" Carla says. "Can I have a hold?"

Jen's auntie gets her the black coffee she asks for and the four females and Joseph sit at the kitchen table. Jen and Carla work out their connection. She is the sister of the groom.

Then Jen's mum asks her where she lives, what she does, how old she is, and - Jen's mum style - pretty much everything else other than her inside leg measurement. But her sister has that on file now so all good there.

It turns out she doesn't live in Leeds, she lives just north of Manchester. She had a meeting in Doncaster earlier that day so it had been easy just to crack onto Lincolnshire for the dress fitting. She was used to driving, had been a medical rep for a healthcare company after leaving nursing, so had many miles on the clock of her four-door silver Vauxhall Astra. She says that strong black coffee always helps on long drives. She has just turned thirty. She has been married for just over a year. She has no tattoos. Jen's mum doesn't like tattoos.

"Mum, will you stop asking all the questions," Jen says, embarrassed at the intrusion. But even more embarrassed about her own appearance. Carla is very smart and perfectly put together. Jen looks like something one of the cats dragged in after being attacked by the geese, pecked by the hens, been hauled through the straw shit mountain and accidentally fallen into the septic tank.

"It's fine, honestly," Carla says smiling. "I'm in marketing now, for the same healthcare company, so am much more office based. But still have to travel a bit." She sips her coffee and adds, "It's really busy, to be honest. I've been looking for a graduate for a little while now to join as a marketing assistant. To help me. I Just can't find the right person."

Jen doesn't think anything of this casual comment in her post baby brain fog, but her mum literally pounces on it like a tiger. "Jen has just finished her degree in Marketing. Where's your office?"

"Mum! Leave her alone for god's sake. She came for a bloody bridesmaid dress, not the Spanish Inquisition," Jen cringes.

"It's ok, honestly," Carla laughs while proceeding to give the address. It is totally and completely randomly just over a mile away from the little town where Jen, Jen's mum and Joseph now live.

Jen's mum literally has kittens. Tiger kittens. It is really rather embarrassing to witness.

Jen and Jen's auntie hold their heads in their hands at Jen's mum arranging a meeting between Carla and Jen the following week. Unsure whether Carla is being rigorously railroaded in a random kitchen in the middle of the countryside one hundred and fifty miles east of her place of work, or whether she is actually interested in having a chat with Jen - but it is planned.

Arranged for the following Thursday. July the 13th. Jen hopes this isn't an omen, like the flags. In fact, after Carla hands Joseph back and leaves, her travel mug filled with more black coffee for the two-and-a-half-hour drive home, Jen almost strangles her mother - a little like a scene from The Omen.

"Mum," she shouts. "He's not even three weeks old!"

"But you need a job, don't you?" she replies quite sternly. "You don't want to be on the dole forever, do you?" It has literally been just over a week since she signed on.

"Remember how you were feeling when you arrived here?" Jen's auntie reminds her. "Just go and see what she has to say. You never know. And it would show that bitch health visitor, wouldn't it?"

"Yes, you're right," Jen admits, switching her perspective in an instant. Like the Wasjig jigsaw. Like her auntie had made her do when she filled her in. Like the instant black coffee may have changed her potential future. "What the hell am I going to wear?"

"That's the spirit!" Jen's mum says. "We'll go shopping this weekend."

"Thanks mum," Jen laughs, not sure how either of them were going to be able to afford anything particularly nice or suitable.

She feels immediately stimulated. Energy levels increased and mood significantly improved. She feels invigorated.

Like she's the one who's had the black coffee.

Black coffee.
All Saints.

-31-
THE QUARTET: SUMMER OF LOVE

8th July 2000
Jen, Joseph and her mum go shopping for 'interview clothes', whatever they are. They go out first thing so they can get back home for the Wimbledon women's final. Venus Williams is playing. It is already a really very warm and rather humid day.

"Why are we going so early?," Jen asks. "It's not on until two."

"The early bird and all that," her mum says, making no sense at all. They need a new wardrobe, not a worm. But Jen rolls with it.

Em just loves tennis, having played in summer a lot as a child at the local lawn tennis club. She has invited the girls over to watch it at hers. Pimms, strawberries and cream all on tap. Lou was a straight yes due to the tap and seeing her troupe, not the tennis. Said she would jump on the train from Liverpool after lunch and be with her just before it starts. Kate said she would come over too on the train, but she would miss the tennis as 1) she was working until 1pm, and 2) she couldn't give two shits about tennis.

Kate is staying in Chester with Will. She has decided to take up his dad's offer of work experience for the summer, but has also picked up some late night and weekend shifts at Dolcis in Chester to earn some much needed money. She is starting work at the legal firm in a week or so and doing a half day at the shop on Saturday. She needs money to generally live but also to fund a few trips back up to Glasgow over summer to see her family. Will's parents said she could kindly stay with them for the summer, they can see how much her being around is helping Will with his recovery, both mentally and physically. Their summer of love.

Jen had said she couldn't, she was watching it with her mum. And she also didn't want to spoil their afternoon or evening taking a baby along, but she didn't say this.

Em had called Jen's mum the night before to ask her if she could take care of Joseph for the afternoon so Jen could come. It would be a nice surprise for her, and the other girls. She had said yes, that would be absolutely fine. And why didn't Jen stay over and come back home in the morning?

"The joys of bottle feeding!" she had said. "It's not a problem at all. I have no plans and no man, so I will have a lovely time with my little man."

She also added that her new neighbour, a single lady a few years younger than her (yes, she had been curtain twitching on 'flag-gate') may pop over with a bottle of wine. "Don't you be drunk in charge of a baby," Em had teased.

"Ha!" Jen's mum replied laughingly. "I'm sure we'll have the night of our lives."

In House of Fraser 'Rackhams' in Altrincham, Jen's mum picks out a grey pencil skirt and matching fitted bandeau top with a zipped back, both with bright pink stitching, and a matching hot pink fitted boxy cardigan.

"Are you absolutely joking?" Jen says, shocked as much by her mum's choice as the shocking pink and the boob tube.

"You only get one chance to make a first impression, and you properly messed that up didn't you?" she reminds Jen of her appalling appearance in Lincolnshire.

"But what impression will this make?" Jen asks. "I don't want to look like a tart or like I'm going to a flippin' fiesta. It's very 'loud'."

"Just trust me and go try it on," her mum encourages. "Joseph and I will be waiting out here. Won't we, little man?"

In the few short weeks since giving birth, Jen has zipped straight back into her size six clothes. She is just twenty-one so it was easy. Her abs are on fire again, Britney style. She looks in the mirror and smiles. Her mum is right, again. Annoyingly right. The outfit looks amazing. Smart with a hint of sass, creative with a wink of congeniality. Just calves, feet, hands, hint of upper chest (no cleavage), neck and face showing. Surprisingly sombre from her first impressions. Not fiesta at all. It is perfect. It is also expensive.

She leaves the dressing room to show her mum whose face is immediately a mix of pride and annoying 'I told you so'.

"I have some nice grey heels that will look perfect with it." Jen is only half a shoe size smaller than her mum so insoles are always an option.

"I can't afford it, Mum."

"Your Grandpa gave me some money last night to help with the outfit shopping today," she says. She had popped in for a brew on her way home from work. Jen and Joseph had met her there for an hour. "If you want to pay him back when you start working, that's your choice."

"Thank you," Jen is, yet again, almost in tears. This joyride adventure of life is having some raging highs and lows, rather like her hormones still are. This is a real high.

"And I have another surprise for you," she adds. "We are going home now and you're going to pack a bag. You're going to watch Venus at Em's and stay the night. I'm having a date night with Joseph."

"I can't," Jen says, eyes wide open.

"You can, and you are," her mum confirms. "Isn't she Joseph? … See, he's nodding."

Jen eye rolls at the ridiculousness of a three-and-a-half-week-old baby nodding, but he kind of looks like he is. She laughs.

"Forget your tomorrows for the night," her mum says. "Go and be just Jen for a few hours."

So it is sorted. Jen is like a child getting giddy before a party. In fact, in many ways she is still a child. Like most twenty-one-year-olds. After hanging her grey and hot pink non-fiesta purchase on the clothing rail in her room, packing a bag and having a quick shower, she sets about making sure everything is ready for Joseph for the night.

"But he's only three weeks old," Jen is now back-tracking, doubting her decision.

"Do you think I've never looked after a baby before?" her mum laughs. "Leave me to sort everything. Go! Have fun."

She kisses Joseph goodbye and hugs her mum. "Thank you, I think."

She climbs into Honey, her Fiesta, and heads into Manchester, feeling really strange without her little man. On the motorway she looks at the horizon and there's not a cloud in the sky. It is clear, like her head has become recently. It has only been twenty-three days and nights, but she can barely remember life without him. She is totally smitten. It is genuinely turning out to be a summer of love for Jen. She turns the blowers on as she feels the temperature rising even further as she enters the city, but they just seem to turn up the heat by blowing hot air back at her. It is a sweetly sticky, sunny summer day. She feels alive.

It's just before 1pm when she arrives. "Been colluding with my mother, have we Emily?" Jen accuses, grinning.

"Collusion is a particularly great skill of mine," Em admits. "As are cocktails, conspiracy and cock."

"Get me a bloody drink, then," Jen laughs, seeing where this is going. Also seeing that Em is wearing a tiny white skirt and a cropped white t-shirt. "Match ready?" she asks.

"Always! My summer of love starts here. De fruta la vida!" Em replies with a cheeky grin, mixing the Pimms in a ginormous jug with cucumber, mint, strawberries and orange slices. "Oh fuck!"

"What?"

"I've bought ginger beer instead of ginger ale," Em says with frustration.

"Why do we need either?" Jen replies. "Surely we just need lemonade."

"No we don't, you heathen!" Em says indignantly. "I am making my famous Pimmbledon. It needs ginger. And it needs ginger ale, not ginger beer."

"Lashings of ginger beer," Jen laughs, taking her back to George, Julian, Dick, Anne and Timmy the dog of her childhood. The Famous Five. She always desperately wanted to be George. "Are you fucking Aunt Fanny?," she cajoles her friend, referring to George's mother.

"I am not fucking anyone's aunt, Fanny or not," Em replies haughtily.

Jen dissolves into giggles. "I've missed you, Em."

"You too," Em says, hugging her friend. She has missed her in more ways than one, for longer than she knows and in more ways than she knows. "You can just be Jen today and tonight, right? Just our Jen. Forget about tomorrow just for the night? Not pregnant Jen, not mum Jen. Just Jen."

"Ok, I'll try," she responds, not knowing how she could now be 'not mum Jen', but knowing she should try. That was why her mum had given her this time, she knows that. And she could also feel that Em, and probably the other two girls, need her to just be her for a

187

few hours too. They probably also want to forget about tomorrow just for the night. "I'll run to the shop and get some of your ginger shit. Do we need anything else?"

"Crisps," Em replies. "I've only gone and eaten most of them. And maybe some chocolate and some biscuits. Get loads in fact, we'll need snacks later. And may as well get another bottle of Pimms, just in case."

Jen looks at her, not knowing quite what to say. Not wanting to look like the dole tramp who can't afford to buy some snacks. She only just about managed to put petrol in her car earlier. "There's some money on the side," Em quickly adds, reading her friend's expression. "I'm still getting my allowance. May as well take advantage of it while I can." Jen makes a mental note to ask her what she means later.

As Jen is heading back bearing Pringles, two bottles of ginger ale, a packet of Wagon Wheels, some Milky Way bars, two large bottles of lemonade (Jen doesn't really like ginger), a packet of Trio bars, a multi-bag of Golden Wonder crisps and some orange and green Club biscuits, she spots Lou dancing her way down from Piccadilly Station in cute little denim dungaree shorts, living her vida loca.

"Lou," she shouts.

"Bloody hell, Jen," she says shocked and with worry on her face. She didn't know Jen was coming, and is thrilled that she is there. "What are you doing here? You shouldn't be carrying all that! Where's Joseph?"

"I'm not pregnant any more, you wally!"

"Oh yeah! But how's your fu-fu and boobs?"

"A lot better, actually." As Jen says this she realises that they both (or all three) really genuinely are. "And Joseph is with my mum. She's having him for the night."

"That's amazing," Lou smiles at Jen, super proud of her and ridiculously pleased she has just Jen for the night. "Let's get back. We need to properly catch-up." She grabs half the bags. "It's so great to see you!"

Settled in at Em's, all three squished onto the small sofa even though there is another chair and a pouffe, the girls sip Em's Pimmbeldon. Lou chokes slightly. "It's quite bitter," she says, without really meaning to say it.

"That'll be the ginger ale," Jen explains, also slightly gagging.

"Why does it have ginger ale in it?" Lou questions, swallowing hard and reaching for her throat. "Why not just lemonade? Or 7UP?"

"For fucks sake, you two," Em says. "I try to do something nice and civilised, and you just want bloody Pimms and Panda Pops."

Lou and Jen glance at each other and then back to Em, laughing. "Panda Pops sounds great to me," says Jen while Lou says, "I bloody love Panda Pops."

"If you've got any Sunny Delight we'll have it with that," Jen adds with a wink.

"I give up," Em says, shaking her head whilst pretending not to laugh. "You are both past saving," she resolves as they completely agree with her. "I'd make another jug with lemonade if we had any," she adds. Jen grins. Em shakes her head again.

A few minutes later, all three again squished onto Em's small sofa, Em sipping her Pimmbledon and the other two sucking the newly named Poppedon through straws, Sue Barker introduces Venus Williams and Lindsay Davenport to Centre Court.

"Give me a sec, I'm just going to call my mum," Jen says, jumping up and heading out onto the balcony with her phone.

"For fucks sake," Em says, covered in her Pimmbledon from Jen's jump. Her Wimbledon whites now more Brixton browns. "Can we not just watch the bloody tennis? It's not like we can pause live TV!"

"Can you imagine?" Lou mused. "How cool would that be?"

A few minutes later, all three are once again squished onto Em's small sofa. The twenty-year-old Venus beat her eighteen-year-old sister Serena just two days earlier in the semi-finals. Even though they were already fairly well known, the UK has become hopelessly obsessed with the Williams sisters over the past few weeks.

Venus is victorious in two sets. 6-3, 7-6. Her very first Grand Slam. She dances around the court like she's at a fiesta, lost in the dream she dared to dream as a little girl in Compton. Tasting paradise and treasuring every single moment of her first big win. It is absolutely amazing to witness.

Lou has actually enjoyed it more than she thought, helped by the vividly vivacious, victorious Venus. Also assisted by the rather punchy Poppedon. And it only lasted about an hour and a half -

bonus! She had thought she would have to watch it for hours.

"Strawberries and cream?" Em offers as the intercom buzzes.

"I've just had a cheeky on the train," Kate updates the girls as she notices the huge jugs of Pimms and hugs them all one by one. "It is over, isn't it? The stupid pingy pong thing."

"Yes, it's over," Jen laughs.

"Hang on, what are you doing here?" Kate questions. "And where is Joseph?"

The girls explain the situation. "We've got just Jen? All night? Until tomorrow?" Kate clarifies in question form.

"Yes," Jen confirms, smiling. Still feeling very guilty.

"Sweeeeet! Bloody love this!" Kate whoops. "Get the tunes on, Emster!"

For tonight they forget their tomorrows and dance to the music Em plays.

Summer of love.

Steps.

-32-
THE QUARTET: SPINNING AROUND

8th July 2000 – continued

The girls have the very best afternoon in the sunshine on Ems' balcony, Pimmbledonning and Poppedonning. Kate more than happy with the Pimmble version. Apparently loving ginger in every way.

"I'm Scottish," she reminds them. "Irn Bru. Made from girders!".

The rest of the quartet have absolutely no idea what she is going on about or what the relationship with ginger is, but with Piccadilly Key 103 blaring summer tunes from Em's lounge and Lou straddling Kate whilst flipping her red curls and asking her if she loves her ginger too, they feel no need to ask. They just enjoy the crazy vista, and each other.

"I've got something to show you," Jen says after regaling the bitch health visitor visit. "Fill us up Em?"

"What is it?" Lou asks as Em Pimmbles and Pops their glasses up.

"Well, I was in the car with Joseph two days after 'health visitor bitch-gate'. On the Thursday. On my way back from picking up my dole, free baby milk vouchers and baby milk. Feeling monumentally shit about myself," Jen explains. "And did I tell you what some old cow said to me in the Post Office with Joseph in his travel system?"

"No," all three reply, trying to keep up with Jen's story and what on earth she is going to show them. And where and how this old cow has popped up. And why could she not just call it a pram or a buggy? She was spinning around with her story so much, it was hard to keep up.

"Well, I'd just been given my dole and vouchers by a miserable bitch behind the counter. She barely even looked at me. Her name badge read 'Joy'. She was anything but joyful. And then, as I was leaving, nearly out of the door, this equally miserable cow said, "You gymslip mums with your illegitimate children taking money off the state. It is an absolute disgrace," Jen says with such fury it is really quite funny.

"But you're twenty-one," Lou says, slightly horrified. "You're not exactly a child doing your GCSEs are you? What an opinionated bitch."

"I spun around and said exactly that to her!" Jen replies, full of rage and indignation.

"Did you? Well done you!" Kate praises Jen, like she is a child.

"Erm, well, no," Jen admits. "That's what I wish I'd said to her."

"What did you say?" Lou questions.

"Nothing," she shakes her head and smiles sheepishly. "I just turned round and gave her a really rather childish bitch stare and walked away, pushing Joseph."

"That will have told her," Em said, pseudo seriously. "You will have really made her think about her behaviour with that."

"Here's to Jen and her super scary staring," Lou raises her glass.

"To Jen," Em and Kate say, raising their glass and laughing. "And her super scary staring."

Jen laughs along too, knowing she is really rubbish at confrontation and also glad she can now see the funny side of the opinionated old cow's comments. And what the hell does 'illegitimate' mean anyway? That Joseph is not legitimate, not legal? That a baby can be unlawful? What a ridiculous word. Bitch cow. She sits back in her chair and sips her drink through the straw.

"So what is it you have to show us?" Kate asks, intrigued and confused. Going back to where Jen started her winding, spinning story.

"Oh yeah, sorry," Jen sits back up. "So I was in the car with Joseph on my way home when Randy Crawford's 'One day I'll fly away' came on the radio."

The girls know this is one of her fave songs and that she had had a moment with it when she was pregnant and highly hormonal.

"And I though 'fuck it'. I don't actually want to fly away, Randy. I don't want to leave the world 'til yesterday'. Fuck off bitch health visitor. Fuck off opinionated old cow. And fuck off any other fucker that thinks I can't fly. I'll make it alone." Jen is a little Poppedon pissed, randomly spinning Randy's lyrics into her slightly sloshed, frenetic soliloquy. "So I decided to mark the occasion."

"What did you do?" Em asks, wide eyed.

Jen proceeds to stand up and pull her jeans down to show her arse.

"Did you hurt yourself?" Lou asks, confused. Looking at a white plaster-like dressing on the top of her right cheek.

"Oh yeah, sorry," Jen wobbles slightly as she tries in vain to spin her upper body around so she can see her arse. Seeing her arse in her inability to be like an owl and actually see her own arse, she impatiently says, "Just rip it off."

They are all now staring at her arse in bewilderment.

Em goes in for the rip.

"Oh wow!" Kate says. "It's a bird!"

"It's a plane! It's superman!" Lou can't help completing the lyrics.

"It's a swallow," Em says in awe.

"It's bloody brilliant is what it is," says Kate. "I absolutely love it!"

The little bird tattoo flying on Jen's upper right bum cheek is celebrated by all.

"It's symbolic," Jen clarifies, unable to actually see it. But being able to see in the reflection in the glass that her three friends are peering at her bare arse, also seeing a man on his balcony peering at the strange view too. She laughs.

"And Em, it is not a symbolic swallow," she chirps. "Don't mock me. I do not have a swallow anywhere near my crack!"

"It's a Mockingjay," Lou says.

"What the hell is that?" Em asks.

"No idea," Lou replies. "I'm a bit pissed, and maybe it's hunger. I'm starving. And I have limited 'game' knowledge. But, you know, mocking for people mocking her and J for Jen. Mockingjay."

"Well, Jen, let's drink to your new addition," Kate raises her glass to Jen's arse, ignoring Lou's rampant rambling.

"To Jen. A beautiful bird. Inside and outside. And on her arse!" Em cheers while the others repeat, in some form.

"I am not on my arse!" Jen laughs, pulling up her jeans. "That's the whole point of the bloody bird!". The tattoo becoming even more symbolic to her but thinking what a shame it is that she has to look backwards in a mirror to see the symbolism. But maybe that is the point. Maybe it denotes things that are behind her, to help her focus on things that are ahead of her. Focus on tomorrow.

"And what an arse it is," Lou cheers to Jen's cute behind while the rest of the balcony whoops as Kylie's 'Spinning Around' comes on the radio.

The quartet spin around. Celebrating themselves, their friendships, Venus, the Kylie comeback, impending exam results, swallowed bottoms, gold hot-panted bottoms, Jen's scary stares, the sunshine and the weird chap who is still staring at them from his balcony.

They tease the poor innocent chap with their singing and dancing. He was just sitting on his balcony minding his own business, enjoying the sunshine. And the birds.

Slightly dizzy from spinning, the quartet go inside. "I need something to eat," Kate says, sozzled.

"We've got snacks!" Lou grins.

With Pringles, Milky Ways, Wagon Wheels, Trios and Club Biscuits extravagantly spilled out of the plastic bags and onto the floor, the girls dig in. Steve the Cheese watches on in disgust, spotting no decent Swiss chocolate anywhere.

"The red car and the blue car had a race," Jen starts.

"All red wants to do is stuff his face," Lou excitedly replies.

"He eats everything he sees, from trucks to prickly trees," Kate builds, beaming.

"But smart old blue, he took the milky way," Em finishes, in fits of giggles.

"Where did that come from, Em?" Lou is pissing herself.

"What about this one?" Kate asks, picking up a green Club Biscuit.

"If you want a lot of chocolate on your biscuit," Em sings.

"Join our club!" Lou, Kate and Jen sing back to her.

The girls are bouncing on the sofa, chair and pouffe, reliving their youth in daft yet brilliantly developed adverts and their juvenile yet enduring jingles.

"That's enough," Jen pleads, half bent over. "My bladder can't cope."

"Just one more," Lou yells, grabbing a Trio. "Suzie's goin' to sing about a different chocolatey biscuit."

"Trio! Trio! I want a Trio and I want one now!" Jen, Em and Kate yell back to her. Doing the spoilt sassy brat Suzie actions and moves, falling about laughing.

"Not one, not two, but three things in it!" the quartet scream as

Em bounces (falls) off the sofa crying 'Oospidaisy'. "A chocolatey biscuit and a toffee taste too."

"Did Susie actually realise she was screaming for a threesome?" Em hollers, trying to pick herself up from the floor by grabbing a leaf from Steve.

"Emily, why do you always have to take everything to the floor?" Lou laughs as she drags her friend up from the floor, apologising to the long-suffering Steve and his licit leaves.

"I've brought a few little gifts from Hairy Potter," Kate admits with a wry smile. "Anyone fancy?"

"Fuck yes!" Em says, newly upright.

Back on the balcony, Em, Kate and Lou share the spliff. Jen politely declines to no counter from the girls. While Em is smoking, Jen spots some old scars on Em's right wrist and a fresher, newer one. She has a flash back to the night before her hospital scare, a few months ago. She has not thought of it since, had clearly forgotten in the exhaustion of the night and the following few days.

After a little while, Jen braves, "Em, we really do need to talk about you."

"Do we?" Em replies. "Not now, I'm chilling."

"When then?" Lou pushes.

"I don't know," Em slurs. "Soon, I promise."

Jen takes Em's phone from under her stoned nose and goes inside to the loo. She finds Charlie in the contact list. It is 'Charliebobs'. She presses call.

"Emster?"

"No, it's her friend Jen," Jen responds. She has never met Charlie, none of them have. They have never met any of her family.

Jen proceeds to ask Charlie what is going on. Does not mention what she has seen on Em's wrist. What she thinks Em has done or is doing to herself. He says he doesn't really want to go into details, but that it was a really bad Easter. It has been two and a half months since Em had apparently spoken to any of her family.

"Will you please come up and see her?" Jen asks. "I think she's in a bad way."

"Ok," Charlie replies, letting out a sigh. "I'll come up as soon as I can. She had better be willing to listen, though."

"Thank you," Jen says. "One question. When is the baby due?"

"Due late October, I think," he replies. "In fact, I think I remember dad saying it was due on Halloween."

"Do you know what she's having?" Jen asks.

"No," he replies. "They might but I don't. And Jen, Eve's really really nice. She's done nothing wrong. Em needs to get over this - and soon. Otherwise I'm not sure what dad will do."

Jen gives Charlie her number and he agrees to call or text her when he knows when he's coming up. She tells him that their graduation date is the 18th of July.

Jen feels really shitty and underhand calling Charlie without Em knowing, but she doesn't regret it. She quickly deletes the call from Em's call list and leaves the phone in the kitchen, knowing Em is far too pissed to know where she left it, and heads outside.

"Where the hell have you been?" Em asks her.

"Calling my mum," Jen lies. Then kicking herself because that's exactly what she wants to do now. She looks at the time. Just after 8pm. She decides she'll give it half an hour then call her. She knows her three friends will not really remember her lie by that point.

"All ok at home?" Kate asks.

"Absolutely fine," Jen lies again, having absolutely no idea. "Results on Monday for all of us but you, Kate," she deflects, not wanting to lie again about the non-phone call.

"I'm scared," Lou admits, her teeth biting her lips.

"I'm terrified," Jen confesses. Her hands on her cheeks, her wrists cupping her chin.

"I'm stoned," Em declares, her head spinning.

Spinning Around.
Kylie Minogue.

-33-
JEN: AGAINST ALL ODDS (TAKE A LOOK AT ME NOW)

10th July 2000
Results day.
 Rest of Jen's life day.
 She waits for the postman to come.
 She is bouncing. In fact she is one legged bouncing.
 "Why am I hopping?" she asks Joseph.
 She just hopes to God he has her letter. She can't have another night where the few hours sleep she gets between feeding Joseph are taken by purblind panic and fear of the unknown.
 "Keep everything crossed for me," she says to Joseph as he stares up at his one-legged bouncing mum from his bouncer. She's sure he smiles, but he is not yet a month old so assumes it is wind.
 She decides to lie on the shaggy rug on the stone tiles and do some sit-ups, just to pass a bit of time. And to stop herself hopping like a maniac. To make her feel a little more in control.
 After about fifty sit-ups, she looks over at Joseph who is looking at her, like she's completely mad. "Want to join in?" she asks him.
 "Are you mad? I can't do sit ups. I can't even sit up yet," Jen replies for him in a very bad Bruce Willis 'Look Who's Talking' voice. "I'm only three and a half weeks old, you fool."
 She picks him up and lies back down. She puts his bum on her stomach, she bends her knees and rests his head on her legs.
 "There you go," Jen says as she crunches towards him counting, up and down, over and over again. He stares at her, never takes his eyes off hers. Sucking his dummy. He barely blinks. And when he does, it is super exaggerated. He looks inside her somehow, again like she's mad. Jen smiles. "I probably am, little man."
 At one hundred and forty-six sit ups the letterbox rattles and there's a little thud on the mat.
 "Shit," she says, paralysed in an 'up'.
 She finally goes down again and puts Joseph in his bouncer. "Shit."
 She heads to the front door, a door that is rarely used. A big old cottage door. She again thinks of Gwyneth Paltrow and her sliding

door. She also thinks of her ex and the big old Victorian door.

She picks up three letters and two flyers.

One flyer for a local plumber called Bob with 'Bob the Builder' smiling below 'Can I fix it?' and above 'Yes I can!', both in a cheesy bubble font. She assumes local Bob has not paid any license fees.

The other is for Saga holidays featuring a highly heterosexual middle aged couple clinking wine glasses, Tenerife tanned and dressed head to toe in whitish cream, grinning at each other in a rather disturbing, demonic way.

She takes them all into the kitchen and decides to bin both flyers. The cottage needs no plumbing and she is very confident her own personal plumbing problems will work themselves out super soon, and she thinks her mum will shoot herself if she realises she is now being targeted by Saga.

So she is left with three white letters.

One is for her mum.

She is now left with two letters.

She sits at the kitchen table and looks at them both. Then over at Joseph. Then back to them both.

She goes and puts the kettle on. Makes a cup of tea and heats up a bottle for Joseph in a jug of boiling water. She tests it on her wrist.

"You're being ridiculous, Jen," she says and then looks at Joseph. "I can't change what's in it now, can I little man?"

Joseph stares back at her with a knowing look in his bright blue eyes.

"Ok, here we go," she agrees with him.

She opens the first one. It's about her student loan. "Fuck off," she says to it, then says "Sorry," to Joseph.

She is now left with one letter. The letter. Or maybe not.

She takes a slurp of tea as Joseph starts to whimper. He's hungry.

She opens it.

She reads it over and over and over again, not quite taking it in. Not quite believing it.

Name: Jennifer Jones
Award Type: Bachelor of Science
Subject: Management Science (BSc Hons)
Classification: First Class Honours

She bounces around the kitchen with the letter. Tigger bounces. She literally whoops. Against all odds, she has gone and got herself a first!

Then she cries, then Joseph cries. She picks him up and dances him round the kitchen before heading into the snug with him and his bottle.

She gets them both comfy on the sofa and starts to feed him. He stares up at her. Rhythmically bouncing to the sucking beat.

"Take a look at me now," she says, staring back at him. Grinning from ear to spock ear.

13th July 2000

Thursday. Interview Day.

Jen is terrified.

Em had asked for her results to be sent to her flat, not her Hertfordshire home. She got a high 2:1 and is satisfied with that. She is due over shortly to look after Joseph while Jen goes to her interview as Jen's mum is at work.

Lou got top of her class. Distinction. She is thrilled and the girls are thrilled for her. too She just needs to work out what she wants to do with her fabulous results.

Em is terrified. She has never looked after a baby before, and has certainly never prepped a newly babied friend for such an important meeting before.

She arrives a few minutes early. Her Clio clock tells her it is 13:13. She hopes this isn't an omen and doesn't tell Jen. Jen had asked her to give her a little time to get ready, for Em to role play some interview questions with her and also to ensure that Jen does not leave the house with a baby milk feature on her hot pink boxy cardigan.

Jen's interview is at 3:30pm.

As Joseph is happily sucking his dummy, Jen's hair already washed, mascara on and clothes hung up in her room ready for hot pink action, they decide to focus on the interview prep.

"Love a role play," Em says, twinkling.

"This is serious!" Jen admonishes.

"That's what I say when I'm a pushy police woman," she grins. "You should see my baton!"

"Emily," Jen yells. "I'll baton you in a minute."

"Ok, ok," Em concedes. "Right, let's get started."

Jen is as tight with tension as her virgin birth canal was. Em proceeds to ask all the right questions. She went to the library yesterday and took out a book. 'How to perform successfully in interviews'.

She has taken it really seriously and spent most of last night writing the questions she feels are the right ones to ask Jen. Had added in some curveballs, just in case. Knobhead ones like 'give me three words to describe yourself and why', 'if you were an animal, what would you be and why', 'what makes you better than the other candidates?' and 'what is your greatest weakness?'.

They decide to take ten minutes alone to do the 'knobby' ones and then compare notes.

Em's version:

Three words to describe yourself and why:

1) Goofy: because I'm hilariously ludicrous

2) Dipsy: because if it's going to happen, it will happen to me. I'm 'that' Teletubby

3) Tigger: because bouncing is what I do best

If you were an animal, what would you be and why?:

See above. All three.

What makes you better than the rest?:

- Great abs
- Bangin' arse
- Supernatural Spock ear

Greatest weakness:

- Will do anything for anyone to own detriment sometimes
- Shit at confrontation
- Gets emotional when drunk

Jen literally laughs out loud when she reads Ems' version of herself in 'knobhead question' form.

"Seriously," Jen asks, still laughing. "Is that who I am?"

"Well, not exactly," Em replies, glad Jen is laughing. She needed to do something to alleviate the tension in her. "On the animal front,

I'd have you as a labrador if I was to write it again."

"Why?"

"Because you're brave, bright, instinctive and loyal."

Jen smiles at this. She has always wanted a big dog, and especially an Old English Sheepdog or a labrador. A black labrador.

She had a little West Highland Terrier as a kid called Snowy. His shortened name from the ridiculous Kennel Club name her parents had given him. 'Saxifrage of Snowdon'. Snowdon. That very famous mountain in the Scottish Highlands? Her parents had promised that Snowy the Westie would grow into an Old English Sheepdog like the one that lived at the often frequented wine bar down the road from Blockbuster. He never did.

She adored her Snowy the dog nonetheless.

Final version:

Three words to describe yourself and why?:

1) Brave

2) Instinctive

3) Loyal

If you were an animal, what would you be and why?:

Labrador - because of the three reasons above

What makes you better that the rest?:

- I don't know the other candidates so I don't want to be cocky and assume I am better, but I can genuinely turn my hand to most things

- I am a great team player

- I am very industrious and bright, good at problem solving and storytelling

- I am also very passionate and people tend to warm to me

Greatest weakness:

- Personal confidence

- Dealing with conflict

"Thank you Em," Jen says when they finish the prepping. "You've made me laugh, if nothing else."

Em is a tiny bit pissed off with this. She had prepped a lot for the prepping. But she can see Jen is still tight with nervous energy so she lets it go.

After another thirty minutes or so of prepping with Em's pre-prepped questions, she looks at her watch. "You need to leave in ten minutes. Go on and get dressed. I'll watch him."

After a few minutes, Jen comes back into the kitchen.

"Wit woo. Take a look at you!" Em says. "You look amazing! Do a twirl."

Jen does a twirl, laughing. Joseph stares at his mum from his bouncer, sucking his dummy like Maggie from the Simpsons. Making the same funny noise.

"Honestly Jen, when you explained this outfit I was frankly a little horrified," Em admits. "But you absolutely bang in that!"

Jen laughs again at Ems Northern 'banging' and says, "Thank you. And thank you so much for today. You're an angel." Em knows she is absolutely no angel, but she hugs her friend and wishes her all the luck in the world.

"Right, here is the list of everything you need to know and do," Jen gives a piece of paper to Em. "He just needs feeding in about fifteen minutes, or whenever he starts to cry. Remember to burp him in the middle of his feed. You remember how to do that right? Otherwise he may puke it all up. His spare dummy is here. Spare clothes are there. The changing mat is over there with the nappies and wipes…"

"I've got this!" Em assures, interrupting her. "We won't need any spare clothes, we aren't going anywhere. And we've been through this so many times Jen. Just go. It's way past three. You're going to be late."

As Jen drives off in her Honey, Joseph starts to cry.

"Shit," Em says. "I so haven't got this."

She pops his dummy back in and follows the bottle heating instructions. She touches the teat then remembers she can't do that. She doesn't really know why. She gets another ready made bottle from the fridge. She is all fingers and thumbs, and Joseph starts to cry a little more indignantly now. "Shit. Shit," she repeats.

She finally gets it to a temperature she thinks is ok after it becomes too hot in its jug of boiling water and she has to sit it in the same jug, now full of cold water. She can't get a third bottle of milk from the fridge. That would be just inept. She hasn't touched the teat this time, which is a small success. She double checks by testing it on her right wrist, like Jen had said to do, and watches the milk running down the wounds and scars. She shakes her head.

As she goes to get the now screaming Joseph, she smells an almighty stench.

"For fuck's sake," she says. "Oh, sorry Joseph". She remembers Jen saying he will have a nap after his feed so best to change him before his bottle if he's wet or smelly.

She grabs the changing mat and puts it on the rug on the floor as she has seen Jen do. She then puts Joseph on the mat. The poo is smeared all up his vest and a browny yellowish liquid has escaped and infiltrated his baby grow. Poo water? What the fuck is that? He is now screaming.

She just stares at him and the poo water, and then looks for some gloves. There aren't any. Surely you need gloves for this sort of crap task? She somehow removes all his clothes and his nappy but ends up with poo and poo water all over her hands and arms. He is really screaming now and looking very cross with his little bird face scrunched up and bright red.

She grabs the wipes pack but can't open it. She rips the fucker open and, by mistake, drags out about thirteen wipes in one. She uses the full baker's dozen extravagantly and manages to de-dung his tiny body while he writhes resentfully, and then de-shit herself. She decides to de-poo-water the rug later.

"Now, where are those spare clothes?" she asks the wailing Joseph, realising she hadn't listened when Jen gave her the now needed advice and instructions.

She locates them and puts on his tiny little vest, having a proper quarrel with the poppers. "Little bastards," she shouts at them not realising she has put his little vest on the wrong way round. Back to back.

She abandons the prestigious pile of poo-ed wipes, popping the poppers and the shitty shaggy rug. She picks up Joseph in his open vest and his now truly tepid bottle, and heads for the snug.

"Well I think we completely smashed that," she laughs to the now quiet and happily sucking Joseph.

She stares down at him as he stares back up at her, rocking his rhythm. Totally content and trusting. She is completely relaxed in an instant, loving the purity and simplicity of it. Instinctively and beautifully moved by the force of nature she feels bubbling and growing inside her. Her eyes start to well. She feels a little overwhelmed, but is happy being whelmed. She thinks about her unborn baby sister or brother.

She is at peace for this short while, feeling flabbergasted that this little person is totally relying on her. And that she is clearly doing something right. She is giving him what he needs. She doesn't really realise that he is giving her exactly what she needs too.

"Just take a look at me now," she whispers to him proudly as his eyes start to flicker and close, very slowly.

14th July 2000

Em stayed over in the cottage.

By the time Jen got back it was nearly 5pm and her mum had already arrived home from her shift at the hospital. She had found the three of them sitting happily outside in the cottage courtyard with two large glasses of wine, one empty wine glass, a half emptied bottle of wine and an empty baby bottle.

The space was filled with sunshine.

She watched them for a little while through the criss-cross blue fence and smiled. Joseph was on her mum's knee and Em was telling a story with exaggerated arm movements and pretend crying. Joseph was clearly involved in whatever tale she was telling. "There was literally shit everywhere," she heard. "It was like poomaggedon." Her mum was laughing and ever so slightly shaking her head.

She opened the blue fence. Em suddenly stopped when she spotted her.

"What?" Jen asked.

"Absolutely nothing," her mum said, winking at Em. "Come and sit down and tell us all about it."

Jen regaled the last few hours with a slightly annoying summary of, "What will be, will be."

The foursome spent a lovely lazy evening drinking wine and chatting about not a lot. Jen didn't ask about poomaggedon. Em didn't tell.

Jen's mum left for work early this morning so it is just Em and Jen drinking tea in the kitchen. Jen and Joseph have been up for hours. Em stirred at just after 10am. It is now just past 10:30am.

Jen's phone rings. It's an unknown number. Jen just stares at it.

"Answer it!" Em insists.

"Hello," Jen says as she fast walks into the snug.

"Hi," unknown says. "It's Carla."

"Hi Carla," Jen says, not knowing what else to say.

"How are you this morning?" Carla asks warmly.

"Really well, thank you," Jen replies. "How are you?" The forced formality is awkward. She is aware she is speaking robotically.

"I am really well, thank you," Carla replies humanly. "It was really lovely to see you yesterday and to get to know you a bit better."

Jen is just about to jump on the pregnant pause when Carla continues.

"I am pleased to tell you that we would love you to come and join us," Carla says.

"Sorry, what did you say?" Jen fumbles.

"I would like to offer you the job," Carla says. "If you would like to accept it."

FUCKEDY FUCKEDY FUCKEDY FUCK !!!

"Really?" Jen questions, with all frames of fuck in her head. "Why?"

"Because you're by far the best applicant for the job," Carla says convincingly. "And I believe in you."

Against all odds (take a look at me now).
Mariah Carey & Westlife.

-34-
EM: OOPS!...I DID IT AGAIN

18th July 2000

Graduation day for Em and Jen. Lou's is later in the week.

Kate starts her summer work experience at Will's dad's law firm today. "Are you joking?" Em had said incredulously. "Isn't it spring still?"

Neither Em nor Jen have any family coming to their graduation. Em for her green reasons, Jen because her mum is attending her sister's graduation up in Scotland.

Neither Em nor Jen are particularly fussed, they both insist. They are happy to don their rented robes and go together. They are more excited about a new TV show launching tonight on Channel 4. 'Big Brother'.

"Big brother is watching you," Jen had quoted from George Orwell's novel 1984. Written in 1949. A little like when they saw 'The Beach' and didn't initially understand the reference to Orwell's Animal Farm, they currently have no real idea what 'Big Brother' is all about.

It has been advertised heavily over the last few weeks. The peculiar pixelated eye and Paul Oakenfold's masterpiece pervading homes across the country.

TV producers Joop van den Ende and John de Mol launched the first one in their native Netherlands last year under their, unknown to Brits, company Endemol. Apparently the 'housemates' have been in the first British 'Big Brother House' for a few days already. The devilishly cool Davina McCall from MTV and Streetmate is the host and it is being termed 'reality TV' and a 'social experiment', whatever that means.

One of Jen's old friends who had been in the tent (but not puce puked) is back home for a few weeks and offered to look after Joseph for a few hours while Jen goes into Manchester for her graduation.

The day goes without a hitch. Jen and Em wildly clap for each other when they respectively go up to receive their degrees, then they head to the newly opened Wagamama's in St Peter's Square

PAPER OVER IT

for a quick bite to eat before Jen heads home to pick up Joseph and stare at her certificate for the night with the company of her little baby and Big Brother.

Em is now alone in town. She has a good few hours to kill before Lou heads over from Liverpool to spend a few nights with her before her graduation on Wednesday. They are going to watch Davina and 'Big Brother' together. Lou's parents are just coming over for the day on the train. Kate has promised she will come over on Saturday to celebrate their graduation with them. She and Lou will stay over at Em's with the recently rescued Hairy Potter from the recently released No. 52 in Withington. Em has no idea how long her flat will be an option. For her, the quartet, Steve or Hairy.

She decides to go for a mooch in town, still in possession of daddy's plastic fantastic. She wanders aimlessly and buys yet another pair of trainers. Oops, she does it again. She has shit loads of trainers.

She finds herself in Mothercare, randomly. She looks around at all the cute clothes and gets a little emotional. She is not sure why. Whilst admiring the cutest little pink cord dress and matching pink tights she ponders how long it has been since she spoke to her dad or Charlie. Since 'Bad Friday'.

"It must be nearly three months now," she ponders to the pink.

She had thought many times about that day. Had wanted to pick up the phone and call Charlie, or her dad. She couldn't quite believe that neither of them had been in touch. Had not even texted to ask her how she is, how she has done in her degree, when her graduation was. Her stubborn is possibly even stronger than her green. She has spoken to her mum a few times, but she is now living in France and Em had not told her until the last minute when her graduation was so she couldn't make it back in time. Em knows she had done this on purpose. It was Charlie and her dad she had wanted there. She didn't realise how cruel this was to her mum. Her mum had been really quite upset. She had upset her mum numerous times over the last few years and oops, she had gone and done it again.

The bitterness between her parents means she can't ask her mum about her dad. She doesn't even know whether she knows about Eve's pregnancy. She hasn't asked her mum and her mum never said anything. They could, however, talk about Charlie. After graduating last year he has been living in London working in the City at an investment bank. He is doing really well, making a lot of money. If that is 'doing really well'. Something to do with mortgages. He still has no particular girlfriend, but has plenty of girlfriends.

She randomly buys the little three-month-old pink outfit. She is really not sure why.

It is just before 3pm, still three hours before Lou's train pulls into Piccadilly. All the baby stuff reminds her of Ally McBeal. Her legal mind hallucinating in the boardroom of Cage & Fish imagining a funky baby dancing on the table. Symbolic of the fear she has of her biological clock.

Not biology, chemistry or physics, but computer science was guilty of creating the similar dancing internet baby. Baby Cha Cha. The 3D rendered nappy clad sensation still makes Em laugh.

She decides to grab a bottle of something and head back to her flat. She thinks she will go on the internet and check out Baby Cha Cha again. And maybe look to see if there is anything interesting or useful on being a step-sister.

Beep-boop-bop-beep-eeeeekkkkrrr-ding-dang-dong-pshhhhhhhhhhhhhhhkkkkkhhhhhkkkkkhhhhh

Em sits and waits for the internet to load, glass of white wine in hand. Listening to the dulcet tones of the 56k dial up connection.

You have to have an email to 'surf' at uni. All four girls had created their own at university in the computer labs. Their 'monikers'. It was a battle between Hotmail and Yahoo. Some chose stupid names. Some didn't. The ones that chose stupid names tend to have to put numbers after their names, because they are in a pool of other people sharing the stupid monikers.

The quartets emails are as follows:

em.luvscock69@hotmail.co.uk
kate.bigtits3@yahoo.co.uk
jennifer.jones@hotmail.co.uk
lou.dancing12@yahoo.co.uk

Some monikers have a future. Some don't.

She goes outside and finishes the half spliff in the ashtray while thinking about Monica from Friends quotes. "We're supposed to start having fun in fifteen minutes!" is one of her favourites from the latest season. Season six. Em really relates to Monica. Her friends say they see similarities. Controlling, stubborn, hot headed, compulsive and slightly annoying - yet loveable.

When she gets back inside, the internet is finally working. It feels like it has taken longer than Monica's fifteen minutes to fun. It is all scrunched links, pixelated images and shocking search bars. It's brilliant and game changing!

She has always used either Yahoo or Ask Jeeves as her search engine, but there is a new kid in town. Google. It hasn't been around long but the computer geeks at uni had told them about it and had said, "It's really fast and delivers highly relevant results", whatever that means. She goes to Google and types in 'step sister'. She trawls the results for a few minutes not finding anything of particular interest. Nothing highly relevant.

She then goes to www.britannica.com, the biggest encyclopaedia website, just to pass some time. It has something flashy on it. It asks her to update her flash player. She is confident she did this only yesterday. She updates it, again. She has no idea what she is doing and why.

As she takes a sip from her vino she hears her buzzer buzz.

"Hello," she says.

"Open up, Emster."

Em's heart literally races. It's her brother.

"Ok," is all she can say. She presses the button.

She is half hyper-ventilating, half terrified.

She opens the door.

"Hi Emster" he greets her.

"Charliebobs," she falls into his big arms.

"You ok?" he asks.

"Not really," she says honestly, slightly crumbling.

"Got a drink?" he asks. "It's been a hell of a drive up."

"Wine?" she replies.

"No, a proper drink."

"Like what?"

"Whiskey."

"No." When the fuck did he start drinking whiskey?

"Well go for a whiskey walk then," he doesn't ask, he tells. She can feel he is still furious with her. "I need a shit. We can talk properly when you're back."

Em goes to the shop.

Back at the flat, Charlie's kids happily dropped off at the pool, the siblings sit in the lounge.

"You ok?" he asks for the second time.

"No," she answers honestly for the second time. "What are you doing here?"

They spend the following hour or so catching up while sipping whiskey on the rocks. Or rather Em catching up on how much she is on the rocks with her dad. And with Charlie. She learns that her stepsister is due to be born on Halloween. It's a girl. She is getting a sister. They are getting pink and tights. Charlie tells her how pissed off her dad still is with her. How disappointed he is. Hurt, angry, cross and disappointed. How he is really serious and will not back down. Em tries to put forward her point of view, but it is in vain. She knows she is defeated.

"Does he know you're here?" Em asks weakly.

"No. But this is it this time, Em. You've done this so many times and he's finally snapped. You can't just paper over it this time. No more 'oops I did it' again shit. Eve has told him to call you quite a few times, but he just says no," Charlie says. "You can both be so bloody stubborn, but Em it's you that's being stupid too."

"I know," admits Em, starting to cry. She knows she's done it again. But for the last and final time. It's serious shit. "What do I do?"

"You have burnt a lot of bridges, and a lot of water has run under the burnt bridges. It's fire and water. The most destructive things on the planet, but also the most needed," Charlie has an amazing way with words, annoyingly so. "You need to work out how to rebuild things. Dad is like fire and Eve is like water. Together they are perfect, and you have spent a long time being destructive, trying to destroy them. This is not just about saying oops and sorry now. You need to grow up and come up with a way of genuinely showing...."

Before Charlie can finish, Em's buzzer buzzes. "It'll be Lou," Em says through her tears.

Charlie gets up, presses the button to let Lou in and heads out to the balcony for a fag.

"To be continued," he promises Em.

Em stands up and dries her eyes whilst looking at her puffy face in the mirror above the fireplace. Lou's mirror. She looks slightly pathetic. She feels pathetic too. She hates both of her pathetics.

There is no more 'Oops' or 'Oopsy daisy'. She realises this now.

She can't do it again.

She needs to get a grip.

She needs to grow up.

Oops!...I did it again.
Britney Spears.

-35-
LOU: LET ME BE YOUR FANTASY

18th July 2000 – continued

"What the hell is the matter?" Lou asks her clearly emotional friend when she walks through the flat door, concerned.

"I'm fine."

"Looks like it," Lou replies.

"Drink?" Em offers.

"Always," Lou responds as her red curls and aquamarine eyes automatically turn towards the balcony door as it opens.

"Hello," Charlie says.

"Hello," Lou synchronises.

"Fuck," Em says, almost being bolted backward by the sudden energy in the room.

"Hi," Charlie repeats his greeting, using a different H.

"Hi," Lou responds, repeating his alternative H.

"Charlie meet Lou. Lou meet Charlie," Em muses, acutely aware of the sexual tension that has instantly pervaded her flat. Also glad it has taken Lou's attention off her.

"Pleased to meet you, Lou," Charlie flirts. Something like ecstasy inside him rising, firing. He hopes he doesn't mistakenly make an Eton mess.

"Ditto," Lou robs Em's 'Ghost', something inside her smoking. Something way down inside. Her fanny is on fire. Not in a cystitis way - in a good way. She clenches her suddenly clammy clunge.

"Get a fucking room, you pair," Em teases. "I'm going to bed for a bit."

Em is shattered by the day. The parent-less graduation, Charlie's unannounced visit, their difficult chat, what she now knows she has to do, but unsure exactly how to do it. Conflicted and confused. The wine, the whiskey, the Hairy Potter, her green. It's not yet six thirty but she heads to her bedroom. She is one hundred percent sure her big brother and friend will not miss her for a few hours. She laughs at what she has just witnessed. She can't wait to tell Kate and Jen. But for now, she just needs to lie down and think.

"I always get to where I am going by walking away from where I have been," said Pooh.

"Fancy going out for a bit and playing pool?" Lou asks Charlie. "I'm pretty good at it. A bit of a legend, in fact."

"Are you challenging me?" Charlie replies, raising one eyebrow James Bond style.

"Yes," Lou challenges him, grinning her cheeky grin. The first of many times she will challenge him.

"Ok," he accepts the challenge. He loves competition. He can tell she does too. It is the first of many times he will accept one of Lou's occasionally crazy challenges.

They walk down Deansgate to a pub Lou knows. She explains that she is a dancer and a performing arts student. He could tell from her amazing toned body and strong, muscled legs and arms that she was some sort of athlete. He now understands where her clear fire and competitiveness comes from.

With Charlie towering about a foot higher than Lou in her trainers and short dungarees, they are immediately comfortable in each other's little and large company. Jen's little dancing steps going faster and faster as he strides out to keep up with her. They end up running, racing each other. Already in competition.

In the pub, Lou asks for a pint. "It'll be nearly as big as you," Charlie teases, ordering two pints.

"You are a knob," she replies easily, used to references to her small frame. "Got some twenty pence pieces? You're paying for the pool now too."

"Say pool again," Charlies asks.

"Pool," Lou says. "Why?"

"Pee-oool," he mimics her scouse. "Liverpee-oool."

"Are you taking the piss?" Lou admonishes spiritedly. "That's why I never go for the posh twats. Always think they're a cut above."

"I'm really sorry," Charlie realises he may have upset her, that he may have been rude. "I didn't mean anything by it. I think your accent is adorable! Just like Cilla Black."

"Cilla? Is that meant to make me feel better?" Lou's fire is burning stronger. She doesn't really know where this over-passion is coming from. She starts to think that this very impromptu non-date date is a mistake. "Piss off you dick," she looks away, weird emotions interfering with her.

"I'm honestly sorry. Can we please start over?" Charlie takes her hand. He is surprised by his retreating reaction to this defeat, he is usually really competitive. He also usually couldn't really care less if he pisses off a girl. But he really doesn't want to rile this fiery dazzling dancer. Or does he?

Lou looks up at him, into his gorgeous blue eyes. "If you promise to never call me Cilla the dwarf again, I will consider it." She knows she has probably over reacted.

Charlie laughs out loud. "I did not call you a dwarf," he clarifies. "Or a Cilla," he adds.

"Pygmy promise?" she asks, sticking out her little finger. Not really listening to him.

"That is actually really offensive," Charlie says, jumping on the opportunity to take back an element of control. His competitiveness rising. He is totally bemused and fascinated by this red ringleted stunner and her scouse sparkiness.

"What's offensive?"

"Pygmy."

"Is it?" She had no idea. Her dad calls it her all the time. "What about dwarf? Isn't that offensive? You called me a dwarf!"

"I did not call you a dwarf," he says for the second time.

"Did you not?"

"No!" he is now laughing out loud again. "For the third time, I did not call you a dwarf."

"Oh right," it's Lou's turn to accept defeat as she remembers it was her small offensive word. In fact both offensive words had been hers. She knew she was fiery, but this boy created more fire in her than anyone she had ever met. "Start over?" she asks.

"Ok," Charlie agrees. "Let's go play pee-oool."

Lou pushes his chest, feeling the strength and size of his pectoralis major. She wonders what the strength and size of his penis major is.

"You are a knob," he laughs, repeated her northern insult, while he grabs her wrists and kisses her. Not a long, tongued kiss. Just a quick yet perfect simple kiss.

It is not yet 7:30pm. They have known each other just over an hour.

In that time they have had their first race, their first argument and their first kiss.

They take their pints over to the pool table in surprised silence. Two lads have just started a game on the pool table but they have placed no money on the side so Lou puts down the three twenty pence coins Charlie gave her on the way over. Manchester and Liver-pool etiquette means they will have at least three uninterrupted games.

They play beer mat flipping while they wait.

One of the lads pots the black well before he intends to pot the black to the hilarity of his mate, and then annoyance as he realises their game is now over. "Dick 'ed," he calls his mate.

Lou puts a twenty pence coin into the metal mechanism and pushes it. The four balls the lads managed to pot tumble down to the end of the table. Lou grabs the triangle and starts to sort the spots, stripes and black.

"That's not right," Charlie says, taking over the sorting of the balls. Much to Lou's annoyance.

"Twat" she says under her breath. "Dick," he replies under his. They lock eyes and grin. Both pretty certain the two vulgarisms will meet at some point fairly soon.

Lou, much to her frustration, epic fails at the first game. He overwhelmingly whips her. She just can't get her angles. She is discombobulated, somehow. Out of balance and sync. She tries desperately to combobulate herself. She is highly frustrated as she is normally really good at this, has often beaten her dad at their local since she was about fifteen. She is almost shaking with chagrin in the second game.

Charlie has got them another pint each. She necks half of it.

"Would you like some help?" Charlie asks cheekily when her little legs and arms mean she has to perch on the table for a tricky shot. "You have to keep at least one foot on the floor at all times," he preaches.

"Fuck me, you are your sister's brother," Lou chastises. "I'll show you keeping your feet on the flippin' floor!"

Knowing she is in no state to beat him today at pool, but with a carnal need to win, she jumps up on the pool table and executes a perfect box split, her fu-fu hitting the green felt. Her dungaree shorts defending her dignity. She then leans forward in her wide legged split and puts her elbows on the felt, cups her chin in her hands and looks up at him under her eyebrows with a mixture of provocative prostitute and charming child.

Charlie can't cope. It really very nearly is an Eton mess.

Lou wins. Hands down. The boyish, excited smile she's put on his face is her trophy.

He leans down to her face, unaware the full pub is staring at the sexy scene, and kisses her. Kisses her properly. She takes her hands from her own face, cups his and kisses him back in his warm embrace. She knows instantly she's got what it takes to make him hers. To make her his fantasy.

Their little trip to wonderland is a fantastically electric moment, for everyone in the vicinity.

Let me be your fantasy.
Baby D.

-36-
THE QUARTET: GO LET IT OUT

1st August 2000

Brad and Jen have just got married and Big Brother has been on for exactly two weeks now. The quartet is hooked. On both BJ and BB.

Anna the brilliant guitar playing Irish lesbian ex-nun, Andy the adorable scouse builder, Nick the nasty stockbroker and a flock of cheeky chickens. Melanie, Darren and Tom. Just ordinary people. Plus a few more less memorable housemates.

All let in, not wanting to be let out. For now.

Kate, a big George Orwell fan, has educated them on why this is so aptly titled. The divine Davina is fabulously holding the fort.

"You are live on Channel 4, please do not swear."

Potter's wheel wheeled, shopping lists listed, housemate facts remembered, stripping sessions and wall body prints completed, first nominations placed and the housemate termed 'self-centred', tofu loving Sada was the first to be evicted on Friday. To be let out.

The quartet have never seen anything like it. It's mental. Do they not realise that everything they say and do is being shown to the nation? They are all like clowns capering in a sawdust ring. It is annoyingly addictive viewing.

Jen has been given her start date for work. The 4th of September. Five weeks away. Joseph will be just eleven weeks old. Her salary is £12,500 pa. She is excited and terrified. She has been invited to a conference at a hotel in Manchester the week before she starts. A day and night away. She needs to work out what to wear. She needs to sort a nursery quickly. She needs to work out her finances. She needs to sort some form of wardrobe to wear to work generally. She needs to tell the dole people she no longer needs their welcome weekly support. She needs to understand if there are any benefits for a single working mum. Her ex clearly adores his son, but is frankly no help at all. She is not surprised. There is an awful lot she needs to do. She feels out of control. She needs to let it all out. She has been sick most days this week.

Kate is really enjoying her work experience at Will's dad's law firm in Chester. Loves the name badge and lanyard she was given on her first day. Kate Karam. Legal Intern. She kept looking at it. Made sure it was on display and the right way round when she went out on a coffee run.

Will's dad decided to pay her a small amount so she can focus on this rather than worry about money. It is not a small amount to Kate. She sacks off the summer Dolcis job. Even in a short time she has become a much liked asset to his team, more than worth the money. She has a naturally talented way of looking at things in a way that the rest of his team doesn't. A different perspective.

He also likes her being around generally, as does Will's mum. She is like the daughter they never had. And she is a clearly bright light in their son's life, helping him through his recovery in a way they are acutely aware they can't. Kate could not feel more lucky.

Will is improving every day and has decided to go back to Manchester Uni and re-do his final year. He is unlikely to play any contact sport like rugby again, but has started to try and play standing tennis with Kate and his parents on the court in their garden. Kate had never picked up a racket before, had hated tennis, but is now learning to really enjoy it. Finding it rather therapeutic. And swimming has become Will's daily physio too after his head injury and multiple broken bones.

Will and Kate have had sex numerous times in the outdoor pool at night, thinking they were being discreet. Will's dad clapped him on the back one morning before going to work saying, "Now that's what I call water sports, son." Kate nearly died when Will told her.

Will will be at uni with Kate as she is doing her final year too. They are inseparable. Not in a competitive, slightly toxic Charlie and Lou way. They are hopelessly different but amazingly connected. Like two jigsaw pieces. They have been in touch with the landlord of No. 52 in Withington to see if the recently released house is still available. They would want a bedroom each for them to have their own space when they need it, and for when either want to have friends to stay. Surprisingly it is. Some well-deserved luck. And he has another pair in their final year interested too. Sorted. Will will live between his home in Chester and No. 52 in Withington depending on how he feels and what appointments and meetings he has, both medical and academic. The university is fully supportive. They don't sign on the line yet, but in principle they tell the landlord they will take it.

Kate went home last weekend to Glasgow to see her family. They are super proud of her working for a legal firm, but also miss her dreadfully. They had assumed she would go back up for the summer. They had been really worried about Will, had met him a few times and were as surprised as Kate how much they liked him. "Even though he is a toff," her dad had said. She had an amazing time with her family and promised to take Will up next time.

Lou didn't have sex with Charlie on night one. They both stayed over at Em's, on her sofa. The threesome watched Big Brother after Lou and Charlie got back from playing pee-oool and box split snogging. They did everything other than penetrate. Lou treated Charlie to her lavishly long tongue.

They have been in touch daily since and Lou went to see him in London the following weekend. He had sent her a train ticket from Liverpool Lime Street to London Euston for the Friday afternoon so she couldn't really refuse, and didn't really want to. She was just a little annoyed at the control he had stamped on the situation.

She let him in on night two, Friday night. Incredible competitive sex. They were very ready to. Eddie who? They also fought both nights, about something ridiculous. Had really let it out. First an argument about whether pasta was better served on a plate or in a bowl. Then an argument about whether you should put cheese on a pasta dish that contained seafood. Another time a squabble about whether Posh Spice was actually posh, and whether Ginger Spice's growler was actually ginger. And the obvious heated conversation about whether pineapple should exist on pizza.

But the make-up sex was hot like a cacciatore spicy Italian sausage. Sometimes long and firm like a fettuccine fantasy, sometimes short and slightly twisted like a fusilli fantasy.

Lou absolutely loved London. She had been once as a child but doesn't really remember it. She insisted on going on an open-top tourist bus. Charlie said that the best view was from the bottom of the bus, not wanting anyone to see him. Lou bounced up the steps to the top and perched herself right in the middle in full view. Five minutes later he conceded and joined her. He watched her joy as they drove past Buckingham Palace, Big Ben, Downing Street, The British Museum, The Tower of London, Baker Street,

Madame Tussauds and Pudding Lane. She listened intently to the guide, Mike, on his mike. She asked him loads of questions. She was transfixed, mesmerised. Mike was actually really funny and very well informed. Charlie's initial embarrassment turned to genuine interest as Mike described and explained things he never knew.

She jumped up as they approached Covent Garden and bounced down the stairs. "Bye, Mike, and thank you," she grinned as she went. Mike laughed with her and at Charlie as he rolled his eyes and followed her like a slightly sulky teenage boy following his mother into a clothes shop to buy something 'smart'.

Covent Garden was somewhere Charlie never went as it is apparently "for tourists", but the baseball cap that Lou insisted he bought her earlier on from a street trader with 'I Love London' written in a heart shaped Union Jack, and the huge map she kept opening and closing, made the couple look like tacky tourists anyway. She looked super cute in it with her red curls bobbing from underneath it. He rolled with it all, laughing.

They had al fresco pasta watching the street performers. Jen was transfixed like a child. She asked for parmesan on her seafood linguine, and didn't say 'when' like the waiter had asked her to 'say when'. He just carried on grating, slightly awkwardly. Her prawns and mussels were swimming in the rich, nutty cheese. Charlie shook his head at the fishy fromage farce.

Post her parmesan with a side portion of pasta pescatore, she walked to the Royal Ballet School following her map as he followed her, then to The Royal Opera House and theatreland. Starlight Express, Cats, The Phantom of the Opera, Les Miserables and The Rocky Horror Picture Show. Lou's excitement was palpable. She didn't want to leave this city, this place or this vibe. Stood in front of the Lyceum Theatre, looking up at the big shiny Lion King sign, Charlie was pleased he had bought tickets for the pair on a whim a few days ago to see the show that night.

Em would normally be heading out to Barbados for the summer to the family beach house. She would not see her beach this summer. Charlie had told her that Eve was having some difficulties with morning sickness. It just hadn't gone away in the second trimester like with most women. She had been diagnosed with hyperemesis gravidarum. It sounded serious. Anything with hyper and grav in it sounds serious.

At six months pregnant Eve still feels horribly nauseous daily and does not want to fly long haul so Barbados is out for her and Em's dad too. She had even left her thirtieth birthday party early a few weeks ago grumbling to her friends about the stupidity of it being called 'morning sickness'. "Well, it's always morning somewhere, I suppose," she quipped.

Eve rarely complains, so her friends knew how bad she must feel. She was pleased when the summer holidays had started and she could finish work at the school. Teaching groups of thirty rowdy kids algebra, probability and statistics while feeling sick had not been easy. Her husband was also pleased. He doesn't understand why she chooses to work, she certainly doesn't have to. But she loves it, and he massively respects her for it.

Em has done a lot of soul searching and Big Brother watching over the last few weeks. The revolutionary live feed meant she could watch at any hour of the day. She has watched people make fools of themselves on TV, make mistakes. Break the rules. Be selfish, angry, petulant, stubborn, bitchy, hot headed, green, kind and supportive. BB has helped her come to terms with her own mistakes in a quite crazy but constructive way. She realises she wants her own eviction to stop now. Her self made eviction. She wants to be let in, not out.

After a long chat with Charlie the day after the Big Brother launch, she decided to write her dad a letter so that her emotions can't get the better of her. So that she can explain, apologise and propose action all in one, removing all anger, green and stubbornness. She has also decided to write a letter to Eve too. She realises now she needs to let it all out to be able to be let in again. She does not know which letter she will find more difficult. So far she has written 'Dad' at the top of at least thirteen pieces of paper, and hasn't written Eve once. She decides to swallow her pride and enlist some help. To finally explain what is going on. Time is running out.

Jen is coming over on Friday night for a few hours to watch the Big Brother eviction. She is getting the train in and out. Last train home is 23:13. Jen's ex had asked to have him for the night but Jen is not ready for it, and she knows he probably isn't either. He has taken him for an hour or so a few times, but that had been with his lovely mum too. Jen says maybe in a few more weeks. He agrees. His new accepting, agreeing self. Joseph is staying at home with Jen's mum. Em has also asked Kate and Lou over. They haven't confirmed yet.

They have all set a date for their next quartet big night out. With babies and holidays, geography and money, work commitments and family things, it is not until the 2nd September. A whole month away. The Saturday before Jen starts work and two nights after her big work conference night. Three weeks before Kate starts her final year. Nights out used to be so spontaneous! What the hell has happened?

Jen asks her mum if it's ok to let her out for two nights in the same week. She has no problem with it at all. She is just really proud of her and pleased she is sorting her life out for herself and Joseph.

Above all, if she is brutally honest, she is relieved.

4th August 2000
Big Brother Eviction night.

Jen's mum gets home from work at 4:15pm and Jen gets the 5:12pm train to Manchester Piccadilly. She gets to Em's at just after 6pm. She is thrilled to find out that, last minute, Kate and Lou are coming too. They won't arrive until about eight thirty. So the quartet will be all together sooner than September. How very spontaneous!

This gives Em over two hours of Jen. Just Jen.

She seizes the opportunity. Jen is a great storyteller and writer, far better than she is. She had done English Literature A-Level and work experience in the northern office of The Guardian in Upper Sixth form when she thought she wanted to be a journalist. She needs her help.

"I have a challenge for us," Em says, popping open two bottles of Sol and pushing a wedge of lime in each.

"Like a Big Brother challenge?" Jen asks, intrigued. Sipping her Sol.

"Well I suppose so, if the challenge involves writing an apology letter to your dad and your pregnant step-mother."

Jen chokes mid slurp and bubbles start frothing from the bottle neck and onto the rug. "Shit," she says. "Sorry," still slightly gagging from the Sol going down the wrong way.

"For the fact I have to write two awful letters, or that you've beered my rug. Again?" Em smiles ruefully.

"Both?" Jen answers with a question tone. "Tell me everything, Em. Let it out. It's time. Let me in."

Jen had loved hearing Lou talk about her and Charlie, how they had met, the pee-oool, the trip to London, The Lion King. And how it is genuinely all like a lesson in chemistry. Competitive conflict chemistry. She isn't sure that this level of passion and intensity is the foundation for a lasting relationship, but she can see how much fun Lou is having. How bright her voice had sounded on the phone, especially when she spoke about theatreland.

She is also really pleased that Charlie had come up north to see his sister. He called her a few days before to tell her he was, as he promised he would, but they had both agreed to keep both of their conversations to themselves. She got a vibe that Charlie may feel a bit guilty that he hadn't been in touch with his little sister, that it had taken a call from her friend to stir him into action.

Em proceeds to tell her everything. She obviously doesn't tell her absolutely everything. Who ever does? Just the 'everything' she chooses to tell her. She finally lets it all out.

It's enough. Jen gets the gist and understands the gravity of the situation. She doesn't interrupt or ask any questions. She just lets Em talk. She is sure Em is not telling the whole truth, but she can see how difficult this is for her. How the pride she is swallowing is causing her pain. The length of time it has been since she last had any contact with her dad is what adds genuine gravitas to the gravity of the situation. Fifteen weeks. A long time. Not far off a third of a year. And the time until her baby sister is born is not that long. Time is ticking and slowly running out.

When Em comes to a natural end, she asks, "What is it you want to say, Em?"

With that, Em's flood gates open. Her water flows, her destructive water. Jen is shocked by the honesty, the self-deprecation and the emotion. No fire, just water. It is so not Em, the lack of fire. But it is clearly so very needed.

"That I'm sorry. I'm scared. I'm lonely. I miss him. I miss Charlie. I feel so excluded and ignored. I have for ages. I am actually really excited about the new baby now. I want to be part of her life. I want to try and be a good sister. To be part of the family. To be wanted. To be loved. I don't want them to hate me. I want to make it better. I want him to understand how everything has affected me since I was a little girl. I want to feel less angry, less jealous. I want him to love me like he used to love me. I want to understand why I have been like this, why it hurts so much, why I think he has chosen her over me. Why haven't I been able to talk about it? Can things ever be ok again? I want to make it better. I just want to make it better." Em is now full of tears, but empty of her water. She has finally let it out. "I've been so, so sad, Jen. For such a long time."

Jen pulls her friend into her and hugs her. She can feel her quietly sobbing. Her words are juvenile, regressive and bordering on self pity. Her saturated soliloquy is vulnerable, childlike and slightly pathetic. In the almost three years she has known her, she has never experienced Em show any sort of emotion like this. It is quite shocking to witness. It has literally poured out of her in a tumbling, bubbling tide. Like an Olympic whitewater canoe course. Erratic, rapid and intense. A heady mix of upstream and downstream. A slalom of raw, infantile sorrow.

She knows it has taken a lot for her to open up like this. She can't quite believe the strength of despair and grief Em is feeling and has felt for such a long time. This must be very deep rooted. This is far more than simple jealousy of Eve. This is a lifetime of papering over it. These are adolescent tears which have been in her for many years.

They stay like this for a little while until Em's sobs slightly subside.

"Em, tell me about your wrist," Jen says, softly.

Em admits to what she has been doing and how horrified she has been with herself and her self-harm. Still is mortified with herself but has been struggling to stop doing it. She does not self-pity or make any excuses as her lowered head slightly shakes and her eyes stare down.

"Promise me that you will never, ever do anything like that again," Jen says seriously. "And if you ever feel like you might, that you call me immediately."

Em keeps her head down but her eyes look up at her friend. She nods.

"I'm being really serious, Jen. It's frightening. In fact, it's terrifying.

If you go too deep you could kill yourself."

"Please don't tell anyone, Jen," Em pleads.

"It's a difficult secret to keep," Jen says, but then thinks how she would feel if she finally ever confided in anyone about her bulexia/anoremia and they let it out. Her own self harm. But that won't kill her, right? She thinks for a second, having an inner turmoil, and says, "If this ever happens again, Em, I will call your father myself. Is that clear?"

"Yes," Em nods. "Thank you. I swear I will never harm myself again. I promise." She doesn't know if she can keep this promise, but she knows she will try.

"Right. Where's a pen and paper?" Jen asks. Knowing that even if Em doesn't ever harm herself again, she absolutely will. Harm her knuckles, her insides and her teeth most days.

Just not her wrists.

Go let it out.
Oasis.

-37-
THE QUARTET: THONG SONG

1st August 2000 – continued

Jen and Em sit for nearly two hours and collectively craft two letters. No mention of Em's last admission and promise.

"Let's start with some key bullet points for each letter," Jen says practically. "Try to get your thoughts and objectives down, and into some sort of sensible order and key actions."

"We're not writing a fucking strategy document," Em says laughing, having collected herself. Grateful for her friend and her help.

"Yes, Em," Jen replies. "That's exactly what we're doing. We absolutely are."

The bullet points are written. One set for her dad, one for Eve.

Then Jen starts to work them into a constructive, rational flow. As prescriptive and primary school as it is, it genuinely helps….

- How do I feel?
- Why do I feel like this?
- What am I sorry for?
- Why am I sorry?
- What am I going to do about it?

Jen leads and Em edits. Then Jen edits Em's edit. Connects the dots. Tells the story.

By 8:02pm they have finished. Both edits complete. Both letters re-written neatly. Both pieces of paper tippexed in a couple of places. Both end with 'Love from Emily'.

Both girls are exhausted. Em by the emotional effort of it. Jen by Em.

"Envelopes?" Jen asks wearily. "Stamps?"

"No, sorry," Em replies, equally wearily. "I'll get some tomorrow."

"No chance!" Jen affirms. "I'll move my butt and go to the shop for stamps and envelopes, and find a post box. These letters are leaving this flat tonight! Write your home address on this piece of paper."

With that Jen leaves the flat on a mission, the letters burning a hole in her pocket a bit like the fag had in her bag all those months ago. She buys two envelopes and two first class stamps. Twenty-seven pence each. So scandalous! She considers buying second class, but plumps for the more expensive Queen.

While Jen is out, Em busies herself rolling some big fat Hairy Potters. Thinking. Wishing she had a wand and could cast a spell. Make everything better. Like a wizard. She stores the spliffs safely in a cup in the little cupboard where she stores her cups in her kitchen.

She wonders why a cupboard is called a cupboard. And why do we not have a plateboard or a panboard or even a shoeboard? Or, in fact, just a board? You say plate cupboard, pan cupboard and shoe cupboard. But it sounds stupid to say cup cupboard, when that is exactly what it is. She ponders for a while and thinks she may ask the girls later. She clearly needs them here to take her mind off such totally irrelevant, mindless things. Like cupboards.

Jen asks the miserable man behind the counter at the shop to borrow a pen for a sec to write the addresses on the envelopes.

"No. But you can buy one," he replies, without looking up from page three of his newspaper.

"Dick," she replies, under her breath. Followed by a louder "Fine".

She copies Em's address with her new orange Bic biro, licks the envelopes, gives herself a tongue paper cut, licks the stamps with her stinging tongue, manages to stick both of the stamps on a little wonkily, so the Queen looks like she has had a few bevvies, and heads for the post box she saw on the way on Deansgate.

As she approaches the scarlet cylinder with its impressive girth and protruding cap, like a circumcised bell-end, she notices the Queen's royal cypher ER on the trunk. She laughs to herself for a second as she posts the letters through the urethra. Emily Roberts' initials printed on this crimson, cast iron cock. Of course they are!

Back at Em's flat, Lou has arrived. It's just after 8:30pm.

"Where have you been?" she asks Jen. Em has clearly not updated her on the last few hours, and it is not Jen's story to tell. Even though she has just very eloquently written her story for her.

"Just had to pop out for a pen," she panics, pulling the Bic out of her pocket and purposely displaying it like the puerile prop it is.

Lou looks at her strangely, head cocked, then eyeballs the random orange ballpoint, then her gaze shoots back to Jen. Eyebrows raised, theatrically questioning.

Before Lou can ask anything, Em deflects Em style. "Anyone any idea where Kate is up to?"

"Yes, I've just spoken to her," Lou is dutifully deflected, always loving to know more than others. "She'll be here in about five minutes."

More Sols are cracked open and the trio go out onto the balcony. They have fifteen minutes until the Big Brother eviction night starts. Andrew and Caroline have been nominated by their housemates.

"How's Charlie, Lou?" Em asks cheekily.

"He's your big brother, Em" she sasses back, slurping her Sol.

"Yes, but thankfully I've never spent the night on my sofa with my big brother," Em shoots back, a little too sharply. She is still unsure about this romping budding romance. Her Charliebobs. Her gruesome green is a little grown, her terrible teenage mutant ninja mildly nudged. She hates herself for it and collects herself quickly just as Lou opens her mouth. "Sorry Lou, I'm sorry. Please ignore me."

"Who is this person?" Lou asks, stunned at Em's self-deprecation. "Jen. What the hell did you do with Em?"

"Dunno," Jen laughs slightly ludicrously. "I just went out for a new pen and came back to a new Em."

"Back to the pen," Lou is now totally confused with new pens and new Ems.

Just at this moment Em's buzzer buzzes. Both Em and Jen shoot up, saved from the new Em and the new pen by Em's bell.

Lou stays seated on the balcony, befuddled. Until Kate comes outside. "Lou!" she goes in for a cuddle. "Come on in. It's about to start."

Before Lou can even start to regale the strange conversation she has just had, Kate goes back inside. "Will and I have been watching every second, we are right sad bastards we are," Lou hears her tell Em and Jen as she bounces onto the sofa, copping her Big Brother spot.

Lou knows she will get no pen or pal answers now, so concedes and makes her way inside. Copping her own spot next to Kate on the sofa, in the middle. Em is already sat in the chair. Jen, heading back from a wee, bounces over the back of the sofa to plant herself next to Kate. Knocking Kate's Sol in the process. "For the sake of fuck," Em berates from her chair. Steve the Cheese is happily viewing from his pot spot next to his old pal the pouffe and his new, slightly pungent acquaintance Hairy Potter.

The Big Brother housemates have collectively ridden their exercise bike 1,800km, the same distance as Land's End to John O'Groats, have written and performed a play, succeeded at their Shakespeare shenanigans and won the right to watch a movie and had chosen to watch 'Happy Gilmore'. All in a week.

It's Andrew versus Caroline.

The pixelated eye is dilating. The Paul Oakenfold tune is pulsating.

Davina time.

George Orwell time.

Big Brother time.

The quartet and Steve the Cheese watch the madness, gloriously glued. Unlike the haphazardly stuck Queen on the way to her home county, Hertfordshire.

Andrew is evicted from the house getting 68% of the public vote. No-one will ever remember Andrew. Not even Steve the Cheese will remember Andrew.

"I've got to catch my train," Jen says. "I've only got twenty minutes."

"Stay for a bit Jen," Kate pleads. "We'll all club in for a taxi? Girls?"

Lou stays quiet, broke.

Em says, "I'll book one for you, Jen."

"Ok, just a while longer," Jen replies, knowing a cab home will be far quicker than a walk, the train and another walk. "Midnight?"

"Done," Em says, calling a man she knows.

"Outside for a cheeky Potter?" Kate asks. Will's mum and dad are rather regular with their reefers and are always happy to share. Will has found it is an excellent form of pain relief.

"You read my mind, you legend," Em jumps up from her chair and retrieves the pre-rolled Hairy spliffs from the double named cup cupboard in the kitchen.

The quartet sit outside enjoying the cloudy yet balmy August Manchester night.

No-one talks for a few seconds, surprisingly.

"I'm thinking about moving to London," Lou breaks the silence. "I want to try and be in a show in the West End."

"Yes, Lou," Jen says. "That is exactly where you should be."

Kate says, "Lou, I'm so pleased you're saying this."

Em completes the simultaneous trio response. "Yes, Louisa!"

"You think it's a good idea?" Lou asks.

"Yes," the trio confirm in complete harmony. Like a synchronised double pike tuck dive.

Lou pops inside and brings a copy of 'The Stage' magazine back outside with her. "I bought this in the newsagent at the station," she updates the girls. "It shows when and where all the open auditions are. And Charlie says your dad may know some people, Em."

Em flinches at the mention of her dad. Jen notices, but Lou and Kate don't. Charlie and Lou have not spoken about Em much at all in the short amount of time they have known each other. They have been far too busy frolicking, flirting, fighting and fucking. Em rises above it choosing to assume that Lou knows as little as Kate does. She does not want to get into the family fight conversation again today.

"That's great, Lou. Really exciting" Em says genuinely. "Let's take a look," as she takes the magazine and starts to look through it. It genuinely is exciting.

"You all have a plan! I'm so proud of you all. Jen sorted with her fab new marketing job, Lou going to live her dancing dream in London, Kate going into her final year and already starting her career in law... just leaves little old bumhead me," Em laughs.

"Do you have any idea what you want to do yet?" Kate asks.

"Maybe I'll marry a rich landowner, live in a massive country estate and wander around my extensive gardens hoping to see a wet Mr. Darcy in one of my numerous lakes," she quips.

"You'd be bored shitless," Lou laughs.

"I do quite like the thought of working outside, though," Em says. "I think I would like to work with animals."

"Where the hell has this come from?" Kate asks. "You're doing a management degree."

"I've always loved animals," Em insists. "And its Management Science, thank you." As if that makes any difference at all.

"You love animals, as pets," Jen says, also surprised. Ignoring the second statement. "But you've never said anything about actually working with them."

"I know," Em responds, starting to laugh. Knowing this is crazy new news. "I think I want to look after big animals too, like James Herriot," she explains. "It's clearly an epiphany," she adds.

"An epiphany!" Kate shouts, laughing too. "You want to look after elephant fannies?"

The other girls laugh at Kate's immediate wit, but also her Herriot ignorance.

"James didn't look after bloody elephants. There's no elephants in Yorkshire," Lou shrieks. "He put his hands up cows' arses."

"He pulled out their stuck calves, Lou. From their fu-fus," Jen shrieks back. "He didn't find them up their bum holes!"

As the girls laugh, the cow and arse confusion makes Jen think about her own bovine backstory.

"Did I ever tell you about cows chasing me half naked?" Jen asks.

"No," they all reply, immediately intrigued.

"Well," Jen starts, taking a Sol slurp. "My ex and I were in a field down a country road near where he used to live. We were having a picnic. It was all quiet on all fronts. Trees and hedges all round. A totally secluded spot."

"What happened?" Kate interrupts.

"I was in a crop top and denim shorts and we got fruity on the picnic blanket. If I remember rightly it was his mum's, a Union Jack one with a plastic underside," Jen continues to explain, explaining more than she needs to. Just like her mum. "My shorts were removed and we cracked on. No, to be totally honest, I just closed my eyes and he cracked on."

"And?" Em asks.

"Well, I opened my eyes at one point and was faced with about thirty dairy cows with a look in their eyes so devilish," she explains. "I told him to stop, shut up and look. For the first time in his life he did what I told him. I must have sounded very serious. He just said "fuck" fairly quietly and very slowly."

"What happened next?" Lou asks, totally engaged with the farcical field frolic.

"He told me to stand up slowly, leave everything, and follow him."

"And?" Kate asks. "Did you?"

"Well of course I fucking did. But as we started to move slowly, the herd moved slowly too. Mooing. And if you haven't been surrounded by a herd of moos, you'll never know how frightening it is," Jen explains. "Their eyes were like the Big Brother eyes, mental and freaky."

"What did you do?" Em asks.

"We left everything on the United Jack blanket, including my shorts, and headed towards the nearest fence. He said to me "They won't follow us, and they can't really run." I was like "Of course they can run, you prick!""

The girls are now all laughing at Jen's nightmare.

"They were literally heading in on us as we pelted across the field. Then they started to canter, then gallop," she relives the rodeo. "He shouted "Run Jen, fucking run" as the black and white herd gathered speed. It was totally terrifying. I literally ran as fast as I could to the nearest fence and jumped up on it. It was like when I had to do the high jump in a national athletics competition."

"You did what?" the small Lou asks the even smaller Jen.

"Oh god, that's another story, for another day," Jen says. "One of the cows missed me and my thong by about as far as a long ruler!"

The girls all thought about their 'long' pencil cases always bought from WH Smiths to house their 30cm bendy rulers. They really weren't that long.

"You were wearing a thong?" Lou asked, wide eyed.

"Yes," Jen replies. "Just a tiny red thong."

"And you nearly got trampled?" Lou asks. "In just a thong?"

"I still had my top on," Jen says to the relief of the girls.

"Bet they were all aggressive boy cows," socialist, slightly feminist Kate says.

Em and Jen cock their heads towards her in a slightly bullish way.

"What happened then?" asks Lou, ignoring Kate's dairy cow

ignorance.

"I caught my fu-fu on the fence," Jen replies. "It full on hurt"

"Where was your ex?"

"On the other side of the fence, panting," Jen explains. "The road was on the other side of the fence too."

"What did you do?"

"What could I do?" Jen says. "I was in a bright red tiny thong and a crop top by a road with a crowd of crazy cows between me and my shorts. It was scandalous. I told him to go back to his house quickly and find something for me to wear. I wasn't going to walk down the road, country road or not, showing my booty."

The girls are now really laughing. Imagining Jen half naked. Stood alone by a fence on a country road. Desperately hoping no-one drove past.

"I found a tree to hide behind and sang to myself for a while to take my mind off the crap situation, but it was all fine in the end," Jen assures. "But I really liked those denim shorts, and his mum really liked her Union Jack picnic blanket. He obviously never told her." It became a family mystery, a little like how his mum's prized mahogany lounge speakers had got oil marks on them or how Jen's dad's office wall had fallen down. "I will never look at a cow again in the same way."

"It was a cow-trastophe," Lou spouts, out of nowhere.

The other three girls moan, but actually quite impressed with her bovine banter.

There are loads more questions the girls have about Jen's G-string jaunt and what song she sang in her thong, but it starts to rain. The quartet head inside and plonk themselves on the sofa and chair.

"Why don't you train to be a vet?" Jen asks Em. "You've got the right A-Levels, haven't you? Sciences? And you're definitely clever enough."

"But it's like I've wasted three years, though," Em replies. "And it will cost a fortune."

"So what?" Kate says. "I've got another year to go and then I'm going to spend years training to be a lawyer."

"And if you hadn't met Jen on your course, we may never have met you," Lou adds cutely. "So it's not a waste, really."

"Yes, I suppose you're right," Em lightbulb moments.

She decides to look into it, as soon as humanly (or animally) possible.

She needs to do it quickly, though. Needs to move her butt, butt, butt.

Thong Song.
Sisqo.

-38-
EM: SAME OLD BRAND NEW YOU

11th August 2000

Em is driving home to Hertfordshire.

It's Friday lunchtime and her Clio is flying down the M1.

Em wonders why the A1 never became the M1, like she thought the A6 had become the M6. Or had it? She is a little delirious.

She hasn't slept properly for a few nights. It had felt like a blur of dark and light. Another night then another day. So two empty cans of Red Bull are on the driver's seat and she has just opened a third. She feels a bit wired, it is definitely giving her some form of wings.

She opens the window for some air.

Her dad had called her on Tuesday night.

"Hi dad."

"Hi Emily."

Awkward pause.

"Thank you for your letters," he said factually and formally. "We need to talk."

"Yes," she replied, meekly.

"I don't want to do it on the phone," he said. "I'm away from tomorrow for a few nights, but I'm back on Friday at about lunchtime. I'd like you to come home please, so we can talk properly."

His tone was neither warm nor harsh. It was flat. It made Em shudder.

"Ok," she said.

"Eve is not feeling well. I will not have you upset her. Is that clear?"

"Yes dad," Em said. "I promise I won't. Is she ok with me coming home?"

"Emily, she has been pestering me to get in touch with you for quite some time now," he admitted, thinking Em was having yet another dig at his wife. "It is her idea that you come home this weekend. We have cancelled our plans."

Em knows she deserves his distrust and the assumption she is being a green bitch. "Thank you," she says simply. "And please thank Eve too."

She also had hoped maybe he would be a bit more understanding after her letters. After she had said she wasn't going to be the old her, she was going to try and be a brand new her. But deep down she knew she had a long way to go.

Her dad detects a tone in Em's voice he hasn't heard before, a mixture of sorrow and defeat. She sounds small. She sounds weak. She sounds slightly broken.

He has always adored his daughter, his little star. The last few months have been awful for him, but the mixture of her behaviour over the past few years with their collective hot headedness and stubbornness, meant the absence was inevitable. She needed this time to reflect, learn and accept. The well-constructed, thought through, self-deprecating and honest letters show to him that maybe she had. But he is worried she will just break her promises, in the two letters, in two.

It also had made him think a lot about why she thought she had behaved as she had, though he still didn't really understand why she was so awful to Eve. He did understand more how much her formative years filled with fighting and divorce had actually affected her. He feels ashamed he hadn't really realised. Never actually asked.

Listening to his little girl sound so sad tugged at his heartstrings.

"It will be ok, Em. As long as it's not just lip service. As long as we are not just going to get the same old brand new you." His tone warmed and he added, "I have always loved you, my little star."

"I love you too, dad," Jen said, her voice crackling. A large lump lingering in her throat.

"See you Friday then?"

"See you Friday," Em just about got out before she hung up and sobbed.

Friday came round slowly. She had wanted it to come, but had been terrified of it.

This week's number one 'Rock DJ' by Robbie is blasting from her Clio speakers. Happily filling her mind with 'sleazy' and 'tease me' rather than the queasy, uneasy thoughts she has been having.

She stops at the service station on the M1 just north of Milton Keynes. She buys some actually fairly decent flowers and some chocolates, then gets herself a coffee.

Back on the road she knows she is about fifty minutes away. She has been through the worst part. The M6 through Birmingham and M5 junction. "Roll on the new relief road," she had said when she got through, but knows the new toll road won't be open for a few years yet.

She punches in the code on the pad next to the gate. 2709. Her birthday. He hasn't changed it. She is pleased about that.

She drives in and notices her dad's car isn't there. It's just before 2pm. Just the gorgeous dark green Audi TT convertible roadster. "Where the hell are you?" she asks her absent father. She brakes, not knowing what to do. Stupid gates. If they weren't there she could have seen her dad wasn't there and driven around the block numerous times.

But it's too late now. The gates are closing behind her. And the massively grown Joey and Chandler are racing towards her car, barking excitedly.

Inside the house Eve says "Shit," as she sees Em come through the gate from her bedroom window upstairs. "Where the hell are you?" she asks her absent husband. She watches Em stop and realises that she is probably thinking exactly the same thing.

She watches Em park up and get out of her car, being almost knocked over by her two boisterous boys. She thinks, for the millionth time, how much she needs to take them to a trainer. Especially in advance of her impending baby girl.

Em fusses them and laughs, loving the lolloping licky labs. She somehow relieves herself from them enough to open her boot and takes the flowers and chocolates out. She turns to face the house and Eve quickly dives away from the window, not wanting her to know she has been watching.

Em takes a deep breath and walks towards the front door. She finds her key in her bag and starts to put it in the lock when the door opens.

"Hi Em," Eve says.

"Hi Eve," Em replies.

"Come on in." Eve waits for Em to say something snide like, "Well thank you very much for allowing me to enter my own home," but it doesn't come.

"Thank you," she replies instead. Em thinks she looks really tired. Annoyingly stunning still, but a little puffy and rather drained. Her normally beautifully toned dark skin a little sallow. She knows she has not been well throughout most of pregnancy. "You're looking great. Really glowing. I got you some flowers and chocolates."

"Thank you, Em," Eve says genuinely, knowing she certainly isn't glowing. But she appreciates the kind words and positive intent. "That's really lovely of you to say."

The dogs bounce in, nearly knocking Eve over, and Em shuts the front door. She follows Eve, Joey and Chandler into the kitchen.

"You've had a long drive, do you fancy a drink?" Eve asks. "I've got a nice bottle of white wine open. We had a few friends over last night. I can't wait until I can drink again. It's bloody boring being the only one not pissed."

Em laughs. "My friend just had a baby in June. I know all about that. We lived it with her for months."

"Your friend had a baby? A friend from uni?" Eve asks, clearly a little surprised and very interested.

"Yes," Em replies. "She's called Jen and her baby is Joseph. He is adorable. She had him just a few days after our last final. I looked after him on my own a few weeks ago when she went for a job interview. I was terrible at it. I mean, he was fine. But I was a mess. As was the house. Shit all over me, him and the rug. Thank god her mum came in before her and helped me clear up. If she hadn't I'm not sure whether Jen would have ever let me near him again."

This warm, funny, self-deprecating person in front of Eve is unrecognisable. She is talking fast and is clearly nervous.

"Right, let me get these flowers into water and you get yourself a glass of wine. It's just in the fridge…" Eve says, stopping herself last minute from telling her where the drinks fridge is or where the glass cupboard is.

She has obviously read her own letter, and has also read her husband's letter. She intends to make an effort. She is committed to trying to be a brand new person with Em, like she is clearly trying to be with her.

She understands more now, and how she can help with the situation. She still doesn't really understand the level of Em's past cruelty, why she was so often dismissed and ignored by her. She

PAPER OVER IT

feels there is something more to it. She intends to ask her some questions over the weekend. "And then we can sit in the garden and I want to hear all about Jen and Joseph," she proposes. Then adds, "If that's ok with you?"

"Perfect," Em says heading for the fridge in the utility room. She is pleased they have something to talk about to fill the time before her dad gets back. She is not ready to talk honestly and openly to Eve until she has spoken to her father.

They walk out to the garden together and sit down. Joey and Chandler follow them and then head off chasing something, anything.

"They are bonkers," Eve says.

"They are fab," Em replies. They smile at each other.

Em proceeds to tell Eve all about Jen and her story. Eve gets quite emotional at times. She touches her lovely little six-and-a-half-month bump absently.

She chooses to share something she didn't in any way think she would, especially at this stage. She isn't really sure why, but thinks it may be that she wants to offer Em something. "I had a miscarriage last year," she divulges. "It really affected me. I was devastated."

Em looks at Eve in surprise. Why is she sharing this? With her? Such a personal thing. "I'm so sorry, Eve," she says. "I didn't know."

"Only your dad, my mum and my two best friends knew," she reveals, looking sad. "I didn't want to talk about it with anyone really. I have been massively worried and nervous throughout this pregnancy, thinking I'm going to lose her. It terrifies me. I think that's what has added to me feeling so tired and awful."

Em looks at Eve like she is meeting her for the first time. For the first time she isn't blinded by her green. It's like the slate is being slowly wiped clean, as if on the horizon there is a baby bridge building machine heading their way.

"Do you want to talk about it now?" Em asks kindly. Not wanting to pry with unwanted questions, but giving her the option. Her emotional intelligence growing by the second.

"Not really," Eve replies. "I'm not sure why I told you to be honest... Sorry - I didn't mean you. I really don't mean you," she quickly realises how this comment could be interpreted, it sounds a little cruel. "I just mean I haven't spoken about it to many people, and for such a long time."

"I understand, I think," Em says softly. "Although I don't really understand, obviously."

"Tell me more about Jen and Joseph," Eve asks, moving the conversation on. Or back. "I would really love to meet this pair."

Eve pours her some more wine like a pro. With her left hand. Em has never noticed this before. Or cared to notice. Is she left-handed? Has she been a waitress in the past? So many things she doesn't know.

As Em sips her wine and regales what Jen said to the doctor while he was stitching up her snatch, Eve starts to laugh. The girl is actually really funny and engaging. Though she clearly has a wickedly funny, quite tough shell, she is softer, warmer and more inviting than Eve had previously thought. She's not like the Mint Imperial she thought she was, hard through and through. She is more crispy on the outside, but chewy on the inside. Like a Trebor Softmint.

When she gets to the 'cone head' and the 'big fist trying to get into what a little finger should', Eve is laughing hysterically. Holding her bump while clutching her sides. "Is that your ring or your watch I can feel?" Eve suddenly asks cheekily. Em is now the one to laugh out loud, shocked at her crudeness. It's like she's sat talking to one of her friends. It surprises her.

It is at this moment that Em's dad enters his kitchen. He notices the flowers freshly placed in the vase. He watches the two girls through the window, his two favourite girls in the world, for quite some time. He smiles. There is a lot Em needs to do and prove she is not the same old green, but this is a start.

Starting to feel a little pervy, and definitely not wanting to be spotted looking a little pervy, he pours himself a large glass of red wine and goes out into the garden.

"Hello girls," he booms. "Oh and yes, you boys too," as the playful, panting pair almost push him over.

Eve is still laughing but Em stops. She watches her dad kiss Eve. "You ok?" he asks her.

"Yes," she answers, kissing him back. "Not too bad today, thank you."

Em is not surprised he greets his wife before the daughter he hasn't seen for months. It hurts obviously, but she gets it. He is perhaps proving a point, testing her. Or maybe she is overthinking things, like she has for many years.

"What are you laughing about?" he asks them while kissing Em on the top of head. Like he did when she was a kid. He can feel Em slightly freeze.

"Em is just telling me about her friend who has just had a baby," Eve updates him.

"Really," he says surprised. "A friend from up in Manchester or down here?"

"A uni friend," she explains. "Do you remember me talking about Jen? She's on the same course as me."

"Yes, I do vaguely," he remembers. "Well please carry on Em. Whatever you were saying was clearly amusing. I haven't seen Eve laugh like that in quite some time." He was planning on immediately taking Em off and having a very serious talk with her, but the time does not now feel right.

Em is beaming internally that she has managed to make her dad happy by making Eve laugh. She still cannot be as pleased that she is making Eve happy, but she is getting there.

Em carries on with her story, after giving a bit of background and context to her dad. She is nervous as she knows this is not going to be this easy, that the 'chat' will come at some point. But she enjoys the moment for now. Entertaining her dad and his wife, making them laugh.

When she has finished, her dad says, "Charlie is going to be here later."

"Really?" Em says, closely followed by the same word from Eve.

"Yes, sorry princess. I called him last night. I should have let you know."

Em's green starts to gurgle, at his prioritising Eve in his response and ignoring her in the process, and the word 'princess'. She thinks about the promises she has made to herself and the mirror. Both back in the flat above her fireplace, in her rear view on the way here and in the downstairs loo a short while ago.

Eve notices Em's very subtle, almost unnoticeable, reaction and quick catch. Thinking about some of the words in her dad's letter, she is kind.

"Is that ok, Em?" she asks her, ignoring her husband. "That Charlie comes?"

Em can see what she is doing. She is teaching her dad something. And making her feel included, prioritised - or rather not excluded, not deprioritised. She is being educated herself on the real Eve. The possibly left-handed Eve.

"Yes, absolutely, it will be lovely to see him," she replies to Eve. Then she bolts on, "And to be all together."

"That's all sorted then," Eve replies warmly to Em. "I'm doing a lasagne for dinner with salad and garlic bread so there's plenty of food. I've got berries, meringues, fruit and cream for an Eton Mess and we've got loads of wine. And I thought you could have some Pimms in the garden later too. It's such a lovely day. I may even have a small glass myself."

"Jen taught me to make a wicked lasagne," Em says. "And I have perfected my Pimms recipe too. I call it Pimmbledon."

"Well, you can be head chef if you like?" she offers. "To be honest, I am a hopeless cook. Burn everything. I can be your commis chef. I just hope I've got all the ingredients you need."

"Ok," Em is surprised how much she genuinely likes the thought of this. And, if she is to be honest, likes the thought of Eve being shit at something. "When do we start?"

Eve looks at her watch. A beautiful silver diamond set Rolex. Em has never seen it before. It must be new. Yet another gift. Eve clocks Em clocking the watch. "Well it's gone three now so we nearly need to get cracking."

As the girls stand up and head into the kitchen, Em's dad says, "Right then. I'll get my bags from the car. Are your bags still in your car Em? And let me know, princess, if you're missing anything for the meal."

But they have already gone. Neither respond.

Em's dad feels a funny feeling.

He doesn't like it.

He is being deprioritised and ignored.

Em and Eve start to busy themselves in the kitchen. "Do you like it?" Eve asks after a short while, showing Em her watch. Em tries not to rise to Eve rubbing her nose in the tinselled timepiece. Before Em can respond, Eve adds, "It was my mum's. She couldn't believe it when my dad brought it home one day. We aren't wealthy in any way. Not Rolex people at all. But he had saved and saved for it. Apparently he had promised her he would get her one the day they got married. It took him over twenty-five years to get it. He gave it to her seven years ago on their silver wedding anniversary. It was a massive surprise to her and us all. She died a little while ago. She left it to me in her will."

"I'm so sorry," Em says, something doing a complete 360 in her head. "I had no idea."

"There's no reason why you should," Eve says. "I kept it very much to myself, didn't want to talk about it. It wasn't long after my miscarriage that she went. I couldn't even look at the watch for a while, but now I get comfort from wearing it. It's like a little piece of her with me all the time. Organising me, like she always did."

Em nods as Eve wipes a tear from her eye. She even looks stunning crying. "Anyway," Eve says firmly. "Let's crack on. What's first, chef?"

Eve puts some music on. Eminem.

Em's dad heads back into the kitchen after fetching the bags. He can't stand Eminem. Doesn't understand him at all. It's just rude, offensive noise to him. And seeing his girls seemingly happily working together, neither wanting nor needing him, he excludes himself and heads into his study with his glass of wine. Suddenly deep in thought. He hopes they need something for the meal, that one of them comes and asks him to go to the shop.

Over an hour and a half later, with Em having no doubt that Eve is indeed left-handed and that she bought the racing green Audi TT convertible herself from a funny story she told about the sleazy man in the shiny suit she bought it off, the pair are starting to layer the cooled ragu, bechamel, lasagne sheets and cheese. They hadn't needed anything from the shop. She had even found a random bottle of unopened ginger ale. Both sauces are far tastier than Eve's version, she admits this very openly. She can't wait to taste the finished dish later.

As Eminem, Eve and Em belt out 'The way I am' with Chandler and

Joey dancing around them, Charlie enters the kitchen.

He feels like he has entered a parallel universe. His sister and his step-mum working as a team, singing together like two schoolgirls. It's like the same old Em, but brand new.

They don't notice his arrival. What the hell is going on? Whatever it is, he wants a part of it.

He puts his weekend bag down and joins in, loudly.

"Charlie!" Eve shouts over Marshall Mathers. She goes to run towards him, but checks herself. She has no idea when the last time Charlie and Em have seen each other. It could be months. Em just looks up.

"Good to see you little sis," he bear hugs her and rubs her head annoyingly, like he did when they were younger.

"Get off, you dick," Em says.

Then he heads to Eve and gives her a kiss. "Hello sexy step-mother, and even littler little sis," looking down at her bump.

"Do you know how strange and slightly twisted that sounds," Eve says as Em thinks it.

"I'm like Eminem," he laughs. "Strange and slightly twisted."

The girls laugh as he asks, "Can I help?"

"Yes," Em says. "You can make the Eton Mess while we finish this and start on the Pimmbledon."

"The Pimmble-what?" he asks, whilst childishly smiling to himself about making an Eton Mess.

As 'Stan' is starting, Jen's dad comes into the kitchen. Bored of his almost two hour childish self-exclusion. He is starting to realise how similar he and his daughter really are.

He sees his two children and his wife singing and working together. Looking just like three young friends.

"What is this bloody racket?" he asks. "It's not real songs like in my day. Can you not put on some proper music."

"Hello, old man," Charlie greets his dad with a veiled insult. "Got any Vera Lynn or Glenn Miller Orchestra for dad, Eve?" he cajoles. "He hates anything this century."

Eve and Em laugh. "I might have some Peggy Lee," Eve offers, giggling at her husband.

"I'm not that bloody old! I wasn't even alive in the forties," Jen's dad berates. "Maybe something from the seventies or eighties?"

He realises that the conversation he wants to have with his daughter is unlikely to happen tonight. He thinks about taking control and asserting himself, telling her to join him in his study. Remove her and have her to himself for a while to talk things through. But he rethinks, thankfully. He needs to think differently, generally.

Charlie goes and checks the huge CD collection next to the even huger DVD collection in the TV watching lounge.

"Dire Straits or Queen, dad?" he shouts over Dido and her cold tea from the kitchen door, holding two CDs. One in each hand.

"Dire Straits," he shouts back over Dido's cloudy windows. "Is it Brothers in Arms?"

"Yes," Charlie shouts back over the picture on Dido's wall.

"Crack it on then," Em's dad says.

Eve has been watching her husband and reflecting on the past few hours. After reading the letters she has a slightly different perspective.

Maybe the man's too hot headed and stubborn. Maybe the man's too strong for his own good.

Maybe he needs to look a little more at himself and his behaviour too. Maybe he has some changing to do too.

Same old brand new you.
A1.

-39-
EM: WHY DOES MY HEART FEEL SO BAD?

12th August 2000

Em wakes up with a stonking headache.

"Shit," she says to herself after the previous night starts slowly piecing itself back together. "Fuck. Shit. Fuck." She pulls the cover over her head. Trying to hide from the memory. She absently touches her right wrist with her left hand.

After dancing to Dire Straits' money for nothing and their river, deep and wide, the four had sat down to the meal. Pimmbledon flowing.

Charlie, Eve and her dad all congratulating Em on both her lip-smacking lasagne and her terrific take on the Wimbledon classic, before they toasted her degree. Even Charlie's Eton Mess was a ten on taste. A six on presentation.

Em's dad had had a late night the night before. "He was out in London at some posh twat thing, where the twats act anything but posh," Eve had explained, much to Em's amusement.

She knew how much her dad hated the 'tw' word, nearly as much as he hated 'see you next Tuesday'. Maybe the one glass of Pimmbledon had got to her, or maybe this was just the real her. She liked her more for it either way.

At about ten o-clock, and after numerous Pimmbledons and a whiskey with his son, he had admitted defeat and gone up to bed.

She remembers asking Charlie, "How's Louisa?"

"Who is Louisa?" he had replied.

"Louisa Armstrong. My friend who you have been banging for weeks, you idiot!"

Em had suddenly started to pay attention, intrigued.

"Lou?" he replied and asked simultaneously. "Is that her name? Louisa?"

"Jesus, Charlie," Eve joined in, head in hands.

"Well she never said," he defended himself. "She didn't ask if I was actually called Charles. I just assumed she was a Louise."

"But what the hell could Charlie be short for otherwise?" Em mused, laughing at her big brother.

"Charlton? Charlotte?" Eve offered.

"Not helping, stepmother," Charlie laughed. "In fact, I need to go and ring her."

"Thumb and under," Em laughed, pissed.

So it was just Em and Eve left. Em felt a little woosy and wonky, but when Eve asked her, "Do you want to talk?" she decided to seize the moment.

They sat together on an outdoor sofa. Started to talk. Em opened up about how much her parent's mess of a relationship and divorce had not only broken her heart but hadn't shown her what good relationships and love were. The soul of her family had been slowly and systematically screwed. She also spoke about how she had felt so left out when her father and Eve had got together. Rejected and unwanted.

They talked for a while, Eve asking Em questions, Em answering honestly, and then vice versa.

There was a natural pause.

Em leant forward and went to kiss Eve.

"Oh no, Em." Eve pulled back. "No."

"Oh shit, I'm so so sorry," Em sobered almost instantly, pulling herself away. Retracting. "Fuck. I don't know what happened there. I'm so sorry."

"Em, it's ok," Eve assured. "Honestly, it's fine."

"But this is so fucked up," Em was now stood up. Totally confused with herself, appalled with herself. She felt so bad, so wrong. Slightly hysterical. "I have just tried to kiss you. What have I done?"

Eve stood up and took Em's hands. "Em, it's fine. Please try to calm down and sit down with me."

The jigsaw pieces started to fall into place for Eve. It wasn't Charlie that had a thing for her, that was just banter. It was Em. Maybe that had been the root of some of her behaviour. Maybe her jealousy was two-fold. It was all so complex and bewildering. She, all of a sudden, felt desperately sorry for the confused, mortified girl in front of her.

"But, what will my dad say?" Em sat down, guided by Eve.

"Your dad will never know," Eve replied. "I promise you. He will never know."

Em sat with her head in her hands.

"Do you want to talk about it, Em?" Eve offered after a little while, taking her hand.

"I just don't know," Em replied, removing her hand. Totally disorientated. "I don't think so."

She remembers crying and Eve hugging her. "It's ok, Em," she vaguely remembers her saying. "It really is ok. Let me know if you want to talk. Any time. I'll be here. It will be just between you and me. You can trust me, I promise."

She then very vaguely remembers Charlie coming back outside. "What's going on here then?" as he saw the hugging pair. "Nothing you need to know about, nosey," Eve had laughed, making light of the situation. "I am exhausted. Em, you must be knackered too. Shall we all go up?"

It is then a bit of a blur.

Em peels the covers away from her head and sits up. Her head bangs even more. From embarrassment and inebriation. Her heart and her soul feel as bad as her head. She is mortified.

She hears a knock on the door. "Tea?" she hears Eve ask.

"Yes please," Em replies, unsure what else she can say. She can't pretend she's not there and hide under the cover, like a child.

Eve opens the door and places the steaming mug on Em's bedside table. "I'm doing a fry-up," she says. Em doesn't look up at her. She can't, her shame prevents her. "How do you like your eggs?"

Em doesn't want to be rude. "Scrambled, please," she says. Then adds ruefully, "A bit like me."

Eve smiles and then laughs while shutting the door. "We're all scrambled in our own ways, Em. I'll tell you about me one day. Things even your dad doesn't know."

Em raises her head and looks at Eve. She nods slowly.

"I meant what I said last night," Eve recounts. "I know I am not exactly your favourite person, but I am here as someone you can talk to. Anytime. Maybe I can help in some way. As we both know I am not much older than you," Em had made it very clear in her letters that this was one of the reasons she had found accepting Eve difficult. They both now knew another reason. "I am a good listener and I am also very trustworthy. My word is my word, I promise you."

"Thank you," Em says. All she really wants to do is forget it happened. Bury her hand in the sand, ostrich style. And not think about why it happened.

"It will be ready in about twenty minutes. Gives you plenty of time to have a nice shower," Eve says before she turns and leaves Em's room, shutting the door behind her.

Not long ago this would have royally pissed Em off. Eve in any way even having an opinion on what she should do. She would have thought it was her way of having control over her, like she did her dad.

But Em weirdly quite likes it. She feels part of something, rather than fighting so furiously against it.

She desperately needs some protein and carbs. And she most definitely needs a shower. She knows she stinks.

As Em enters the kitchen with wet hair, her dad is sitting at the table reading The Financial Times. Eve and Charlie are cooking. And giggling like naughty school kids.

"Em," Charlie greets her. "Thank the lord! Please take over. This woman is so shit at eggs."

Eve whacks him with the spatula she has in her left hand and then flicks him with the tea towel she has in her other hand. She chases him round the kitchen island, both laughing. Joey and Chandler are chasing around after them as well.

Again, Em knows this would have really pissed her off before. Seeing Eve and Charlie having fun, enjoying each other's company so much. But she sees the scene with fresh eyes, through a new lens. From a different perspective. She laughs at Charlie's squeals. "Child abuse! Em, our wicked stepmother is abusing me. Call Childline quickly."

Em's dad is also enjoying the scene, especially seeing both his children interact with his wife and hearing Em laugh. It is a sound he hasn't heard before last night and this morning for a very long time. It's good for the heart and the soul.

Sat at the table a little while later, he picks up a sausage with his fork. "Well I'm not going to get food poisoning from these," he points out. "The one benefit of burnt pork."

"I'll bloody pork you in a minute," Eve waves her knife at him playfully.

"He's clearly porked you first," Charlie says, pointing his knife at her bump.

"Charlie!" Eve and Em shout just before Em's dad adds, "You know how she likes her eggs in the morning?"

"Stop it!" Eve berates her husband, thinking it's too soon for Em. After yesterday and especially last night, she feels all of a sudden quite protective over her. Not like a mother of course, but maybe more like a big sister. But Em is not reacting. "At least you've all got some nice eggs. Thank you Em."

Em smiles. She is finding the situation a little stressful and odd, especially after last night and also the fact that she is yet to have the proper dreaded conversation with her dad, but she admits to herself that she is also finding it quite warm and fun. Her green is shifting to amber. "Nothing quite like a good scramble," she says, knowingly looking at Eve.

"To a good scramble," Eve toasts the eggs, raising her orange juice.

"To a good scramble," the rest reply.

"Shall we play Scrabble after?" Charlie part rhymes, always eager for any sort of competition.

"Em and I are just going to pop out for a bit together," Em's dad says. "Then I suppose we can. Eve?"

Em is again being left out of any decisions, even those that include herself. "I'm fine with that," Eve replies. "Em, ok with you?"

Em smiles at Eve, she is again aware what she is trying to do. "Can't wait to win at both scramble and Scrabble in the same day," she challenges. This will be the first time the foursome have ever played a game together, and the first time in years she has played a game with Will or her dad.

"Game on," whoops Charlie. Chandler and Joey bark with excitement.

Em finds herself in the passenger side of her dad's car driving down the country road from their house to the local village. Her dad parks outside the little cafe and asks Em what she wants. "Are we not going in?" she asks.

"I thought we could get a takeout and go and sit on that park bench we used to sit on by the lake and feed the ducks. I've brought some bread," he points to a full Warburtons loaf on the back seat.

"I'm not a kid anymore, dad," she laughs.

"You'll always be my kid to me, Em," he says while opening his door. "So what's it to be?"

"Hot chocolate?" she asks. Even though it is a hot summer's day, she plays the game.

"Cream and marshmallows?"

"Yes please."

Sitting on the park bench, sipping their matching hot chocolates and throwing bread to the ducks, they start to talk. They talk for over an hour and a half. They are both honest, brutally so at times. They don't get angry. They don't even get too sad. They both try to keep their emotions in check. They communicate in a way they haven't for years. Or maybe ever. They both listen.

Talked out and with promises made, both ways, Em's dad puts his arm around her and they sit silently for a while. Looking out over the small lake.

"I'm proud of you, my little star," he says.

"Thank you, dad," she replies. "I'm proud of you too."

He kisses the top of her head and stands up. "Come on, let's go home."

On the way back, he asks her what her plans are next. She doesn't know whether to tell him her crazy vet plan. It will be years more of studying, not earning. He had told her in their talk about how he thought she could be ungrateful and it could seem she was only interested in his credit card. And that she took the piss at times. But it is just an idea, so she goes for it.

"What a brilliant idea!" he grins. "I always thought you would do something with animals. You were obsessed as a child. And you always loved the sciences. You never really used them for anything."

"Do you not think it's a waste of the last three years?" she asks.

"Well somehow we have wasted the last three years, haven't we?" he says philosophically.

Em laughs. "Yes, I suppose we have."

"Hang on a minute. I play golf with a chap from the Royal

Veterinary College just down the road in Hatfield," he has a light bulb moment.

"Of course you do," Em teases him for his ridiculously brilliant network of connections.

"Want me to ask a few questions?" he asks her. "I'm sure we have donated money to them. Nothing like a bit of bribery and nepotism, eh?"

"I don't want to get in because of you and your cheque book," Em insists, knowing she has never really said no to this before. She has been a spoilt, taking brat. But wanting to change. "But if you can get me a contact or even an interview at this late stage, I wouldn't be daft enough to say no."

"You got an ology. You got an ology. You're a scientist," he recites Maureen Lipman's old BT advert from 1988. His accent is terrible.

Em laughs even more. Feeling lighter, freer. Her heart haltingly beginning to mend, to feel less rotten, less bad - and her soul slowly starting to shine.

As they approach a set of traffic lights on the way out of the village, the lights turn from green, to amber and then red.

"Enough," Em says to herself, absently feeling her right wrist. "Enough now."

Why does my heart feel so bad?
Moby.

-40-
JEN: MOVIN' TOO FAST

14th August 2000
Monday.
 Just three Mondays before Jen starts work. Two and a half weeks before the work conference where she will meet everyone.
 Eeek.
 She is feeling really good. Positive and in some semblance of control. But everything is moving so fast. Too fast.
 Her mum has rearranged her shifts so she has the morning off. They are going to have a look around a nursery together. Jen has already been and verbally committed to send Joseph there. She really liked it. Thank god. Because it is the only nursery in the area with a full time space available at such short notice.
 She wants to show her mum, and her mum wants to see it. She is confident she will be picking Joseph up fairly regularly for Jen. She can't drop off as she starts work most days at 7:30am.
 It is just a six-minute drive from the cottage and set in lovely countryside. Jen and her mum travel separately so she can go straight on to work after. It is a massive old hall with tall ceilings apexing up to the roof. The huge space is split into three sections by cute little fences. One for babies, one for toddlers and one for pre-schoolers. The space feels bright and buzzy, packed with colour and fun. The baby section has ten lovely cots.
 Outside there is a huge garden with a big lawn, a woodland area and a playground in a concrete section. There are a number of prams outside with babies asleep in them. "We like to get them outside as much as possible," the lovely lady manager said. "Even in winter we wrap them up nice and warm and bring them out. Fresh air is best."
 There are kids racing around fast on trikes and bikes, while others are playing on the sturdy plastic climbing frames or tracking the snakes and other animals painted on the floor.
 "It's perfect," Jen's mum says. "Isn't it Joseph?" He smiles in agreement back at her from his travel system.
 He had smiled at Jen for the first time last week, at just six weeks.

She mistook it at first for wind, but he kept doing it. Showing off. It was the most beautiful thing she had ever seen.

She had raced for her camera hoping it had film in it. It did. She snapped away as he continued to perform, to show off. "You are so so clever!" she grinned back at him and kissed his head. She found the red baby book and added in the date next to 'smiles for the first time'.

She couldn't wait to develop the pictures. She has spent quite a lot of money on photo development since he was born, sending off at least one film a week to Tripleprint and receiving the exciting wallet filled with one big, two little prints on each of the twenty four, and the new film for the following week. She loves looking at the photos, never quite remembering what she has taken. She wants to capture and record everything. He is growing so fast. She always crosses her fingers that the pictures don't come back blank or have any big, recurring black marks on them.

"Thank you Joseph. I think it's pretty perfect too," the nursery manager says, smiling at Jen's mum and Joseph. "Shall we go into the office and get everything sorted?"

Sitting at the office desk, the warm woman goes through everything. She moves too fast through the detail and Jen has to ask her to repeat certain things a few times to make sure she one hundred percent understands. She wants to get everything right.

The nursery is £580 per month. Jen needs to bring five ready-made bottles of milk every day in a cool bag, all named. She must provide the nursery with nappies. The bags should always be named. She must also bring a set of spare clothes every day. Again, these should all be named, in a named bag. If she wants them to give him Calpol if he has a temperature, she will have to provide them with that too. Again, named. They will always let her know when they need more of any of the above, or if the nappies they have are too small.

She goes through the new Working Families Tax Credit which replaced Family Credit last April. Jen has to apply to the Inland Revenue and it gets paid to her through her employer as part of her pay packet. She thinks Jen may get about £160 a month as a single full-time working parent, but can't be sure. It's all a bit new and in the nursery's wealthy location, it is rare for people to claim this

PAPER OVER IT

benefit. Jen is also now doubling the number of single parents she has. She doesn't say this with any form of judgement, just states it factually. She adds that lots of the children in the nursery are there just a few days a week to give their non-working mums some free time.

Jen's head is a little blown with all the information and necessary action. She asks Jen if she has applied for the universal Child Benefit. Jen says she has. At least she has actioned something. As a single parent she gets £76 per month.

As Jen finishes filling in all the forms, the manager asks, "So all set for the 4th of September then?"

"Yes, thank you," Jen replies, smiling. Handing her the pen back.

"We will have a 'settle in' for a few hours for him the week before," she adds. "Is it ok if I give you a call next week to let you know what the best day is?"

"Yes, of course," Jen says, overwhelmed but trying not to show it. "That would be great."

After they all say their goodbyes, Jen and her mum chat in the car park.

"What do you think?" Jen asks.

"I absolutely love it," she replies.

"Me too," replies Jen, smiling.

"See you both later," she sings as she climbs in her car and drives off to work. Jen pops Joseph in his seat in Honey and leaves too.

Later that day, after Jen and Joseph visit the excellent charity shops in their little town and manage to dole fund some actually rather decent work clothes to get her started, and a pair of fake glasses with tortoiseshell rims, Jen does her sums.

Her salary of £12,500 per year means her monthly take home pay will be about £1,041. With the WFTC and child benefit that leaves her with £1,277 a month. After the nursery fees she will be left with £697 a month. She cannot rely on her ex giving her anything.

Her car and petrol cost her about £100 per month. Milk, nappies and all other Joseph related things she budgets to be about £150 per month, but she thinks this may be too low. She is to pay some of the bills at home including the council tax. This will be about £120 per month. She has budgeted £150 a month for food and any other essentials like toiletries, again she thinks this may be a little low. So in total at least £470 a month.

This will leave her with £177 per month, or about £41 per week, for everything else she or Joseph needs. It is tight and there certainly isn't much left for fripperies, fashion or fun, but it is doable.

"I'm not going to worry," she tells Joseph. "Because I know if I worry, it only upsets you." She remembers the letter her ex had sent her on Mother's Day before he was born. "It is all going to be ok."

He smiles at her, as if he knows. As if he's saying it's going to be ok too.

Later Jen is sitting with her mum in the snug with Joseph in her mum's arms. They are waiting for a new TV show to come on. The Weakest Link. Anne Robinson is taking the reins.

The three had gone to see Jen's Grandpa on Friday, the day Caroline was evicted from the Big Brother House, and he had given them a massive bag of pistachio nuts and some feta cheese brought back from his recent holiday to Greece.

He is in love with his Great Grandson, as is his wife. They spent ages making funny faces at him. They are all sure that Joseph giggled for the first time when he did it on Friday. It was adorable. He took him outside and showed him his prized sweet peas. Putting one under his little nose so he could smell it. Jen took a lovely photo of the pair and the peas before Joseph sneezed about seven times.

A little later she caught her Grandpa giving Joseph a fudge bar to suck on instead of his dummy. He sucked on his pipe at the same time, emulating Joseph's rhythm. "It never harmed you," he said, unperturbed by Jen's shocked reaction.

"Grab those pistachios from the kitchen will you, Jen? And the feta." her mum asks. "And get a bowl for the nut shells."

"Are you sure the feta's going to be ok? It wasn't in the fridge and he was travelling for hours."

"It'll be fine," she assures. "We would take a picnic with cheese and Greek yoghurts when you were young on holiday in the heat, and eat it hours later."

Jen wonders whether this was the cause of the endless bouts of diarrhoea they suffered as kids on holiday. Not mistakenly drinking the local water, when they were specifically told not to, in ice cubes, on washed salad or brushing their teeth with water from the tap instead of the bottled water always placed next to it.

They sit transfixed at what a bitch Anne Robinson, in her little round glasses, is being. It is just brilliant. "You are the weakest link. Goodbye."

The salty nuts and equally salty, slightly bitter feta transport Jen back to her holidays in Greece as a child. She was very lucky to have been to a number of the Greek Islands. They went on many day trips on these islands to visit 'interesting ruins'. They tended to end up being dull piles of stones and rubble of 'historical importance'.

However, she had a luminous love for Greece and its culture, people and colours. Donkey rides on Santorini and snorkelling in the beautiful clear blue sea were amazing. And one place of historical importance particularly sparked her imagination, even as an eight-year-old child. An old leper colony called Spinalonga off the island of Crete. An ancient Venetian fort with huge boundary walls that ensured the lepers couldn't leave. Or couldn't be seen. Or both.

They were abandoned, but not in a shipwrecked 'Swiss Family Robinson' way. Food and supplies were sent over on little fishing boats. They could see people and life, if they climbed to the top of the fortress, just a few hundred metres away in the village of Plaka on the northern coast of Crete. People were terrified of them and their cruel deforming disease leprosy, so for the first few decades they were just left there to rot, to die. 'You are the weakest link. Goodbye'.

The last inhabitants had it better as people understood the illness more and a cure was found. The last leper left only twenty-two years before she was born. In 1957. Jen, her family and another family they were on holiday with got a little fishing boat to the island and were all alone. The buildings were all fairly in-tact and completely abandoned. A society, a community - just abandoned. Houses, detached and semis, flats, a bakery, workshops, a church, a hospital, a pharmacy and a school. It was very eerie and impossibly sad. Unforgettable for Jen.

While watching Robinson, Jen ruminates on their bitter fate. And whether they were sent its slightly bitter anagram, feta, in their food delivery.

She also thinks about how she feels trapped sometimes of late. Then realises how absolutely ridiculous, self absorbed and slightly narcissistic her internal thoughts are. Sat there in the lovely cottage with her mum and gorgeous baby. She has a good, strong word with herself. Again.

After forty-five minutes their mouths are super salty from the pistachio nuts and the feta, and the nut bowl is full to the top with shells. They have somehow nearly finished the huge bag and the whole block of cheese. They have been so fascinated by the new game show and how much the victims are being abused by Anne, plus Jen's internal thoughts of the leper's abuse and her ridiculous self-absorption, that their nut noshing has been unregulated.

Jen feels sick. She has been trying really hard over the past week to regulate her bulexia/anoremia, but she hasn't been doing very well. She feels out of control. Everything is moving too fast. She feels anxious.

She goes upstairs telling her mum she is going to get her pyjamas on. Regurgitating salty pistachios and bitter feta is not new for her, but the combination is. It is absolutely revolting. She looks in the mirror after she purges, and after taking numerous slurps of water straight from the tap. She hates herself in this moment.

She looks into the toilet after the flush and can see there will be no just papering over this one. The mix of bile, sheep / goat milk and oily nuts have left a strange skim she has never seen before. She knows her mum is still tucked away downstairs in the snug, out of earshot, so she flushes for the second time. Before papering over it.

Looking in the mirror again while washing her teeth, she knows this is not good for her. Not good for her insides, her teeth or the sore hard piece of skin on the knuckle of her right index finger. The giveaway sign which no-one has ever noticed. Almost as invisible to her mum as the bird tattoo she has yet to admit to. Jen can spot a bulimic straight away, just by looking at their knuckles. Unless they are that brilliant type of bulimic who can bring it up without abusing their fingers.

Back downstairs, her mum says, "I thought you were getting your pyjamas on?"

"Oh yeah, I got distracted."

Her mum looks at her suspiciously, but then Joseph starts to cry.

"Grab him a bottle, will you?" her mum asks.

Jen heads into the kitchen, very annoyed at herself for her mistake. She never makes mistakes like this. Never raises any form of suspicion. She is always in control.

But she is not in control. Everything is daunting and seems difficult. She is a little scared and a lot sceptical about her ability to pull all of this off. Every time she feels like she has everything sorted, something else crops up to concern her. To remind her how out of control she is.

She just wishes things would slow down a bit. That she hadn't agreed to start working when Joseph is so little. That she could have some more time with him. That her ex would help her a bit more. That there isn't so much to do. That time isn't running out to do it all.

That everything isn't moving so very fast.

Movin' too fast.
Artful Dodger.

-41-
KATE: YELLOW

18th August 2000

It's late afternoon on Friday. Will and Kate are carving up the magical and majestic Cumbrian countryside on the West Coast Mainline.

Beautiful rambling fields and mountains, some covered with yellow flowers which make them look like they have been dusted with gold. The evening sun makes them glisten.

Will is not ready yet for the long two-hundred-and-forty-mile drive, and Kate has never learned to drive.

"Next stop, Carlisle," the conductor announces.

"How long until Glasgow?" Will asks Kate.

"About an hour and a half-ish," Kate replies.

"Want another drink?" he offers.

"Rude not to, I say," she replies. "We can toast the border."

Kate always gets excited when she crosses over to Scotland. She starts to give Will a highly expressive and passionate geography and history lesson.

Carlisle is just ten miles from the Scottish border. And from Gretna Green. The haven for young lovers following Lord Harwicke's 1754 Marriage Act was introduced in England and Wales forbidding anyone to marry under the age of 21 without their parent's permission. If a parent objected to the young person's choice of bride or groom, they could veto the marriage.

So Gretna Green, just two miles from England, became the place for eloping couples and clandestine weddings, shotgun or not. The West Coast Mainline rolls right past the town as it tracks the M6, snaking its way over Hadrian's Wall, the border and on to Scotland.

Hadrian's Wall marked the boundary between Roman Britannia and the unconquered Caledonia to the north. Built by the Roman army on instruction of their emperor Hadrian, it took six years to build and was finished in 122 AD. It lies entirely in England and, unknown to some, has never formed the Anglo-Scottish border. Although on the west coast the wall is just ten miles from the border, on the east coast it is a huge 160 miles south of it.

PAPER OVER IT

"It was not built to keep the Scots out, you prick. What did that posh school teach you?" Kate exclaims loudly in reaction to his ignorance and the fact he is ensuing that the Scots needed to be 'kept out'. "And it absolutely isn't the border. It's like saying the Chester Wall is the border between England and Wales."

"That's not comparable," Will says, pretending to be argumentative. But his smirk giving him away. He is always surprised how knowledgeable Kate is on British geography when she is so monumentally shit at directions and map reading. "The Chester Wall was built in a circle around the city by the Romans to protect it."

"Protect it from who and what, exactly?" she asks, indignantly.

"I'm not actually sure," he admits, laughing. Holding his still sore ribs. "You are just too cute when you get mad," he teases her. "You get all passionate and fiery."

"Fuck off, Mr. 'I'm not sure'," she says, pretending to be annoyed. "Thank god you're pretty. Now make yourself useful and go and get those drinks."

Will knows he is not as intelligent as Kate, however much expensive private education he had. He has absolutely no issue with this, is in no way felt threatened by it. He smiles at her veiled compliment. "Yes, ma'am," he says, performing a little salute.

"Good boy," she says saucily, like a sexy schoolteacher. "Off you go," she adds with a whisk of her hand.

He hobbles back with a can of Heineken, a bottle of Smirnoff Ice and a bag of Haribo Starmix.

It's Kate's little sister's eleventh birthday tomorrow so there is going to be a big party. He is genuinely looking forward to it and seeing her 'crazy Celtic crew' as he calls them.

As they cross the border, just south of Gretna Green, Kate puts both hands straight out in front of her. "I'm first in Scotland," she announces.

"Weirdo," Will says, amused. Sipping his can of Heineken. "Marry me," he says, taking her still extended left hand and putting a Haribo ring on her finger. "We can elope."

"Elope?" Kate grins. "You hopelessly soft dope."

She takes the ring off her finger with her mouth, then pushes her

261

tongue through the opening and pulsates it.

"Is that supposed to be sexy?" he asks, slightly offended by the rebuff, however much in jest the sweet Gretna Green inspired proposal had been. Sometimes he can be like Mr. Soft who has overdosed on Trebor Softmints taking the slow train to soft land. However, he does find the tongue ring action framed by her blow job lips really sexy.

"Yesh, shuper shexy," she manages through her ringed tongue as she pulls his mouth towards hers and transfers the ring to him before kissing him. He kisses her back, and then almost chokes on the ring.

She has to bang his back to help him get it up. It clearly really hurts him and his recovering ribs. The ring ends up projectile flying over the table in front of them and hitting the chair opposite. Thank god the elderly couple who had been sat there since Preston had got off at Carlisle.

"I survive a big ski-ing accident 3,000 metres up a Swiss mountain," he recounts, coughing. "And you nearly kill me with a Haribo on a train passing a sleepy Scottish town."

"You're very welcome," Kate is laughing. She retrieves the ring. It is sticky with saliva and sugar, and a little fluffy now from the seat. She puts it in her pocket. She is not sure why, but she wants to keep it. She will give it a good wash and dry later. "You know I love you so," she says to him.

Will sings back to her the line about bleeding himself dry for her, genuinely meaning it.

They arrive at Glasgow Central just after 6:30pm. There is yet again a welcoming committee and her little sister has upgraded from a banner to a flag. It is made with a bamboo stick and a large piece of yellow paper.

She knows yellow is Kate's favourite colour. To her it doesn't mean anything melancholy, it means happiness, sunshine, warmth and devotion. She is waving 'Welcome Home Kate' as the train pulls in. Kate waves madly back at her. She loves her little kid sister.

She once asked her mum if she was planned, seeing as there is ten years between her and her little sister, and eleven and twelve years between her little sister and two big brothers.

Her mother, honest as the day is long, simply replied, "No hen, she was totally planned. It was you that wasn't."

"Really?" Kate had asked, slightly aghast.

"I had a one year old and a two year old," she had explained looking pensive. "Why the hell do you think I'd want another?"

"Oh," Kate had ohh-ed.

"Sorry lass," realising how it had come across. "I was only upset when I was pregnant. When you came out I was thrilled. You were my first girl, and you were so bonny. Can't imagine how I'd have felt if you were another bloody boy."

"Oh," Kate repeated. Privately praising her dad's sperm for not producing a penis. "Well, that's out there then. Never to be back in."

"You asked," her mum had said practically.

"Wish I hadn't now," Kate had replied under her breath.

As Kate steps off the train, her sister piles into her. She bear hugs her and then spins her around, her yellow flag still flying. "I've missed you," she yells into her ear. "I've missed you too, hen," Kate yells back, laughing.

Kate's dad shakes Will's hand with his enormous hand. He is massive, nearly six foot five, with impressive shoulders and strong arms. His striking Arabian features are framed by a thick mane of black hair, gently peppering on his temples. "Let me take the bags, son," he says. "You've been in the wars, haven't you? Dangerous business, ski-ing."

He has a very eclectic accent mix of Lebanese and Glaswegian. Will struggles to understand him. "Give him the bags," Kate translates, "Hi dad," she adds, reaching up to give her much loved dad a hug and a kiss.

Driving from the station to Kate's home in her dad's black cab, Kate's sister is up front with her dad. She has, like Kate had when she was little, spent many happy hours in that seat from being a small child. In fact, it's crazy how shocking Kate is at map reading after all those years spent driving around Glasgow and its locality with geographically ignorant and sometimes rude passengers expecting her dad to know every corner of Scotland's largest city and the surrounding counties of Lanarkshire, Dunbartonshire and Renfrewshire.

Kate's little sister spends even more time with her dad in the school holidays when her mum is working at the shop from 10am until 3pm. It is the last day of her school summer break.

Kate and Will are in the back with their bags. Kate's dad starts telling stories about passengers he has had in his cab. It is his favourite topic. In fact, it is his only topic. Some stories are very interesting and funny, whereas others sound like they are completely concocted. Kate translates his stories to Will in the back.

"Had Tony Blair in the cab two weeks ago," he says. "Lovely chap. Cherie was quite nice too. Very cheery, but with quite an annoying voice. And she definitely wears the trousers."

Both Kate and Will are unsure that the PM and his wife would thumb a black cab down in Glasgow city centre, but they roll with it. His random bullshit an endearing and harmless part of the kind, giant of a man.

At home, and after a greeting from the extended family which made Will feel like they had been on the International Space Station for two years, not a few hours away in England, Kate and Will head upstairs to Kate's childhood bedroom. Bunk beds feature Kate's childhood Teenage Mutant Ninja Turtle duvet on the bottom bunk and her sister's Powerpuff Girls duvet up top. Kate's little sister is spending the next two nights in her parent's room.

"Top or bottom," Kate asks Will, eyes twinkling.

"You asked me that last time," he asks. "I'm Ninja all the way."

"I'll put my hair in bunches later, like a Powerpuff Girl" Kate teases. "If you're lucky."

"Reins," Will replies, grinning. "I can't wait."

As the pair get a little fruity on the bottom bunk witnessed by three Powerpuff Girls and four turtles, Kate's sister bursts in.

"What you doin?" she asks, innocently.

"Just checking whether the bed can take us both," Kate replies quickly. "Want to see if it will take all three of us?"

She doesn't answer and just piles on top of them. Will tries desperately to protect her from his hard with his hand. He succeeds, thank the lord of powerpuffs and the god of turtles.

"Mammy wants you both to come down," she says after she is one hundred percent sure the bottom bunk can handle the trio. "It's teatime."

Will, since being at Manchester Uni, has got used to people calling lunch dinner, and dinner tea. At home and at school he had lunch at lunchtime and dinner at dinner time. If there was a snack later in the evening, it was supper. When Kate had first said in their early days, "Come over for tea, if you'd like," he had expected a cup of tea. Had got himself something to eat before he headed over. Had been surprised when she handed him a bowl of pasta with Philadelphia, tinned tuna and sweetcorn. He had eaten it all even though he was full. And he hates tuna. Had a bone incident as a child in Marbella. It had terrified him. He told her a few weeks later about his two teas and his tuna trauma.

Downstairs the table somehow has six chairs and and two stools squished around it. Kate's dad, two brothers and auntie, who lives a few doors down, have collectively bagged the best seats.

"Hope you like tuna pasta bake, Will?" Kate's mum asks as she places a substantial, steaming and slightly smelly dish on the table.

Will squeezes Kate's leg to keep her quiet. "Looks great, thank you!" he evades the question. "Can't wait."

In the middle of the meal, Kate's dad perks up.

"I have a plan I want to tell you all about," he announces. "Have you ever heard about the company Apple? They make computers."

"Yes," most of the table say.

"Why?" Kate asks.

"I've been in this country for nearly thirty years now. Been driving a cab for a lot of that time," he says. "I'm not going to stop driving, but I am going to try a new road."

"What road, dad?" Kate's biggest big brother asks, mildly intrigued what the next madcap scheme is that his dad will never go ahead with.

"I'm going to remortgage the house and put the money into an Apple gamble."

"But you don't play fruit machines," his sister-in-law says, not knowing what Apple is. "And you don't like gambling. You've always been dead against it. You won't even go to the bingo with us."

"I know. But we are still here," Kate's dad explains, ignoring his sister-in-law's tech ignorance. Clearly not happy with where 'here' is.

His family is everything to him, and he occasionally has these moments where he feels he hasn't done enough for them. But he never actually goes through with anything. Never actually takes any form of risk. "I want more for us. I've made my mind up. I'm not going to be yellow-bellied anymore. I'm going to invest in Apple. Ted at the rank is going to do the same."

"Mum?" Kate laughs, not taking him seriously. "You're surely not going to let him go along with this"

"I don't really understand the money stuff, hen," her mum replies. "That's his area." This annoys Kate. She wishes her mum was a bit more independent, less the old-fashioned wife. But she knows her parents adore each other, and that the team is solid and works well.

"The only gamble you've ever taken is singing Kenny Rodgers at the karaoke down the pub," Kate's littlest big brother claims.

Kate's dad starts to sing about knowing when to hold them and fold them. Kate's biggest big brother continues the chorus, knowing when to walk away and when to run.

While sitting at the table, everyone but Kate and Will finish Kenny's classic about time for counting after the dealing is done. Kate is far too bemused. Will doesn't know the famous 1978 anthem, The Gambler.

"But dad, you know nothing about technology," Kate interrupts the Kenny choir. "You and mum don't even have mobile phones. And I've only just got one."

"Apple doesn't do phones, ya dafty," her dad replies, laughing at Kate. "They do computers. And little computers. Lab tops."

"Laptop, dad. Lap. Top," Kate's littlest big brother snorts at his dad. "For sitting on your lap, not on a big dog."

"Whatever," he replies dismissively, but having been educated. Having clocked his mistake. "But, as I said, Apple does computers. Not phones."

"Ok, you're right. But you know nothing about computers either," Kate says. "We don't own one and I doubt you've ever been on the internet." Only about a third of households own a computer in the UK and less have home access to the internet.

"Why does that matter, Catherine? I'm not going to be making them or selling them am I? I'm just going to invest in them," Kate's dad is getting uncharacteristically annoyed, using Kate's full name. "Anyway, I've made my mind up. I'm going to do it. What do we have to lose?"

"Just everything," Kate laughs, still not believing he will actually go through with it. "And how will you afford the extra mortgage payments?" she asks, practically.

"I'll work more hours in the cab," he says. "And your sister's eleven tomorrow, starts high school on Monday. She's growing up. Your mum is going to increase her shifts at the shop, aren't you love?"

"So you're in on this too, mam," Kate's biggest big brother asks, surprised.

"I was always going to up my hours when she started high school," she replies. "So it doesn't really make a difference to me."

"I think you're both mad," Kate says, stupefied. "You're like bloody Del Boy with your hair brain schemes, dad. 'This time next year we'll be millionaires' and all that."

"Maybe not next year, maybe the year after. Or the year after that," her dad ponders. "But who knows? It could turn into something beautiful. He who dares wins," copying Del Boy's take on the British SAS motto.

"How much are you talking, dad?"

"Fifteen thousand, maybe twenty," he says.

"Wow," Mexican waved around the table.

Will just sits and listens, concentrating on swallowing the terrifying tuna.

Later that night, just before Nasty Nick is ejected from the Big Brother house for cheating and vote manipulation, "or just playing the game," as Kate's biggest big brother suggests, Kate's parents and little sister go to bed.

"Big day for you tomorrow little miss eleven," Kate says to her little sister as she kisses and hugs her goodnight. "Don't let the bed bugs bite."

"Nightie night Katie Pie," she says. "Night everyone else," she says to Will and her big brothers, clearly none are as important as Kate.

"What do you think?" Kate asks her big brothers and Will.

"I'm not sure it's a good idea," Will says. "But then again, I'm not sure it's a bad idea either."

267

"Very helpful posh boy," Kate's littlest big brother laughs while her other brother asks, "Is that fence digging into your dick?"

Will rolls his eyes and smiles, knowing there's no point in defending his daft, pointless comment. Also knowing there's no point in going up against these two big, boisterous Scots. They frighten him a bit.

Kate adds, "Thanks for your pearls of wisdom Will Shakespeare. Very insightful."

"Don't you gang up on me too," Will says, pretending to pout. "I'm just saying I honestly don't think it is the worst idea in the world. As long as they can afford to pay the mortgage. My dad has some investments and has made quite a lot at times. Isn't Em's dad something to do with stocks and shares?"

"I think he is," Kate replies. "And I'm sure her brother works at a bank. I think Lou said he does anyway."

Seemingly less interested than Kate at their parents' precarious plan, Kate's biggest big brother asks, "Pub for last orders?"

"I'm in, if you're paying," her other brother says.

"Not for me tonight. Definitely up for it tomorrow," Kate says. "Will, you go with them if you like?"

"To be honest I'm feeling a little tired," a migraine starting to melt over him, an aura on the horizon.

The brothers call Will a 'wee fanny' and a 'soft southerner' and head out.

"It's only still quite early," Will says. "Call her if you're worried. See if she can talk to her dad or brother. You may as well ask, see if they know how risky it is. But it looks like he is really sure about doing it."

"Ok I will," she says. "Are you ok?"

"I don't feel great to be honest," he answers. "I'm going to go up and lie down in the dark. You come up when you've spoken to Em."

After Em agreed to do some digging on Apple investments, Em says she had wanted to talk to her anyway.

"You will never guess what!" she says.

"What?" Kate asks. Intrigued by the excitement in her voice.

"I've got an interview at the veterinary college near me," she exclaims. "I might be on my way to being a vet!"

"What? How? You didn't even apply."

"I am so bloody lucky. My dad knows some people, has given to some charity thing in the past. I already have the right A-Levels, and obviously a degree now too. He made some calls, and although I am far too late to apply… I've been given a chance!"

Kate hates the fact that money can buy people and privilege, and that this privilege breeds privilege. That her parents are going to risk a lot of the little money they have, all currently safely saved in their home, on a gamble which might not pay off. Just to try and get a better life after working so hard anyway. An amount of money that Em's dad probably has in his current account. An amount he has probably just gifted to the veterinary college so he can gift his daughter a place she is seven months late in applying for. It is all so crudely and crassly Conservative.

But she loves her friend, has never heard her so excited. She bites her lip and clears herself from her capitalist contempt.

"Oh my god," Kate says. "That's amazing." She can't help herself add, "And you're right, you are one very lucky cow."

"I certainly am. I genuinely know I am Kate. I did not expect this and probably don't deserve it," she replies. "I'm terrified, but I can't wait. I feel like I finally know what I'm going to do. Like you and your law."

Kate smiles to herself. It is like listening to a different Em. Self deprecating, unguarded and super excited. For so long she has sounded a sad mixture of green and blue. She now suddenly sounds yellow.

She had spoken to Em after her weekend at home in Hertfordshire and she had said that everything went as well as it could have done. Said she would update them all properly on their night out in a few weeks.

"When's the interview?" Kate asks.

"Next Wednesday," she replies. "At 9:30 in the morning."

"No way," Kate exclaims. "That's the same day as Lou's audition in London."

"She's got an audition?" Em asks, news to her.

"Yes, she only found out earlier today from that new agent she got a few weeks ago. Apparently it's really quick to get a first audition.

She's stunned. It's for a musical. I can't remember which one. I didn't recognise it so don't think it's a big one. She's really excited and nervous, like you," Kate explains. "I think she said she's staying at your brother's place."

"Bloody hell," Em says. "Big day for both of us then. I'll call her first thing. One more thing, Kate. How do you fancy renting my flat for the next year with Will?"

"Where has this come from?" Kate asks, confused.

"Well, I won't need a flat in Manchester if I'm down here, will I? And even if I don't get in, I'm going to stay down here for a while."

"But, won't you sell it?" Kate asks.

"No, but I can't leave it empty either. I'd give you mate's rates. There's the parking space too so super easy for Will. However much you pair are planning on spending on No. 52, I'll match it. No deposit. You'd have to look after Steve the Cheese and Hairy Potter. You're planning on getting two rooms in Withington right? There's only one bedroom in the flat as you know. Anyway, think about it. Speak to Will. I've got to go. I'm due out in ten minutes and I haven't even dried my hair. I promise I will get on that Apple thing in the morning. Find out what I can."

After she hangs up, Kate suddenly feels knackered. It has been a long yet really good day. A yellow day. With work, the long train ride, the candy carnage of Haribo-gate, excitement in seeing her family, Em's news, Lou's news, the offer of Em's flat and the Apple bombshell.

She heads up to talk to Will about Em's offer. They are late to sign for No. 52 so have not yet committed or paid any deposit.

She finds him fast asleep on her bottom bunk with her four turtles. He hadn't even managed to undress or shut the turtle curtains before he passed out on the bed. She looks out through the window into the clear dark sky brimming with billions of stars shining their brilliance. She pulls the ninja pair over the night sky and looks at Will for a second. He is lightly lit by her little turtle bedside lamp. He really is beautiful, she thinks.

She snuggles into him underneath Leonardo, Donatello, Raphael and Michelangelo. He is slightly feverish and sweaty, his skin a slight shade of yellow. This always happens when he gets the hideous headaches which started after his accident.

She kisses his hot head, whispers "I love you" and closes her eyes.

Yellow.
Coldplay.

-42-
EM & LOU: STRONGER

23rd August 2000
Lou. London. 07:50.
 "You'll be fine," Charlie says to Lou. "They will love you."
 They had a semi argument last night when Charlie was tired after a particularly stressful day at work and then, after a lusciously long copulation session, he plugged in his PlayStation and started to tackle the tee offs with Tiger Woods.
 "Can't we watch a movie or something?" Lou had asked.
 "You can watch me play this if you like?"
 "Are you serious?" she pouted. "I've come all the way down from Liverpool to see you."
 "No, Lou," he replied, his thumbs vigorously pressing the controller. "You came down for your audition and it suited you to stay here. And you said you wanted an early night. It's nearly midnight."
 "Well, can I play with you?" she couldn't disagree with him. He was annoyingly right. "I might not be very good at it though."
 "You just have," he replied naughtily. "And you were very good at it. Excellent in fact. Like a pro."
 Lou laughed. He made her laugh a lot. He just annoyed her a lot too.
 "Go on then," he conceded and handed her the controller. "Here you go."
 He explained a number of times how she should do it. She didn't really listen to him. Didn't want his help. She was shit at it. Even after about fifteen minutes, she was still monumentally shit at it.
 "You are monumentally shit at this," Charlie laughed.
 Lou hated that she was so clearly shit at it.
 "And you are monumentally annoying," she replied, going into a sulk. "I'm going to bed now anyway. Don't want to play your stupid little boy game."
 Charlie laughed at her petulance. She turned around mid sassy strop walk and stuck her long tongue out at him.

PAPER OVER IT

"Twat," she said, smarting.

"Dick," he replied, laughing.

"I've got to go," Charlie says, picking up his work bag. "I'm going to be late for work. The keys are there. Lock up when you leave. Make sure you don't lose them. Call me when you're done." He kisses her and adds, "Good luck" as he flies out of the flat door.

Lou is left alone in the small one-bedroom flat. Probably worth more than her parent's whole street, she thinks. She flips through Charlie's Loaded magazine. It is so laddish, so full of smut. She laughs at the pornalikes. Especially one which is supposed to look like Britney Spears. She really doesn't. Looks more like Lisa from The Simpsons.

She moves the sofa in the combined kitchen and living area to one side to clear a bit of floor space so she can stretch. So she can get her muscles moving, contracting, become more flexible. She knows it will calm her mind. Help her feel stronger.

The audition means so much to her. Hours upon hours of pliéing and perfecting, years upon years of classes and competitions, piles upon piles of trophies and triumph trinkets. A young lifetime of injuries, strain; no pain, no gain. Of over-tight hair buns and sticky-in grips, smiling through her painted lips.

But she just loves it. Always has. Always will. It's what makes her feel strong.

She looks at her phone. It is just before 8:00am.

She has already had a shower and sorted her hair. Her audition is at 10:30.

It will take her only about fifteen minutes to get there on the tube. The station is only a two-minute walk away from Charlie's flat and it is just a seven minute walk to the address from her destination station.

She wants to be there fifteen minutes early, and wants to give herself an extra twenty minutes for the journey. Just in case.

She decides she will leave at 9:00 to be super certain she makes it on time.

That gives her an hour.

She presses play on Charlie's hi-fi and becomes stretch Armstrong. Hertfordshire. Em. 09:20.

Em is at the Royal Veterinary School Hawksmead complex in Hertfordshire waiting to go in to her specially arranged / paid for late interview. She is holding her bag tight, it is somehow helping to control her bouncing bag of nerves inside.

She sips at her trembling water. Nothing has really ever mattered this much before. She sailed through school, passed her one and only driving test, got into a very good course at Manchester Uni and got a 2:1 with minimal effort. Except at the end. But she only really revised because she was helping Jen. All without really caring about herself or her future.

"Be strong, Emily," she says to herself.

She has tried to research the questions she may be asked, like she had with Jen's interview. But this is so specific, too specific. The library and internet gave her nothing. She has filled in a long form she was sent in the post with personal information, education history, and plenty more, and has written a personal statement. All very similar to the UCAS application she had done in upper sixth form four and a half years ago. She really has absolutely no idea what to expect. She assumes people normally interview at seventeen or eighteen, that she is three years older than the majority of applicants.

"Emily," a lady says. "Emily Roberts."

Em is taken off guard. She was not expecting a woman. Maybe she is the secretary.

She stands up and extends her arm, "Hi, I'm Emily."

"Pleased to meet you, Emily," the lady says in a Scottish accent, an eclectic mix of curious and curt. Taking her hand and shaking it, she adds, "I'm Doctor Campbell, one of the senior lecturers here at the RVC."

Em is immediately appalled at herself for assuming she is support staff. She hopes one day she, or anyone, will not pre-judge. Be so sexist, so misogynistic. That her baby sister will not live in a world of gender-based roles where the successful, high-flying woman is perceived as the exception. That the strong woman at work is not considered a bitch. That the angry woman is not deemed on the blob, hormonal or menopausal. No more 'isn't it amazing she's doing that as a woman'. Not to undermine support staff, but to not undermine women generally. But for now she knows misogyny still exists in a big way. She has just proven that to herself, to her personal dismay.

"Lovely to meet you too," Em replies. "Thank you so much for seeing me. I know this is a very late interview. I'm surprised you could see me."

"I'm as surprised as you are, to be honest," she looks at Emily in a knowing way. "Come on, let's see what you're made of. No-one gets a free pass into this place."

As Dr. Campbell walks away, Em assumes she is to follow. She feels like she has just been told off, slightly sneered at. She is desperate to make a good impression on her, but quickly understands that her situation, and the way she has found herself here, has not made a good impression at all so far. Is nepotism as bad as misogyny? She imagines this woman hates them both in equal measures.

In the interview room, an office with a large table and numerous chairs, Dr. Campbell takes a seat next to a man and points to the chairs opposite for Em to sit down.

"This is Doctor Garcia," Dr. Campbell explains. "There would normally be three of us interviewing, but in this exceptional circumstance there are only the two of us available." She labours on 'exceptional'.

"Hi Emily," he says. "Pleased to meet you. I met your father once at a fundraising event."

"Hi," Em replies. Suddenly feeling in no way strong at all. Embarrassed about how and why she is here. She has always taken whatever her privilege has offered her without a second thought. Has never even contemplated that any of the opportunities she has had or achievements she has made aren't one hundred percent because of her. This is a brand new feeling for her. And it makes her feel quite sick inside. "I could not be more grateful for you both taking the time to see me. It is hugely appreciated. And I just hope I can prove to you that I genuinely deserve a place here."

"Lots of people who genuinely deserve a place here don't get in," Dr. Campbell says. "Because we can't take every single deserving person. It is why we have a strict process."

"Shall we crack on with the interview?" Dr. Garcia says, giving Dr. Campbell a sidewards glance.

This is not how Em had imagined it. Even when she had tried to envisage the worst, she had not thought of this.

The interview consists of three general themes: personal, ethical and specific. Em answers the numerous questions to the best of her ability. The nods and the scribbles on notepads builds her confidence, makes her feel stronger.

One specific question, at the end of the interview, is, "What work experience have you had within the field of veterinary science?"

Jen has to admit she has none, but she explains confidently all the experience she has had with animals. Big and small. Dr. Garcia nods, writing on his notepad.

"Ok. What other work experience have you had? More generally I mean," Dr. Campbell asks. "You are, let me see, almost twenty-two. What can you tell me about your general work experience?"

Em is stumped. She has never had a job. Never earned a penny of her own. She knows her three friends at uni have all had jobs from being mid-teens right through to university and throughout their summer holidays. In shops, at pubs and restaurants, temping on receptions, working in warehouses, spending hours filling envelopes and delivering Yellow Pages door to door to name just a few she remembers them telling her about. Most of her home friends hadn't worked, like her. She is not judging them but she suddenly personally feels quite stupid, horribly spoilt, highly inexperienced and overwhelmingly undeserving.

Her confidence takes a mammoth nosedive again. She thinks about lying, but decides against it. She has lied so much in the past. Made so many things up to make her feel stronger, appear stronger. She is sick of it, tired of it.

"I'm a spoilt, wealthy, privately educated pony club girl who has never had to work and has been given everything she has ever needed or wanted. I understand that I may not deserve this opportunity, and I also don't want to be given it if I don't," Em just lets her feelings out in a way she has never done in the past, but is learning to do more recently. It is actually quite cathartic. "I have already spent three years at university doing something I didn't really care about because I never bothered to sit down and really think about what I wanted to do or be. If I had, I would have applied here when I was seventeen. I lazily assumed it would all work itself out. I am in the incredibly fortunate position that I can stay in education, that I don't have to go out yet to work to earn a living. That I can change my mind and go after something I am genuinely passionate about. I understand what a huge privilege that is."

The pair sit and listen, Dr. Campbell's face softening ever so slightly. Dr. Garcia nods at Em to carry on.

"I would work so hard, I promise," she adds. "I know now this is exactly what I want to do, where I want to be. But I totally understand that I probably don't deserve it."

After waiting for a few moments to see whether Em has finished, and after seeing her head go down, Dr. Garcia says, "Well thank you very much, Emily. Have you got any questions for us?"

Em knows she should have, but she hasn't. She doesn't even want to ask what the next steps are as she knows there won't be any. "No, thank you," she replies, defeated. "Thank you very much for your time."

"Thank you Emily," says Dr. Campbell. "We will be in touch as soon as possible."

London. Lou. 10:20.

Lou is waiting to go into the audition for the ensemble.

She looks around at her competition in the queue. There looks to be about thirty people. Strong looking people. She starts to feel a little overwhelmed and slightly panicky. There are lots of conversations going on. It is clear that some recognise or know each other.

She has done countless auditions in the past, but none had felt so important. She starts to do the breathing techniques she has been taught.

This is the start of the rest of her life, not just part of her journey.

Once inside, she mentally lists the audition rules which have been drummed into her. Hearing her uni tutor and her agent's drilling in tandem.

Be confident.

Be gracious.

Be prepared.

Be kind.

Be focused.

Be powerful.

Be engaging.

Be fierce.

Be seen.

Be strong.

Be fun.

Above all. Be you.

They are taught a choreography combination which Lou finds fairly simple. She can see that the creative who is leading the session is watching her. 'Be gracious'. Lou smiles at her and she smiles back.

They are then split into smaller groups of five. Each group is to perform the dance to the panel of creatives. Apparently the director and producers will be involved at a later stage.

Lou takes her place in the middle of her quintet and smiles at the four people facing her. 'Be seen.'

She tries her best but for some reason her concentration, that has rarely left her in all the years she has been dancing, suddenly fails her. 'Be focused'. She can't quite understand it and panics. This has an immediate impact on rule number one, 'Be confident'. She knows she is fluffing the steps, steps which normally she would find so easy. She is usually so strong at learning new choreography. But not today, when it really matters. It is embarrassing and heart breaking, and no fun at all.

'Be you'. The one person Lou doesn't want to be right now is herself.

Unsurprisingly Lou is not called back to the next stage. She just wants to run away and hide. Her brain and body have never let her down in this way before, they are usually both so strong.

As she packs up her bag and heads for the door, tears starting to prick her eyes, the lady who lead the choreography session approaches her.

"Louisa, isn't it?" she asks.

"Yes, that's me," she says, wishing it isn't.

"First audition?" she asks, kindly.

"No, I've done loads before," Lou admits. "But not as an adult. I mean not as a graduate. Not like this. I've never really felt nervous before."

"My first audition like this was an absolute car crash," she explains. "Slipped and fell flat on my face. Took out the girl next to me. She was fuming. I was floored and so embarrassed. I went so red the proverbial egg on my face was literally frying."

Lou looks up at her through teary eyes. "Really?" she asks.

'Really," the lady nods. "Try to learn from this. It will make you a stronger applicant and performer. If you have never really had nerves before, you need to learn about them. How to control and handle them. How to use them to your advantage to make you stronger. To treat them like the adrenaline they are."

"Thank you," Lou says, genuinely appreciating the advice. Taking it all in.

"I know your agent," she adds. "She told me how impressive you are. I could see that in the practice session. And if she says that, you must be. She's a bit of a battleaxe, isn't she?"

Lou smiles, the feedback improving her mood slightly. "Yes, she is a bit."

"Today wasn't your day, hun," she smiles back at her. "But you will be snapped up soon. You're not only very talented but you're also super striking and clearly very strong. You have an awesome presence and you very much command attention. It's a brutal business, cut-throat. And rejection is just part of it, I'm afraid. Keep your chin up. Make sure you sizzle and sparkle!"

"Thank you," Lou says for the second time. "I really appreciate this, honestly I do." She flashes her a sizzling, sparkling smile. "And I will."

"That's the spirit," the lady says before returning to her fellow judges.

Lou walks out into the London heat and smiles to herself. A rueful smile, but a smile nonetheless.

She is even more certain that this is what she wants, even more driven and motivated to succeed.

She decides to go and have a wander around Covent Garden. Watch the street performers. She opens her trusty London map. She hopes one day she won't need it. As she walks down Russell Street she catches a reflection of herself in one of the windows of The Theatre Royal Drury Lane filled with pictures of the recently premiered 'The Witches of Eastwick' musical.

"One day," she promises herself, feeling somehow stronger than yesterday. Even with the rejection.

Hertfordshire. Em. 11:10.

Em has driven the long way home. Needed time to think. To process what has just happened. But more importantly, how it has made her feel.

Have her friends in Manchester only wanted to be her friend for what she could give them? Did her privilege actually rile them as it clearly had Dr. Campbell? She had loved living in an environment where it wasn't all about what you had, a space where what you could do for people was less to do with influence and money. She is totally overthinking everything, but the last few months have made her genuinely reflect. Huge questions are rising in her head.

She had asked her dad and brother about Kate's Apple question and got back to her saying they actually both thought it wasn't a terrible idea. But it carried risk as any tech investment did. The memory of it has compounded her thinking that maybe her friends were only her friends for what she could do for them. She is totally confused.

What she isn't confused about is that she needs to start taking responsibility for herself. Not be so reliant on her dad's wealth and her own pompous privilege. Start to stand on her own two feet. Grow the fuck up.

She keys her birthday into the pad and drives through the gate. The Audi TT is the only car in the drive. Oddly she is relieved.

Weirdly and incomprehensibly, the only person she wants to speak to right now is Eve.

She feels immediately stronger.

Stronger.
Britney Spears.

-43-
JEN: DON'T CALL ME BABY

1st September 2000

Jen just lies there. Stunned, horrified, mortified and confused.

She hears her hotel door opening.

"Hello, baby," Mr. Senior Specs says as he walks back into her room. "Knew I would forget something. That's why I took your key."

He retrieves his glasses from the bedside table next to where he slept.

"I'll see you, baby Jennifer, next week when you start." He leaves without a care in the world.

She casts her mind back to the day before. The night before. The night she's sure she fucked up before she even started.

The day had started well. She had arranged for Joseph's settle-in at nursery for the morning and was to drop him off any time after 8am. Her mum had arranged to leave work early and pick him up just after lunchtime. She had prepared his bottles the night before so she just put them in the cool bag her mum had found and she had named with an indelible marker. She just needed to grab and name the bag of nappies she had bought the day before from Tesco, and the bag of spare clothes she had already packed in a non-cool named bag.

She and her mum have a well-practised morning routine now. When Joseph wakes up at about 6am, Jen gets up and takes him into her mum for a cuddle while she goes downstairs and pops the kettle on to heat up his milk and to make two cups of tea. She puts the warm bottle in her dressing gown pocket and takes the two mugs upstairs. She places the two mugs down on each of her mum's bedside tables and hands her mum the bottle. She gets into bed with the two of them and they talk about the day to come. It is a lovely, calm, perfectly planned process.

Yesterday, when her mum got up to get ready for work, she cuddled Joseph even more than normal. She knew she would miss him massively. She has never spent such a long time away from him. Over twenty-four hours.

A little while later he giggled at her as she blew raspberries on his bare tummy while she changed him and dressed him in the clothes she had picked out for his big day.

Her bag was already packed and her clothes for the day hung up. She had a quick shower with Joseph happily lying on the carpeted bathroom floor. Watching her.

She got changed into her interview outfit. Carla had told her it was work wear for the day and dress up at night. Her shocking pink and grey had been lucky last time, she just hoped it would be this time too. She had packed her much loved little black dress and a pair of her mum's black high heel shoes. Thank goodness they had nearly the same size feet. A pair of insoles made them the perfect fit. She also packed a pair of little pink shorts and her old blue childhood Snoopy nightie t-shirt to sleep in, and a tracksuit and trainers to travel home in the following morning.

She was to be at the hotel near Manchester Airport at 9:30 for registration. The event started at 10am. The drive from the nursery should only take about twenty minutes but she didn't want to risk being late. She got herself, Joseph, her bags and his numerous bags into Honey by 7:50.

Joseph was in his seat on the passenger seat next to her. Honey has no airbags so he is perfectly safe.

"Let's go, little man," she said to him as she jabbed into first gear. He smiled and gurgled back at her. "I have a feeling this is going to be a really good day for both of us."

Dropping him at the nursery was difficult and he cried when she left. The kind nursery manager told her it was perfectly normal. He would be fine as soon as she left and he started to be distracted, looking around at all the new things, people and experiences. Even though she did believe her, Jen cried when she left.

She waited in her car in the car park at the hotel for about half an hour. She was very early. She took the fake tortoise shell rimmed glasses out of her handbag and put them on. Looking in the rear view mirror she was sure they made her look older and more intelligent. They also felt like a mask to her. Like she could be anyone she wanted to be. That was the plan, anyway.

As she entered the hotel lobby there was a desk filled to the brim with name badges. An older lady, probably in her forties she thought, was standing behind it.

"They are all in alphabetical order so should be easy to find," she advised. "Let me know if you have any problems."

She didn't say whether the order was first name or last name, but being Jennifer Jones meant it didn't matter. She found her badge easily and attached it to her pink boxy cardy.

"Jen," she heard from behind her. "You're here! How's Joseph?"

It was Carla. Jen was relieved and happy to see her. Carla took complete control and explained what was going to happen in the day and night before introducing her to everyone they bumped into. Thank god for the name badges as Jen could not remember any of the multiple names she was told. Hers said Jennifer. She always felt she was being told off when anyone called her Jennifer.

The day was great. A massive conference room with big round tables seating ten people each. There must have been about twenty-five of these tables. A huge screen and amazing lights and sounds. The presentations were as inspiring as the people delivering them. It was all very exciting for Jen. Exhilarating.

A guy, who Carla explained was 'The Big Boss', introduced everyone and then a senior guy stood up on the stage and started his presentation. Jen couldn't make out who Carla said he was. He looked about in his early to mid-forties, Jen thought. But she couldn't be sure. For an old guy, he was really quite attractive with cool glasses and a sharp suit. She called him internally Mr. Senior Specs. He had a huge presence. Some of his jokes were bordering on rude, crude or both, and a story he told about his wife had misogyny written all over it. But he was entertaining, commanded respect and was a great orator.

Jen was made to stand up in the middle of the Marketing Director's bit. The whole room welcomed her. "Hi Jennifer," two hundred and fifty people said in chorus. Two hundred and fifty people she will now have to tell that her name is Jen. She doesn't want to feel like she is being told off by two hundred and fifty people every day.

She called the nursery on a break. Joseph was, as expected, perfectly settled and happy. Not missing her at all, like she is missing him.

After the day finished, Jen headed up to her room to get changed for the evening. She called her mum. As expected, Joseph was perfectly settled and happy.

She checked herself out in the mirror and was happy with what she saw. She had zipped back also immediately to her pre-pregnancy body, as young mums tend to. Just a few stretch marks on her outer thighs and boobs are tell-tale signs. Although quite old now, she knows the little black dress is a winner. She loves it. Is her banker, her go to. Not too tight, too low or too short. She feels good in it and her mum's high heels. Grown up. Almost elegant.

There was a seating plan on a big board in the entrance to the same room they had been in that day. It had been transformed, in just a short time, into an amazing evening venue. She scanned it and found her name. Jennifer Jones. She was sat on a table towards the back with some lovely people including the name badge lady from the morning. Straight after dinner, there was an annual awards section which was compered by the 'The Big Boss'. Jen missed the first few minutes of it as she was papering over it. Controlling it.

The awards were just brilliant with trophies, lights, photos, music and standing ovations. Jen hoped one day she might be up there on the stage receiving an award. She was really excited and exhilarated by the whole event.

After the awards, an up-and-coming comedian called Peter Kay did a hilarious set. He was from up the road in Bolton and had won 'North West Comedian of the Year' a few years back, and had won a few more awards since.

After the Peter Kay thing, a band started to set-up on the stage. They were absolutely brilliant. Jen danced with Carla and her friends for ages. She was sweaty and the ill-fitting fake glasses kept falling down her nose. But it was so much fun.

At about 11:30pm Jen felt totally exhausted physically and mentally so thought she might head up to bed. She thought no-one would notice her departure, they were pretty much all pissed by this stage. She headed out of the room.

As she approached the lobby she heard her 'in trouble' name being called. "Jennifer."

She swung round and saw the senior chap from earlier. Mr. Senior Specs was standing there, smiling. Or rather, kind of smirking.

"Not going up yet are you?" he asked.

"Yes," she replied. "It's been a long day."

"Come and have a drink with me?" he asked. But it wasn't really an ask. He was very senior and she was very junior. In fact, she had not even started the job yet.

Jen looked around, but they were alone. "Ok, just one," she said.

She followed him to a quiet corner and sat down. He went to the bar and came back with two large glasses of red wine. He didn't ask her what she wanted. Jen hates red wine. Has done ever since the tent puce puke incident.

"I've been watching you all night," he said.

Jen felt uncomfortable but knew deep down she had to play the game. She can't fuck this up before she even starts. Can't piss him off or make an enemy of this super senior man.

"Really?" she replied, taking a sip of the rancid red. It tasted strange and slightly threatening to her, a little like this situation.

He removed her fake glasses and said, "Let me take a proper look at you."

Jen was shocked by his space invasion, but just smiled. She was not sure what else to do.

"Gorgeous," he said. "And I hear you have a baby. You're just a baby yourself."

Jen suddenly felt vulnerable. A few people had asked her about Joseph, but they were friends of Carla's. She hadn't actively said much to anyone else as she didn't want to be just known as that girl with the baby. She knows how much some people can and will judge. Assume she won't be able to cope. She has first-hand experience of this. Being a young single mum is unfortunately still looked down upon. Even Posh Spice got some unfair shit last year when Brooklyn was born out of wedlock. She adores Joseph but she wants to make sure she sets herself up for success for him and her too. It is a massive conflict.

"I'm twenty-one," she replied. "Not a baby at all."

"You're a baby to me," he said, slightly weirdly.

They started to chat and he was actually very amusing. She told him she preferred to be called Jen. Jen was laughing at one of his stories when the name badge lady walked past, clearly looking for someone. "All ok?" she asked the pair when she spotted them. Jen felt like she was asking her rather than him. She also thought she could sense an element of suspicion in her tone. Jen smiled, not sure what else to do. She was aware how bad this might look and just wanted to get away from the situation. But she couldn't say she wasn't ok, could she? And in fact, at that, moment, she was ok.

"Yes, absolutely fine," she answered. "Why wouldn't we be?" he added in a marginally micro aggressive manner.

The lady nodded slowly, slit her eyes ever so slightly and walked away.

Jen said, "I think I may head up now."

"I'll walk you up, baby," he grabbed both wine glasses while she retrieved her fake glasses from the table. Feeling like the fake she is, the fraud. "We can take these up with us."

Not knowing what to do, totally inexperienced at any kind of situation like this, Jen got up and started walking to the lift. She hated being called 'baby' and wanted to tell him, but she didn't want to be sacked or branded a troublemaker before she had even started.

He followed her.

Mr. Senior Specs followed her right into her room.

"I promise we won't do anything," he said. "I just thought we could have a cuddle."

"I'm not sure this is a good idea," Jen said. Slightly panicking.

"It's fine," he soothed her. "Just get yourself ready for bed and I'll go and get some stuff from my room."

He took her room key from the side and let himself out.

Jen froze. She didn't have a clue what to do. She couldn't tell anyone. She didn't really have anyone to tell, anyway. Apart from Carla, and that was not going to happen. She would not put her in a difficult situation or get her involved in this mess. But she didn't want to look like 'that kind of girl' either, though. She had ultimately allowed him into her room. What if someone had seen? Seen the single mother slut leave the lobby with him in the lift? Seen him go into her room? Seen the door shut?

She was in a lose lose situation, and knew it. She had no option but to accept it.

She changed into her little pink shorts and her childhood blue

Snoopy nightie t-shirt and got into bed, under the covers. Hiding herself. The 'self' she knew looked like a baby sporting her Snoopy. Wishing she had brought proper grown-up pyjamas. Or, even better, her no access onesie.

As he let himself back in she shuddered, or shivered, or both. He changed into his shorts and t-shirt too and hung his trousers, shirt and jacket on the trouser press. She could hear him place something on the bedside table.

He then slid into the bed next to her. Much worse space invasion than removing her fake glasses.

True to his word, he didn't try to have sex with her, or even properly kiss her. But he held her close and kissed her head a few times. "You really are a beautiful baby, aren't you," she remembers him saying.

She was frozen with disbelief and shame. She lay awake for a long time as he fell asleep and started to snore. Trying to work out what she had done wrong, how she had let this happen? How had she been so misunderstood? Had she come on to him? Made him think that she wanted this? Was it the dress? Too short? Too revealing? She could see her much loved little black dress hanging over the dressing table chair, and suddenly hated it. Was it the way she had danced? Had she laughed too much? Or too loudly? Encouraged him? If he had seen a certain vibe in her she was unaware she was giving off, had other people seen it too? Was everyone laughing at her? Appalled at her behaviour? She tried to understand how she had fucked up so much. How she had let it happen.

She must have fallen asleep at some point because when she wakes up it is morning and she is alone in her bed.

She just lies there. Stunned, horrified, mortified and confused.

She hears her hotel door opening.

"Hello, baby," Mr. Senior Specs says as he walks back into her room. "Knew I would forget something. That's why I took your key."

He retrieves his glasses from the bedside table next to where he slept.

"I'll see you, baby Jennifer, next week when you start." He leaves without a care in the world.

"Don't you dare call me Jennifer," she cries when she is sure he is gone and out of earshot. "And never, ever call me baby again."

Jen can't believe it. She is shattered in more ways than one. Has been totally undermined and underestimated. Is it because she's vulnerable? A single mum? Does she smell of desperation? Or worse, smell of slut? Desperate slut? Did anyone see him go in and out of her room this morning? Or last night? Does he know how he has made her feel? Or even care? What she does know is that there is nothing she can or will do about it. And she knows he will think that, estimate that, too. If he has any thoughts about it at all. So she hasn't been underestimated, or even overestimated, after all. She has been accurately estimated. She just wants to be at home. With her family. With her mum and her baby.

She gets changed out of Snoopy and into her tracksuit and trainers, leaves the hotel with no makeup on and without having breakfast, and gets into her car, her Honey, as quickly as she can.

On the drive home her mind is in overdrive. She can't understand why she keeps being let down by so many of the men in her life. What is she doing wrong? It must be her fault, she must be to blame. She feels stupid. She feels dirty. She feels very, very small. Weak. Vulnerable. Like a baby.

At home she relieves her mum of Joseph and tells her she can get off to work. Her mum just thinks her lack of words means she's tired and says, "You must tell me all about it later."

"I will," Jen promises. She lies. She digs a fake smile out of the substratum of her slightly broken self.

Cuddling Joseph on the sofa in the snug, she promises herself and him that she will steer clear of men generally. She clearly has a bad effect on them. And the effect they have on her is not helpful either. She needs to focus her strength on herself and her baby. Not on trying to understand what she never will, control what she can't and change what is seemingly unchangeable.

She needs to try and rise above it. Whatever 'it' is. Find the strength within to hold her head up high. To not be, or at least not appear to be, broken. To not be underestimated, or at least not be misunderstood. With her fake glasses, the fake wedding ring she still intends to buy, some fake bravado she will source from somewhere and her fake smile.

She never, ever again wants to feel as fraudulent, shitty, filthy and shattered as she feels right now.

Don't call me baby.
Madison Avenue.

-44-
THE QUARTET: STEAL MY SUNSHINE

2nd September 2000
Kate and Will moved into Em's flat last week.

It makes perfect sense for all involved. The new residents start back at uni next week.

New friends Will and Steve are getting on very nicely, as are old friends Will and Hairy.

Em drove up at lunchtime today from Hertfordshire in the blazing sunshine for the big girlie night out, and to collect her clothes and personal things. She is going to leave all the general flat stuff, like the cups in the cup cupboard, Steve the Cheese and Hairy Potter, for Kate and Will to either use, abuse or simply look after. Hairy is now tucked away tightly and brightly under his fake sunshine in the cupboard by the front door.

The moment she passed Stoke, the rain started. 'Up north' had yet again stolen the sunshine.

Will is staying in Chester. He is very happy to leave the quartet to it. They can get a little scary when they're all together. If he is to be totally honest, they collectively give him a headache.

Jen is due at Em / Kate / Will's at about five-ish. Her mum is having Joseph for the night, for the second time this week. Jen does not in the slightest bit feel like going out. She just wants to stay at home with her little family. Her mum and Joseph. But her mum is insistent.

Her ex is giving her a lift into Manchester. Honey started making some very strange spluttering noises and broke down first thing this morning. She doesn't want to risk not getting to nursery and work on time on her first day. She will get her sorted on Monday after work. Her ex has 'a friend'.

She was with Joseph on a country road about ten minutes from home. She had only popped out to Halfords for some oil to put in Honey to make sure she didn't break down.

Is that irony, Alanis?

Honey just stopped going. As she sat there pondering what to do, she said to Joseph, "You're not yet three months old and you've

PAPER OVER IT

already broken down twice," she laughed. He gurgled back. She thought about the M62 breakdown and how much nicer it was to breakdown in the sunshine on a quiet lane rather than on the highest motorway in England in the pouring rain. She then had a brainwave. She remembered that she still had her mum's AA card in her glove compartment.

After a fairly short time, and after she had tried to shoo away the scary cows straining their heads over a fence to take a look at what was going on, she again saw a bright yellow van overtaking her and then reversing down the lane back towards her. It was like sunshine to Jen. She had pulled the 'single woman with baby' card on the phone, this was likely to be the need for their speed. "There has to be some advantages of being a single woman with a baby in the year 2000," she had thought to herself, not feeling guilty at all.

"Hello," the AA patrol man said jovially. "What seems to be the problem?"

"She just stopped," Jen answered equally as jovially, plastering on her fake smile. Thinking to herself, "Isn't that your job to tell me?"

"Let's have a look, shall we?" He got into the driver's seat and said 'hello' to Joseph who smiled back at him.

"Well 'you' can," Jen thought to herself. "There's no 'we' in this. Joseph and I have absolutely no idea. That's exactly why we've called you."

Then she stopped herself and her defensive, chippy, shitty thoughts. This nice man was just trying to help her. Didn't want or need anything from her. She was the one who needed him. He neither underestimated nor misunderstood her. "Stop being a dickhead bitch, Jen," she berated herself.

After a short while under the bonnet, he said. "You need a new battery, love. I'll get it going for now but I wouldn't trust it to go for any longer than a few more days."

"Ok, thank you," she said to him brightly.

"And you need a change of oil. It's filthy and really low," he added. Her oil was a bit like she felt. She hadn't even made it to bloody Halfords. Had been on her way. She should have sorted all this after the last breakdown. She just hadn't found the time. There had been so much to do. "Want me to pop a bit in just until you can get it sorted?"

"Yes please," she replied to the kind man. "That's really kind of you."

After he had bounced her bust battery and topped up her soiled oil, he said, "Right, lass, you'll be fine to drive for a good few miles. But you need to get the battery and oil sorted asap. Let's go through your details shall we? And then I'll get on my way."

This was the bit she was dreading.

"So you are Mrs. Jones?" he asks, looking at his notes, then up at her.

"Yes," Jen replied slowly.

"AA member since 1984?"

"Yeees," Jen replied even more slowly. That would make her a member since she was five years old.

"Born on the 17th January 1949?" he raised one eyebrow.

"I am going for 'yes'," Jen answered slowly, scrunching her nose. She is nowhere near fifty-one. She knew it. He knew it. Even the crazy cows in the field knew it. She looks nowhere near half that age. The bovines just chomped on their grass while cocking their heads, chewing their cud, like a pile of kids munching on popcorn watching an awkward scene play out in a movie.

He looked at her for a split second, then looked at Joseph gurgling in his car seat, then back at her. "Right then, Mrs. Jones," he said purposefully, putting away his equipment. "I think we're all done here." 'We' again, but Jen had no issues with it this time. "Hope you both have a lovely day."

"Thank you, you too," she replied to him, knowing the kindness he had just shown her. The non-member, unpaid for recovery he had just executed, could get him into trouble. "Thank you very much," she added. Her faith in humankind, or mankind to be more specific, slightly improved.

As she waits for her ex to pick her up, she considers telling him about Thursday night, but then rethinks it. She thinks he would kill him. Wouldn't put it past him. He is still very protective over her, but in a good way. They are no longer split, they are now connected by blood. But she doesn't want any blood spilt.

He had offered to have Joseph for the night, but Jen is still not sure. He is going to have him for a few hours tomorrow morning.

Pick him up from Jen's mum. He is happy about that. Em and Lou are going to drop her home tomorrow at about lunchtime on their way down south. She is dreading starting work on Monday now.

She has a word with herself on the way into Manchester sat next to her ex, heading through the Moss Side rain which has stolen the earlier sunshine. It's quarter to five by the time they pass the Asda on the left and the big brewery on the right. She needs to just forget everything for the night and try and have a good time. If she lets herself think too much, she will ruin it for everyone. Steal their sunshine too.

It's 4:50pm and Kate is at the flat with Em, helping her sort out the things she wants to take back home with her and creating a pile of things she doesn't want which she will offer up to the girls. Or Jen could just take to the tip. The girls know all about Jen's tantric tip fetish.

Lou is on her way down from Piccadilly Station lugging a huge suitcase in the downpour for her stay down south with Em. She is super excited about their road trip and seeing Em's home in Hertfordshire for the first time. She has never met Em's family, apart from Charlie of course. She has 'met' every inch of him. She is very interested in meeting Eve.

By quarter past five the quartet are all together again. Hugging and already slugging the champagne Em has brought up with her. That Eve had given her yesterday.

She means to broach the questions she had after her interview with the girls at some point, face her demons. But for now, she resists the temptation of self-absorption and focuses on the celebration.

Lou goes into Kate's new bedroom with her and Jen seizes the moment. She grabs Em's arms and turns them both over. To Jen's relief, only fairly old scars are visible on her right wrist. No new wounds. "I promised, didn't I?" Em says, suddenly very serious. Jen smiles up at her and nods. She drops her arms and then hugs her.

A few seconds later the quartet are back together in the lounge, Lou and Kate piling in on Jen and Em's impromptu hug. Not questioning it at all.

"To Kate, and the absent Will's, new home," Em starts the celebration toasting, giving Jen a little extra smile. The girls all repeat back to her. They chink glasses and toast Kate and the absent Will.

"To Jen's belated twenty-first birthday, her adorable little man and her new job on Monday," Lou continues the celebrations. Again, this is repeated and chinked to. Jen smiles brightly, hiding the chink in her armour.

"To Lou. Her upcoming auditions and new life in London," Jen toasts.

"Fingers bloody crossed," Lou replies laughing before they all chink her.

She is going to stay with Em in Hertfordshire for a while as she has two auditions coming up over the next week or so. The one she really wants is on Wednesday. She had confided in her dad that she really wanted it. Didn't want anyone else to know.

Charlie offered for her to stay but it's a bit crowded with him, her, her tigger and his Tiger. And she doesn't want to be with him all the time either. It's not like Will and Kate. Not even like her and Eddie-twat-gate. But she's really content and happy with that. Wants to find her LondonLou. Doesn't want anything serious. She knows LiverLou all too well and now wants to spread her liverbird wings. LiverLou will, however, more than likely go and stay the odd night with Charlie for a shag or two while she finds her LondonLou.

"To Em," Kate says. Then stops. "Sorry Em, not sure where I'm going with this. Can we just generally toast you?" she laughs, ever so slightly embarrassed.

"Well you can, of course," Em replies. "But I have news."

"What?" they all ask.

"Did they get back to you?" Kate adds.

"Yes."

"And?"

"I'm only fucking in!"

"Oh my god, are you?" Jen cried. Literally feeling like crying. She is so in need of some lovely news.

"Yes, they called me yesterday," Em shouts a little loudly. "I start a week on Monday. On the 11th." Her excitement is palpable. Her 'new Em' very present too. "I wanted to tell you all together in person. Have been dying to say."

"Fuck me!" Lou says. "That is just amazing. The best news ever!"

"What did they say?" asks Kate. Em had been quite honest to all three of them separately about the interview. Eve has been encouraging her to start sharing. To be more open and honest. She had told them all pretty much verbatim what had happened, what they had asked and what she had replied. How she knew she wasn't in, but was ok with it.

"Well it was that Dr. Campbell who called me, you know the one who clearly didn't like me. The one I really wanted to like me," she explains. "She said that she wanted to talk to me directly, so I obviously expected the worse. She said something along the lines of "I want to personally thank you for your honesty. As you are probably aware, I was uncomfortable with the circumstances surrounding the late interview. It was highly unusual. However, you proved yourself to be a very worthy applicant. A deserving applicant. So, as out of process as this is, we would like to offer you a place here at the RVC. Starting on the 11th of September"."

Em is literally beaming. Like sunshine.

They all head in on her, surrounding her with arms and covering her with kisses. The foursome end up on the floor, a loud and loyal pile of limbs and laughter. Steve the Cheese looks on, one eyebrow raised. Bracing himself for the inevitable soaking.

"To Doctor Roberts," Kate shouts as she picks up her flute and lets it slip a little.

Steve gets a posh shower this time. Moet. The crispness and bubbles make it a great partner to any cheese. Camemberts, Gloucesters or Bries.

"To Doctor Roberts ," Lou and Jen reply.

"Well, I've got a long way to go until that. But thank you," Em glows. "I can't wait to start."

Jen's mood is lifted immediately, a little like the weather. The rain is no longer stealing the sunshine. A huge rainbow signifies their recent tussle, but the sun has won.

A day without sunshine is like, well, night.

And this night is going to be about her friends and their achievements. Their highs. Not her lows. They have been there for her so much this year. She will deal with her emotions another time. She is not going to miss a million miles of fun with her friends. She will not allow any man to steal her sunshine tonight.

"Right, what's the plan then?" Lou asks.

"It's your belated birthday, Jen," Em says. "What do you want to do?"

Jen honestly doesn't mind. Is just enjoying the freedom. From her life and her mixed-up mind. But she does want to go dancing.

"As long as we end up dancing, I genuinely really couldn't care less," she replies.

"Why don't we get ready and head down to Castlefield for a few drinks by the canal in the sunshine and make a plan?" Kate offers. "It'll be winter soon. May as well enjoy the al fresco while we can."

"Perfect," Jen says. It does sound perfectly perfect to her.

The end of the Champagne is quickly caned and alcopops start to reign. They go outside on the balcony, to the sunshine still reigning over the rain.

"How's Em's brother, Louisa?" Kate asks cheekily.

"Fine thank you, Catherine," Lou sasses, lips sealed.

"What's it like having sex with your friend's big bro?" Jen asks, boldly building.

"I really don't want to hear any details about my brother's abilities, thank you," Em hides her head in her hands. "Any bedroom action for you, Jennifer?"

"Are you joking?" Jen laughs. "The only male I have shared a bed with in a year is Joseph," she lies convincingly.

"When do you think you'll be ready to think about it?" Kate asks. Genuinely interested.

"No time soon," Jen replies honestly. "I am a one little man woman right now. I don't need any more complications in my life. Although my rabbit has started to be rather regularly rampant."

"Yes, Jen!" Em shouts. "I knew he would come in useful one day."

"Is it a 'he'?" Kate asks.

"It's a huge cock, Kate. Of course it's a 'he'," Lou spits out her Moscow Mule. "How can it be a 'she', you idiot?"

"But Will always calls my rabbit my 'girlfriend'," Kate replies indignantly.

"Do you use it with him?" Jen asks inquisitively. She has only ever used hers alone.

"Yes, of course," Kate answers. "He likes how wet it gets me. Then just before he heads down to check, he says "Watership down"."

"What the absolute fuck?" Em screams. "That is just ridiculous. The saddest fucking film ever. Dead bunnies everywhere."

"Does he look up at you with 'bright eyes'?" Jen laughs. Also not quite believing that Kate and Will include one of the most forlorn films ever in their foreplay.

"Does he have 'hares' between his teeth?" Lou builds, bubbling at her own quick wit.

"Oh Lou, that's just disgusting," Em scrunches her nose at the pubic 'Watership Down' herbivorous villain reference.

"We all know you have a sex toy shelf, Em," Jen says.

"A shelf?" Em replies. "More like a cupboard. My clit and cock cupboard."

"Em, you are so unladylike," Kate says.

Em laughs. "Yes, but I certainly know what this un-lady likes." Although after the Eve-cident, she is not now too sure.

The early September evening sunshine is slowly setting on the city, still stealing the rain. It is beautiful and peaceful.

Lou's phone rings.

It's her mum.

She answers it.

"No, not my dad," she says quietly. Frozen apart from her slowly shaking head. "Please, please not Len."

Steal my sunshine.

Len.

-45-
LOU & JEN: STAND TOUGH

4th September 2000
Lou didn't go to Hertfordshire with Em.

She just needed to get home to Liverpool. To her dad. To Len.

Em had had too much to drink to drive and she was the only one with a car close by. Or even a working car. They didn't want Lou to be alone on the train, and she was very clear that she didn't want any of the girls going with her. She just wanted to get home as quickly as possible. Silently. To her family.

Jen rang her ex. He came within fifteen minutes and drove Lou silently and quickly home to Liverpool.

Len died before the ambulance arrived. Before he had a chance at the Liverpool Royal. Before Lou got the chance to say goodbye.

A heart attack was what the paramedics had said, though it would have to be confirmed by the coroner. Just a few weeks before his fiftieth birthday. He just wasn't tough enough for the strength of it. No warnings - unless he just hadn't said. Had kept it from them. Been too tough.

Lou's heart is broken, just like her dad's. Like Len's.

She sat in his greenhouse, hour after hour. The rain beat down on the glass roof. Wearing his great big, well-worn garden coat. Smelling him. Hearing "You're a tough one, kid," in her ears. Gripping him close to her through his coat. Silently sobbing. Not feeling tough at all.

That was Friday night. Another Bad Friday. A really really tough Bad Friday.

The Armstrong family did not have a good night. Sleep evaded them all. His absence was palpably present. The thunderstorm somehow signified his vast vanished presence. The shock was shudderingly overwhelming.

In the middle of the night, when the storm had calmed, Lou took her Garfield duvet into her mum and dad's room. She found one of her sisters already there in bed with her mum. The other soon came in. The grieving quartet held each other for hours. The thunder and lightning returned. Was it a new storm or the same one revisiting?

Coming back to the same place? It really didn't matter, they didn't care. Len wasn't coming back.

One of Lou's sisters started singing about raindrops on roses and whiskers on kittens.

The forlorn foursome continued to sing about how favourite things made things feel less bad. Bright copper kettles, warm woollen mittens. Brown paper packages, cream-coloured ponies, blue satin sashes. Doorbells, sleigh bells and wild geese. Snowflakes, white winters and white dresses.

Although it didn't make them feel better, any less bad, the sound of their collective music did make it easier for them to find some form of fitful, fantasy filled sleep.

The following two days were even more of a nightmare. So many important, practical things to do when they felt the least capable of being practical in any way.

Lou's uncle, Len's big brother, his wife and their Fu-Fu camped out at the house with them. Being practical and tough for them all. The police came over. Apparently normal practice when someone dies suddenly and unexpectedly at home. They said there may need to be a postmortem. That they would be informed by the coroner.

Lou's first audition in London is on Wednesday. Her mum tried to encourage her to go. "Your dad would want you to go, Louby Lou. You know he would."

"I just can't," she said. "It just doesn't feel right. It wouldn't be right. It just wouldn't be right."

"But maybe that's exactly what you need. A reason to succeed. This is the one you really want right? The one you told your dad you really wanted? He told me not to say that he told me," her distraught mum said, remembering the very recent conversation. "Please, Lou. Think about it for you, for us and for him. He would hate it for him to be the reason you didn't go. Didn't have the chance of getting it. He would want you to be tough. To stand tough. There is nothing you can do here, love, until the funeral. And that could be weeks away. Please Lou? For him?"

Em hadn't driven back down south on Saturday as planned. She had waited to see if and how she could help Lou. She had driven Jen, and her things from the flat including the cute little pink outfit she had bought in Manchester, back home on Saturday morning and stayed with her at the cottage.

On Sunday Lou called Em and asked her where she was. Her entire family had encouraged her to go to the audition. Just one day and night away was not going to make a difference. He was gone. Her dad was gone. Len is gone.

"I'm still up here, Lou," Em had answered. "I'm at Jen's. What can we do? How can we help?"

"I'm going to go on Wednesday to the audition," Lou replied. "I think if I don't go, my uncle will kidnap me, lock me in the back of one of his ice cream vans and bloody jingle me all the way down to London. Not sure I could cope with that."

Em smiled at her friend's humour in the face of such devastation and sadness.

"Well, we can't have you turning up in a chiming Mr. Angelo, can we?" she replied. "Want me to drive you down south? Could pick you up on Tuesday and you can stay at mine? I'll get the train into London with you? I could ask Charlie to be there too? How does that sound?"

"Perfect," Lou said, feeling anything but perfect. Her internal torture dominating her tough. "No Charlie for now, please. Just you and me if ok? Thank you."

Monday morning. Jen's first day at work.

She could not feel more shit, more shattered. About Mr. Senior Specs and her friend's awful, terrible loss.

Her gorgeous early alarm clock wakes her.

She kisses him and says "Good morning, my little sunshine."

As she pops him into her mum and heads down to sort his bottle and make their tea, making sure she isn't too loud and wakes the sleeping Em in the snug, she sings the song quietly.

You are my sunshine
My only sunshine
You make me happy
When skies are grey
You'll never know dear
How much I love you
So please don't take my sunshine away

It makes her feel better. More in control. More tough.

An hour later, with Em still asleep in the snug, her mum already left for work and Joseph dressed with everything he needs for day one at nursery and ready to go, Jen is still nearly an hour too early. She can't go for a drive. The troubled Honey has only a few miles left in her before her battery needs replacing and her oil needs cleansing. Jen relates.

She is not yet dressed in her charity shop work gear, so she decides to put on a trackie (a tracksuit for anyone outside of Manchester) and take Joseph for a walk in his travel system. Just for ten minutes. To pass the time.

The fresh air invigorates her, cleanses her.

Em is still fast asleep when she gets back, and when she is ready to leave. She leaves her a note.

The drop at nursery is no drama at all for Joseph. He goes in like a pro.

Jen is less like a pro and cries in the car park for a good few minutes after. Again. She has a good, strong word with herself. Again. Tells herself to be strong, be tough. She fixes her mascara in the rear-view mirror she has just had a conversation with her reflection in, yet again, and grinds Honey into first gear.

Arriving at her new job she is filled with emotions. It should be the start of an amazing adventure, but Mr. Senior Specs has stripped her of that. Even though, thank all the gods and their lucky stars, he hadn't actually managed to strip her.

She puts on her fake glasses, stands tough and walks into the reception.

"Jen Jones," she says to the lady behind the counter.

"Yes of course," the lady says. "You're here to see Carla?"

"Yes, I am," Jen replies. "I'm really nervous," she admits.

"You just said Jen. Is it Jen and not Jennifer?"

"Yes, I much prefer Jen. I always feel like I'm in trouble when people call me Jennifer."

"You just leave that with me." She taps her nose twice with her right forefinger whilst adding, "I will spread the word."

"Thank you so much!" Jen smiles. She likes this lady.

"Have you just dropped your baby off for the first time?" she asks kindly. "I'm a friend of Carla's. I wasn't there last Thursday but she's told me all about you."

"Oh," Jen says. Not long ago 'told me all about you' was always positive. Now it isn't necessarily. Doesn't feel like it is, anyway. She is now far more reserved now, more sceptical. Less positive, less trusting.

"In a really good way, hun," the lady replies, noticing Jen's nervousness. "You just let me know if you need anything. I can be very helpful, you know. For people I like anyway," she winks. "I can be a right bitch to people I don't."

Jen warms to her even more. "Thank you," she says, smiling. She is clearly someone Jen wants, or needs, on her side. She reminds her a bit of Em. "I really appreciate that."

Her first day is just brilliant. No sign of Mr. Senior Specs. Just Jen being shown her desk, meeting her team and Carla generally and genuinely looking after her. Showing her off. Jen forgets all her fears and just feels proud. Feels almost at home.

At the end of the day she feels good. Feels invigorated. Feels a little like her long lost Tigger.

"How was that?" Carla asks her as she packs up her things.

"Brilliant," Jen replies honestly. "Thank you."

"No," Carla responds. "Thank you."

The relief is overwhelming. The nightmare she envisaged has not come true. The unsightly and highly inaccurate slutty version of herself she had created in her mind after last week is nowhere to be seen in anyone's eyes. At twenty-one, she has only ever slept with one man so not a slut in anyone's eyes. She is not made to feel like 'that girl' in her mind in any way at all.

Such a positive day. A sunny day. A bouncy bright day.

She picks Joseph up from nursery. His little face is a picture as she heads into the baby section. She is told all about his day. How much milk he drank, his bowel movements, what games he had apparently played. It is all written down in a little blue book. He is happy, too. Bouncing. Smiling. He was clearly not branded 'that boy with the slutty single mum'. Babies don't care anyway.

Jen gets home. Her mum is already there chatting to Em drinking tea sitting at the kitchen table. They ask her about her day and Jen tells them all about it. Every second. She has nothing to hide. They both listen, smiling.

PAPER OVER IT

"How's Lou?" her mum asks them.

"She's in a mess to be honest," Em replies. "But she's coming down south with me tomorrow and going to the audition in London on Wednesday. They've been told there doesn't need to be a postmortem but the funeral won't be for at least another week."

"It's good to keep busy," her mum says. "There's not much she can do right now."

"That's what her mum said," Em agrees.

"Tomatoes on toast for tea?" Jen offers as she pops Joseph in his bouncer next to them. "Oh no, wait. They're a bit old and soggy. I could whip up a bechamel sauce with cheese and we could have some sort of Welsh rarebit? We've got some Worcester sauce, I think. And a beer in the fridge."

"Sounds great to me," her mum replies. Longing for a rare fillet steak, but life can sometimes gives you tough stewing steak. Or rotten tomatoes. She is, for now, perfectly happy with the rarebit of the Welsh, not the cow.

"What's a Welsh rarebit?" Em asks.

"Wait and see!" Jen's mum replies. "Jen makes a really good one. She may even go mad and pop a fried egg on top."

"Can't wait," Em dubiously declares.

After their really rather tasty tea, Em pops out to the shop and Jen rings Lou.

"How's you?" she asks.

"Shit," Lou replies.

"How's your mum?"

"Bad, really bad. She's at breaking point. It's the shock, I think. It's really tough." Then she adds, "Em's picking me up tomorrow. Taking me down south just for a day or so. For my audition in London."

"Ok," Jen replies. Lou has obviously forgotten Em is staying at the cottage. Her mind understandably elsewhere. "That's good, right?"

"I suppose so," Lou says. "Jen, I'm not in a good place."

"What can I do?" Jen asks.

"Nothing," Lou relies. "Just be there."

"I'm here," Jen confirms. "I'm always here."

"Thank you," Lou says. "I need to find my tough for Wednesday."

"You are tough," Jen replies. "Your tough just needs to find you. And it will. I promise."

Stand tough.
Point Break.

-46-
EM: WHAT A GIRL WANTS

11th September 2000
Em's first day on her course.
 She is bricking it. Shitting bricks.
 She just hopes to god it goes as well as Lou's audition had on Wednesday. Em had been waiting for her outside. When Lou came out crying, Em had assumed the worst. But it was emotion rather than rejection.
 She had been called back for a second audition in a few weeks. Had got through the first stage. Was hopefully on her way to what she really wants. Although all she really wants right now is her Len back.
 She hugged her and, after Lou said she fancied some fresh air, Em walked with her the thirty minutes to Euston Station past The British Museum. Arms looped.
 Lou needed to get home, back to her family. Back to Len's greenhouse and his big garden coat. The two hour and forty-minute train ride home seemed to last forever. Milton Keynes - the garden city. Crewe - the railway town. Runcorn - the industrial inland port of the Manchester Ship Canal. Then Liverpool. Len and Lou's Liverpool.
 When she let herself in the front door, she could hear funeral plans being formed in the kitchen, songs being selected and readings being ruminated. She listened in the hall for a little while. Sadness consuming her.
 In amongst the sadness she heard a little smidgen of joy, of the real Len. "We are not having 'Danny Boy' and bloody Everton's 'Spirit of the Blues'," Lou's mum said to her brother-in-law, allowing a little laugh to slip out.
 "Yes, shut up you old oaf," his wife said, smiling. Knowing how hard her husband is taking the loss of his little brother. Mourning the big bro in him also. "Not helpful. You can let your pipes call at the wake. Not in the church."
 "Can't wait for that," Lou's mum said, eye rolling while patting the furry, white Fu-Fu on her lap.

"What about 'I did it my way' by Sinatra?" Lou asked as she entered the kitchen.

"Hello love," her mum said. "I think that's a perfect idea. Now tell us all about your day. We can carry on with this later."

She was grateful for the distraction. She had always loved planning events and parties, had revelled in it. This event was not one she wanted to organise. Is not what this girl wants. At forty-six she still thinks of herself as a girl. Thinks, or thought, of Len as a boy. Didn't think she would have to plan this for decades.

Em assumed she would start studying at the Hertfordshire campus. But she isn't. She will begin her studies at the North London Camden campus. She will be studying mostly there for two years before her base will be in Hertfordshire for the rest of her course.

The 'Teaching and Higher Education Act' of a few years ago, July 1998 to be more precise, had introduced tuition fees for students in England and Wales. A massive change. Tuition was free before this. It is now capped at £1,000 a year. If she smashes it and graduates in five years this will still be £5,000 in fees, before any living expenses. A huge amount of money, she now realises. Especially hearing the detail of Kate's dad's potential Apple investment. Even though she will now spend the first part of her studies in North London rather than Hertfordshire, she will live at home with her dad, Eve, impending baby sister, Joey and Chandler - and commute in. That's the plan for now, anyway.

Not knowing what to wear, she rang Kate on the Sunday morning. She did answer but the signal was shocking. All Em could hear was "We… tied up….. …..minute... ok?" She tried to fill in the gaps and, as she knows Will and Kate are both starting back at uni tomorrow, she assumed it was something to do with that.

Her next port of call would have been Lou, but she didn't want to disturb her with fashion frivolities.

In desperation she rang Jen.

"Why would I know what you should wear?" Jen laughed. "And when on earth have you ever asked my opinion on what you should wear, anyway?"

"Well, I don't know what the fuck to wear either," Em replied. "And I am asking your opinion now."

"I assume I wasn't your first choice of call?"

"Yes, you were," Em lied, unconvincingly. Her amazing ability of evasion and lies had been evading her of late.

"A sassy grey and puce pink ensemble, just like me?" Jen laughed. Knowing Em was lying. That she was a last resort. Finding it funny.

"You are being highly un-helpful, you dick," Em laughed back.

"I'd go with cargo pants and a t-shirt," Jen relinquished.

"You know I don't own any cargo pants."

"Well go and bloody buy some then," Jen replies. "Or ask Eve if she has any. Or wear something else. Jeans, maybe. I'm fairly confident you becoming a vet won't be dependent on whether you wear dungarees, double denim or a dressing gown decorated with ducks on your first day."

"You are not taking this seriously," Em is clearly not busy. Overthinking things. Rambling and ruminating. "Double denim, now that's a thought."

"I've really got to go. Joseph needs feeding. Let me know how it goes?"

Why hadn't she thought about asking Eve? Maybe she still found it awkward. When she did ask her, she said she could either borrow a pair of her cargoes, or they could go shopping. She said she could do with getting out, wasn't feeling too well. The fresh air would do her good.

They had never been shopping together. Never really been anywhere together, just the two of them. Or if not just the two of them, without Em being under duress. Or in a green bridesmaid's dress.

They went in Eve's Audi TT with the roof down. It was a lovely early autumn day. Jen felt like Bridget Jones heading for a dirty night away with Daniel Cleaver in his 1969 Mercedes-Benz convertible, minus the lost head scarf. She realised that it sounded odd just before she said it, so thankfully stopped herself.

Eve asked Em how she met her three uni friends.

"I met Jen in the registration queue. You know we were on the same course? Kate and Lou were put in halls together in their first year and got along straight away. The rest of the people in their flat were a little odd," Em explained.

"I had exactly the same thing," Eve said. "But pretty much all the people in my flat in halls were odd. And there were a few who were really quite racist."

"Really?" Jen said, appalled and intrigued. "In what way?"

"In a subtle way, so other people may not have noticed," she explained. "Being micro-aggressive. Things like asking me where I was 'really' from and how I managed to brush my hair. I also felt that one in particular didn't like using the toilet or the bath after me."

"Are you joking?" Em said.

"No," Eve replied. "With some people it's always there. Like calling afro hair 'unkempt'. For some it's like a white saviour complex. For others it's racial profiling. I honestly remember once hearing, "She's black but she's really quite articulate and clever"."

"Wow," Em said. Thinking how white her school and upbringing was. Thinking whether she had ever done anything like this to anyone. Whether she had ever racially profiled or denied white privilege. Especially middle-class white privilege.

"And my brothers," Eve continued, staring forward as she drove. "Well they had it far worse. Arrested for no reason on a number of occasions. Just for the colour of their skin. And questions like, "Do you have a big cock?" Do you think Linford Christie liked being objectified? Liked the phrase 'Linford's lunch box'? It was racist fetishisation of his genitals. Sexual discrimination and racism all boxed up for people to read in 'The Sun' for fun while grabbing their soggy cheese and chutney sandwiches and putrid pork pies from their own lunch boxes."

Em didn't know what to say. She just stared at Eve's exquisite profile.

"Sorry Em," Eve said after a little while, turning her head to look at her. "I lost myself for a moment."

"Can I ask you a question?" Em asked. "But now I don't know if it's racist or not. I really don't want it to be. I think I may need educating."

"Go for it," Eve encouraged. "I'll be honest and tell you if it is."

"Do you ever think about what colour her skin will be? Your baby, I mean. My little sister."

"Well firstly, I don't know if someone else may think it's a racist question, but I don't," she clarified. "I don't as long as the question is simply about the shade of the skin colour, not the lightness of the colour. My two brothers and I all have different skin hues. As do both our parents. Like you and Charlie are different. You're more fair like your mum and Charlie is a little darker skinned like your dad, right?"

"Yes," Em agreed, nodding. She had always wanted Charlie's more golden skin, wanted to tan like him.

"And secondly yes, I do think about it. I have thought about it a lot. I can't wait to see. It's exciting. But I also think about what colour her hair and eyes will be. Will her hair be super curly like mine? Or more relaxed. Will she be a tomboy or a girlie girl? Will she love maths like me? Will she be left-handed like me? I don't think about what I want for my girl, I just think about what she will be. What our mix of genes, personalities and foibles will create. Not just mine and your dads. All of ours. Will she look like or be like you or Charlie at all? Or like my brothers? I certainly don't just think just about her skin colour."

"Oh god. For her sake, and yours, I hope she's not like me," Em laughed.

"I hope she is," Eve replied.

Em was taken aback. Not sure what to say, she ignored it. Deflected. "Thank you, for being honest in your answer. And for sharing such personal things."

Eve smiled at her as she pulled into a parking space. She has learnt to give Em time to speak. That she really opens up if you don't reply immediately or cut her short and stop her flow, like her husband often does.

"And for being so kind to me after everything I've done… and said. And not done," Em added.

Pulling on her handbrake, Eve simply said, "Water under the bridge, Em. And you know I get it. I don't completely understand yet, but I get it. Now let's go shopping."

They both genuinely enjoyed it, enjoyed each other and each other's company. It was what both girls needed, wanted. Made them both happy. Further sealed their fledgling relationship.

Eve never found out how Em met Lou and Kate, realised she had been the one to stop Em's flow. Berated herself for it. They did, however, buy some cute things for the soon to be met baby to add to the gorgeous little pink outfit Em bought from Mothercare in Manchester and had given to a delighted Eve a few days earlier.

Em enters the classroom for the first time in Camden in her new khaki cargoes, with pockets by the knees, and tight white t-shirt. She scans the room the room from the back. Spots a spare seat next to a girl with curly brown hair. As she sits down, the girl turns to face her.

"One day it'll happen to you – it'll be like 'boom' and it'll hit you right in the chest like a carthorse back buck," Kate once said to her.

It literally just does.

What a girl wants.
Christina Aguilera.

-47-
LOU: FLOWERS

15th September 2000

The day after Joseph's three month check. It went really well, he is progressing brilliantly in every way. He's apparently had a really great start to his young life.

Jen and her mum are delighted.

But like in the magnificent 1994 Lion King film, it's the circle of life. A circular movement of despair and hope, faith and love. As one being's path is starting to wind, another's is unwinding.

It's the day of Len's funeral.

It is also the day of the Big Brother final and the opening ceremony of the Sydney Olympics.

This is not lost on Lou. The end of something and the start of something else. Like a race around a circular track, a handover in a relay. A baton handed from one person to the next.

Lou has always loved the Olympics. Had been obsessed with the 1996 Atlanta games and even more so with the 1992 Barcelona games. She was fourteen, she thinks, and was mesmerised right from the opening ceremony showcasing a flaming arrow lighting the Olympic torch.

Derek Redmond's dad embodying Olympic spirit when he helped his injured sprinter son over the finishing line to a standing ovation. The stunning city silhouette behind the open-air diving board. Her mum had bought her a tape single of Freddie Mercury and Montserrat Caballé's dazzling duet because she had loved it so much. She and her sisters took turns to be Freddie and Montserrat as they dueted Barcelona in full voice.

But she doesn't want this Olympics to begin. It's start somehow signifies the end of her dad. Her Len. The end of family life as they all know it. She doesn't want any race to start, the baton to be passed or the Olympic torch to be lit. Because the lighting of that flame will mean the choking of her dad's. The extinguishment of Len's light.

She gets up early and goes downstairs. Everyone else is still asleep. Or pretending to be asleep. The front room is filled with flowers.

She hates them. Despises the smell of them. The intense scent of lilies reminds her of the funeral home they had visited the week before. She shuts the door on the putrid pop-up florist shop, heads into the kitchen and pops the kettle on.

Charlie had called yesterday, but she wasn't really in the mood to speak to him. Didn't have the energy for him. She had texted him and said she would call him as soon as she could. The girls had all said they would miss respective work and lectures to come to the funeral. But she had said 'thank you, but no thank you' to that too. She just wanted to get through the day. Get it over with.

With a brew in hand, she puts on Len's big garden coat and heads out to his beloved greenhouse.

It smells a lot better in there. Of him, his plants and his cigar.

It's a cloudy morning and she thinks what her dad would say. "It's threatening rain, Lou," as if all the clouds were one living being having a laugh with us mere mortals below. Playing with us. Provoking us.

She smiles up at them, at him and his weather obsession, and then just sits and stares up through the glass roof for quite some time. Watching the clouds slowly fight for space, playing their ethereal cat and mouse game.

Her mum's loud question from the open back door breaks her trance. "Another brew, love?"

She stands up, leaves the greenhouse and starts to walk to the door. "Yes please, mam."

Her mum is putting on a brave face for them all, but her eyes are slightly sunken into her head framed by deep, dark circles. She looks almost skeletal. It makes Lou shiver and shudder.

"Come on, love," her mum reacts to her involuntary reaction. "You're cold. Let's get you inside and get a warm cuppa in you."

It's not cold outside, and she has her dad's big garden coat on, but she lets her mum steer her inside.

Later, as the hearse pulls up outside the house housing the coffin covered in white flowers spelling out DAD, LEN and BRO, the family file out of the front door and towards the funeral cars behind.

Lou wishes they hadn't been all placed next to each other so tightly, or at least not in the order they had been set. It looks like they are mourning the loss of a fictional Russian city. BROLENDAD.

She laughs to herself knowing her dad would find this amusing.

As they drive the short, slow drive to the church, it starts to rain. As Len had threatened it would to Lou this morning in the greenhouse. Lou smiles. It feels right. A pathetic fallacy for her and her grieving family.

The church is packed full of this family, their friends and Len's work colleagues. It is also replete with the remnants of the recent harvest festival. Handsome autumnal flowers and foliage grace the pew ends and altar.

When asked, the family had asked to keep them there for the service. Len had died in the very early Autumn of his life, the harvest of his life, so it felt apt. He will never get to meet his mid or late Autumn, will never witness what his winter would bring him. Wonderland or not. At just forty-nine it is all so desperately sad. The church is also filled with peoples' mixed emotions around their own mortality.

The service is beautiful. Len's brother gets up to do a speech. He has been so stoic and solid these last few weeks. Had done a great job of papering over his feelings for the family. Wanted to write him a proper send off. As he tells some funny stories about him and Len growing up, the daft things they got up to, and then continues to talk about his obsession with the weather and Michael Fish, people laugh.

But, half way through his speech when he starts talking about Len the husband and Len the dad, he stops. Chokes. Can't carry on. He walks from the pulpit and puts his hands on his little brother's coffin, lets his head drop down and starts to cry. Cry for the first time. It is heartbreaking and devastating to witness.

His wife stands up and walks over to him. She places her hand on his arm and gently takes his piece of paper. She stays by him with one hand still on her husband and the other holding the paper. She continues where he left off and finishes his speech for him. Beautifully. The relief and gratitude on his tear-filled face is clearly visible. Like Derek Redmond's dad, she helps him over the line. Helps him finish what he needs to finish, but is not capable of doing alone. There is not a dry eye in the church.

Lou and her two sisters share a reading from the bible, still reeling from seeing their uncle's distress. They get through it together, holding hands.

As Frank Sinatra starts to sing about living full lives, travelling every highway and final curtains, the family are encouraged to be the first to walk past the coffin and say their goodbyes

Later, in the pub at the wake, the mood lifts for many. The celebration of his life begins, rather than the mourning of his death. Tepid sausage rolls, burnt vol-au-vents and soggy sandwiches are wheeled out as is the old upright piano, which is normally tucked into the corner. Songs begin to be sung, stories begin to be told and laughter begins to be unleashed.

But Lou and her sisters are not in the mood. They aren't kids happily relegated to the little room with the dart board and games, neither are they 'proper' adults getting pissed and reminiscing on their dad's younger self. They are somewhere in between. Inbetweeners. Too young to lose their dad and be able to focus on good times past, too old to be distracted by games, crisps and fizzy drinks.

They tell their auntie, in case their mum asks where they are, and head home. Just a short walk in the rain.

They plonk themselves together on the sofa in the lily infested lounge and put the tele on. Not caring that they are soaking wet.

They also don't care that Craig wins Big Brother ahead of Anna the singing nun, but it is a better distraction than the games in the little room in the pub or 'Danny Boy' being destroyed on the piano.

A little while later, Lou notices that both her sisters have fallen asleep. It is just the three of them in the house still. She gets up to remove herself from the foul-smelling flurry of frightful flowers, which are driving her insane, and heads out to the greenhouse again. To a place which has a right to be over-filled with flowers, sweet smelling flowers.

She curls up on her dad's chair, with his big garden coat wrapped around her, and sobs.

As her tears start to dry, with nothing left inside her, she slowly lets sleep consume her whilst listening to the rhythmic pitter patter of the rain on the glass roof.

Flowers.

Sweet Female Attitude.

-48-
LOU & EM: CAN'T FIGHT THE MOONLIGHT

27th September 2000

Em's 22nd birthday.

Sixteen days since she first experienced her Kate termed 'carthorse back buck'.

Twenty-five days since Len died and twelve days since his funeral.

The Olympics have become a momentary and much needed thief of grief for Lou. But as soon as each program ends, it all comes flooding back. Especially in the middle of the night, deep in the dark of her mind. She just doesn't seem to be able to fight the bright flood of moonlight through her thin curtains. She keeps surrendering to it, waking up in a sweat. She prefers it when it's cloudy and it rains. She sleeps better. But while she watches the swimming, diving, gymnastics, athletics and everything in between, she is transiently transported away from it all. It's a relief from the grief. It helps paper over it.

Her call back audition is in London today. She got the train to stay at Em's yesterday. Like she was supposed to go and stay the day after her dad died.

She had said to Em that she didn't want to spoil her birthday with her self-described depressive self, that she would just get the train up and down in the same day. Em had heard none of it, had insisted. Had also insisted she stayed Wednesday night, tonight, too for her birthday. Lou didn't have the energy for the fight. Em won.

Eve and Lou got along immediately, from the moment they met when Em brought her home from the station late afternoon yesterday. In fact they buzzed off each other. So much so that Em felt a little glimpse of her green giant rising. She laughed it off knowing what a ludicrous, limp dick she was being. It was just brilliant to see Lou laughing, even though it was Eve who had managed to make it happen. Not her. She had barely got a smile out of her on the drive back from the station. "Maybe Lou is just being polite," she said silently to her inner dick.

Lou also made an impact on her dad. He loves the arts and is fascinated by all things theatre and ballet. They talked for ages about her dance history, her degree and her plans for the future.

"Happy Birthday, my little star," Em's dad grins as he goes in for a big hug whilst eating a piece of toast.

"Thank you, daddy," she responds like a child.

Lou watches, sitting on a bar stool. Elbows propped on the kitchen island, as Eve walks, or kind of waddles, in from the utility room and tries to calm down the excitable Joey and Chandler whilst navigating the handling of a large wrapped box. "Happy birthday, Em. We thought you might like these," she says a little nervously. It is clearly her idea, Lou thinks, whatever 'they' are.

As Em starts to unwrap the box carefully, she hears a little squeak. She rips at the paper, desperate to discover the squeak's owner.

"Oh wow," she says as she releases the most adorable grey kitten from its brief incarceration. "And there's another one," Em squeaks as she pulls out another equally beautiful, squeaking chocolate brown kitten.

"They're Burmese," Eve explains, still not completely sure of Em's reaction. "They're sisters. Apparently Burmese cats hate to be alone, they should always be kept in pairs."

"They are absolutely perfect," Em is bowled over. "The most perfect pair. I can't believe it. Thank you so much, both of you. Best present ever."

She tries to hug Eve whilst holding two kittens with two young labs bouncing around and sniffing at the strange smelling little toys, and then tries to do the same to her dad. Lou starts to laugh. It is a ridiculous yet radiantly happy sight.

"What are you going to call them?" asks Lou, relieving Em of the grey one and cuddling her.

"Well this one is like chocolate," Em replies, looking at the one she is holding.

"What about Coco?" Eve offers.

"Coco Chanel," Lou builds.

"Perfect!" Em agrees. "Done."

They all then look at the gorgeous grey kitten. She has blue eyes with a slightly mis-shaped pupil in her left one. Or a black spot in her iris. They are not sure.

"She looks like David Bowie," Em's dad says, scrutinising the infant feline.

"Well she's not exactly going to call her Dave, is she?" Eve laughs at her husband.

"No, fair enough. Good point, well made, princess," he laughs back at himself. He loves making Eve laugh, even though he is acutely aware she is often laughing at him not with him. "What about Ziggy, then? Ziggy Stardust?"

"I love it!" says Em. "Ziggy Stardust and Coco Chanel. Ziggy and Coco. But what am I going to do with them? They're too little for me to leave them all day while I'm out at college."

"I'm here for the next however many months, aren't I?" Eve replies, having already thought it all through. "I'll be their day care when they're still little, if you like? I've already got most of the things they need like a litter tray, litter, carrier and kitten food. But we can take a look later at what else you think they will need?"

"I would really like that," Em says. "Thank you, Eve."

"Right girls," Em's dad addresses Em and Lou, interjecting the still peculiar love-in between his wife and daughter. "If you want a lift to the station, you'd better get showered, dressed and sorted quickly. I have to leave in about twenty minutes."

The girls get ready immediately, Em into her college clothes and Lou her audition ensemble.

Em can't wait to get to Camden for more reasons than one. She decides she may tell Lou and Eve why later. She is not yet ready to speak to her dad or Charlie, who will both be home tonight for her birthday meal. She wonders what Lou will think. She thinks Eve will not be surprised.

Lou is quite pragmatic about her call back. The rejection from her first audition and the last few weeks have changed her outlook on things. How sometimes things will just be what they will be. 'It is what it is'. She also remembers the kind words and constructive advice from the lady in her first audition. Her competitiveness is now channelled in a contrasting way to before with the knowledge that things can change in an instant. That you can't control everything, and you most certainly can't always win. However hard you try.

Lou calls Eve from the station later that day, a few hours before

Em's day finishes. Lou said she could make her own way back, but Eve insisted. "Just give me a holler when you're ready. I insist," she had said. Lou is intrigued by how much 'insisting' is going on lately. But she decides to stop fighting it. To let the insisters win, if that's a real word. Like she had when her mum, uncle and little sisters became insisters when they insisted she came down to London for the initial audition.

"How did it go?" Eve asks on their way back, thankful that Em and Lou didn't finish at the same time as she surveys the tiny space in the two-seater convertible. Knowing she needs to trade him in for a much more family friendly, less fun and frivolous vehicle asap. Unfortunately.

"It went well, I think," Lou replies. "They said they will let us know as soon as possible. They didn't give timings which is annoying. I'm not counting any chickens. What does it actually mean, to not count chickens? Why would you want to count them in the first place?"

Eve laughs at Lou's randomness. "I think the full phrase is 'don't count your chickens before they hatch'."

"Why? Because they might not hatch?"

"Yes, I assume so. Though, in fairness, I've never really thought about it in too much detail."

"That's really sad," Lou ponders. "There are lots of sayings about chickens, aren't there?" she adds whilst taking in the stunning home county scenery.

"Are there?" Eve laughs again. "Again, I have not ever really thought about it. Go on, name a few more then. And I'll think of some too."

"Well, there's 'don't put all your eggs in one basket'," Lou starts, smiling. Her attention back inside the car. Looking forward to the childish chicken competition.

"Pecking order," Eve adds, happily rocketing to Lou's poultry planet.

"Don't be such a chicken," Lou laughs, loving the game.

"Walking on eggshells," Eve shouts after a little think.

"Rule the roost!" Lou blurts, rather proud of herself.

"She's no spring chicken," Eve offers. "Although I don't really like that one. I am definitely on the turn from spring to summer chicken," she adds, patting her swollen tummy and her little unhatched chick.

Lou laughs. "If I look as good as you, heavily pregnant and in my 'late spring', I'll be winning. As fab as my mum is, she kind of stopped caring too much when she had us three girls. Don't suppose she had the time, or the inclination. Just became a bit of a mother hen."

"Mother hen!" Eve spits out. "Yes, Lou. Did she just cluck around you all day?"

"She so did!" Lou is literally laughing out loud at her accidental chance chicken reference and Eve's clucking brilliant quick response. Genuinely enjoying the giggles and escapism. She feels like Ginger in the recent film Chicken Run, trying to escape from Tweedy's Chicken Farm. She laughs to herself at the similarity between her and Ginger, both physically and emotionally.

"Which came first? The chicken or the egg?" Lou adds, more question than saying. But she is running out of ideas.

"Right now I wish no-one had cum, first or not," Eve laughs, moving her constricting seat belt away from her bump and even more constricted bladder.

Lou has really got the giggles now. Not wanting the daft, turning rude, departure from the recently depressing day to day to stop. She asks, "Why did the chicken cross the road?"

"I don't know," Eve replies, shaking her head whilst chuckling at the continuation of the crazy conversation. But really pleased at Lou's lifted mood. "Why did the chicken cross the road?" she replies, obediently.

"Because she wanted to show off her poultry in motion," Lou performs a perfect sitting down chicken dance.

"Oh god, Lou, will you stop," Eve begs, holding her stomach. "That is so shockingly bad it's hilarious. I need a wee so much! I need this seatbelt off me."

The two newly formed friends just about get back to the house before there is an accidental toilet torrent in the 'needed to be traded in' Audi TT.

After relieving her extended bladder, Eve lets Joey and Chandler out whilst Lou checks on Ziggy and Coco.

A little while later, sitting outside the back of the house in the late summer/early autumn sunshine, Lou sipping her second glass of white wine, they hear someone shout. "Who let the dogs out?"

"Who.. who, who, who?" a lightly lubricated Lou sings back Baha Men, lolling.

"Oh shit," Eve says, pushing herself up. "They must have got out. I didn't check that the gate had closed. They've been dodgy lately."

"Stay there," Lou insists. Instantly sobering and becoming the insister. "I'll go and help."

She runs around the side of the huge house to the front drive to find Em's dad with Joey and Chandler gambling around him. "All ok?"

"They were half-way down the lane," he replies. "It was like the bloody 'Great Escape', or more 'The Incredible Journey'." Lou smiles at the reference to one of her favourite Disney childhood films.

"But they're ok, right?" Lou says in a slightly sassy, short manner. Her scouse boldness bouncing in. Sick of drama. Emptied of patience. Not wanting the heavily pregnant Eve to be distressed about not checking the gate. Realising too late she is being a tad rude to her hospitable host.

"Yes, they're fine," he says, ignoring her sass. Knowing she is going through a really tough time. Also having learned more and more about his hot headedness and stubbornness over the last few months. Eve had made sure of that. Also quite taken with this northern sassy dancing girl who his son is also apparently quite taken with too. "How are you? How did the audition go?"

As they walk round the side of the house and meet Eve making slow progress towards them, Lou explains her day. She realises that Eve knew pretty much as little as he did as their car convo had been overrun by chickens.

Later that night, following a Chinese takeaway (Em's choice), a bottle of Champagne, a wish made by Em blowing her candles out and after Charlie had asked Lou for a chat before he drove back to London, Em's dad excuses himself to his study. He has a few calls to make.

It has suddenly gone dark outside but it's still warm. They can see through the large glass doors that the thousands of fairy lights that Eve spent hours putting up last year, even though her husband said she should get 'a man' in (as if only 'a man' can do these things), have just come on through the timer. They look stunning, fighting for attention with the moonlight and star dusted sky.

"It looks like a sparkly wonderland," Lou says in awe. They went to bed really early last night so she hadn't seen them, or hadn't noticed them in her nervous pre-audition state. She is still in total awe of the house and garden. It just keeps getting better.

"We can go and sit outside, if you like?" Eve asks the pair.

"Let's light the fire pit," Em says.

"The what?" Lou asks.

A little later, with Lou loving the big fire pit and asking if they have any marshmallows (they don't), Em says, "I'm glad it's just us three. I've got something to tell you both."

"What?" Lou asks, intrigued.

"I've met someone," Em shares. "On my course."

"Who?" Lou shouts excitedly, and far too loudly. "What's his name?"

"Or her name?" Eve asks, astutely.

Lou's head spins round to Eve and then back to Em. "What?" is all she manages to say. Not sure whether it is a question or not.

Em smiles at both her perceptive stepmother and her perplexed friend.

"Her name is Melanie," she says. "Mel."

Lou's eyes widen as she takes a huge gulp of her wine.

"We met on our first day," Em goes on to explain. She can see that Lou is quickly processing and needs more info quickly. "I sat next to her in class. A pile of us went for a quick drink after to celebrate our first day. Mel and I ended up talking for hours outside a pub in Camden. It was only when she pointed out the reflection of the full moon in the pub window that I realised it had gone dark."

Lou listens intently. Her larger-than-life friend and resident of planet Venus with a persistent penchant for regular mini-breaks to planet Mars is suddenly telling her she is on a moonlit staycation.

"I'm not going to lie, Em," Lou says. "I have all the questions."

"She's twenty-four. So even more 'mature' than me," Em says.

"Well that's not a great benchmark," Lou laughs.

"Ha, ha," Em replies. "You know what I mean. In fact I'm really surprised the mix of ages on the course. I thought I'd be the oldest but I'm definitely not. In fact there's a man who…."

"Back to Mel, Emily," Lou curtails her Jen like rambling.

"Well there's not much more to say. We've had a few little moments, but apart from that, we're taking it slow. I really like her." Em then stares into the crackling, dancing fire and talks like she's thinking out loud. "I've never met anyone like her before. I'm trying to work things out in my head. She's so sure of herself. Really understands who she is. We talk a lot."

Eve takes Em's hand to get her attention back from the fire.

"Take your time," she says. She thinks there's probably been an unlit fire inside Em's pit for years. Waiting for the right fuel. Unsparked until the night outside, sat exactly where they are sitting now, just over six weeks ago. And now Mel. "Let it breathe for a while. Give it air. Fire doesn't just need fuel, it needs oxygen too. And when you're ready to bring her home, if you're ever ready, we'll be here to welcome her."

"Welcome who?" Em's dad asks, heading over to them..

"Just a girl Em met on her course the other week," Eve explains. Knowing her husband will have no interest in asking any more about this girly friendy female stuff, and the fact that Em chose to talk without him being there means she doesn't want him to either. For now.

And with that Eve swiftly and skilfully papers over the previous enlightening conversation and changes the subject to the new kittens, Ziggy and Coco.

Em gives her a grateful look and realises that this is the best birthday she has had in years. If not ever.

She is studying something she really cares about with someone she is starting to really care about. She's at her home, but feels at home for the first time in years. She has two new gorgeous kittens. She's about to get a little sister. The person she thought she hated most in the world is turning out to be a person she is really starting to care about, and she feels this is reciprocated. She knows she doesn't deserve all this, but it feels good. It feels real. It feels right. She is very grateful.

She's not out on a bender for her birthday, yet she's happier than she's been in years. It's all a revelation. She thanks the moonlight and stardust that she came to her senses. Finally. And that her dad and Eve let her back in.

Lou loads her brain with all the questions she wants to ask Em, but for now she is just happy to be here. To celebrate Em's birthday with her and to not be at home in her room alone, fighting her own moonlight.

Can't fight the moonlight.
LeAnn Rimes.

-49-

THE QUARTET: SHOW ME THE MEANING OF BEING LONELY

14th October 2000
Saturday in London.
 Lou got a third call back from the musical production team for yesterday, Friday. It is costing her a fortune in train fares, even though she is taking the slow train which takes nearly four hours each way and she has to change at Crewe.
 She stayed at Charlie's on Thursday night as it is far closer to her audition location than Em's. And also because Charlie had asked her to. At Em's birthday dinner a few weeks ago, before he drove back to London, he had told her that he really liked her. He didn't tell her he felt lonely without her, that he missed her every time she left him. Like something weird was missing in his heart. She had said she liked him too but was not in the right place for a serious relationship. She was actually tired of the constant competition with him, but she hadn't said. Was too tired to go into it. They had agreed that they would still see each other, but not as a couple or anything like that. In fact Lou had said that, and Charlie, for once, had not contested.
 She got the job right there on the spot. It was apparently some final checks with the senior producers and the director. They had to perform one more time, both dancing and singing. They all moved and harmonised perfectly together. The group of twelve who were called back were asked to wait for a while after they had finished. Just fifteen minutes later they were all told the great news.
 Rehearsals start on the 6th November. Just over three weeks away. Shit! Lou needs to find somewhere more permanent to live. She asked around the group and found out that two of them were in the same boat as her. No current permanent residence in London. Now urgently in need of somewhere to live. They asked one of the production team who gave them some numbers to call, very used to the question. The three share their numbers and email addresses so they can work together to get their living arrangements sorted. Thinking how easy it would be if there were a way to be on a text chat together, the three of them.

lou.dancing12@yahoo.co.uk

Lou was thankful she doesn't have 'luvscock69' or 'bigtits3' in hers.

She has her first adult professional job. In a musical. In London. In a fairly small theatre, but on the west end. Just four months after she finished uni. She was and is absolutely buzzing. She knows she may feel lonely living in London, at least at the start, and that she would really miss home. But her heart tells her it is the right thing to do. To find her LondonLou.

She rang her agent to give her the good news, then went to call her dad. This still happens quite a lot. Just short of a month since she lost him, she feels his absence like a huge hole inside her. An excruciating chasm. Like there's something missing in her heart. Sometimes it makes her physically gasp in pain.

It's especially tough when she wants to talk to him. To tell him something good, like today. Or get his guidance and counsel on something bad or sad.

When the person you have always chosen to talk to about difficult or painful things is the same person you have lost and this loss is what has caused the pain, it is a double hit. Doubly shit. You grieve both the person and the guidance, the counsel.

Em decided that Lou, Charlie and she would go to the cinema on Saturday night to see a new film called 'Billy Elliot'. It seemed a perfect celebration for Lou's new job. Described as a 'coming of age comedy drama' so not a musical as such, but all the adverts had a kid dancing in them. Plus Julie Walters is in it. There has never been a bad Julie Walters film, ever, so she decided it must be good. Em texted Kate and Jen to see if they could come to London too, last minute. Plus Will of course, she decided. They are all welcome to stay at hers in Hertfordshire, but she decided that Will and Kate would probably stay at Will's brother's flat. Far more central. As she decided that, and before she knew whether they could all come, she decided that she, Jen and Lou would stay at Charlie's. Again, far more central. She decided a lot in the space of a few minutes. For a lot of other people. She feels a bit more like the old Em. It is exhausting, she decides.

"We're on our way!" Kate says to Em on the phone. It's 9:20 in the morning.

"No fucking way. That's amazing!" Em says back. "We who? Just you and Will, or Jen too? She said she would try and make it."

"Just me and Will," Kate replies. "Jen can't make it."

Em had booked six tickets to the cinema, or rather Eve had. She really wanted to come but didn't want her waters to break over someone's popcorn. "Soggy popcorn is like off crisps or soft Jacob's Cream Crackers," she had told Em. "None have any place in your mouth. Reject them all immediately."

Em had told Eve about a variety of mouth rejections she had actioned. Eve had laughed, somehow managing to not share her own younger experiences of going down. Not appropriate for a stepmother.

"So, that's Will and Kate a yes. Jen a no," Em says to Eve, stroking Coco. "How many are we on now?"

"Am I your personal party planner?" Eve asks, laughing. Rubbing Ziggy's ears.

"It would appear so," Em grins.

"Ok," Eve eye rolls. "I'm only doing this because I'm bored, fat, can't be more than ten metres from a toilet, or a fridge to be fair, bloated, hormonal and frankly flipping jealous. In fact, why the hell am I doing this?"

"Because I will do this for you when you are none of the above," Em replies.

"Ok," Eve concedes, pushing one of her baby's limbs from her ribcage. "So we have you, Lou, Charlie, Will and Kate."

"So five," Em says, counting on her fingers.

"Yes. You have five people and six tickets," Eve says. "Invite Mel?"

"Do you think?"

"I think you should."

"Ok, I'll see if she's free," Em smiles. She pulls Coco the kitten up to her face and says to her, "That'll put the cat amongst the pigeons, won't it."

Kittens, cats and pigeons aside, at 8:15pm all six enter the cinema to watch 'Billy Elliot'. Will and Kate have never met Charlie, no-one but Em has ever met Mel. But after two hours of pre-Billy drinks, they were all blended and brewed like a perfect brandy sauce.

Jen is at home in the cottage. Her mum is out - she has been randomly out a bit more lately. Her home friends and uni friends are also out - out, out. She makes and eats a cheese and tomato toastie.

She was asked to go out to two places tonight. And three places today. She is not short of options. They are just options she can't do, or doesn't want to take a baby to. They rarely include the option for a family pass. Why would they? Her friends are all around twenty-one with no real responsibilities.

Each time she is asked and can't go, she pretends she is busy, rather than saying she can't. Because she is sick and tired of saying she can't, and she knows her friends are also sick of hearing it. Even though they never say. She cannot continue to rely on her mum to 'paper over it' through endless baby-sitting, she has to create some form of life which is family friendly too. And anyway, her mum seems to be creating more of a life for herself as well, so is not as 'available', which Jen genuinely thinks is brilliant.

She wants everyone to keep asking her out, to do things, but deep down she knows they won't. Her lack of ability to have any sort of spontaneity in her life is dawning on her. Mixed with the fact she doesn't really 'fit' any of her friends anymore, on a day to day basis. No one else has a baby. As much as she loves them and they love her, their lives are very different now. She knows they will always be her friends, but her world is completely different to theirs. She, all of a sudden, starts to feel very lonely.

It's 8:30pm on Saturday night. "Come on," she says to Joseph. "Let's get our Tigger on and get out of here."

She grabs a bottle of milk from the fridge, warms it and puts it in a cool bag. She was stunned when she found out from one of the nursery nurses that cool bags also keep things warm. She was even more stunned by how interesting she found this imparted information and how much she wanted to find out how this actually worked. She really does need to get out more.

She picks up Joseph and kisses his gorgeous face before popping him in his car seat in the passenger seat of her now fixed Honey.

She heads onto the M56, down the Princess Parkway and into Manchester city centre. She drives around the city to nowhere in particular, showing Joseph all the places she used to go. The life she used to lead. She is not sure why she is doing it, but it weirdly makes her feel better. She genuinely doesn't want to be out getting wasted every night, like the young people she is watching walking down the rammed city centre streets. Doesn't even necessarily want to be where her friends are right now - out, out. But there's something missing in her heart which, as much as she loves her baby, he just can't fill. She's feeling lonely.

Joseph is happily gurgling at the bright city lights and music pumping from the pubs, bars and clubs.

As she drives under the passenger bridge on Corporation Street next to the red post box, opposite the huge Arndale shopping centre near Marks & Spencer, she shows him where the IRA bomb had gone off four years earlier. In 1996.

Jen knows all about the bomb. Had, like most other Mancunians, been heartbroken at the devastation to her city. Right bang in the heart of her city. It was like its heart had been ripped out of it in an instant. She had become a little too obsessed with the bomb, its repercussions, and the subsequent clean up and complete remodelling and transformation of her city's heart.

She was also doing work experience at 'The Guardian' in its northern office in Manchester when it happened. Had been allowed press access into the deserted, devastated heart of the city filled with the eerily haunting sound of thousands of office and shop alarms.

She parks up for a minute and starts to tell Joseph all about it. In a sing-song way. Like she is reading him a fairytale or a bedtime story.

"At about 9:20am, on a busy sunny Saturday morning in June, in one of the busiest shopping areas in the UK, the IRA planted a huge explosive device in a white lorry, not a red or yellow lorry, a white lorry. It was parked on double yellow lines with its hazards on. Flash, flash, flash. Just over there," she points to the still standing, apparently bomb proof red post box. "Two naughty men left the lorry after setting a timer and walked behind the Corn Exchange to Cathedral Street, over that way, where a third naughty man was waiting for them in a car. A Ford Granada. The naughty men abandoned it later, thirty odd miles north of here in a place called Preston. Yes, Preston."

Joseph is listening to her intently. Taking it all in.

"A few minutes later a traffic warden gave the seemingly abandoned lorry a parking ticket and called someone, ring ring, to get it removed. Thank god the removal people were not very good at their jobs, really really rubbish at them in fact, and didn't move it quickly."

"About twenty minutes later, Granada Studios (where 'Coronation Street' is filmed, you know, the programme your Nanna likes) received a call calmly saying there was a bomb on Corporation Street and that it would explode in one hour. They gave an IRA codeword so that the police would know the threat was genuine. I mean, real."

Joseph looks like he's nodding.

"Yes they did," Jen confirms. "Then other television stations and a hospital got calls too. Do you know how many people were very close to here at that time, shopping and working?"

Joseph's face is blank.

"Well, let me tell you, there were a huge amount of people. About eighty thousand in fact. That's a load more people than can fit in Old Trafford football stadium. You know, where your daddy's team Manchester United play."

"Then a short while later, at about 10 'o'clock, lots of brave police men and women began evacuating this whole area while the hunt for the bomb began."

"Mummy was working that morning about ten miles that way." she points south. "In the Oasis clothes shop in Altrincham. I picked up the shop phone and it was a girl from the Arndale Oasis store, just over there," she points the other way. "She told me not to send anyone into Manchester if we didn't have the right sized item of clothing for them. This was what we normally did. Just to get rid of them to be honest. I asked why and she said it was yet another bomb scare and they had been evacuated. Nothing to worry about. At the time the Arndale was quite often evacuated for IRA scares. Mummy had been evacuated once, just a few months before."

Joseph's dummy falls out of his mouth. Jen likes to think his mouth had opened as he was in such awe of her amazing story, but knows he is just getting a bit sleepy. She pops it back in and carries on, talking him to sleep.

"Do you know what happened next? Well let me tell you. As

loads of emergency vehicles, nee-naws, started screaming into the city, people got scared and panicked, they began to run. Carrying kiddies, dragging shopping and pushing prams and travel systems, just like your tartan one. Then a heroic policeman looked inside the white lorry, you know the one the naughty men had left, and he spotted wires running from the dashboard through a hole into the back. Thank god it hadn't been moved anywhere else. It would never had been found."

Joseph starts to yawn but is still staring at Jen. Still taking it all in. Sucking on his dummy like Maggie Simpson.

"The police cordoned off a circle more than half a mile from the lorry, from here. They thought that would be more than enough. The bomb disposal team was quickly dispatched from its base in Liverpool, you know where Auntie Lou lives, and they planned to diffuse the bomb with a remote control robot. Yes, a robot. But, Joseph, they were too late. As the little robot made its way to the van it only got to just about there," Jen points to a just a few dozen metres away. "At just after quarter past eleven... BOOM. The bomb exploded."

Joseph jolts with Jen's big BOOM. His eyes widen and he sucks even harder on his dummy.

"A massive mushroom cloud rose three hundred metres into the air. Right up there. Up to the moon. And the blast could be heard up to fifteen miles away, that's further away than where mummy lived at the time. It left a crater, like on the moon, fifteen metres wide. Piles of glass and masonry were thrown up into the air. Behind the police cordon more than half a mile away, people were showered with falling debris. It was like Armageddon."

Joseph is now falling asleep. His eyelids bouncing up and down as he fights it. Jen smiles and starts Honey's engine. She knows she will get moved on soon anyway. As she drives off she finishes her story. Just in case he has taken any of it in and has nightmares about the bomb.

"But don't worry, miraculously no one was killed. Although there was some brief confusion when quite a few mannequins, like 3D Charles Hetherington-Smythes, were blasted out of shop windows and mistaken for real bodies," Jen explains. "But hundreds were slightly injured, unfortunately. One man, in his flat high up in the

Arndale Tower back where we were just parked, slept right through it. Like you are doing to the end of my story," Jen laughs to herself.

Although some beautiful and historic buildings were severely damaged like Manchester Cathedral, the Corn Exchange and the Royal Exchange, many Mancunians believe the bomb is the best thing to have ever happened. Not for the injured, of course - but for Manchester. The city was rearranged, repaired, replanned, remodelled and reinvigorated.

Joseph is fast asleep, only taking a single suck of his dummy occasionally. She feels sightly uneasy in her beloved city. Detached in a weird way. She starts to drive south, out of it.

As she crosses the inner ring road and onto the Princess Parkway, out of the city centre, a strange cloud descends over her.

The M56 is just lights and sounds in the darkness. She feels tears starting to pour down her face. She isn't sure why. Her vision becomes a little blurry. She doesn't feel very well, she feels unsafe. She gets off the motorway at the airport junction and takes the country lanes back to the cottage. She gets herself and her baby home. Safely.

Her mum is still out, somewhere. Has been a little cagey of late. She puts her beautiful sleeping baby boy to bed upstairs, goes into the silent snug and cries quietly. "If a tree falls in the middle of a forest and no-one is around to hear it, does it make a sound?" she remembers the question from a lecture. She can't remember the actual answer, but right now she feels like the silent falling tree. She is lonely.

She tries to puke up the cheese and tomato toastie she ate a few hours earlier. It's just bile now. She knew it would be. Bile tastes vile, she knows this. She papers over it and brushes her teeth, trying to rid her mouth of the metallic taste.

She kisses his sleeping face goodnight and goes to bed on her mattress on the floor, right next to his cot. She tells him how much she loves him. She quietly sings him the sunshine song as she stares up at the beams in the ceiling of their bedroom. Lightly lit by Joseph's night light.

The cottage is way over a hundred years old and the four old beams which span the width of her and Joseph's room go right up into the apex roof of the pitched ceiling. Joseph's cot is in the eaves. She ponders about the stories the beams could tell. How many people and pageants they have silently looked down upon. She wonders how many babies they have viewed being created, how many they have seen being born. How many tears and tantrums they have witnessed, how much love and laughter they have observed, and how many people they have watched die.

All this wistful wondering and pensive pondering. She really needs to get her shit in gear.

"I really really need to get my shit in gear," she says to the sleeping Joseph and Cherish, the sloping ceiling and the silent beams. She's sick of her self-absorption. She dreams about the beams and the stories they could tell. It is comforting.

Back in London, the sextet are heading out of the cinema in the most amazing spirits. Spontaneously deciding where they are going to go next. The night is young!

"Well that was absolutely brilliant," Kate says about 'Billy Elliot'. "Such a shame Jen wasn't here to see it. She'd have loved it."

And she absolutely would have.

Show me the meaning of being lonely.
Backstreet Boys.

-50-
EM: I PUT A SPELL ON YOU

25th October 2000
It's the middle of reading week at Em's college and she is, for once, doing some actual reading in reading week. Getting up at about eight in the morning to start. In Manchester her 'reading weeks' meant get pissed all week, like her 'Wednesday sports afternoons' meant get pissed all afternoon.

She has known Mel for about six weeks now and has become more and more attached to her. There is a magnetic, magical attraction, like she has cast some sort of spell on her. A good spell. Her uni friends and brother had instantly warmed to her when Em had introduced her on the night out in London as her 'friend from college', even though they were all (apart from Lou) a little confused as to what their relationship actually was, seeing their interaction with each other. Feeling the magic and the magnetic force. Especially Charlie.

Lou had not told him, or anyone, about the discussion on Em's birthday with Eve. It was Em's story to tell. Lou knew that she would open up more when she was ready. She also could see that she had now, in Eve, a real confidante. Which came as quite a surprise after how Em had clearly despised her for as long as she had known her. A confidante who Lou imagines she has opened up to more already.

Eve's baby, at thirty-nine weeks, is apparently the size of a mini watermelon. By next week, forty weeks, she will be the size of a small pumpkin. Very apt as she is due to be born on Halloween. In just six days.

Eve had looked up Halloween to see if there is any significance of the date being someone's birthday. Like baby showers, she thinks of it as a rather silly American tradition, but discovers it is actually the night before All Saint's Day, or 'Allhallows' in older times. The 1st November. A feast day observing the lives of saints who don't have a specific feast day for themselves. Poor buggers. Like kids who don't get their own birthday parties, or are born on Christmas Day and dickheads buy them 'joint' birthday and Christmas presents wrapped in Santa paper.

Halloween, or Hallowe'en, is the day before Allhallows. Short for Allhallows Even. Apparently Christmas Eve was originally Christ's Mass Even. It could have turned into Christmase'en. But it didn't. Who the fuck knew? Or, let's face it, cares. She needs this baby to come before her brain is addled by too much time and far too much useless information.

So, her baby is due to be born the day before the day that celebrates the Saints who have no personal parties planned. Those who are clearly not important enough, or that no-one gives enough of a shit about. Rather sad, actually.

She now prefers the rather silly American version. Much better. Less sad. Full of magic, paganism, costumes, parties and spells.

Last Friday night Em and Eve's friends hosted a little party for Eve at home. She is the first of her friendship group to have a baby. They all brought little gifts for Eve like magazines, moisturisers, a Jo Malone candle, some face masks and a book on meditation. One of Eve's friends, who had lived in America for a while, had tried to call it a 'baby shower'. Eve had said how she thought it was a silly American tradition, and some of the other girls didn't even know what a baby shower was.

Her friend explained that it can cost thousands to have a baby in America for prenatal, labour and postnatal medical care for both mum and baby due to almost absent maternity pay, no government help with childcare, no free pre-school places, etc. That baby showers were traditionally a way of people helping to pitch in when expectant mothers genuinely needed help buying the things they needed. Essential things. Yet again, Eve had to reconsider her thoughts on 'silly' American traditions.

The rest of the girls started to look around the vast kitchen and marble topped island, then through the bank of glass doors to the immaculately manicured expansive gardens and onto the stables and lake.

"Really looks like she needs help buying the essentials," another of Eve's friends, a teacher from her school, quipped. Ever so slightly cruelly. Em did not warm to her as she felt that she gave off a green vibe, clearly quite jealous of Eve. Then she realised how ridiculously ironic these feelings of hers were.

Is that irony, Alanis?

Although Eve was tired and still sick, she had a great time with her friends not showering her baby. Only one of said friends did have to shower after she got really pissed and decided to jump into the swimming lake and try to swim to Bob the little rowing boat. In October.

Another friend regaled a story about an older woman from her work called Beverley, a bit of a cow, who had just got married to a guy called Roger Hills. "There is absolutely nothing Hollywood about her," she bitched as the girls clocked on and laughed out loud. This got them onto asking Eve what the baby will be called. When Eve said they still hadn't made their minds up, they started shouting out more ridiculous first and last name combos.

"Theresa Green!"

"Chris Peacock!"

"Jen A Taylior!"

"Mike Hunt!"

"Annette Kirton!"

"Ben Dover!"

"Ivor Hugh Johnson!"

Pissed and pissing themselves, the girls got more and more silly and giddy. Especially at the last one. Although she found it funny, Eve was suddenly really tired. Em noticed. Not long after, on Em's instruction, they all piled into their respective taxis and left.

On breaks from reading, whilst trying to stop Ziggy and Coco from attacking her pen, books, hands, feet or anything else that even slightly moved, Em is helping Eve make sure everything is completely right and ready for the impending addition to the family and her birth in just six days. Her dad is in London for the day. He will be back later tonight.

At just after ten in the morning, Eve checks her hospital bag for the hundredth time, lets Joey and Chandler out into the garden and calls up to Em.

"Do you want a quick break and a brew?" She has started using Em's northern term for tea. She likes it.

"Yes please," Em says. "Give me a few minutes and I'll be down."

By the time she gets downstairs, Eve is doubled over.

"Oh fuck, shit," Em says, slightly panicking. "Are you ok? Is she coming?"

"I don't know, but it's very painful. It's like a really bad cramp."

"Have your waters broken?" Em asks.

"No, I don't think so."

Em is still in her pyjamas. Perfectly suitable reading attire. Not perfectly suitable hospital attire as a non patient.

"Right, sit down here," she guides Eve to the sofa. "Where's your hospital bag?"

"It's just there," Eve points to the kitchen island where she was checking it a few minutes before. "I've got everything but something to put on my feet."

"Ok. Just relax. Give me one second to find you some trainers so we have everything ready," Em orders as she races out of the kitchen and up to Eve and her dad's room and then onto her own.

Eve does exactly as she is told. The contraction stops, only lasted less than a minute. She feels her fu-fu to see if it is wet. It isn't. It's the first time she has ever felt her fu-fu with clothes on to see if it is wet. Even when wild weeing she checks before pulling her pants up.

Now she is thinking more rationally, she remembers that she shouldn't go to the hospital until the contractions are about five minutes apart. Or her fu-fu is wet. Would probably be sent home anyway.

She reaches for her phone and calls the maternity unit to double check the contraction timings and her thoughts on her double fu. They tell her exactly the same thing. Just as the call stops, she is violently sick. Regurgitated Special K Red Berries is now all over the sofa and herself.

Em comes in at this moment. "Oh fuck, shit," she says for the second time.

"There's no point in me going in yet," she tells Em, wiping her mouth. "It's such an early stage. I think I'll just have a nice warm bath and get cleaned up. Could you run one for me please? And I'll call your dad."

"Yes, of course." Em races up the stairs again and shouts halfway up, "I'll get dressed while I'm up here. Do you want bubbles?"

"No," Eve shouts back. "I'm sure I've read it's not good in labour."

Eve gets up to let Joey and Chandler back in as they are barking at the back door after hearing the shouting. Joey immediately starts to eat a pile of fresh poo in the kittens' litter tray. "For fucks sake," she shouts as she pushes him and his nose, which now looks like it's been dipped in chalky coloured fowl smelling sherbet, away from the tray with her leg, removes the half-eaten poo with a little plastic bag and ties it up, locates Ziggy and Coco, puts both kittens, their tray and a large blanket from the non-puked on sofa into the warm utility room, checks there is some water for them and shuts the door.

She finds Chandler hoovering up her Special K Red Berries vomit from the sofa. "For fuck's sake," she shouts at him. He looks up in surprise. His mum rarely shouts at him. Then goes back to his fruity feast. At least she doesn't now have to clean the wheaty red marbled chunks from the sofa. Silver linings and all that. Not so much a Special K day so far. More sherbet shit-show sick bay, anything but ok, day.

In the five or so minutes it has taken her to sort the animals, she hasn't had another contraction. So no need to panic. She calls her husband. His phone goes straight to answer machine so she leaves a message. She tries to be calm and tells him not to panic, it could be days. She is, however, aware that her pitch is elevated. Like her stress levels and unlike her sugar levels. She feels a little faint.

She gets into the nice warm bath and lies down. She watches as her tummy ripples with the movement of her baby beneath. She tends to get active when her mum is in the bath and Eve normally likes to watch. But she feels another contraction coming and realises she may not know if her waters break as she is in the bath. She gives herself a quick wash all over and heaves herself out. At least she doesn't stink of puke anymore.

She gets changed into a tracksuit and heads downstairs to find Em clearing up the remnants of the mess on the sofa that Chandler has somehow not managed to hoover up. She thanks her and checks her phone to see if her husband has called back. No missed calls. Another contraction is starting so she leans on the island and braves it out. Like islanders during a freak, temporary yet wild and all consuming coastal storm. It is almost eleven.

It's been eleven days since Jen and Joseph's trip into Manchester and her late-night beam dreams. She and Em had a long phone conversation a few days after, and Jen opened up a little bit about how she is feeling. She didn't tell the full dull tale, was not woe is me. That would have been boring. Too lonely moany. Boring, boring, boring. So boring she's started to bore herself.

She didn't let on how hard she was finding things, and how much she feels she has to continually prove herself. Not that anyone is telling her to, her boss certainly isn't and neither are her friends or her mum, but it is just in her somehow. She can't get rid of it, like the chip on her shoulder she has felt grow from a skinny French fry to a thick cut wedge. She also didn't tell Em that the other day, for some reason she couldn't really explain, she called Carla and said she couldn't come into work as she was ill when it was actually Joseph who was poorly. She doesn't want anyone to think her baby is an issue in her ability to do her job. That her being a single mum is a problem. What she doesn't realise is that most working mums, single or not, are the primary child carers. That they would be in exactly the same position as her, husband or not. She is a little too blinkered, too consumed by her chip. No-one is saying what she is thinking, but she feels that people are feeling it. Rightly or wrongly.

She didn't say anything about Mr. Senior Specs, she hadn't seen him recently anyway thank God, but what she did say was that she is going to have to try to create more of a day-to-day life around her reality, and her geography. A young, single, working mum living in a small Cheshire town. She is not sure how, but knows she will have to at some point. But for now, she is going to focus solely on her job, her career, her baby and their future.

Em has been so wrapped up in her own progressing and evolving personal life, her new course, her kittens and her impending baby sister, she has not checked in as much as maybe she should have with Jen. As much as she had promised herself she would. She made a mental note to make sure she checks in on her more often, and to try and arrange some things where Jen can bring Joseph.

At about three in the afternoon, Eve's contractions start to come thicker and faster. Both Eve and Em have called their respective husband and father several times, but the phone just keeps going to answer machine. It's not unusual to be out of signal, but five hours is a long time.

It is seven hours later when Eve remembers the kittens. In the hospital. In her delivery suite.

"They're in the utility room, Em. And the puppies have been on their own for hours. They might start eating each other" Eve is a little delirious with drugs. Em is not sure whether she means Joey and Chandler will start munching on each other, or they will miraculously make their way through the shut door and into the utility room to the kittens.

"They'll be fine, Eve. They'll be fine." Em has no idea how the quartet will be. But has no way of finding out. Pretty sure 'Animal Farm' or a feline/canine version of 'Watership Down' will not play out right now in Hertfordshire.

But she is genuinely starting to panic about the whole situation.

Em finally gets in touch with her dad just under an hour later. Through the eleventh person she tries from her and Eve's contact list. She knows Charlie has tried at least eight others.

It is past eleven at night and Eve is in the thick of labour.

"For fuck's dad," she half shouts at him on the phone in the corridor outside Eve's room. After 'Frank hubby work' from Eve's list picks up and hands the phone to her dad. Whoever the hell Frank is. "Where the fuck are you?"

He replies, clearly in high spirits. Very clearly full of high end spirits.

"Language, Emily," he berates merrily. She can hear he's been on the sauce. "I'm in London. Where I said I'd be. Just closed possibly the best deal of my life. What's the problem?"

"Get your fucking self in a fucking cab now and get to the fucking hospital," she adults her father. "You are just about to miss possibly the best deal of your fucking life."

Momentarily on the cusp of admonishing his daughter again for her extensive expletives, sense quickly kicks in.

"She's in labour?"

"Yes she's in fucking labour," Em fuses. "Has been all day, dad."

She knows she is letting out a world of fucking frustration on her frankly fettled father, but she will not have him miss this. Not on her watch.

"Shit! Fuck!" his turn to curse now.

"Are you moving, dad? Are you on your way? Put me back onto Frank, whoever the hell he is."

Frank sorts everything. Frank has a driver. Of course he does. In fairness, Frank is frankly brilliant. Whoever Frank is.

As Em's hand is being squished to within an inch of its kitten scratched life by her recently hated stepmother's powerful left hand, and the midwife tells Eve to push, Em's dad races into the room.

Eve's scared, haunted, fiery eyes pounce on him. "You fucking twat! Where the fuck have you been?" she furiously gasps.

He tries to take her hand from Em's grasp.

"No, fuck off," the normally controlled, quite serene Eve shouts.

Em doesn't know what to do. But the feeling of her near broken hand bones can feel she has no option. She is penned. Caged between wanting her dad to have the moment yet loving the moment herself. But having no control over it.

Eve lets out the most curdling noise Em has ever heard and grabs her husband's hand with her right hand. It is guttural. Brutal. Em has never heard anything like it. She is frankly terrified. As is Frank who is now leaving the room he should never have entered.

"That's the head, Eve," they hear the midwife say. "You're doing brilliantly. Just one more push. One more. Big. Push."

As Eve clenches everything, including Em's maimed hand and her husband's fresher one, and lets out a soundless yet very obvious wave of pain, the baby's shoulders and body are set free.

Em has never witnessed anything so amazing and significant in her life. She watches as the cord is cut, the placenta is delivered and the baby is handed to Eve. She is totally and completely overwhelmed. Never in a million years thought she would be here. Witness this. Be part of this.

Completely uncharacteristically, she retracts. Moves herself to the corner of the room. Spellbound. Watches as her dad and Eve celebrate their moment, their new baby. She is in awe. Silent, unobtrusive, no drama, total, unselfish, non-green awe.

A few minutes later her cornered existence is remembered.

"Em," Eve says. "Do you want to meet your little sister?"

"Yes please," Em says, starting to cry. Totally overwhelmed. "Yes please."

She sits down as her dad brings her little sister over and hands her to her. As she stares down at her, something jolts in Em. Like a spell, a shutting door.

A shutting door of a holiday hotel room. A magical whole life for a family for a week, ten nights, a fortnight. One room. Their paper palace. Gutted to leave their few hundred square feet. Or not. Their imprint soon to be erased like the sandcastles they spent hours making. With the turrets and moats. Replaced by another family, their sandcastle of dreams that everything will be ok for these few short, shallow end, sheltered days. It will surely paper over it, won't it? Make everything ok. Won't further establish the lie. Surely not? It will be like a spell. A spell of harmony and happiness.

Much loved and laid on, yet now limp, lilos just left. Safe code, someone's birth year, cracked for the final time. Passports and shreds of local currency removed. Hopefully enough for a soggy snack and non-alcoholic drink at the airport. Unobserved alliances secretly made inside the seemingly tight knit family unit. Tight lipped, quiet arguments formed of too tight close quarters and too much time spent together, not fretted upon but not forgotten. Half empty, or half full, bottles of shampoo and shower gel abandoned on the shower shelf. Appalling and repetitive aloe vera parrot jokes put down to a plethora of pina coladas. Frog masks broken and forgotten. Bikini diets buried, for another twelve months. No more looking right, the wrong way, and nearly being taken out by a quad bike full of other tourists. Dread of the flight, the letters on the mat, the price of the taxi home from the airport and the kennels, and the heavy weight of the humdrum of life on the horizon they see through the small window over the wing.

But Em is happy to leave the transient, small, stifling hotel room she has been inhabiting for many years. No more looking the wrong way, not seeing what is good and right in front of her. Can't wait to unshackle herself of her past, her half empty. Her papering over it. She is going to be half full from now on. Can't wait to press in the safe code holding her passport to a new life.

"Smile, Em," Eve commands as she points her retrieved Nikon Coolpix at her.

She already is. Widely. Almost wildly.

"Thank you Eve," she says. "And dad."

"What for?" Eve asks.

"For being you. For understanding, forgiving and accepting me. For me being here," she replies. "And for her."

Neither know what to say. They both just smile at her. Have both seen Em change and grow in such a significant way. Were not expecting Em to be part of this in this way. For her to watch her sister be born. It was not in the plan.

Fuck the plan. This is a far better unplanned plan.

"You're my little sister and I'll do anything for you, I promise," Em says softly as she kisses her soft head of little dark brown curls. "Because I'm yours and you're mine."

I put a spell on you.

Sonique.

-51-
JEN: SHE BANGS

4th November 2000

Saturday night in Lincolnshire.

Jen, her mum, auntie and uncle. A roaring fire. Two male cousins, both well over a foot taller than Jen. Her Grandpa and his wife are also in the shire. Two packs of cards carefully checked by suit. Certainly no suits. Instead a pile of dirty wellies, filthy fleeces and battered Barbours. Guns safely locked in the cupboard. Drowsy post hike dogs, lazy cats, horses tucked up in stables listening to the perpetually angry honking of geese. A jive round and round the kitchen by auntie and niece. A finished jigsaw with its one missing piece. Free range chickens waiting impatiently for the remnants of ham and chicken pie. Dire Straits and their 'chicks for free' blaring. Lots of swearing.

Pissed yet genuine joviality. Joseph watching on, bemused by the jocular scene and his mum's bounciness. Until his bouncer is knocked by the jiving duo and he starts to cry.

Jen stops dancing and watches as her Grandpa picks up his abandoned dummy and dips it into his whiskey, then puts it back in his great grandson's mouth.

"Dad!" Jen's mum shouts before Jen can react.

"What?" he says stoically, like his Volvo would if it could verbalise. "Never did any of you any harm."

"Debatable," one of Jen's cousins quips, the really really tall one. A bit like the BFG. This is quickly followed by the inebriated agreement of his father and the whipping of a wet tea towel over his and his tallest son's heads by their respective wife and mother. Jen's auntie looks like a flower, but she can sting like a bee.

Joseph very happily sucks on his drunk dummy. Like Maggie Simpson on a pub crawl.

Perfect. Picture perfect perfection for Jen. Her happy place.

Just one thing missing, apart from the ham and chicken pie inside Jen. Her sister. She stayed up in Scotland after graduation and is now living with her boyfriend. Jen has spoken to her a lot recently. She will be home for Christmas.

"Chase the ace?" the other of Jen's cousins asks. It was always going to be a card game or the well-worn pub quiz DVD. Monopoly has been left untouched in the cupboard for years, gathering the dust of the ghost of Christmas past.

Jen loves the game. 'Ace' is supposed to be the best. 'She aced it', 'That was ace'. In poker it is like Gemini. A two-faced ace. Can be high or low. But in this game, it's the worst card you can be dealt. If you are left with it, you've lost. It should really be called 'replace the ace'. Recently Jen has certainly not been chasing 'ace', she just needs a sense of belonging and place. And here, she has it. For a few nights, at least.

She can forget about the world and the future for the night as she Tiggers it up, papers over it and palms off the unwanted ace onto her Grandpa's lovely wife sitting to the left of her who is, for the first time, struggling to keep up with the game. And the conversation.

Later that night, with Joseph tucked up in his travel cot, Jen sits in the lounge chatting shit with her cousins and drinking wine. Jen's mum and auntie are in the kitchen. As Jen walks in to go through to the downstairs loo, she stops as she hears her auntie say quietly to her mum, "Give Carl a chance. You've enjoyed his company so far. What have you got to lose? And let's face it, your pride left you years ago when your husband pissed off over the Pennines."

They have not noticed her. She stands still, not wanting to eavesdrop on the sisters, but not sure now what to do. She slowly reverses and goes to the upstairs loo making a mental note to be Miss Marple when they drive home first thing on Monday.

Back in the lounge, she rather stupidly tells her slightly sozzled cousins what she's just heard, but makes them swear not to say.

"I swear on my knob," BFG one says.

"What the fuck?" Jen laughs. "Who swears on their knob?"

"My most valuable asset, I'll have you know," he replies. "Needs to be intact to populate the planet with more giants in the future."

"You're so fucking weird," the other cousin replies. Still annoyed his younger brother overtook him at sixteen and, even though he is tall, now has over four inches on him.

At this point Jen's mum and auntie come into the lounge.

"DVD pub quiz?" one asks. Standard.

5th November 2000
Bonfire night.

No fireworks allowed at the house. Too many bangs. Too scary for the animals.

Jen's Grandpa and his wife are going to stay in to make sure they're ok. Or at least they said that when they heard about the daft proposal for the afternoon.

The plan is to go to the beach, have a BBQ and set off some fireworks there. Sunset is around 4:30pm so they pack up the trailer with the BBQ, gas cylinder, camping stove, general food, a pan of spicy lentil dahl Jen's uncle has knocked up "to keep us all warm", a bottle of mulled wine also to keep them warm, a pan for the mulled wine, fireworks, a football, a frisbee found in the garage next to the football, some deck chairs, torches and lanterns, blankets, plates and cutlery. The fire pit, sparklers, wood and coal. It's a perfect early November day. But they are still all mad.

Jen calls Lou as she moved into a house share in London yesterday with some other people from her show. She wishes her good luck as she starts rehearsals on Monday. She is still reeling from the death of her dad, and found it very hard to leave her family. But she knows this is what Len would have wanted. Jen says she can't wait to see her on the 25th for her birthday. Her actual twenty second is on the 23rd, but the quartet have all arranged to go out in Manchester two nights later on the Saturday night. Lou promises to call Jen on Monday night and let her know how her first day goes.

In Lincolnshire they all get wrapped up and squeeze into two cars. The bigger one pulling the trailer. They hit the road east at just after 3pm.

Twenty minutes later, they are unpacking onto the beach. At the amusement of a duo of dog walkers who want to tell the crazy trailer crew that it's the middle of winter. Not BBQ season.

The football is fairly quickly stolen by the wind and the sea. They are foolish enough to BBQ on the beach in winter, but not enough to dive into the freezing waves of the North Sea to rescue a ball. They wave it off on its nautical journey to get hairy pottered in Amsterdam. After only a few brief flings and flights in the picking up coastal wind, the frisbee soon follows its garage mate, hoping to be flying even higher very soon.

"For fuck's sake," one of Jen's cousins shouts at his brother for the unfortunate overzealous fling. They fight it out, like the moon is now starting to fight it out with the sun.

BBQ and stove are set up and firing, the mulled wine is heated and shared out and the firepit is roaring. Deck chairs and blankets are carefully positioned and then fought over.

Jen notices another set of dog walkers watching the ludicrous scene. She laughs at the ridiculousness of it. "They must think we're mad," she says.

"Well they would be right," her auntie replies. "It's bloody freezing. Pour me some more mulled wine."

A large pre-made salad is dressed and the pan of delicious smelling dahl has replaced the now empty mulled wine pan.

"Who the hell wants salad? In the freezing cold on the beach in November?" a cousin asks.

"I do, actually," his mum replies, having insisted on bringing it. Knowing she will now have to eat some of the cold, now really rather uninviting salad.

They stubbornly and stoically persist with their grilling of sausages, chicken drumsticks and corn on the cob. Then one of Jen's cousins starts grilling her mum about what he'd sworn on his knob he wouldn't.

"Any dates recently?" he asks her.

"No," she replies to her cheeky nephew. "You?"

"Loads, thanks. I'm clearly irresistible. But how about you? A little bird told me the news that you may be having a romantic rendezvous some time soon."

"Oh yeah, they're forming an orderly queue outside my door," she says, giving her sister an evil eyed sideward glance. "Lady luck has never been on my side with men."

"I didn't say anything," her sister yells indignantly as she stands up to give her huge son a clip round the ear. Stinging like a bee again. Jen's mum copies her, confused about how her Carl confession has been cat out of bagged. In the process she stumbles and knocks the pan of dahl over onto the sand.

"Well done," the same cheeky BFG nephew says saucily. "Just what we want to eat. Sandy dahl."

"She'd rather eat Randy Carl," the other nephew quips, quick as a flash.

"Stupid boy," Jen's mum replies. More ear clipping and tea towel flipping ensues as she pretends she is genuinely upset at all the attention.

"Go on, mum," Jen asks, laughing. "You may as well tell us now. Who is Randy Carl?"

"No-one," she replies to her daughter. "Just a friend of a friend. And he's not exactly randy. He's actually rather dandy."

"Oooooh! Randy Dandy Carl," the BFG cousin quips. "Is he from Cumbria? Is his surname Lyle?"

"Carl Lyle," Jen spits out her mulled wine.

"Don't be so childish, Jennifer," her mother berates her instead of her nephew. "He's not from Carlisle, he's from Warrington. Anyway, we should be talking about your potential love life. Not mine," she tries to divert the unwanted yet rather enjoyed attention.

"Yes, Jen," one of her cousins accepts the diversion and ploughs on down the new path. "Anything to tell us? Banged anyone recently?"

"God no," she replies, laughing at the terminology. "I have absolutely no banging plans. I've got more than enough on my plate, thank you."

"Grab a plate. Grubs up," Jen's uncle interrupts returning from having a wild wee over the sand dunes and checking the BBQ. Completely missing the last few minutes. "What the fuck has happened to my dahl?"

"It just rolled off," his wife lies.

"Pans of dahl don't just roll off." He is a bit pissed off. Loves his dahl. Took hours making it for them all "to keep them warm".

"Rolled Dahl!" Jen's BFG cousin wisecracks. He is really on form tonight with his Dahls and his Carls.

A little bit of wee escapes from Jen as she doubles over in laughter. "How has Randy Carl turned into bloody Roald Dahl?" she screams.

"Who is Randy Carl?" Jen's uncle asks. Completely confused and still upset about his sandy dahl. Fully acquainted with Roald Dahl.

"They're just being a bunch of bloody twits," Jen's mum replies, having no idea how clever her choice of word is.

"She wants some of randy Carl's marvellous medicine," one cousin helpfully explains, smirking.

"And his magic finger," the other quickly builds. "The woman's got one thing on her mind, dad."

"Oh, you're all just awful," Jen's mum says, thinking at least they are all fairly well read, even though they are shockingly crude and have a general lack of respect. "Anyway, I'm hungry," she again attempts to divert. "I'd like a sausage, please," she says to her brother-in-law.

"I bet you would," he replies. Quickly catching up and adding in some banger banter. Still having no clue who Randy Carl is.

"Thank god dad isn't here, hearing all this filth," Jen's auntie says while Jen, her cousins and her uncle laugh a little uncontrollably. "Wash your mouths out, the lot of you."

A little while later, when it's really dark, they light the sparklers and set off the fireworks. A battery of comets and rockets fill the beautiful buxom night sky. She bangs with crackles and brocades. Joseph is mesmerised wrapped in a blanket in his mum's arms. Doesn't moan or cry. Just stares up in awe under his little red bobble hat and above his chubby red cheeks.

It has been a great few days for Jen. She hasn't felt so normal in a long time. So like Jen. Wrapped in the blanket of love, madness, belonging, sense of place and easy contentment of her family, she can be completely herself.

She has laughed and Tiggered her way through the two days. She promises herself to try and emulate this feeling at home. To find a way to be herself again in real life, not just here. To belong. To somehow transport her 'here' happy place to bang on the door of her 'there'.

"If it's not Here, that means it's out There," said Pooh.

She watches the last of the fireworks bang and fizzle. Looks as the glow lights up Joseph's little face.. and she smiles.

She bangs.
Ricky Martin.

-52-
THE QUARTET: INDEPENDENT WOMEN

25th November 2000
Saturday. The long-awaited girls' night out for Lou's twenty-second birthday.

Her actual birthday was on Thursday, but they are celebrating today in Manchester.

Em drove herself and Lou up last night through the dreadful Midlands traffic and shocking, just north of Stoke, storm.

They both stayed with Kate at Em's flat. Kate and Will's flat. Will has gone home to Chester for the weekend. Knows he is surplus to requirements. And their inevitable collective screeching would probably give him a headache anyway.

He has however, yet again, come up trumps on sorting the cinema tickets. 'Charlie's Angels' premiered a few weeks ago and has been packing cinemas ever since. Men and women alike hankering after the ridiculously hot trio. The Manchester trio, Em, Lou and Kate, chatted about the film at the pub.

They are really looking forward to watching Cameron, Lucy Lui and their girl Drew independently and collectively boss it. Or get told what to do and be completely controlled by a faceless, older man 'apparently' called Charlie and his assistant John (Bill Murray) in a massively misogynistic "Good morning Angels", "Good morning Charlie" way. Were they actually free-range hens, or free to range only within the chicken run confines of Charlie's Farm?

Either way, Jen can't wait either. To see the girls and to get out of her chicken run for the night, more than the actual film itself. She would, however, have preferred adult time to screen time for the whole night. Have had two more hours of girlie chit chat, chewing the fat and harmless spat, than be silently sat. She doesn't say this, of course. Doesn't want to appear ungrateful. Happily accepts it would not even enter their heads.

She has realised that these girls, and her home friends, can no longer be her day to day friends in her new world. It just doesn't work. Due to either geography or activities, or both. That doesn't mean they can't still be great friends. Mainly in their worlds, though. In worlds without babies and responsibilities each evening and each weekend. Jen just needs to work out some more adult company in her new world. Somehow.

Her mum is going out with Carl tonight. She is refusing to call it a 'date', as she had the previous nights out. "I'm a Grandmother. Grannies don't date," she had said to Jen. "It's more of a 'meeting'."

"Well whatever you want to call it - consultation, appointment or encounter of the third Carl - enjoy," Jen had laughed when she left the house and packed Joseph and his paraphernalia into Honey on Saturday afternoon. She headed to her ex's house where Joseph is going to stay the night with him and his new girlfriend.

Jen is nervous about leaving Joseph overnight, but her ex has promised her everything will be ok. "He is my son," he reminds her. "You know I adore him and would never let anything happen to him." She feels bad as she knows both are true. And it's her issue, not his.

As she drives Honey down the Princess Parkway and into the city centre, she feels excited. The quartet haven't been all together since September as Jen couldn't join them in London in October. That was the last time she had gone into her beloved Manchester. Where she used to feel she belonged. Had avoided it since her feeling of detachment from it on her last visit and her slight crisis on the motorway on the way home. But now she is excited.

She arrives just after 5pm.

Her three friends are already on one. Destiny's Child's 'Independent Women' blaring. Steve the Cheese surveying the scene, tutting and glaring.

"Jen," Kate shouts as she opens the door. She has met up with Kate a few times. She came on the train to see her and Joseph at the cottage. Jen understands she is wrapped up in uni life, her studies, Will, his ongoing treatment and some new friends they have made. She genuinely really appreciates her coming out of town to see her.

After they hug it out, the foursome quickly and easily snap back into their comfortable closeness and collective belonging. They turn down Beyoncé, Michelle and Kelly so they can catch up.

"How's stardom treating you, Lou?" Jen asks proudly.

"I'm absolutely loving it!" she sings. "It's only been, what, three weeks? Still in the thick of rehearsals. It's tough and super demanding, but I honestly could not be happier. Feel like I really belong."

"How's your house going?" Kate asks, sipping her Bacardi Breezer through a straw. Feeling suddenly a little nostalgically blue for their Withington No. 52. "And your housemates?" A wave of what feels something like jealously laps over her. A rare emotion for Kate.

"The place is a shit hole, to be fair. But it's our shit hole. And honestly they are just fab. We have so much in common. Couldn't ask for a better bunch of people to live with."

Kate's face must have let her down.

"I mean, no-one could ever replace you or our 52," Lou adds, giving her slightly crestfallen friend a hug. "Sorry mate."

"Aww Kate's jealous," Em says, with a hint of her old stirring Em.

"Emily!" Jen admonishes. "You've got no room to talk. How's bitch Eve?"

"Do you know what, she's great. Really great. Not a bitch at all. I can't believe what a bitch I was for all that time. I feel like such a dick."

"You are a dick," Lou says, laughing. "Once a dick, always a dick."

Em retorts by wanking off an imaginary penis protruding from her forehead.

"How's Mel?" Jen asks, laughing. She is the only one of the quartet who hasn't met her. But Em had talked her through her feelings and the budding relationship to a stunned Jen on the phone a few weeks ago, as she had to a slightly less surprised Kate. Kate had seen them together in London and had had her suspicions.

"She's great, thank you," Em replies very coyly, like a carp hiding behind his bashful bro. She stops there.

"Our Em, not explicitly sharing her dalliances," Jen laughs. "What's come over you?"

"Maybe this isn't just a dalliance," Em replies. Unusually ignoring the opportunity to sexualise Jen's question.

Jen plucks up the courage after downing the remnants of her Hooch. "So do you think you're gay? Or bisexual? Or what?"

Neither Kate nor Lou have managed to ask the question they have both been wanting to ask. Intrigued, they both turn to Em for her answer. They are not used to this person. This new, no wild cock story, coquettish Em.

"I'm not going to put a label on it. I just know I really like her. Fancy her. And she makes me laugh. And I think I like her as much as she likes me. Which is a weird feeling. I've never really actually liked anyone before," she says thoughtfully. "Eve tells me to let it be what it will be. To give it space and time to grow. To breathe. To not put any pressure on it, me or her."

"Wise Eve," Kate says. "Well, Will and I thought she was just fab."

"Me too," Lou agrees.

Jen can't comment so asks, "And your little baby sister. How's she?"

"She's just adorable. In fact, she's a month old today."

"Bloody hell, that's flown hasn't it," Lou says. "How old is Joseph now Jen? I haven't seen him in ages," she adds with a flicker of guilt.

"He's about five and a half months, now," Jen replies, smiling. "Full of cheek, laughs and sass."

"Do you get out much?" Em asks. Also aware she hasn't found the time to really catch up with Jen lately either.

"I'm out now," Jen replies, a little too defensively. She does not want her friends to feel in any way guilty. She does not want to be a burden like that. To cover it up, she tells the girls as much as she knows about her mum's budding romance. They scream with laughter when she regales the 'Randy Carl' incident at her aunties.

The girls decide it's time to start getting ready. They cop their spots.

On Em's suggestion, fully aware she will be the least independent of all of them, they play what she christens 'The Independence Game'.

"What is it?" Lou asks, starting to apply a thick layer of concealer over a fresh, angry looking spot on her chin. Looking in the fireplace mirror. In her spot.

"Just play along," Em responds from her new spot on the floor by Steve the Cheese. Kate's old spot. Kate is just a few metres away in her, Em's old, bedroom. Her new spot. Jen is comfortably in her long lived spot. In the bathroom. All doors wide open, as they always were.

"I'm in, whatever it is," Jen winces, ridding her nose of a very satisfying blackhead.

"Me too," Kate calls, debating whether her recently purchased push up bra is too much for her naturally pushed up breasticles.

Em shouts about shoes on her feet.

Lou and Jen shout back that they bought them. At the same time Em sings, "I didn't." Then Kate gets it, a split second after the others, and adds, "I stole them."

"Kate!" Em says.

"It was over a year ago," Kate replies. As if the time absolved the Dolcis crime.

Then the game went on to the clothes they're wearing.

Lou sings back that she bought it. Em replies, "I didn't," while Kate hollers "Will bought it" and Jen admits awkwardly "It's Emster's."

They are all laughing by now. Em and the fact she has so far bought herself nothing, Kate's ability to get things either from other people or in rather dubious ways, and Jen realising she is wearing a dress that she never returned to Em after borrowing it 'just for the night' quite some time ago.

Rocks and rocking are next.

"What does that actually mean?"

"Diamonds, I think" Em admits. "Anyone got a hidden rock? Kate?"

"Ha, ha!" Kate replies, remembering the Haribo ring from the train which she, for some reason, has safely cleaned, dried, wrapped and placed in one of the pockets of her bag. "No."

What watches they are wearing continues the daft game.

A mixture of "Not wearing one" and "Don't have one" are sung back. They realise that their phones have made their watches redundant. None can remember the last time they rang 123 to call the speaking clock either.

"At the third stroke, the time sponsored by Accurist, will be.. five forty-six and ten seconds," Lou parrots in a terrible BBC accent.

"Beep, beep, beep," Jen adds, grinning.

"Can you imagine having your phone on your wrist?" Kate asks. "Mental. Like something from 'The Jetsons'."

"You'd still always be late, Kate," Em laughs.

They continue onto houses they live in and cars they're driving. Of course none live in houses they bought themselves, Lou and Kate don't own a car, Em's Clio was gifted by her dad - 'Papa, Nicole'. Jen did buy her Honey, but with a mix of the proceeds of a summer job she had and selling the old Fiat Tipo her parents bought her after the Victorian wall felling Jeep got stolen. So apparently that doesn't count.

"So basically, I'm a spoilt brat. Kate's a thief. Jen's an even worse thief as she stole from a friend. Leaving Lou the nearest to Beyoncé," Em summarises.

Lou responds, quick as a flash, that it isn't easy being independent.

"I've missed you girls," Jen says from the bathroom. Feeling a little guilty about the stolen dress, but not guilty enough to give it back. She feels great in it.

When they are all ready, and Jen has successfully checked in with her ex, they sit in the lounge and each have another bottle of something rum or vodka based.

"Seen much of my brother, Lou?" Em asks. Knowing from Charlie she hasn't.

"No," Lou replies. "Been really busy. He has called a few times."

"You know he really likes you," Em admits.

"And I like him too. It's just with Len, the auditions, new job, the move down to London, new home. There's been so much going on."

"Yes of course. Sorry to ask. So it's not like you're seeing someone else?" Em continues to pry. Can't help herself.

"Leave her alone, Em," Kate protects her old house mate. Em has told them in the past about her brother's reputation. "Maybe she just doesn't want to be one of Charlie's Angels," she adds with a wry smile.

"Very good, Kate," Jen laughs as Em stops herself from protecting her brother and further prying. She is aware of his past reputation and how she has told the girls about it in the past, in fact revelled in telling them. They are all unaware how much he genuinely likes Lou, though.

"How's work, Jen?" Em asks. Aware her old Em is on her shoulder, nipping away.

"Really good, to be honest," Jen smiles. "I mean, I'm not dancing for a living like you Lou, making a living out of my passion. Or following a dream like you of being a vet or like Kate, going to be the legal eagle for the disadvantaged. But it's really good. I'm genuinely really enjoying it." She doesn't say a word about Mr. Senior Specs. But she is completely honest about how much she is actually enjoying it and being treated really well by her boss Carla, and her close colleagues. "I've been asked to do a presentation at our Christmas conference in a few weeks."

"Wowzers" Kate says. "Are you terrified? I would be."

"How many people will be watching?" Em asks before Jen can reply to Kate.

"I'm shitting it to be honest," Jen admits. "There'll be about eighty people, apparently, for my bit. Just my section of the business. There's about two hundred and fifty in total at the conference. I've planned a lot of our section. There's a massive plenary in a huge room and then we all shoot off to different smaller rooms for our sections. I've planned a boxing theme for us. Fighting for our place in the market. Carla and our big boss love the idea. I've planned a boxing ring. Have got the venue to put up a square stage and have been making the ring corners and the ropes at home with loads of stuff I bought on expenses from B&Q. Mum's been going crazy with the mess. Me and a couple of the team are going to be the ring girls showing the next presenters in signs rather than boxing round numbers, or bouts. Or whatever they're called. Then I'm told I'm going to be a presenter too. Talking about a new innovation we're launching. Terrifying!"

The girls all grin at Jen's enthusiasm. And verbal diarrhoea. None totally confident they understand what she has just explained, but loving her Tigger vibe.

"Bloody hell, Jen," Lou says. "I can dance and sing to as many people as you put in front of me. But to actually talk. That's impressive."

"Well, let's see. I may monumentally fuck it up. I've been on a presentation course. I did a presentation on how to make a good cup of tea, of all things. The trainer said as long as you know what you're talking about, like making a cup of tea, you'll be fine. Just prepare. And that it's best not to have prompts. Makes you look like a robot," Jen says.

"So you have to memorise it? All of it" Kate asks, wide mouthed. "How long is your bit?"

"Just ten minutes," Jen replies. "Although that sounds like forever now I'm saying it out loud."

"That is forever," Lou adds.

"I told a horrible lie the other day," Jen spouts randomly as they all consider how long ten minutes actually is. Most privately thinking that ten minutes is, pretty much always, more than long enough.

"What?" they all ask in unison. Jen never lies, they don't think. Only lies of omission. And they don't know about them by their very nature. Obviously.

"Let's get one more drink and I'll tell you," Jen replies.

"Is Hairy Potter still alive?" Lou asks.

"Yes, he is," Kate cries. "Give me a second."

Steve the Cheese has been living with a really nice couple, called Will and Kate, for a few months now. Far better than his last housemate. She was crazy. He wasn't particularly impressed when she rocked up tonight. The new ones don't make too much noise, don't have crazy parties and they water and feed him with the right things at the right time. And they watch nice movies. Cheesy ones like Pretty Woman, Notting Hill and Love Actually. And they play nice music like 'Prince' He is particularly fond of 'Purple Rain'.

The only time he has been really disturbed is when they moved him, the pouffe and the chair to play a game they called 'Twister'. Will sat on the sofa and spun something while Kate contorted her half naked body on a spotty mat. Numerous times. It was really quite interesting to watch. Senseless, but interesting. He braces himself for his nemesis, Mr. Potter, to arrive. He just wants a quiet life.

"So," Jen elaborates on her lie. "It was a few weeks ago and the guys at work all said that we were going to finish early and go for a drink in one of the local pubs. It was a Friday. I was well pleased to be honest. It was 3:30pm and I didn't have to pick up Joseph until 6pm. Not that I didn't want to see him," she is quick to add.

The girls nod, sharing their Hairy.

"We got to the pub at about quarter to four and ordered our

drinks. It was really nice. Then my phone rang. Joseph's nursery. Shit."

"What did you do?"

"Well I answered it and they said he wasn't feeling too well. A little hot. I asked if it was an emergency and they said it absolutely wasn't. He was fine. But if I could pick him up as soon as I could, that would be good."

"What did you say?"

"Well I have no idea what came over me, but I said I was in Leeds."

"Leeds?" Em spits.

"What, about an hour and a half away? Up the Pennines? On a good traffic day?" The more northern geography educated Lou asks.

"Yes," Jen puts her head in her hands. "Said I was at a work meeting."

"Have you ever been to a work meeting in Leeds?" Kate asks.

"No," Jen admits, head in hands. "Doncaster, yes. Leeds, no."

"What did they say?" Em asks. Finding Jen's clear trauma a little intoxicating and highly amusing.

"Well they asked if my mum could pick him up, as the other 'parent'. But if I'd have said yes, I would have had to tell her about my dreadful lie. She knew I was nowhere near Leeds."

"Then what?" Lou asks, laughing.

"They were so lovely. Told me not to worry. And to drive carefully. "The M62 can be a beast on a Friday". They will look after him until I get there."

"Oh shit," Kate starts to laugh too. "And you were, like, seven minutes away."

"Yes," Jen admits, starting to laugh at her awful admission.

"What did you do?" Lou asks.

"Well, all I wanted to do was leave the pub and go and pick him up. Horrified at myself. But how could I? If I'd have turned up I would either have had to admit I was in possession of a rocket, or forever be the liar. Couldn't go home because my mum was likely to be there. I had to wait it out in the pub, feeling like a piece of shit mum."

"Oh Jen," Kate says in some form of pity. "I'm sorry, but that's hilarious."

"Then, when I finally arrived at a reasonable hour to have driven back from Leeds, they all took pity on me for my long drive back," Jen adds. "Telling me what a great mum I was for getting back so quickly."

"Oh no," Em and the girls are now in stitches, but feeling the need to check on Jen's poorly child. "Was Joseph ok?"

"Yes, absolutely fine," Jen regales. "But I was traumatised with myself and my reckless behaviour."

"Reckless?" Em snorts. "Reckless is my middle name. Not yours."

"I've missed you, Jen," Lou says, giggling at her friend's blatant dishonesty, and how badly she clearly feels about it.

"I've really missed you all," Jen smiles.

Before they head out, Jen calls her ex. Again. To see if he has gone out and left Joseph with his new girlfriend. Then realising, when he clearly hasn't, the irony of her thoughts.

Is that irony, Alanis?

They stop for a drink on their way to The Odeon.

Perched at a high table on four stools, Em says, "I completely forgot to ask. What are you all up to for New Year's Eve?"

"I'm going home for Christmas, but back down to Manchester on the 29th," Kate replies. "Haven't really thought about it to be honest."

"I'm the same, but back in London on the 28th," Lou says. "Will be a really sad Christmas. First one without Len."

"Of course. I'm so sorry Lou," Em says. "I can't imagine how hard it will be for you all. How's your mum?"

"She's ok. Keeping herself busy. Killing all his plants and the veggies in his greenhouse."

"What? On purpose?" Kate asks, her dark eyes as wide open as her blow job lips. Assuming it is some sort of freaky foliage therapy.

"No, you dick," Lou struggles to swallow her mouthful of beer. "Why would she do that? "I'm going to get you back for dying on me, Len, by strangling your strawberries and crucifying your clematises"."

Em and Jen laugh out loud at Lou's quick-witted description of the mock greenhouse massacre.

PAPER OVER IT

"Sorry Lou," Kate says. "Stupid of me."

"No, actually it's really quite funny," Lou laughs. "Len would have loved it. Probably laughing up there right now. Smoking his cigar and happily deadheading his roses."

"To Len," Jen holds up her bottle. She is unsure of Lou's turn of phrase, but goes with it. "Happily deadheading his roses."

"To Len," Lou and the two other reply as they chink their glasses and drink to Lou's dad. "Happily deadheading his roses."

Wanting to move off the subject before she gets emotional, Lou asks, "Why were you asking about New Year, Em?"

"Oh yes, sorry, got side tracked," Em says. "We are having a thing at home. And I promise you, a 'thing' at my house is never just a thing. You're all invited."

"Will?" Kate asks. Knowing the answer.

"Yes of course Will," Em replies. "That's like inviting Juliet and not Romeo, isn't it?"

"That makes no sense," Lou says. "They were never invited anywhere together. That's the whole point of the story."

"For the sake of fuck," Em mock sighs. "Want me to call Will Shakes and ask him to shake up his plotline so Kate's Will can come?"

"Yes please!" Kate giggles into her gin. A tipple recently introduced to her by Will's mum. "And can you please tell him to tell Romeo that Juliet isn't dead. She's just pulling a whitey."

"I'm fairly confident that you like pulling Will's little whitey," Lou teases.

"Louisa!" Kate berates.

"The lady protest too much, methinks" Lou teases back.

"Doth," Em corrects. "The lady doth protest too much, methinks."

"Fuck off Em," Lou and Kate spit back.

Lou adds, "Methinks you are a shrew."

Jen laughs at her friends and their Bard banter. She has been keeping quiet. She has no plans for New Year's Eve. Has not even considered it. But now she has, she feels like the outsider again.

"Jen," Em directs her attention at Jen. "Are you busy on New Year's Eve?"

"No," Jen replies honestly. "No plans as yet."

"Perfect," Em says. "You just need to jump in the car and come down for the night. Or two if you'd like."

Jen stays quiet. Unsure what to say. Eyes starting to prickle with the heat - or the cold - of not belonging. Unsure what temperature it is. Thinking up her excuses already.

"We have a cot so you don't have to bring one. Eve has already bought a highchair in preparation for when she needs it. We have loads of baby bedding and shit. And a bottle steriliser. Eve will be on babysitting duty all night. She can't wait to meet you two. Thinks it's a good idea to set him up in the nursery with my little sis. So you can have a night off. Unless you want him in your room?"

The pre-formed tears behind her eyes now flow down Jen's face. Her emotions have turned on a sixpence. It is overwhelming.

"Jen," Kate asks, visibly shocked and concerned. "What on earth is the matter?"

"Nothing. Honestly nothing," she replies through her tears. "I'm just really tired. We would love to come, Em. Thank you. We would really love that."

Jen's three friends side-glance each other, half believing her 'tired' tale but each independently making a note to make more time and ask Jen more often how she is.

"Right, that's sorted then," Em announces. Kindly changing the tone. "Jen's a yes. Lou?"

"Yes!"

"Kate? You said yes, right?"

"I'll just check with Will," Kate replies.

"Beyonce says you should dismiss a boy who tries to control you," Lou banters. Fully knowing Will in no way controls the independent Kate. And if he tried, she would never accept it.

"What am I thinking? Of course I'm a yes," she says, surprised at herself for her 'check with' comment . "He can come if he's lucky."

"Woo-fucking-hoo," Em pulls a terrible tmesis. "That's all of you! Shit, what's the time?"

"Sup up. Let's go!" Lou checks her phone for the time. "Charlie's Angels are never late."

"Unlike Kate," Jen joshes. Emotions back intact.

The quartet head over to The Odeon, arm in arm. Depending on each other and their other special people, but all becoming more self-reliant and independent women in their own individual, unique ways.

Independent Women.
Destiny's Child.

-53-
JEN: CASE OF THE EX

8th December 2000

The day of Jen's Christmas conference.

Jen is already at the venue. She drove the one and a half hours there yesterday to set everything up in the room, have a practice with her team and make sure everything is perfect and sorted for the 9:30am start.

Her mum is looking after Joseph. Has rearranged her shift hours at work so she can drop and pick him up from nursery. Jen knows she will miss him, and her. Doesn't like to be away from them too much. Or their cottage.

Jen has borrowed a large pool car from work, a Ford Mondeo estate, so she can fit in all the boxing props and everything else she needs. It reminded her of the bitch health visitor's car when she saw it. But it's blue, not grey. That bitch was most definitely grey.

She has had it since Tuesday and doesn't have to drop it back until Monday. As she didn't need her Honey for the week, her ex asked if he could borrow her as his car is in the garage getting some repairs. He was very responsible a few weeks ago with Joseph, when he had him overnight, and has even given her a few quid, so Jen agreed.

"You do have insurance, don't you?" she checked.

"Yes, on my own policy," he confirmed.

"Comprehensive insurance?" she asked. "Not just third-party?"

"Yes, of course," he promised.

Jen is in her room. It's 6:30am.

She is a little terrified for the day, especially her presentation. She is putting an awful lot of pressure on herself for everything to go well. She looks around the room for the ashtray. She finds it and lights a cigarette. She gave up for a while but bought a packet yesterday, just in case she needed one. To calm her nerves. To help her with her control. It helps.

She calls her mum at 7:00am to make sure everything is ok. Of course it is. She knows the call is more for her than them.

She meets Carla and her team, as planned, for breakfast at 7:30am. She is not hungry but manages to swallow a piece of wholemeal toast and half a banana.

They go into their smaller, though not small at all, conference room to check everything. Carla's boss has not seen the room set-up yet. Just arrived this morning. He is thrilled with it.

"It looks just like a proper boxing ring. It's brilliant!" he praises his team.

"All Jen's work," Carla kindly confirms.

Jen beams.

At just before 9:30am all the conference attendees file into the huge room for the morning plenary session. Hundreds of people and faces Jen still doesn't know or recognise. All the head office staff like Jen plus the sales people who work from home, geographically closer to their customers. And the massive field sales forces of three divisions.

The music and lights whip on. It's really exciting. The Big Boss goes on stage with a lapel mike and welcomes everyone to the conference. He goes through the agenda for the day and tells everyone where they are supposed to be and at what time. Mr. Senior Specs then joins him with a hand-held mike and goes through the plans for the evening. He has a great way of presenting, commanding attention. He is funny and attractive, Jen thinks. She also hates him.

Other senior management members join them on stage and say their bits about achievements and targets. Potential bonuses and celebrations. Their stories whip up the massive audience into a menage of morning glories.

Jen, her team and their field sales force then head into their room. The morning goes without a hitch and everyone comments on how great the boxing theme is and how good the dressed room looks. Jen is thrilled. Apart from the little red mark she finds in her knickers and the inside of her white hot pants in the toilet at the morning break. She, and another girl on her team, are wearing little shorts and tight t-shirts in their 'ring girl' jobs introducing the presenters. She has not had a period in years.

She pops in a tampon she buys from the machine in the loo.

At the end of the pre-lunch session, as everyone is heading out of the room, a kind girl, one of Carla's friends sitting at the side of the stage with her, pulls her over. "Jen, you might want to tuck something in. Down there."

Jen realises, through a quick feel, that the tampon string is hanging outside of her small hot pants. "Oh no," she says, mortified. "Do you think anyone else saw?"

"No, I don't think so," the girl says, grinning at her. "But it is fucking funny."

Jen is due to present at 2:30pm. It is 2:15. She is going through her notes while listening to another of her team present. She no longer has a mouse tail dangling from her farthingale. She is wearing a Top Shop dress she found last week in a charity shop. Flowery and floaty. A bit too summery for December, but she loves it. Feels good in it. Demure and pretty. Little capped sleeves, a high-ish neckline and the skirt just skimming the top of her knees.

Five minutes before she is due to stand up, the big doors at the back open silently. Four men from the senior management team walk in very quietly. Lead by Mr. Senior Specs. They sit on some empty chairs at the back of the big room. Carla clocks them too and catches Jen's eye. She gives her a reassuring smile. "It's ok," she mouths. "You'll be great."

Jen gets through her presentation well. She only stumbles once, but quickly regains control and makes a joke of it which the audience respond to with laughter. Her mouth is not dry like the presentation course people said it would be, it has too much saliva in it. She swallows. A lot. The PowerPoint slides she prepared also work really well. The nerves she treats as adrenaline, excitement, like Carla told her to. She is proud of herself and can tell that Carla and her boss are proud of her too. She retakes her seat at the side of the ring to the applause of the audience.

Later that evening, after the dinner and amazing entertainment and before the band starts, Jen walks to the bar to get some free drinks for the people she is sat with. She is wearing a red dress her auntie made her for a wedding a few years ago. It fits her perfectly and she feels good in it. And she feels really good about the day.

As she approaches the bar, she sees two of the senior management team holding it up. Or is it holding them up? The Big Boss isn't there but Mr. Senior Specs is. He, and they, are clearly in high spirits.

"Hi Baby Jennifer," he says. "Great job today."

"Thank you," Jen replies, pleased and proud. Ignoring the 'Jennifer' and baby reference. Hoping it can all be forgotten and she can be the promising new Marketer. The one that did a great first presentation. The talented one. Not the slut single mum who let a Director into her bedroom, into her bed, before she even started.

He adds, "Yes, we were talking about you quite a lot together. In the sauna earlier." He winks. "You looked just great up there. We all thought so." The other guy laughs in agreement.

Jen knows they are a bit pissed. Knows exactly what they are saying. Knows she just has to accept it. She knows she has no choice. Play along, Jen. She needs this job and her career. However the earlier compliment, and her pride in it and the day, slip away like the glorious feeling of holiday sun on your face fades the moment you enter the dingy departure hall of the airport.

She laughs back and says, "Thank you." She adds, not wanting to look crushed, annoyed or vulnerable, "I didn't think I would enjoy it, but I actually really did."

"And we all really enjoyed watching you," one of them says, smuttily. She doesn't know which one. She just wants to get away. "Really enjoyed watching you."

"Sorry, I need the loo," she says, forcing a smile. She walks away, casually. Wants to run. Goes up to her room in the lift and ejects the pate, roast beef and trifle she only half ate just over an hour and a half ago. She doesn't even bother papering over it.

She lights a cigarette and breathes in the nicotine deeply. She enjoys and needs the burn, craves the toxins entering her body. She looks at herself in the dressing table mirror and berates herself. "It was the hot pants. Why did you fucking wear them? It's all your fault. You're bringing it on yourself."

Then she realises they never saw her in the hot pants.

She gets angry. She thinks about her ex. He'd fucking shoot them.

She suddenly wants to see him. She momentarily craves the security blanket of his crazy yet concrete love, however much he cheated and lied. She knows he'd do anything for her and their son. Apart from provide for them and be reliable, of course.

But she knows he'd fucking shoot them.

She sings the Mya song she loves to herself in the mirror about not being able to say no when the feelings start to show, about how you would act if he wanted you back.

She gathers herself. She's being ridiculous. If she said she wanted him back, she would just be playing with him. And it just wouldn't work. It never did. It never could. He's in a new relationship, anyway. Hopefully one where Joseph can feel content and have a father.

It's only just before 10pm. She gets a grip. She handles it. She metaphorically papers over it.

She reapplies her makeup, brushes her teeth and sorts her hair.

Downstairs she sees an older, senior lady she knows. Someone she thinks she can trust. Who will understand. She calmly and concisely explains what has just gone on, been said. Doesn't mention the previous conference and Mr. Senior Specs the Space Invader.

The reply she gets is simple and quite curt.

"Just be grateful for the attention. You're lucky they like you. And it's clear they like you," she winks. Jen's second wink of the evening. She blinks slowly, taking it in. She is starting to really hate winks. "Let me give you a bit of advice. Just accept it. Don't fight it or them. You won't win. Use it to your advantage."

At this moment, yet again, something clicks in Jen. Again.

She never wanted or wants to use 'it' to her advantage. More importantly, she never wants to be told she has used 'it' to her advantage to achieve something. She will never enable anyone to say she has got somewhere because of 'it'. Whatever 'it' is. And she will never, ever trust 'they' or 'them'. She swears Joseph will never ever be either 'they' or 'them'. She will ensure he isn't. She will play the 'it' game because she has to, has no choice. Not because she wants to.

"Who is worse in this situation?" she asks to herself silently. "The men who objectified me or the woman who has just condoned the objectification?"

She is unsure. But her Tigger starts to bounce within, fed by a feast of rising rage and dissolving shame.

She says, "Ok, thank you," to the lady. She gets herself a glass of wine from the bar and goes to find Carla. She finds her with a group of friends dancing. Carla spots her and pulls her into the group, putting her arm around her. She knows she won't tell Carla, she'll never tell Carla, but she also knows she is safe with her. She doesn't

PAPER OVER IT

leave her protective side all evening.

She bounces to the brilliant band with Carla and her crew for the rest of the night. She loves every minute. Is not going to fuck this up by saying anything to anyone else. She wants to belong. She feels like she does.

She goes up to her room at about 2am. Shoeless, slightly shitfaced and shattered. But shame does not follow her up. It remains in the shadows somewhere, unescorted. Hopefully not in someone else's room. Hopefully in its own room, alone. Like she is.

As she climbs into bed, after doing a terrible job of washing her face and brushing her teeth, her mobile phone rings. It's her mum.

Shit. Fuck. Shit.

She sobers immediately and answers quickly. Her mum's voice is high pitched and slightly panicky.

"Jen."

"Mum. What's the matter?"

"Are you ok?"

"Yes, of course," Jen replies, now panicking. "What's happened? Is Joseph ok?"

"Yes, yes, he's fine. He's fast asleep. But the police are here. Your car has been found abandoned. Wrapped around a tree. Totally wrecked. Where are you? What have you done? Why did you just leave it?"

Trying to get a word in edgeways, Jen half shouts, "Mum, remember, I'm not in my car. I have the pool car from work. It's not me. I'm miles away. I don't have my car."

Jen smiles ruefully. Monumentally relieved they are both fine. Her breeding and guidance under her ex's tuition from the age of fifteen has taught her how to deal with the police and him being arrested in her company. Don't panic. Stay calm and quiet. Admit nothing. Say nothing. Apart from pleading ignorance, but only if necessary. Or perhaps offer an alternative perspective to what is being proposed, but only if necessary. Always look shocked and innocent.

Her mum has no such diploma in police management. She is clearly throwing her daughter under the proverbial bus without knowing what bus it is, who is driving it, who is on it or where it is going.

"Oh yes, of course," the relief in her mum's voice is palpable. The shock of the middle of the night knock from the police obviously stunning her. Her memory and sanity are slowly reoccupying her frantic mind. "And you're definitely ok?"

"Yes, I'm fine," Jen replies. "The police. Are they still there?"

"Yes."

"Say nothing more. Put them on."

Jen confirms that the Fiesta XR2i is hers. Explains to the police that she has no idea what has happened to her car. She says it's really late and she's had a few drinks and is confused. She is about eighty miles away and has been since early yesterday. Can she call them in the morning?

She doesn't know what else to do. Why did her ex just leave her Honey? Why is he such a head case? Where is he? If he has the insurance he said he had, why has he just abandoned her? Is he pissed? On drugs? Was someone else driving? Right now she is totally exasperated and exhausted. She realises that she doesn't care. She just needs the police away from the cottage and the local curtains, which she knows will be twitching. And for her mum to feel safe.

After the police leave, when Jen promises to call them in the morning as soon as she is home, she says to her mum, "I'll be back first thing, I promise. I'll sort it. It's fine. Go to sleep."

"Ok," her mum says wearily. Jen knows her mum does not need this.

But neither does she.

She calls her ex. His phone goes to answer machine. Unreliable when needed. She is not surprised. She doesn't want him harmed, but this is why she never wants or needs him back. Just wants to be on her own. Independent. She wants to just depend on herself.

She laughs for some reason. What a day she's had. She has yet again learnt a lot about people, life and herself.

She is exhausted and finds peace in a deep, thankfully lonely, sleep. Mr. Senior Specs and her Ex are somehow excluded from her dreams.

Just her Honey fantastically prancing around in a weird,

psychedelic, colourful fiesta. An XR2i heaven.

Case of the Ex.
Mya.

-54-
KATE: DON'T BE STUPID (YOU KNOW I LOVE YOU)

16th December 2000
Uni finished yesterday for Christmas, so Kate is at Will's in Chester for a few days before she heads up to Glasgow on the North West Mainline for Christmas.

Will's parents have arranged a big Christmas dinner party for tonight. There are going to be sixteen people. Kate, Will, three of his home friends, Will's brother and two of his friends, Will's parents and six of their friends.

Kate took the train to see Jen at the cottage last Sunday and after she had updated Jen on how Will was after a little scare the previous Sunday, Jen updated her on how well the conference and her presentation had gone. She felt that Kate didn't want to talk more about Will. Knows how much she loves him. There was a sadness Jen hadn't seen before behind her gorgeous big, brown eyes. So Jen cracked on with her story to take her mind off whatever was going on in there.

She didn't mention the seniors and their sauna smut. Kate had laughed out loud when she did mention hot-pant-tampon-tail-gate. Then Jen started to explain Honey's tragic fate. She got to the morning after, when she was driving home from the conference.

"Are you joking?" Kate exclaimed, sat on the sofa in the snug, bouncing Joseph on her knee. "What the hell happened to her?"

"Well," Jen took a sip of her brew, crossed her legs under her and explained. "I finally got hold of him. He said he'd been out in the car with a couple of girls. Driving them home from the pub."

"His new girlfriend?"

Jen laughed, "No." Joseph was listening intently to his mum and watching her animation.

"Go on." Kate grabbed a Custard Cream from the biscuit tin Jen had popped on the side earlier. She dunked it in her brew.

"So, he said "The tree just came out of nowhere"."

"Those famous walking, peek-a-booing Cheshire trees," Kate laughed, seeing that Jen was clearly not letting this get her down.

At this Joseph looked round at her. "What?" she asked him,

smiling. "What's the matter?"

"You said 'peek-a-boo'." The story was then halted for a few minutes whilst the game was played with hand actions and piles of giggles.

"So back to Honey and the traversing tree," Jen continued when he got bored of the game. "He said it was just there and he didn't know how it happened. It literally was wrapped around it. He panicked, told the girls to run and ran off himself."

"So they were all ok?"

"Yes, thank god," Jen replied. "And he said I was lucky because he had taken Joseph's car seat out before he drove. "Lucky," I shouted at him. "On what fucking planet am I 'lucky' in this situation?" He actually laughed and said that yes, maybe that was a bad choice of word. And that he would find a way of getting the car seat to the cottage asap. He'd get a lift as he'd obviously broken the car he'd borrowed because his car was broken."

"Shit in hell," Kate replied. Trying not to laugh. It really wasn't funny at all. "Can she be repaired?"

"No chance. I have to go and collect my belongings from some random place where she is. She's a complete write-off, apparently. In XR2i heaven. Bless her."

"So, then what happened? What did he say next?"

"He admitted he wasn't insured, even though he'd promised me he was. He told me to tell the police that I hadn't given anyone permission to drive it and I had left it in the centre of my town. That it must have been taken from there. When I asked him why the fuck I would do that, leave it in the centre of town, and not on the road near the cottage, he said to act blonde and dumb. If my mum or my nosey neighbours were asked by the police if it had been near the cottage, they would all have said no. He knows the neighbourhood watch round us is a full-time job for some curtain twitchers. He said to say, "There was no room at mine with the Mondeo and my mum's. There's only two spaces. And the rest of the road was full. Say you don't understand what's happened. You're really upset and confused. You just want your little car back. In fact, call her 'Honey'. Make it emotional." I said, "I am bloody emotional." He said, "Good. Use it. And say you're a single mum. Have a mini break down. Maybe cry a little'."

"This is ridiculous," Kate laughed again. "My family are a bit bonkers, but this is mental."

"I know. It gets worse," Jen is on a roll now. "About an hour or so later, with Joseph happily at nursery and mum shattered at work, I got back. Instead of calling the police, I went to the station. Thought it better to play the sad, confused, stupid girl card face to face."

Kate nods in agreement at the strategy. She knows Jen is completely innocent in this mad debacle and understands she needs the insurance money to buy a new car. Playing the game is, this time, definitely the correct choice of action.

"They asked me if I would make a statement. As you know, I've done a few of these over the years. All because of the Ex. So I just said exactly what we had agreed. Played dumb and regaled the slightly fabricated facts answering "I don't know" to most questions. And, of course, I turned the waterworks on. It was easy. I was genuinely gutted about Honey. And I was knackered."

"So what happened then?"

"I finished the statement and they read it back to me with a lot of my "I don't knows". They knew they wouldn't get anything else out of me, whether there was anything to get or not. Then I signed it just before they told me they had just arrested someone."

"Oh wow," Kate said. "Was it him?"

"Yes."

"How did you know?"

"He walked past me in cuffs, smirking a "don't say hello" face, as I was leaving the station. Trying to protect me somehow, I imagine, from something. Though I can't understand what the hell from. I have a baby with him. He's on the birth certificate as the 'Proprietor of a Sun Bed Shop'. Of course I know him."

"Is he the proprietor of a sunbed shop?"

"Is that your question in all this?" Jen laughed out loud.

"Actually, no," Kate laughed. But fully intending on asking her about the proprietor of the sun bed shop another time. And what had she put herself as. Unemployed? Student? Never having considered the contents of Joseph's birth certificate. "How did they know it was him?"

"Apparently one of the terrified girls who ran from the car told her mum and she took her to the police station. She told them his name."

"How old is she?" Kate asked, aghast.

"I've no idea. But he will only have been doing them a favour, taking them home," Jen defended her ex, for some reason. After he'd written off her car, ran away from the scene, left her and his son without transport, was responsible for the police panicking her mum in the middle of the night, terrified two young girls and ended her up in the police station, again, making yet another slightly synthetic statement.

"Was he charged with anything?" Kate asked as she took her second biscuit. A Ginger Nut. Not quite a Hob Nob, but stronger and sturdier in tea than the slightly sloppy Custard Cream had been.

"Yes," Jen replied, rolling her eyes. "Driving a vehicle without the owner's consent, driving without due care and attention, leaving the scene, failure to report, having no insurance… I think that's it. Not sure if he was over the limit, but he'd have sobered up by the morning so they couldn't have charged him with that. He was released on bail and will get a court date for his case soon I imagine."

"Case of the Ex!" Kate exclaims, rather pleased with herself and her Mya. "Will he go down?"

"I doubt it. He tends to find ways out of these things. He's a right jammie dodger. But I've honestly got no idea." Jen said impassively. "I'll hopefully get the insurance payout though as he said I hadn't given him permission to drive it. Which of course I had, but with the understanding he was insured. He did have the keys, though, as I had given them to him. Not sure how that'll work itself out. It's all a bit messy. But Carla has said I can keep the Mondeo for a few weeks, at least over Christmas, so I can sort it all out. She just knows my car was stolen, nothing more. So I haven't exactly lied. But she has ensured I have wheels!" Jen smiled. "Woo hoo!"

"How are you so happy and ok about this?" Kate asked, bewildered. "It's a complete and utter shit show."

"Because, my friend, I am past caring about things that don't help me or him," she pointed at Joseph who had dozed off on Kate's knee. "I am going to, from now on, concentrate on what I have. And who I love. Stop being so stupid trying to change things I can't. It's Joseph's first Christmas in a few weeks. I can't wait. I'm going to make it so special, even though he won't remember. But I will." Jen just loves Christmas. Apart from Monopoly Christmas.

Kate smiled, thinking excitedly about seeing her family at Christmas. Also thinking about Lou and her first Christmas without her dad.

"A fierce focus on my wonderful things and people is what is need right now," Jen added. "Apart from Honey, of course. She's dead as a doornail that's been hammered into a deadlock door by my dick head, meatloaf-brained ex."

Kate laughed out loud at Jen's deadpan daftness and her personification of meatloaf. "Certainly not a dead ringer for love, is he? Your ex." Then added quickly, "Sorry, Jen, I don't mean to take the piss and laugh."

Joseph started to wake up.

"Yes you do. It's hilarious and ludicrous. You couldn't make it up," she said, taking Joseph off Kate's knee.

Kate agreed as Jen took Joseph into the kitchen to get him his lunch. She grabbed herself a Jammie Dodger and proceeded to bite carefully around the biscuit edge until just the jam centre was left. She thought of Will as she surveyed her neat nibbling around the red love heart. "Don't be stupid, you dickhead saddo," she said to herself, popping the jammy heart into her mouth.

Back in Chester, Kate giggles to herself at the memory of Jen's story and the Jammie Dodger. She must call her and see what the latest news is.

Will is asleep. He has another headache. He is now under another specialist as they are getting more frequent and more painful. After a brief yet frightening seizure a few weeks ago at home, the day after the 'Charlie's Angels' night, he went to A&E and is now having further tests privately.

Kate's mum asked her last night how he had been as he hadn't been home for a week. She was honest with her. They know each other quite well now. Actually rather love and respect each other. She told her she was really worried about him.

She helps her extend the already huge table in the equally

enormous dining room. They are getting caterers in, and the house has already been professionally seasonally decorated throughout. Inside and out. There are three trees. Three trees! All real. Douglas Firs. The one in the hall must be nearly three times the size of Kate. She thinks it looks like a Christmas wonderland.

"He keeps saying I should leave him and go and have some fun," she admits privately to Will's mum while helping her spread the vast white tablecloth over the table. "That he's holding me back with his illness, whatever it is. That he doesn't know if he will ever be right. I hate it when he says that. What is right? I tell him to stop being so ridiculous."

"Well," her mum thinks before she speaks. "We don't one hundred percent know what the matter is with him, do we? What the future might hold. He might not ever want to feel like a burden to you."

"Don't be absurd. He couldn't ever be a burden," Kate says. "You know I love him. I know I'm still really young and may sound stupid, but I do. I don't want to be with anyone else. I know my own head and my heart."

"Don't we know that, my Kate," she says fondly. She genuinely thinks of her as the daughter she never had. "Let me tell you something. I met Will's dad when I was sixteen and he was seventeen. He didn't have a pot to piss in and neither did I. I left school and worked as a seamstress. I always loved making dresses, but found there was more money to be made making curtains and blinds for wealthy people."

Kate listens intently as they sit down simultaneously on two adjacent dining room chairs. Kate knows from Will that her parents had not always been wealthy. That they were 'self-made', whatever that meant. As if you hadn't 'made it' if you weren't wealthy.

"What the hell is 'it'?" she had asked him indignantly. He had laughed. 'It' and his reaction had pissed her off, and she had told him so. Told him he was impossible. So she never really got to the bottom of the story due to her recalcitrant reaction.

"Will's dad did his A-Levels and started as a kind of clerk in a law firm. He was eighteen and really clever. But he was just doing the admin jobs and the pay was poor. No real progression. A little like Bob Cratchett in a Christmas Carol."

"Didn't Bob work in an accountancy firm?" Kate asks.

"Yes, Kate. Thank you for the helpful correction," she cajoles easily. "I clearly need to brush up on my Dickens."

"Sorry," Kate says, embarrassed at her rare Em-ness. "What happened next?"

"Well, our parents couldn't help with money. So we moved in together when I was eighteen and he was nineteen. Into a shit hole. Like a massive bin. In sin. He quit his job and went to the local University in Chester to study law. I worked as a seamstress by day and did evening and weekend shifts in a local pub. He got a grant and took on some private tutoring work for high school kids, and between us we survived. We laughed a lot. And there were a lot of beans on toast, in fact anything on toast. Sometimes just toast," she laughs at the memory.

Kate's soft, mushy side is literally throbbing. "It's like a novel. So romantic."

"Don't get me wrong, it was tough. And sometimes we would just collapse at night and crawl into bed, exhausted. Or because we didn't have enough for the electricity meter so there were no lights. I suppose the candles were romantic, in a way. Unless it was midwinter and it was both freezing and dark. It was tough, but we were happy. We were a team. We genuinely loved, needed and wanted each other. Planning and working together for our future. It was actually really exciting, on reflection."

"So you worked all hours for money to help him get his degree?" Kate asks, things all falling into place. Even though she has always respected Will's parents, the deepness of this respect has just grown significantly.

"Yes, I suppose I did," she nods. "I haven't thought about it for years. It really doesn't matter. As I said, we were and are a team."

"He must have done really well to get all this," Kate says, looking around the room.

"Yes, there was no stopping him. Youngest partner ever, I think. I started to make quite a name for myself too. Set up a little business on my own and got some really good contracts with interior designers," she reminisces. "I made all the curtains and blinds in this house."

"They're just beautiful."

"Thank you. Then he started up his own law firm. Worked his arse off. I helped him out as I'd been running my own little business for some time by then. We made some investments. Some sound ones which paid back ok, but others a little risky. It was the risky ones that really made the difference. Had a bit of luck, I suppose. And here we are. Still together. And although he drives me up the wall at times, we're still very happy."

Kate thinks about her own dad and his absurd investment idea. Maybe it isn't so stupid after all. She hugs her spontaneously. She laughs as she hugs her back.

"So I can't possibly think you're too young or stupid," She says brightly. "Because that would have made me the same. And much younger than you are now. And I wasn't stupid, was I?"

Kate's affirmation grin beams across her face and she hugs her again. Just at this moment Will walks in looking really quite bright.

"What's going on? Can I join in?" Without waiting for an answer he swoops in and bear hugs both his girls. They both giggle like children as he squishes them tight.

"Right," Will's mum shouts. Liberating herself from the much enjoyed squeeze. "Place cards for the table. Where are we putting everyone? You two love birds are being split up for a few hours."

Later that night, after the delectable catered dinner has been served by the waiting staff employed for the evening, but still in the thick of the uproarious party in the dining room with the big fireplace crackling and glowing, expensive wine and hard spirits flowing and thick closed curtains masking the fact it's just started snowing, Will winks at Kate playfully from the other side of the table and mouths, "See you in a minute."

His glint is exciting, he is on really good form tonight. She has no idea what he is doing, but he is definitely up to something. He leaves the room.

Kate accepts a top up of her white wine from the waitress before Will's dad starts telling a frankly hilarious yet highly inappropriate story about one of his clients. Mid witty tale, there is a loud knock at one of the large windows. A rap, rap, rap kind of knock. A frightening knock. A horror film type knock.

"What the hell is that?" one of the guests asks, startled. "It's past eleven at night."

No-one wants to open the thick curtains. They just all stare at them.

Will's dad looks genuinely concerned. The house is in the middle of the Cheshire countryside, certainly not surrounded by other houses. It is gated. 'Rap, rap, rap' ominously rings out again, even louder this time.

He gathers himself and whips the curtain back quickly like ripping off a plaster. Half the room screams and the other half is deathly quiet. Glaring back at them, with his face pressed up against the window, is a man eerily lit by the outside security lights with sinister looking snow pouring all around him. He has an odd, disconcerting expression on his face. Almost lifeless. He just glares in at them, spookily still. Unblinking. Smirking. He then sways very slowly from side to side. It is terrifying. Like something off 'The Shining' or 'A Clockwork Orange'.

Will's dad quickly shuts the curtains and says, "Shit, call the police someone."

Kate immediately realises what is happening. She watches the fall-out as the party all panic. Thinking there's a serial killer roaming the large gardens. As someone is about to call 999, she knows she has to say something. 'Wasting police time' is not at the top of any lawyer's bucket list.

"Wait," she says, heading over to the closed curtain and opening it. The man has gone. More terror ensues as Will's mum asks her husband if all the external doors are locked.

Seconds later, there is a rap, rap, rap at the other window. The guests are now all properly on edge. Kate goes over to the other window and opens the curtains. They are all shocked at her bravery and courage. The man is again staring back at them all, but the security light is not as strong at this window. He looks even scarier in the dark, more formidable. Then he just disappears. The room is yet again frenzied.

"It's Will," Kate starts to laugh uncontrollably.

"Don't be ridiculous," his mum cries. "It looks nothing like Will. And Will isn't wearing tweed."

"It's Charles Hetherington-Smythe," Kate just about gets out.

"Who the fuck is Charles Hetherington-Smythe?" Will's dad yells. "And what is so funny?"

Kate can't keep it in. She literally cries laughing. At this point Will makes his way back into the dining room smirking, carrying the equally smirking Charles.

"You absolute dick," his dad shouts at him as the room takes in the large cardboard cut-out and takes a massive relieved breath. "You could have given us all heart attacks."

One of the guests says into her phone, "Sorry, no. It was a mistake. There is no intruder. Not a real one anyway." Then she adds, by way of explanation, after the person on the other end clearly asks something, "It's a cardboard cut-out called Charles." A few seconds later, she adds, "Yes, I know that sounds absurd. Yes, I agree, completely ridiculous. I'm very sorry to have wasted your time. I understand. It won't happen again."

The relaxing room falls about laughing as she puts the phone down sheepishly.

They are all introduced to the slightly damp Charles Hetherington-Smythe, his head starting to slightly bend over from his neck as the sellotape loses its stick on the damp Fab lolly sticks. And Will is introduced to a lot of profanities. "You stupid fucker", "Fucking idiot" and "See you next Tuesday" to name a few. With both sets of curtains open, they can see it's snowing really quite hard now. It looks magical.

"Let's get wrapped up and go outside?" Will's mum says after she clips her son round his ear. "Can you please make us some Irish coffees?" she asks one of the two waitresses kindly. "And of course for you two as well, if you'd like to come out into the snow?" The caterers have gone home, but they have paid for the waiting-on pair until midnight.

After a short while, eighteen mugs of steaming coffee, whiskey and cream are transported by their owners into the winter wonderland. Charles stays inside to dry off, and smirk.

Clothed in big coats and blankets, they walk across the crispy carpet of snow and marvel at the beauty of the stunning sparkling sky. It doesn't snow that often in Cheshire. Kate is a little more used to it up in Glasgow.

Kate looks at Will's face as he stares up at the sky and lets the flakes settle on his nose and eyelashes. He looks beautiful. There's something in his eyes that makes her heart leap. A special feeling bursts inside of her. She tells him she needs a wee, hands him her hot coffee and races inside.

A few minutes later she returns and asks Will to go to the bottom of the garden to the big trees. He agrees.

Out of sight from the rest of the party, she says, "Now I've got you all alone." She goes on one knee and pulls out the Haribo ring, from the Scotland train, from her coat pocket. "Marry me?"

"What? What are you doing? Don't be stupid," he is stunned. Still holding the two steaming glass mugs. Was not in any way expecting this. "You said you would never do this. Never ask anyone to marry you."

"I changed my mind," she says, still on one knee. "Marry me?".

"You don't want to marry me," Will responds. "It's impossible, ridiculous even. I'm a mess. Who knows what the matter is with me? What the future holds for me."

"I don't care, you know I love you," she replies. "I need you. And I'm not being impossible or stupid."

"But you may not love me in the future. Get sick of me. Sick of me being sick. You may not want me if I need you too much."

"I will always both need and want you. I don't care what happens. We can look after each other. What if I get sick? Would you not look after me? Whatever life chucks at us, I don't care. And I don't care that we're young. Your parents were young. I know I love you more than anything. Marry me?"

"Yes," Will says, pulling her up and wrapping his blanket around her while the snow envelopes them. "I love you so much, Kate. Even if you can be impossible."

Don't be stupid (you know I love you).
Shania Twain.

-55-
JEN: MUSIC

19th December 2000

The Tuesday before Christmas.

Jen is back at work after a very odd day yesterday. At just after 10:15am Jen and the majority of the head office team were asked, or told, to collect their personal belongings and leave the building immediately.

"It is a dawn raid," a suited, stoic looking man said.

"Who is Dawn?" a few asked. It was about two and a half hours after the sun had risen. Can a dawn raid be late?

Is that irony, Alanis?

Everyone left apart from the Head of Customer Service, someone from logistics and the Senior Management Team who were asked to stay inside. Including Mr. Senior Specs. "He looked terrified," one of the girls said when they were all hanging around outside, some taking advantage of the impromptu smoke break. All unsure what to do next whilst watching other stoic men carry out equally stoic looking box after stoic box.

A short while later, just before they were told they could go home for the day but to be back first thing in the morning, Jen spotted a girl she hadn't seen before with a lady from HR. Tall with a model body. Probably about five foot ten, Jen thought. Long legs which looked great in her tailored trousers and flats, not dumpy like five foot two Jen would look in the same ensemble. Long blonde hair and irritatingly pretty. Jen took an immediate dislike to her.

Jen is sitting at her desk this morning with Windows 98 humming from the computer tower under her desk and her little desk radio, named Ray, softly strumming the Fugees' pain with his fingers.

She is concentrating on creating a PowerPoint presentation from some typed notes Carla's boss had dictated to his secretary. She places each finished piece of paper neatly into the recycling basket by the side of her screen, straddling her desk and the empty desk next to her. Each piece perfectly papering over the last.

"Hello," she hears a posh voice. She looks up from the text box she is populating her bullet points in. "I'm Harriet," posh sings.

It's the girl from yesterday. She looks about the same age as Jen and is even prettier close up. The crisp white shirt she is wearing looks as expensive as her beautifully cut navy capri pants. Neither are blemished by the baby sick and snot Jen noticed on her jumper this morning in the office loo. Obviously a spoilt, rich bitch.

She puts a designer handbag down on the uninhabited desk, confirming her theory, and sits on the vacant chair.

She is clearly her new neighbour. Fuck.

"Jen," Jen replies, glancing at her briefly. "The recycling goes there," she adds to the reluctant monosyllable as she points to the straddling basket.

"Great, thank you," Harriet says brightly, smiling warmly at Jen. "Good to know."

Jen sends her a tight smile and returns to the text box, to bullet point three. With Lauren and Wycleff killing me softly.

Harriet isn't quite sure what she has done wrong. She spotted Jen yesterday in the strange dawn raid escapade and was really pleased when the HR lady pointed out her new desk just before. Next to her.

"Oh well," she thinks to herself. "Maybe she's just a bitch."

A few hours later, after Jen has taken herself off by herself to get some lunch and Harriet has been taken off numerous times to be inducted and meet people, Jen is thinking out loud while searching the slow internet for a specific present for her ex's sister's four-year-old son. The initial inhabitor of Joseph's Winnie the Pooh cot.

The dulcet tones of Hill and Jean are now replaced by an hour of Christmas classics. The Pogues and their New York Fairytailing, Mariah's multi octave, magnificent wailing and Wham's last Christmas gift frankly failing.

"Bay glades? What the hell are they?" Jen asks herself out loud.

"Can I help?" Harriet asks, her ears just pricked.

"I doubt it," Jen replies, assumptively. She's not really sure why she's behaving like this. It's so unlike her. She doesn't dislike Em because she's rich and spoilt. So why this new girl? Maybe it's because she's really tired. Joseph has picked up yet another nursery cold. He was up half the night even though she gave him some Medised to try and help him get some restful sleep. "I'm looking for a present for a child."

"They're called Bey Blades. They're spinning-top type toys," Harriet offers. Then spells Bey Blades out. Letter by letter.

After Jen has typed the letters into 'Ask Jeeves', Harriet adds, "My stepson has them. He's a little too small for them to be fair, but he loves them. Plays with them all the time."

Jen stares at her slowly loading screen, her head spinning like the whirring internet circle, then looks at Harriet properly. For the first time. "Your stepson?"

"Yes, he's called Seb. He's nearly three. We have him most weekends."

"Oh," Jen says. Her mouth still makes an O for quite a few seconds after the Oh noise has stopped. This is music to her ears.

"My partner's a little older than me. I moved up from London to live with him. We have a flat just down the road."

"How long have you been here?" Jen asks. Her already peaked interest multiplying. It's now at three peaks. Big ones. Ben Nevis, Scafell Pike and Snowdon. Her tired brain suddenly awoken.

"About six months," Harriet replies. "I don't know many people yet. I worked just north of Stoke for a few months when I first moved here. When this job came up and I got it, I couldn't believe how lucky I was. I obviously didn't make any local friends in Stoke as its so far away, and we're busy with Seb most weekends. It can be hard sometimes. The lack of spontaneity. And also I'm just working out how and where I belong, and with who. I don't mean the three of us, I mean me. Not partner Harriet, not step-mum Harriet… just Harriet. I sometimes feel like I left her with her friends down south."

She is a little wistful for a few moments and Jen doesn't fill the momentary silence. She is taking it all in. Getting over the shock of her modus-assumous. Getting it. Understanding.

Harriet quickly goes back to her bright, bubbly self. "But we make it work. Seb's adorable and I just love my big man to bits too. I have absolutely no regrets on the move. Bet you're out all the time in Manchester?"

Jen smiles wryly to herself. She has assumed so much about this girl in such a short time. But she is also in modus-assumous, like the guy in the clinic all those months ago. And here is this warm girl opening up to her, assuming as wrongly as Jen had.

"No, I don't get out much," Jen replies. "My little boy, Joseph, is just six months old." She points to a picture of him pinned to the furry felt desk divider behind her monitor.

"Oh," Harriet says. Her mouth still makes an O for quite a few seconds after the Oh noise has stopped. This is music to her ears.

"Jen, where are you up to with the presentation?" Carla asks, cutting through the music in their ears. Neither girl had seen her walk over. "Reckon you'll have it finished by the end of the day?"

"Absolutely," Jen replies. Back in the room. Clocking Carla clock the Bey Blades that have finally loaded on her computer monitor.

Carla smiles kindly, "Great, thank you lovely."

Harriet gives Jen a smile, yeeks her mouth and silently mouths, "Sorry."

Jen smiles back, replaces the Bey Blade Microsoft window with her bullet points and looks back to Carla's boss's notes. Not able to concentrate on them at all.

At just before five, Jen finishes her presentation and sends it over to Carla. She knows the content is good and it looks even better. Her ability to decipher someone's slightly random words and make them into a story is already quite accomplished.

Carla is really happy with it, even though Jen knows it could have been far better if her concentration hadn't been stolen by her three peaks and the music in her ears.

Harriet asks, "Does anyone go for a drink after work?"

It's a Tuesday.

"Not too often," Jen replies. "Sometimes on a Friday."

"When do you have to pick Joseph up from nursery? Sorry, I assume he is at nursery?" This time her modus-assumous correctly assumes.

"By six," Jen replies, confirming her assumption.

"Fancy a quick drink, then? We could go to the wine bar?"

Jen has lived here for longer than Harriet has. She has never been to the wine bar.

Harriet ploughs on, ignoring Jen's slightly raised eyebrows. "I'm meeting my partner there for dinner at six. We tend to go out a bit at night in the week as we are obviously in at the weekend. I just won't go back to the flat beforehand if you come."

She looks at Jen expectantly with a half-smile spreading across her ridiculously pretty face. It makes her eyes twinkle. It's hard to resist.

"If the string breaks, then we try another piece of string," said Owl.

"Ok," Jen concedes. "Just for half an hour."

"Excellent," Harriet lets her smile turn into a full one. "That's a plan then."

Ten minutes later the girls are sitting on two bar stools. Harriet slid into hers elegantly. Jen had to bounce up twice as she missed it the first time. With Jen's pukey, snotty jumper and Harriet's perfect white shirt, Jen thinks they look like the bourgeoisie and the rebel.

They are perched around a high, round table accompanied by the immediately recognisable three notes in the first line of Madonna's 'Like a Prayer', two glasses of white wine and one very flowing, yet concentrated, conversation.

As 'Life is a mystery' is sung for the second time, using its same three notes, they continue to sniff around each other like dogs trying to make friends in a park.

After nearly forty minutes, which feels like seven, Jen checks her phone. Madonna is singing about how music makes the people come together.

"Shit," she says. "I'm going to be late."

She grabs her bag and thanks Harriet for the drink.

"Bye," she says as she bounces off her stool and flies towards the wine bar door. Pushing the pull door with some force. Like Will had when he first met Kate in Dolcis.

Jen turns back round to see if anyone witnessed her embarrassing and slightly painful mistake.

She spots Harriet looking, trying not to laugh. She ignores the inevitable bump already throbbing on her forehead and says, "I'm fine."

She then chooses to give her a big smile and sings, "See you tomorrow, Harriet."

"See you tomorrow, Jen," Harriet sing songs back, laughing over the music.

Music.
Madonna.

-56-
THE QUARTET: MOST GIRLS

25th December 2000
Christmas Day.

Like most girls their age, the quartet are surrounded by their families. Immediate, extended or blended. Or a combination of the three.

It's a strange day In Liverpool. Lou's first Christmas without her dad. The Len shaped hole is still huge. His absence still so present. Palpably present.

Especially this morning when he didn't come downstairs dressed as Father Christmas like he had for years, HO HO HO-ing with his big sack of gifts. Even as his girls became teenagers, and then adults, the tradition remained. And the Father Christmas shaped hole is even bigger than the twenty-one year old tradition.

They are trying their best to make a happy day of it. Lou's uncle, Len's brother, and his family are over with Fu-Fu the poodle. He has really struggled with the loss of his little brother, but he's making an effort. Trying to be dad and husband to them all. His own family and his extended one.

Two hundred and twenty miles north, in Glasgow, Kate's house is bouncing. Tigger bouncing. One of her brothers has brought his girlfriend, so with her other brother, little sister, mum, dad and six other family members, there are thirteen of them.

"Hopefully not an unlucky omen for my big investment," Kate's dad said laughing last night when he counted up the guests and realised they were one plate short. And five chairs short, even if you included the green plastic garden chairs he brought in from the shed.

Kate's little sister was so excited this morning, like most girls her age. She woke them all up at 5:23am excitedly shouting "He's been, he's been."

Kate rings Will a few hours after the pre sunrise present opening. He picks up after four rings sounding like he's just woken up. They haven't told anyone about their engagement yet. There's no real ring yet, just the Haribo, and no actual plan. Unlike most girls,

PAPER OVER IT

Kate has never really thought about what her wedding might look like. She loves romance, the Pretty Woman fairytale. But what she really wants is real love, and a man that understands it too. She has never imagined what her ring, her day or her dress would look like, weirdly. They have agreed they will tell both sets of parents today. And maybe tell other people at Em's big New Year's Eve party next week.

Four hundred miles south, in Hertfordshire, it's Em's little sister's first Christmas. Eve and Em are cooking the meal together. Did all the prep yesterday so today can be easy and enjoyed by all.

Em said, while peeling a potato and after a couple of glasses of wine, "I'm really looking forward to this Christmas, Eve. Sorry, I mean I'm really looking forward to Christmas, space, Eve. I'm not looking forward to today. As in Christmas Eve. Well I was looking forward to it, but now it's today now, I'm no longer looking forward to it as it is today."

Eve laughed out loud at Em as Em equally loudly laughed at herself and her over-explanation. "She's such a different girl, person, than last year," Eve muses to herself silently. "But then maybe I am too."

"I'm really looking forward to it too," Eve says to Em, giving her a hug.

Eve and Em's dad have, for the past few years, invited extended family and friends over on Christmas Day. Made a big day of it. Em hated every second last year. Moped around like a spoilt brat then took herself off to bed early. Didn't even look at Eve all day, barely addressed her father. Embarrassed both of them, and herself.

This year they decided to just have the five of them for the day and the main meal. Just their little blended family unit. Em's dad, Eve, Em, Will and Em's little sister. They are not going to eat at the large dining room table. They will instead eat at the smaller kitchen table. Although this still seats eight, unextended. Extended family and friends will come over later for drinks and canapes.

Em gives Eve a little silver heart locket necklace with a picture of her baby in it. She gets quite emotional when she opens it and unlocks the catch. She is given a gleaming white metallic fully kitted Range Rover by her husband, with a big pink ribbon tied around it. Far more sensible than the small racing green Audi

TT. Eve secretly much prefers the understated necklace than the showy, shiny, snow coloured car. In fact she dislikes it.

Em read her forced reaction when her dad pressed the button to one of the automatic garage doors to reveal it. Eve is not like most girls. Em knows this now. Doesn't want the big overly bling bling things, the multi-carat diamond rings. Is head-strong, independent and understated.

Em plans to talk to her dad about it after Christmas. Tell him that maybe Eve would like to make her own choices. And that, maybe, it's not the car for her.

Eve privately plans to do exactly the same.

Other presents are shared out. Joey and Chandler, dressed in their reindeer antlers, feast on their festive bones whilst Ziggy and Coco, dressed in their little Santa outfits, play with their new toys racing across the shiny kitchen floor. Em's dad and Will busy themselves choosing the wine for later to make sure they let it breathe and Eve dozes off on the sofa whilst bottle feeding her Christmas Angel dressed baby girl.

After spending a few seconds surveying the happy, contented scene, Em goes upstairs and calls her mum in France to wish her Happy Christmas and to say thank you for the pretty bracelet she bought her. She then calls Mel. They spend over half an hour chatting until Eve calls her from the bottom of the main stairs, asking if she has time to help her in the kitchen. Will tries to call Lou. She doesn't answer.

One hundred and thirty miles north, in Lincolnshire, Jen is retrieving a box of Christmas crackers from the Mondeo. The squeeze and tug ones, not the cheese and chutney ones. It's hiding in the corner of the massive boot. She has no idea how she would have fit her, her mum, her sister and Joseph plus all their paraphernalia and everything they need for Christmas into Honey.

She had been so embarrassed when she went to Honey's resting place to collect her belongings the week after she died. They had all been bagged up to the brim into one pathetically thin plastic bin liner. As she lifted it in the porta cabin office, it split at the bottom. Of course it did.

All sorts fell out onto the dirty floor. A soiled bagged up nappy, a pair of sexy knickers (thankfully not soiled) tangled around a horse whip (why? how?), a less sexy pair of not so small smalls, a baby toy which looked frankly phallic like a dildo, a cracked Steps CD with chewing gum and hairs stuck to it, two ping pong balls with some sort of Vaseline-like grease smeared on them, an unused yet tatty and frayed old tampon, the lost cottage key she had got recut at some expense in Timpsons a few months back, a McDonalds bag with one hard chip left in it, three long lost dummies, a pack of extra-large incontinence pads from work, half a spliff, a half-eaten bag of Wotsits, a baby bottle half full of rancid smelling chunky milk, the black bra she lost last year and some empty drink cans. She really is a tramp when it comes to her car.

"Don't worry," the balding, sweaty man pervily winked at her from behind his equally balding and sweaty formica desk. "I know exactly what's in there, love. I had fun bagging it all up for you. I find most girls leave underwear and sex toys hidden in their car somewhere. But the ping pong balls were a particular treat."

She looked at him and his wink in disdain, then asked for two fresh bin bags. She said, "Please," through gritted teeth thinking how 'lucky' her ex had said she had been.

On the case of her ex, he had been charged with numerous violations and is waiting on a court date. Her car insurers are processing her claim. She knows he will find a way of getting out of it. Like the whip, her thong and her smalls had escaped from the bag alongside a chip and a pair of lubed up ping pong balls.

She takes the crackers into the house which is packed full of noise and laughter. There are ten of them for lunch. Well, nine plus Joseph.

Joseph is sitting on his Great Grandpa's knee at the kitchen table being coo coo-ed at by both him and her sister. She imagines he will probably be brew brew-ed later by his whiskey. He had an amazing morning with love and gifts showered on him. Including his first little Manchester United kit from Jen's notorious BFG cousin.

Her cousins are taking the piss out of Jen's mum. Again. Asking about Randy Dandy Carl. She is whipping them around their heads with a damp tea towel, calling them 'Stupid Boys'. Christmas songs are blasting from the CD player in the corner of the kitchen. Her Grandpa's wife and her auntie are peeling potatoes and carrots respectively at the sink. Her uncle is building a fire in the grate in the lounge. Jen grins at the happy scene, gets a small sharp knife from the cutlery drawer and grabs a potato.

"Oh shit," her auntie shouts. "I knew I'd forgotten something. The bloody brandy."

Before the inevitable saucy tale is told and questions like, "Does Randy Dandy know you're not handy with brandy," are asked, Jen says, "I'll go."

She grabs the Mondeo keys she has just hung back on the hooks screwed to the side of the kitchen dresser and heads to the local town where she knows the big garage will be open. She wants a packet of cigarettes anyway. It already feels like it's going a little dark, or dusky. It's only just after 2pm.

One hundred miles west, back in Liverpool, "To Len," has been said numerous times already. With each resulting toast, the mood is lifted. It is also going a little dark outside. They are not eating until about 5:00pm and everything is prepped, in or ready to go on, so they decide to get wrapped up and go for a walk into the local countryside to a pub they know will be open.

As they amble down the country lane, Lou's Auntie's poodle Fu-Fu gambling beside them, they pass the little farm shop next to the pub which specialises in honey. Its neon lights normally shine and flash HONEY. They have somehow knocked off the lights on the N, E and Y and made the H and O lights pulse simultaneously three times and go dark for a few seconds. HO HO HO it flashes at them in the dusky light. They all stop in their tracks.

"Oh my god, it's Len," Lou says as they all stare up silently at the flashing sign. They watch its HO-rotation five times before Len's brother says kindly, "Come on. Let's go inside and get a drink. We'll all catch our deaths out here."

"For god's sake, man," his wife scolds him. "Could you be any more tactless?"

Lou's mum laughs. Really laughs. It makes the rest of her family laugh too. They go inside the toasty warm pub and make another toast to Len and his HO HO HOs.

Two hundred and twenty miles north, in Glasgow, Kate uses a fork to make a chinking noise on her wine glass when everyone is finishing their Turkey dinner either squished around the kitchen table, at the kid's pop-up table in the lounge next door or with plates on their knees on the sofa. "I have an announcement."

"What?" her little sister hollers from the kid's table.

They all squeeze into the kitchen to hear Kate's news. "What?" her mum repeats.

"Are you preggers?" her younger elder brother asks cheekily.

"Are you, Kate? Are you pregnant?" her dad asks quickly, shocked. "What about your degree?"

"Oh Kate," her mum says even more quickly, trying to quickly lighten the mood. "That's amazing news."

"Kate's having a baby. Kate's having a baby," her little sister sings loudly, twirling round excitedly.

"I'm not bloody pregnant!" Kate yells above all the noise. "I can't get a word in edgeways in this house."

"Are you sure?" her other brother asks. Stirring the pretend pregnancy pot. Knowing exactly what he's doing.

"Yes, I'm bloody sure," Kate is getting a little annoyed now. "Do I look pregnant?"

"Well you are looking very bonny," her uncle replies. "Glowing, I would say."

"Oh my god!" Kate yells. "I'm getting married."

"Is it because you're pregnant?" her auntie asks. "A gunshot wedding?"

"It's a shotgun wedding, not a gunshot wedding," Kate corrects her, Em style. "There won't be any gun salutes. I'm not a bloody Princess marrying Prince William, am I?"

"So it is a shotgun wedding?" her dad asks, confused.

Her brothers are pissing themselves knowing they have collectively caused this magnificent mayhem, whilst the rest start rapid firing more questions at her.

"I AM NOT PREGNANT," she screams to get herself heard above the raucous rabble.

"Alright, Kate" her mum says. "There's no need to shout. Calm down."

"Yes, Kate, you'll upset the baby," the initial trouble starting brother says.

"Fuck off, prick," she says to him.

"Language, Catherine," her dad reprimands her. She rolls her eyes.

After the confusion is corrected, the rabble calms down and Kate's little sister is consoled after she cries with the realisation that she is not going to be an auntie, Kate tries again.

"I'm not pregnant, but I am getting married. To Will."

There is general excitement and everyone toasts the happy couple. Well the half of it that's there. Kate's little sister is further consoled by the thought of being a bridesmaid.

The next hour is spent with everyone, especially her mum, asking about their wedding plans, which Kate over and over again repeats they haven't made. Her mum starts coming up with all sorts of ideas. Glasgow venues, local wedding dress shops, what hat she might wear, themes, colours. The lot.

She laughs when telling Will on the phone after. "It was honestly exhausting," she says, smiling.

"Can I put my mum on the phone?" he asks her. "She's desperate to talk to you."

Kate talks to his mum for about ten minutes. She is very excited. Even more so than her own mum, Kate thinks. She starts wedding planning whilst talking to her. Like she is her mum. Chester venues, local wedding dress shops, what hat might wear, themes, colours. The lot.

"Oh fuck," Kate says to Will afterwards. "This could get interesting."

Four hundred miles south, in Hertfordshire, it is just past 4pm. They are sitting down to eat. Just the four of them with the Christmas Angel baby in her bouncer.

"Would you mind if Mel comes over tonight?" Em asks no-one specific whilst toying with a Brussels Sprout, wondering why all sprouts are from Brussels. Was it something to do with the EU? "If we ever did anything ridiculous like leave the EU would they just become 'sprouts'?" she ponders to herself. But that would never happen. It would be ridiculous to think anyone would be stupid enough to think of calling a referendum. So she stops thinking about Brussels, and its sprouts.

"Not at all," Eve spouts quickly. She has not yet met the girl, neither has her husband. Yet she has heard a lot about her. Em has really opened up to her about the sprouting relationship over the

PAPER OVER IT

last month or so. "It will be really lovely to meet her. I assume she'll stay over in your room?"

Em's dad assumes Mel is just a vet school pal. Thinks nothing more of it. "The more the merrier, my little star" he says, forking a pig-in-blanket and parsnip combo into his mouth.

"As long as you two are angelic," Charlie winks at his sister. "No shenanigans on Christ's birthday."

"What are they going to do?" his dad asks, sipping his third glass of red. "Pillow fight? Have an illegal midnight feast?"

Eve looks at Em and can't help laughing at her husband's complete lack of any form of an inkling of a grasp of the situation. And how old his 'little star' daughter really is, even after telling her to grow up many times earlier in the year. "She's not in bloody Malory Towers," Eve refers to the Enid Blyton book about a boarding school for girls. "With matron on a contraband cake patrol."

One hundred and thirty miles north, in Lincolnshire, Jen is less Malory cake patrolling, more calorie intake controlling. She has promised herself, her reflection and Joseph that, for the first time in seven years, she will not eject her Christmas Day meal. Will not let her bulexia/anoremia control her today. Will not have to paper over it. She knows the feeling of 'full' will make this difficult, so she is going to make sure she doesn't get there. She also knows a sneaky cigarette after the meal will help her relax and stay in control.

They have two boxes of Christmas crackers. The one Jen's mum bought and Jen retrieved from the depths of the Mondeo Estate boot earlier and the other bought by one of Jen's cousins. They have somehow doubled up, a bit like the brandy sauce. One set is already distributed on the table.

Lots of "Tug mine" and "Give mine a pull" are sniggered at by the men to lots of eye-rolling by the women.

The crackers are monumentally shit. Stupid little dice, hats that are too small so they rip, snap bangs that snap but don't bang and mini packs of playing cards. Jen's sister's tiny toenail clippers are apparently not shit as they are pocketed by Jen's mum for Joseph.

The first joke, read out loud by Jen, is equally as shit.

"Who hides in a bakery at Christmas?"

"A mince spy."

The second, read out by Jen's uncle, is even worse. And not even Christmas related.

"What do you call a boomerang that doesn't come back?"

"A stick."

The third is read out by Jen's Grandpa. "What does Santa spend his wages on?"

"Playing with his Jingle Balls."

They all look at him, around at each other, then back to him.

"Say it again, dad?" his elder daughter asks, trying not to laugh, whilst his grandchildren openly snigger. He does. It is the same nonsensical, verging on yuletide porn, non-joke.

Jen's sister takes the little piece of paper off him and reads it. "Bills, Grandpa. Paying his Jingle Bills. Not playing with his Jingle Balls."

"Oh my life, this is painful. You even added an extra word, Grandpa," Jen's BFG cousin says as the table dissolves into childish laughter and Jen's Grandpa takes the non semi-porn piece of paper back and studies it more prudently.

"I'll tell mine," the other cousin says, looking at his little piece of paper.

"Why is Mrs. Claus so frustrated?"

"Because she didn't get Randy Dandy Carl for Christmas," his brother answers.

Jen's mum, who is sitting next to him, whips him around the head with her napkin. "Stupid boy." She then turns her attention to her other nephew and repeats his question. "Why is Mrs. Claus so frustrated?"

"Because Santa only comes once a year," he replies.

"Who bought these crackers?" Jen's auntie shouts, appalled. Looking over at her dad who is thankfully still studying his non semi-porn piece of paper.

"I think they're mine," her sister admits. "Give me that piece of paper."

She pushes her chair back, heads over to where her nephew is sitting and starts to wrestle him for it. She is half his size. He does not relinquish the much more tame joke about the lottery winning elf called Welfy. It is hilarious.

About twenty minutes later, after more mayhem and their main course, Jen and her auntie start to clear the plates, "Not hungry, Jen?".

"No, not really," Jen replies, looking at her half-eaten meal. "Think I had too many chocolates before." She hasn't had any chocolates but as the house is full of them, it is a good excuse.

Jen says she's going to the loo but goes outside and has a sneaky cigarette next to the stables. It calms her. Helps her with her control.

A little while later, when the edible crackers, cheese and chutney have been brought out, they open the second box of Christmas crackers. It's a game where eight people get a musical whistle in their cracker. Each one has one certain note so they collectively make an octave. There are song sheets to help them play Christmas carols. Jen's uncle volunteers to be the conductor. Joseph is being passed around like a perky musical parcel.

After the initial conductor is replaced by his older son as he is so shit at it, they all manage to whistle a very wonky 'Little Donkey', a rather bleak 'In the Bleak Mid-Winter' and a, would be better silent, 'Silent Night'. Jen is literally pissing herself as she has the top note whistle and keeps missing her sign to blow. She is really rubbish at it. Joseph is giggling and gurgling sat on his auntie's knee.

At just before midnight, the quartet are all in bed at each corner of their geographical quadrangle.

Lou is fast asleep. The day has actually been quite joyful, even with the absence of Len. Too many toasts to him and his HO HO HOs meant they were all pretty much pissed and passed out by just past 11pm. She is dreaming about the premiere of her new show in just a few short weeks. Knowing most girls could only dream of being on the West End like she will be. About how Len will be watching her from above, proudly smiling at her and telling her she isn't 'most girls.'

Kate is snuggling up to her little sister who has joined her in the bottom bunk. Refused to climb up to her top bunk. Says the bottom is hers now, anyway. Has swapped Kate's Turtles with her Powerpuff Girls. Kate is thinking about how most girls don't get engaged so young, at twenty, but she is not most girls. Her little sister interrupts her thoughts. She thought she was asleep but she was clearly thinking about the engagement too. "I think most girls would want a pink tutu dress as a bridesmaid dress," she loud whispers. "But I want a blue cape like Bubbles." She is referring to her favourite Powerpuff Girl. Kate says it has to be green like a Teenage Turtle, giggling at the memory of Em's recounting of her bridesmaid dress at her dad and Eve's wedding. Kate's sister giggles back at the ridiculous thought of being the green Buttercup Powerpuff Girl, she is her least favourite. What a silly idea it is to wear a green cape as a bridesmaid.

Em is in bed with Mel. They are staying in the same bed overnight for the first time. It is a big moment for Em. She feels excited yet scared. She never cared too much for love before, thought it was all a bunch of mush she didn't need or want. Assumed she would just end up with a man with economic means, neither really understanding what real love really means. But she knows she is falling for Mel. Maybe even falling in love. Mel had said to Em the other day, "I really like you, you know. You're not like most girls I've been in relationships with." She had said the R word. Em's heart had raced. They are not pillow fighting, but they may soon be midnight feasting.

Jen has had the best Christmas Day. Has loved every minute of it. And she only visited the toilet to expel her fully digested meal the right way, the non bulexia/anoremia way, and her over ingested volume of liquid. The first Christmas meal in six years that she has not said bye to by papering over it. The first Christmas Day that she has not tasted vile bile. She looks over at the sleeping Joseph in his travel cot and smiles. She is not like most girls her age, she knows this, but she is absolutely fine with that. Jen is fine. Jennifer Jones is finally completely fine.

She quickly falls into a deep, much needed, contented sleep. Like most girls her age can.

Most girls.
Pink.

-57-
THE QUARTET: REACH

31st December 2000

New Year's Eve in Hertfordshire.

Lou travelled down on the cheap slow train from Liverpool down to London three days ago for her final rehearsals. It chugged away reaching a maximum of fifty-seven miles an hour feeling like it was constantly climbing every non-existent mountain high. She is jumping on the train up to the closest station to Em's house later today.

Kate and Will rode the short train ride first thing this morning from Chester to Jen's hometown. Jen is driving the three hours down to Hertfordshire. Will in the front passenger seat reading the 1994 AA large scale road atlas of Britain Jen borrowed from her Grandpa. Kate sharing the roomy back of the Mondeo with Joseph.

Will can't drive long distances, he gets headaches, but he can read a map. Kate is crap at maps. She is, however, starting driving lessons in Manchester next week.

Jen has taken Tuesday the 2nd of January off work. Will and Kate aren't due back at uni for a week. So they are all staying two nights at Em's. Kate and Will have their own room and Jen is sharing another one with Lou. Joseph is in the nursery with Em's little sister.

"How many bloody bedrooms does your house have?" Jen asked Em on the phone the other night. Only Lou has been before. "It's a big house, to be fair," Em replied.

They take a brief break at Watford Gap Services to feed Joseph and get a Red Bull for Jen and coffees for Will and Kate.

"Gap-uccino, please?" Will asks the bored looking man behind the counter. This is met with a blank face from the coffee server and shaking heads from Jen and Kate. "Back-uccino in the car, you freak," Kate eye rolls. "And I'm up front with Jen after that embarrassment. You're in the back with the bambino."

"Fine," he replies laughing. "But it's the back seat or the map. No back seat map reading for me. Your choice."

Kate is in a quandary as she is aware her map reading skills are nearly as bad as her time keeping skills, but she wants to sit up front with Jen. In the front passenger seat she picks up the AA Road Atlas and studies the page Will left it open on.

Will wonders how long it will be before she makes some excuse, like it's making her car sick.

"I think we'll be on the motorway for quite some time," Jen says, indicating right and checking her mirrors to get back onto the busy motorway from the short service station slip road. "Em said to get off at the St. Albans exit and go left so I'll need directions after that."

Kate nods. Relieved for now. She can't make head nor tail of the map and they have barely even left the Gap.

About an hour and a half later they leave the M1 at Junction 8 and turn left. Kate has no clue where they are. Keeps flicking from page to page, rotating the map left and right then upside down, pointing at it randomly. She wonders if the roads have changed in the last six years, since 1994.

Jen, looking at her friend's atlas antics out of the corner of her left eye, wonders how long it will be before she makes some excuse, like it's making her car sick.

At the first crossroads they encounter, Jen says, "Well?" to Kate. She throws the map into the back behind Jen, to Will, and says, "It's making me feel car sick."

Will and Jen smirk at each other in Jen's rear-view mirror, out of sight of Kate who is hunting for her ringing phone in her bag. If only Lou had called a second earlier, she would not have had to lie about feeling sick.

"Are you anywhere near me? Can you fit me in the car? I'm just about to get to the station," Lou says.

"How the hell do I know where you are?," Kate laughs at her friend, her former housemate. A ridiculous reach to think you would ever be able to precisely locate someone's location through some satellite alien spookiness.

Lou tells her which station she is about to reach. Kate tells Will in the back. Will checks his newly reacquainted map. Slightly sighing and whispering, "Women," to his highly engaged male neighbour.

Will thinks they are currently on the edge of page 17, so goes to page 21 as directed by the little arrow a cm from the edge of page 17, and flips back and forth between page 17 and page 21 to confirm his location suspicions.

"I think I know where we are. Reckon we're just about four or five miles away from her, but I'll need to check the next road sign when it comes up," he tells the front of the car, where no-one is feeling car sick. Back seat map reading is, however, making him feel sick.

"Hang on a sec, Lou," Kate says.

The next road sign confirms that Will is excellent at sick making back seat map reading.

"Turn left, Jen," he says. "It's literally just a few miles up here."

"Lou, you're in luck. We can fit her in, can't we Jen?" Kate says and asks in the same breath. "We will be there in… how long will a few miles take?"

"Less than ten minutes, I reckon" Jen laughs, spotting the national speed limit sign. Her friend really does have absolutely no concept of distance and time. "And tell her we can absolutely fit her in. But only if you let Will come up front again." She smirks again to Will in her review view mirror.

They arrive at Em's at exactly 2:30pm. Best time for the dentist.

They reach their destination and all just stare at the huge gates and rolling vista beyond. Even Will is a little star struck.

"Wow," Jen says, half laughing. She was not brought up poor at all, but this is something else.

"Maybe I should have gone for Charlie and not you, Will?" Kate says. She thought Will's house was ridiculous, but this is something else. "Oh, sorry, Lou."

"You apologise to Lou in this situation?" Will pretends he's pissed off with Kate while Lou laughs, insisting, "Charlie and I are not a couple." She opens the Mondeo back door and presses the buzzer to the gates only she has been through before.

Once they're through, they are greeted by a pair of black bouncing labradors and the most beautiful woman either Kate or Jen has ever seen, carrying a baby.

"Joey, Chandler. For fuck's sake," she yells. "Come. Here."

As the Mondeo crunches over the expensive sounding, expansive shingle and Jen stops it where she thinks is a good place to stop in the car park sized drive, Em dives out of the huge double doored front door.

Kate, Lou and Jen pile out of the car and race to her.

The Quartet re-unite, collectively Tigger bouncing on the shingled drive. Like intermingled, buzzing bees having a party in their personal hive.

Will smiles at the scene and puts the handbrake on with his right hand before reaching over the steering wheel to turn the engine off.

He gets out and is left with Eve, two babies and two labradors. They all immediately bond with Will somehow ending up holding Em's little sister while Eve helps herself to Joseph, still in his seat in the back of the Mondeo. Joey and Chandler gamble around, grinning.

Inside the house, Em's dad greets them all and asks what they want to drink. "Is Champagne ok?"

Stupid question.

He takes his baby daughter from Will and yells to Charlie to come down and get some drinks sorted. Charlie bounces down the steps two at a time and sees Will. They man hug it out. They met a few months ago in London when they went to the cinema to see 'Billy Elliot' with Em, Lou, Kate and Mel then on to a couple of his favourite haunts. They had got on immediately. Even found a few friends in common from their boarding school days. "Pair of toffs," Kate and Lou had said.

In the kitchen everyone is acquainted with people they have never met, like Jen and Eve, or reacquainted with people they have, like Charlie and Kate. Charlie looks over to Lou as she reacquaints herself with his dad.

Jen goes to take Joseph off Eve while they say hello for the first time. "Do you mind if I keep him for a little while?" Eve asks. "It's so lovely to see what I have got to look forward to in about four months. Isn't it, you gorgeous little man?" Joseph giggles at her while Jen smiles at them both and nods.

As Eve is holding Joseph up in the air, Jen's attention is taken by her beautiful sparkly Rolex on her left wrist. Then the tell-tale sign on her left forefinger knuckle a few inches north. To the untrained eye, it is nothing. To Jen it is obvious, even though she normally checks the right one. Opposite to how people check for wedding rings. She is not sure if Eve has clocked her eye moving briefly from her bejewelled wrist clock.

"Would you like to go upstairs and see where he'll be sleeping?" Eve offers, seemingly unaware.

"Yes please," Jen replies.

After climbing the elegant steps of the main staircase, at least twice as wide as normal stairs, and following Eve through what feels like a posh hotel corridor, Jen reaches and enters the most beautiful, exquisite nursery she has ever seen.

There is a moses basket in a stand on one side, with a rocker chair next to it, a made-up blow-up mattress in the middle of the room and a large white cot on the other side. The cot has what looks like a night light attached to the left side. There is a techy looking baby monitor next to it on a little table. Jen recognises it as one of the new, highly expensive video ones she saw the other week in Mothercare,

"Is this ok for you?" Eve asks Joseph, placing him the cot.

"He's going to think he's died and gone to heaven, like all his stars have come at once," Jen laughs. "He normally sleeps under the eaves in my bedroom."

"Well he'll feel right at home then as he'll be sleeping with an Eve tonight," she flashes Jen a gorgeous, twinkling smile. Joseph looks like a pig in shit sat in the big, roomy cot. "I'm going to stay with them on the blow-up. Just to make sure I can keep an eye on them both with all the inevitable noise. And it gives me a great excuse to not be prodded in the back later when I'm doing an excellent job of pretending to be asleep, stone cold sober, by my inevitably pissed husband and his horny dick."

Jen laughs out loud. It feels like being with a friend, not her friend's step-mum. And nowhere near the wicked step-mum Em had initially made her out to be. She adds, quickly, "When I say he's under the eaves, I mean he is in a cot, obviously. And it's a lovely little room. It's just our cottage is a little small. He's not on the floor in the attic, I promise."

Eve laughs, really warming to her. "Nothing wrong with an attic. I slept in the attic when I was growing up. I mean it wasn't like 'Flowers in the Attic' or anything, I wasn't locked up there. I loved it. My brothers shared the second bedroom next to our mum and dad.

I had my own space up top."

Jen slightly shivers and shudders at the memory of V. C. Andrews' first book in her haunting Dollanganger series. "How are you finding it, being a mum?" she asks her.

Eve goes on to say she is loving every second of being a mum but explains that she is the first of her friends to have a baby so it can feel a little isolating at times. There is no ready-made 'friendship with babies' group. She's not sure who Eve is anymore. Especially with her husband working such long hours and being away such a lot. And what a bitch the health visitor had been with her stupid tutting and ticking, especially when she told her she was stopping breastfeeding and moving onto bottles.

She knows she needs to join some baby mummy groups, but the one she went to a few weeks ago was full of local wealthy women talking about AGA recipes, how they think their 'lazy' housekeeper hasn't done a good enough job cleaning the windows, numerous ways their highly giving husbands are annoying them and why, due to the annoying water table, they can't fully sink their hot tub.

She knows she's a local, wealthy woman. But she doesn't belong in that set.

She has an AGA but can't think of anything more boring than talking about recipes (she still can't use it, to be fair), thinks her husband is pretty much perfect in most ways (and the ways he isn't are pretty cute in their own way), doesn't have a housekeeper (even though her pretty much perfect husband keeps saying she should get one), couldn't really give two shits whether their windows have the odd smear here or there (Joey and Chandler make sure they always do), and loves the way the water table naturally fills her much loved cold lake (and balances her beloved Bob).

She admits that Em is great company, but she is out a lot now. Spending more and more time staying over in London either with Charlie, Mel or other course friends. It's like she's just not sure now where Eve, just Eve, belongs.

"I'm really sorry," she says to Jen after she shakes herself back into the moment and collects herself post soliloquy. "I'm not sure what came over me."

"I get it," Jen says. "I really do. I mean, not the wealthy thing. Or the wife thing. Certainly not the AGA thing or the lake thing. I mean the belonging thing. The 'Eve' thing."

Eve spontaneously hugs her, "Thank you."

"No, thank you," Jen replies, hugging her back.

"Now please, Jen, let your hair down. We've got everything covered, I promise. Haven't we, Joseph?" Joseph smiles up from his little white palace. "I'm on babysitting duties. All night," she says firmly whilst picking Joseph up from his idyll. "And you are both very welcome to come and stay with us anytime. I could do with a friend like you, even if you're Em's friend really. Now let's go downstairs."

All Jen really wants to do is spend more time with Eve.

Downstairs Eve and Em take Lou, Kate, Jen, Will and Joseph through the big glass kitchen doors and into the huge marquee. Charlie follows.

"Fuck me," Kate lets out, taking in the oasis.

"Wouldn't mind," Will whispers into her ear from behind.

She looks back and grins, "Maybe."

"Definitely, maybe?" he grins back.

Later, with all four of the quartet dressed up for the night, they have a moment together in Em's room. The radio is playing Robbie's rather humdrum 'Millenium' and the kittens are gambling around, rough and tumbling with each other.

"I can't believe you're engaged," Lou says to Kate. "It's so exciting!"

Kate's three friends start bombarding her with questions like "When do we start planning?", "Where is it going to be?", "When is it going to be?", "Have you chosen the bridesmaids?" and "What about your dress?"

"We haven't got any plans yet," she repeats for the umpteenth time, smiling at her excited friends. "You all sound like our bloody mothers."

"I've got you all a gift," Em announces.

"No, no. Nothing big," Em replies to the cacophony of 'for fuck's sake' in the room. She gives each girl an identically sized wrapped rectangular present and keeps one for herself.

Eminem's Stan replaces Robbie on the radio.

"Oh my god!" Lou is the first to open hers. "I absolutely love it."

The other two girls realise they all have the same gift and hold them up in delight. They are framed photographs of their 'tongues out' photo from the previous New Year's Eve. They all look so young, fearless, bouncy, carefree. So bright. So like Tigger.

"Wow," Jen says thoughtfully. "So much has happened in a year."

"And what a year it's been," Lou adds, slightly wistfully.

"This picture is going to have pride of place on my wall," Kate promises whilst reflecting. "It will always remind me that things are never that bad when you lot are around."

"Me too," Lou and Jen reply. "Thank you, Em."

"No, thank you," Em says. "In the wise words of Dido, thank you. You've all helped me more than you can imagine this year. Thank you."

They all agree. That they could not have got through the year without each other. Spend a moment thinking about what the year 2000 has dealt them whilst the kittens play with the discarded wrapping paper. Privately reflecting on its highs and lows. How they have all felt hurt at times, and have sometimes moaned. Have definitely learnt a lot about themselves and all have most certainly grown.

It's been less 'Four Weddings and a Funeral'. More four girls, three degrees, two births, one break-up, one horrible accident, one massive family break-up then make-up, one new potentially serious relationship, one wedding to be planned, and a funeral.

A knock breaks the silence.

"Em, Mel's here," Eve says as she half opens the closed door.

When Em tells her to come in, she explains, "She's downstairs. Your dad is asking her all about herself. Being his bombastic self. Asking if you've found a special man on your course."

"For fuck's sake," Em grins and shakes her head at her step-mum. Her unlikely friend.

Hours later it is almost midnight. The brilliant band has sung their last song and said "Goodnight" to much booing before they played their actual last song. The DJ is now on his decks. Stars are twinkling outside as brilliantly as Eve's lights in her garden and the professional ones in the marquee. Tunes are blaring to the one hundred plus bouncing people inside.

Lou has successfully performed the Dirty Dancing lift with Charlie after four attempts (his fault, he wasn't reaching high enough) and Kate has hilariously attempted to give Will a lap dance to 'Reach' from Steps ending up with Will in hysterics after she literally climbed on him like she was trying to scale a large mountain. Em is currently kissing Mel in plain sight on the dance floor, rather randomly to N-Sync's 'Bye Bye Bye' to the surprise of her dad who involuntarily sinks back when he witnesses it, looking around in confusion for his wife who said bye bye bye to him about an hour ago.

Jen, a little pissed and very sweaty from too much dancing, laughing and bouncing, needs some air. She heads out of one of the side exits and into the garden. She finds Joey and Chandler having their own little party arguing over the ownership of a large stick.

She walks around the huge house, huge puppies and stick in tow. Deeply breathing in the cold, crisp country air. Outside the slightly open ridiculously huge double doored front door, she stares up at the New Year sky. She closes her eyes for a second and thanks her lucky stars.

Joey and Chandler mash her moment with their madcap madness as the stick smacks into the back of her legs almost upending her.

"Come on then, you two," she says laughing, letting them and herself into the house. Leaving the stick outside.

As her two furry friends lollop into the kitchen in search of more mischief, she heads upstairs to check on Joseph. To see Joseph. She bounces up the steps, two at a time.

She finds him fast asleep in the nursery. Stars from the night light reach every corner of the room and sparkle over Eve gently rocking in the nursing chair. She is half asleep feeding her baby with a bottle. Her left-hand knuckle on show.

She jolts awake, suddenly aware of her intruder.

"Go back down, Jen" she whispers kindly. "Have fun. Be Jen. Be spontaneous. We're fine."

"Can I please stay up here with you two for a bit?" Jen asks, quietly. "And him," she adds, nodding at Joseph.

"Really?" Eve asks. "Why?"

"I like it in here."

"Ok, as long as you're sure," Eve says. "I need a wee anyway. Would you mind taking over?"

Jen sits in the rocking chair and feeds the gorgeous little two-month-old baby, looking at her own sleeping baby through the white cot slats. He suddenly looks huge.

She hasn't even considered papering over it tonight. It just didn't ever reach her mind. She knows she's not 'fixed', but maybe she is on her way. She feels peaceful. Belonging both out there in the marquee and in here.

She quickly texts - struggling slightly using her one unused hand - her sister, her ex, her old home friends and her new friend Harriet.

Hpy Nu Yr x

She will call her mobile-less mum in a bit. She's out with Carl.

When Eve gets back, she lies down on the blow-up bed. Literally crashes. Clearly exhausted. Jen puts her milk-full, sleeping baby carefully into her moses basket and kisses her head.

Jen's phone pings. It's Harriet.

U2. CU Wnsdy x

As she hears Big Ben's dongs start from the epic sound system in the marquee, Jen looks again at her sleeping little man. Reaches over to his little face and touches his cheek. Her perfect Joseph. She sits back on the nursing chair.

"You like writing, don't you Jen?" Eve muses unexpectedly from her blow-up bed on the floor at dong three. The first two dongs must have woken her.

"Yes, I love it," Jen replies, staring up at the mesmerising ceiling stars again.

"Maybe you should write a book about your year? I hear it's been a journey of many steps hasn't it?" Eve questions wearily at dong six. "You could do it at night when you're in on your own. Will keep you busy."

"Hmmm," Jen hmmms at dong eight.

Eve sleepily adds, "I'd definitely read it. Reach for the stars, Jen." As dong eleven dongs, she adds. "Just do it."

At the twelfth dong Jen says, "Maybe I will."

The marquee below erupts with whoops of "Happy New Year" before "Should old acquaintance be forgot" is belted out followed by lots of mumbled singing as no-one really knows any of the other verses of the old Scottish song about times gone by.

"Happy New Year, Eve," Jen says to her lovely new acquaintance.

She is met with a soft snore from the sleeping Eve.

She gets up and gently kisses the also snoring Joseph.

"Happy New Year, my gorgeous little sunshine," she whispers to him before quietly opening and closing the nursery door.

She runs down the stairs and finds her three friends, her quartet.

Together, with no need for any of the girls to paper over it in the moment, their faces shine watching the fantastical fireworks reach for the stars.

They collectively bounce into 2001.

Reach.

Steps.

RUTH GRESTY

Eeyore's Quartet

It occurred to Pooh, Piglet and Tigger that they hadn't heard from Eeyore for several days, so they put on their hats and coats and trotted across the Hundred Acre Wood to Eeyore's stick house. Inside the house was Eeyore.

"Hello Eeyore," said Pooh.

"Hello Pooh, Hello Piglet. Hello Tigger," said Eeyore in a Glum Sounding Voice.

"We just thought we would check in on you," said Piglet, "because we hadn't heard from you and so we wanted to know if you were okay."

Eeyore was silent for a moment. "Am I okay?" he asked, eventually. "Well, I don't know, to be honest. Are any of us really okay? That's what I ask myself. All I can tell you, Pooh, Piglet and Tigger, is that right now I feel really rather Sad, and Alone, and Not Much Fun To Be Around At All. Which is why I haven't bothered you. Because you wouldn't want to waste your time hanging around with someone who is Sad, feels Alone, and is Not Much Fun To Be Around At All, would you now?"

Pooh looked at Piglet, and Piglet looked at Pooh. Pooh and Piglet looked at Tigger and Tigger looked at Pooh and Piglet; and they all sat down around Eeyore in his stick house.

Eeyore looked at them with surprise. "What are you doing?"

"We're sitting here with you," said Pooh, "because we are your friends. And true friends don't care if you are feeling Sad, or Alone, or Not Much Fun To Be Around At All. True friends are there for you anyway. And so here we are."

"Oh," said Eeyore. "Oh." And the four of them sat there in silence, and while Pooh, Piglet and Tigger said nothing at all, somehow, almost imperceptibly, Eeyore started to feel a very tiny little bit better.

Because Pooh, Piglet and Tigger were There. Because They were There.

Adapted from Kathryn Wallace.

Printed in Great Britain
by Amazon